The Courier

ROBERT ALAN WARD

This is a work of historical fiction. With the exception of characters, conversations and events mentioned in the Bible and in other historical records, all other names, incidents, organizations, and dialogue in this work are either the products of the author's imagination or are used fictitiously.

WestBow Press books may be ordered through booksellers or by contacting:

WestBow Press
A Division of Thomas Nelson & Zondervan
1663 Liberty Drive
Bloomington, IN 47403
www.westbowpress.com
844-714-3454

ISBN: 978-1-6642-0574-1 (sc)
ISBN: 978-1-6642-0573-4 (hc)
ISBN: 978-1-6642-0575-8 (e)

Library of Congress Control Number: 2020918001

Print information available on the last page.

WestBow Press rev. date: 10/28/2020

For though we walk in the flesh, we do not war according to the flesh, for the weapons of our warfare are not of the flesh, but divinely powerful for the destruction of fortresses.

2 Corinthians 10:3-4

Contents

Acknowledgements

I wish to gratefully acknowledge my wife Gisela, who patiently listened to this story as it developed and added many helpful ideas that found their way into the manuscript. I similarly wish to thank my daughter Joanna Endermann, who read my earlier drafts and suggested a number of changes that have much enhanced the story.

Cover painting: "Let there be Light" Joanna Endermann

Glossary of Latin and other Words and Terms

arbiter	witness, judge, umpire
assis	bronze coin of low value
atrium	hallway or entryway room
aurei	ancient Roman gold coins
avia	grandmother
avus	grandfather
bireme	an ancient warship with two decks of oars
brevis somnus	brief sleep, nap
caecitas	blindness
century	a basic unit in the Roman army, consisting of about eighty men
cerasus	cherry tree, cheery
Ceres	goddess of agriculture
cisiarii	taxi driver
cisium	taxi
cohort	a Roman army unit consisting of five or six centuries
concilium	counsel
cubiculum	bedroom
culina	kitchen
cultus	privy, toilet
cunae	cradle
curare	nurse
deliciae	delight, pleasure, sweetheart
denarius	a Roman coin worth one day's wages

domicilium	home, dwelling
domina	lady of the house, mistress, wife
dominus	mister, a title of respect
Domus Aurea	House of Gold, Nero's first palace
Domus Transitoria	Nero's second lavish palace that began construction upon the burning of Domus Aurea
euraquilo	a strong, stormy northeast wind that is experienced at times in the eastern part of the Mediterranean Sea
famulus	restaurant waiter
Fedorata Civitas	exemption from Roman taxation and law
festivitas	gaiety, merriment, humor
forfex	scissors
fulgur	lightning
garum	fish sauce
gymnasium	school
gener	son-in-law
hastatus posterior	second in command to a hastatus prior
hastatus prior	commander of a Roman century
Ille Perfugium	the refuge
Ille Forum	the forum, the place of prominence
Isis	an ancient goddess, worshipped as the mother of Pharaoh by the Egyptians and later by the Greeks as the goddess of protection for ships upon the seas
iudices	jury
konnalli	a Maltese dessert consisting of crunchy cubes filled with ricotta, dark chocolate, nuts, and various fruits
kykeon	an ancient Greek beverage consisting of water, barley, herbs and honey
libum	cheesecake made from flour, cheese, eggs, bay leaves, and honey
lictorum	police station
magistratus	judge, magistrate

Magna Graecia	the parts of the Roman Empire mostly inhabited by Greeks, especially the island of Sicily
matertera	aunt
medicus	doctor
Melitene	ancient name for the island of Malta
milite	soldier, a common foot soldier in the Roman army
mulsum	a warm, honeyed, wine drink
officium	office
pastiera	a tart made of wheat, eggs, cheese, and flavored with orange
patrician	a member of the rich upper class of Roman society
Pax Romana	the peace of Rome
peristylium	courtyard or official room surrounded by a colonnade
Pilus Prior	commander of a Roman cohort
pistrina	bakery
Polaris	the north star
portus	harbor, port
praecipuus	a chief
praefectus, prefect	overseer, director, commander
primi ordine	highest ranking centurion in a Roman cohort
princeps	most eminent leader, chief
prinjolata	a domed sponge cake made of flour, eggs, cane sugar, lemon, and pine nuts, topped by cream, almonds, cherries, and chocolate
proconsul	governor
propraetor	governor
publicanus	a tax collector
publicus	a public official
Puteoli	a port city on the west coast of Italy
quinquiremus	an ancient Roman galley propelled by five banks of oars
sambuca	an ancient harp

savillum	a cheese cake covered with dried figs, with a honey topping
servientes ad legem	a person serving at law
shalom	a blessing of peace, prosperity and health
solitudo	quarantine room
spira	a pastry consisting of flour, eggs, cheese, honey, and fruit
stola	a long, loose fitting, pleated dress worn over a tunica
subucula	shirt, vest
sutor	shoemaker
taberna	a business establishment, especially with food, combined with the dwelling of the owners
terra firma	dry land, earth
thermopolium	a restaurant that serves warm drinks
timpana	a blend of pasta in a tomato meat sauce, with turkey, egg, and cheese, wrapped in a flaky crust.
tiro	recruit, the lowest rank of a Roman soldier
togatus	civilian
trierarchus	captain of a trireme
trireme	an ancient Roman warship with three decks of oars
tunica	tunic
tutulus	six locks of hair braided to a coned pinnacle
valetudinarium	hospital
vigilus	policeman
vir honesti	gentlemen
vittae	headband, ribbon

Prologue

The great plague has abated and the messenger of hope has departed by ship from the tiny island of Melitene in the Mediterranean Sea. Bound for Rome to be placed on trial for his life, he knows only to serve and to trust his God along the way, not knowing his earthly fate.

On the same ship is also secretly hidden a hooded figure, indelibly haunted by a terrifying sight he has witnessed near the summit of Scopulus Altus and also by the great misery he has inflicted upon others on the island.

The messenger of hope has left behind a fledgling church under the leadership of young Publius Fabianus, recently married to seventeen-year-old Amoenitas, a healing woman. Little do they foresee the pit-falls that lie ahead that will stretch them, possibly to the breaking point.

Under the governorship of Trebonius, father of Publius, Melitene has a degree of autonomy from Roman rule, but will it last? Sinister forces are at work on the island, determined to destroy freedom and the church by any means at their disposal.

Fifteen-year-old Eletia, younger sister of Amoenitas and new to the Christian faith, is pregnant and wondering how she will care for her coming child. The father of her child is nowhere to be found.

Ille Perfugium, previously a brothel, now under the leadership of the matriarchal Gratiana, is about to open its doors to former prostitutes who seek a better life for themselves. But are all the new tenants so motivated?

"And we know that God causes all things to work together for good to those who love God, to those who are called according to His purpose." Romans 8:28

Will these first century believers truly "know" that truth when faced with seemingly invincible forces arrayed against them? How will they respond to the challenges to the life of faith?

1

Lonely Souls

The Isis undulated easily from side to side as it cut through the dark waters. It was the perfect formula for sleep, but none was to be had for the young man who had stolen aboard the great ship the previous morning. Foul air below decks in the presence of hundreds of sleepers, among whom was a cacophony of snorers, did not help. But for him the problem went deeper. Most distressing was the awareness that there seemed no solution to his predicament. He had escaped the island, but could he escape himself? Regret ran deep in his soul.

He slid from his bunk and groped for the stairway, using the dim light from the open hatch to guide him through the narrow corridor and between slumbering bodies. As he ascended the stairway, fresh salt air afforded a welcome contrast to the stench below.

Once upon the deck he turned full circle, scanning the horizon. No hint of dawn yet appeared as he came to starboard. He gazed upward at myriad stars, visibly brighter and more numerous above the desolate sea in the new moon sky. He observed the helmsman above and before him, steering the Isis northward, guided by lights from the city of Syracuse on the east coast of Magna Graecia. It was still some thirty miles distant by his reckoning. He made his way toward the bow, where he could be alone with his unsettled thoughts.

Abruptly, he halted some fifteen paces short. There before him, silhouetted against the distant city lights, was a familiar figure. A scene near the summit of Scopulus Altus flashed through his mind. In revulsion he drew backward, then turned and fled for the stern. He stopped only when there was no remaining distance he could put between himself and the figure at the bow. He found a bench. His body quivering, his heart pounding, he sat down. Fear was another emotion he had little known until recent months.

As he gradually calmed, a startling realization descended upon him. At the previous encounter he had been excited at the prospect of killing the man at the bow. Now he felt no such desire. *Why is that? He is my mortal enemy. Is it because I don't want to see again what I saw at Scopulus Altus? Is it something else?*

His mind returned to a certain young woman. *I saw how sick she was. How did she ever recover? Does she wonder about me? What will she tell the child in her womb about me? What will become of the child?* Unpleasant, inescapable thoughts—these were his constant companions. Strong drink was the only remedy he knew, but none was to be had aboard the Isis. Strong drink would have to wait until after he reached port.

The first hint of dawn faintly colored the eastern sky. Like a vampire bat scurrying from the day, he rose from the bench and vanished again into the hold of the ship. What little sleep he had known the past few weeks had mainly consisted of ghastly nightmares. But maybe this time would be different. There was always that hope.

*****

A hard kick in her womb jarred the young woman awake. She rose silently from her bed and hastily dressed. Upon filling an earthenware jar with water, she went out the front door, heading for her familiar spot, the same place she had encountered the God who had made her some four months before. Dawn was just creasing the eastern sky.

Ten minutes of navigating soggy trails and dewy grass brought her to the natural seat of the olive tree, her special place. She sucked in great quaffs of sea air in the damp mist before seating herself. The crashing waves below added a comforting ambiance. Everything looked, sounded, felt, tasted, and smelled so much better from her still new perspective. *How close to death and to endless torment came I, but God had mercy on me.*

To her right the grays and lavenders of early dawn gradually gave way to orange hues, reflected in the scattered clouds above the sea. The stars faded from the sky except for the brightness of Venus, above and to the left of where she sat. She peered to her left, where scant evidence remained of the ship that had brought to Melitene the messenger of hope and had saved her life.

Another kick in her womb startled her. She wondered if she carried a boy or a girl. Either way she would be grateful. Yet still she wrestled with troubling thoughts. *How am I to care for my child? I cannot live off my sister and her husband forever.*

Her mind returned to the father of her child. *Where is he? Is he still here on the island? Does he think about me? Does he know about the child within me?* She had once supposed herself in love with him. But he had shown his true colors. *How could I ever have loved such a man?* As she pondered his arrogance and his actions, her heart grew angry. But then she remembered that she too had done much wrong.

She rose again to her feet, lifted her arms heavenward, and verbally cried out. "Lord Jesus, have mercy on him. May he find peace in his heart. May he come to know Your forgiveness, as have I. May he become the man You created him to be.

"I pray for the child within me. May my child come to know You and become mighty for Your kingdom. I ask Your provision for me and for my little one.

"I pray for my sister and for her husband. May You bless them for their kindness. Help my sister's husband to be the pastor You would have him be. Keep him from sin and temptation. May my sister be to him the wife he so greatly needs."

She sat down again, feeling strangely different. *I was angry before. But having prayed, I now feel only compassion for the father of my child. Why is that?*

She looked down to her right at the spindly olive tree, whose roots were still splitting the rock. Against all odds, it was leafing in the early spring. In a flash she grasped the answer to her prayer for provision. *If this feeble olive tree can survive—if it can still split a rock and leaf, then so too can I.*

2

A Fair Young Maiden

At almost the same time as the Isis had left Portus Amplus the day before, it entered Portus Grande from the south. The young man, now obscured in his hooded cloak, gazed again in wonder at the city. He couldn't help but remember Cicero's description of Syracuse as "the greatest Greek city and the most beautiful of them all."

The Syracuse harbor was some three times the size of Portus Amplus. Situated near the center of the Roman Empire, it was the main trading link between its western and eastern parts. Syracuse was by far the wealthiest and most populous city on the great island of Magna Graecia. As such it was the capitol of the Roman government for the island. He knew it also to be the birthplace of Archimedes, a noteworthy Greek mathematician and engineer.

To the right of the Isis loomed Ortygia Island, some two miles in circumference, with its famous acropolis, surrounded by double walls. The Temple of Apollo lay at its northern end. To the north of Syracuse, some sixty miles distant loomed the majestic, snow-capped Mount Aetna.

As the ship neared the wharf, Captain Lucius stood on the top deck by the steering house to address the ship's company and passengers. "This will be a three-day stop. My crewmen have been clamoring for some proper shore leave, and this is the place to get it. For those of you who will disembark here, I hope that your voyage has been pleasant, and I wish you all good luck. For those of you going on with us to Puteoli, please be back here by the seventh hour on Tuesday. We sail promptly at the eighth hour."

Ten minutes later the Isis docked at the wharf. Crewmen cast ropes from the ship to shoremen in loincloths, who secured the ropes to iron moors embedded in concrete. A sizeable crowd that somehow knew of the coming ship had assembled to greet loved ones. Upon securing the ship, the shoremen carried a gangplank to its port side and set it in place to bring ashore the passengers.

Almost as soon as the gangplank was in place, the young man bounded from the ship and evaporated into the crowd, free at last from the people whose presence he found revolting. He had an old friend in the city with whom he had once caroused. *Perhaps we can get together again. My old friend was a man of rising prominence. Perhaps he will help me find a job commiserate with my stature.*

Walking briskly, he made his way down Via Gelone through Acradina, one of the four major sections of the city. The wide cobblestone street was flanked on either side by two story stone structures, with shops below and dwellings above. He came to a large, open air market. The aroma of various foods tantalized his nostrils and stimulated hunger pangs in his stomach, but he kept moving. He passed the great Doric temple of Olympian Zeus, with its massive stone columns, measuring 185 feet one way and 75 by the other.

After a thirty-minute trek he finally arrived at his friend's last known residence. Before him loomed a large, impressive domicile, behind which was a tall, seemingly unscalable wall that divided Acradina from Tycha, a poorer section of the city. He climbed the ten steps and knocked on the front door.

*****

Paul, Luke, and Aristarchus strode down the gangplank, the last passengers to leave the ship. Immediately, they were greeted by a party of twelve; men, women, and children.

"I am Antonius," spoke a man who appeared to be their leader. "Which of you is Paul?"

"I am," responded the shortest of the three. The two clasped wrists.

Following them down the gangplank was Julius the centurion. As he waited his turn to speak, his eyes fell upon a young, chestnut-haired maiden among them, fair of complexion, lovely in form, and with the kindest, sweetest face he had ever seen. For an instant their eyes convened.

"We heard that you people were coming," said Antonius. "As far as we know, we are the only followers of Christ in this city. We are two families. We have quarters where you can stay while you are here. You will not lack for food. We would be honored if you would accept our hospitality."

Paul smiled. "We are much glad to see you people. It seems that wherever we go, there are always God's people waiting to greet us." He pointed to his companions. "This is Luke, our beloved physician, and this is Aristarchus, who brings music to our lives. The centurion here is Julius. He is charged with ushering us to Rome and is also a fellow follower of Christ."

Pleasantries were exchanged, after which Julius reluctantly reverted to his proper decorum as a centurion to address Paul. "You and your friends have the freedom of the city. Please do not go beyond the boundaries of the city and please return here by the seventh hour on Tuesday."

"Thank you for your consideration," answered Paul. "We will not betray your trust."

Julius bade farewell to the group and returned to the ship to give his soldiers their liberty instructions. He found it difficult to concentrate on the task at hand. Several times he stole glances at the departing believers, each time fixating upon the young maiden. Once he thought he caught her glancing back.

* * * * *

To the casual observer, the cobblestone streets, the open-air market, the shops, the chattering children dashing about, and the cosmopolitan make-up of the city made Syracuse appear like any other large municipality in the empire. But Paul found his spirit immediately provoked. Over the door of one shop he saw the Sigil of Baphomet, with the serpent of Leviathan inside an inverted pentacle. Over the door of another was a Talisman of Saturn, a six-point geometric star used to conjure up evil spirits. In his spirit he perceived the worship of false gods, broken families, sexual promiscuity and perversion, sex slavery, alcoholism, crime, poverty, and disease.

"What has been done to bring the gospel of Jesus Christ to this city?" he asked Antonius.

"We are all neophyte believers ourselves—and gentiles. We have no scriptures and no pastor to guide us. We were hoping you could help us with that."

"Then we are here to help. Tell me then, where is the best place to meet and converse with interested, lost people?"

Antonius pointed northward. "There is a large Greek amphitheater on the south slopes of the Temenite Hill in the northern part of the city. It is our cultural center. It has sixty-seven rows of seats, divided into nine sections, with stairways dividing the sections. From the top tier of the theater you can see the Great Harbor and the island of Ortygia."

Paul laughed. "The amphitheater would be great if we had a couple of months here—time to generate a really large crowd. But we have only three days. A meeting place like the Aeropagus in Athens would be ideal. Does such a place exist in Syracuse?"

Antonius thought for a moment. "There is a place on the island of Ortygia that attracts great crowds of people and has a free speech stage. We will take you there tomorrow."

After a twenty-minute walk the group came to a small, humble appearing shop and entered. A long table with several chairs behind it stood off to the right of the large bottom floor business area. At the end of the table on the far side was a weaving loom. A counter for business transactions stood before the back wall. Three of the walls were adorned with stretched out samples of materials in various colors. Light entered through the windows on the street side.

"This is our business," spoke Antonius proudly, "and our home. We are tentmakers by trade. Our two families live in separate rooms upstairs and share the kitchen and a common room."

*****

Porcius bit off another chunk of thick-crusted bread. He was a rotund, slovenly man, considerably more of both than the young man from the ship remembered him. He also lacked any semblance of table manners, a trait that irked his guest.

"So Marcus, how did you get that scar over your left eye?"

"A man took me by surprise. But you should have seen him after I was finished."

It was Marcus' standard answer to all who asked. He sat back in his chair and took another sip of the house wine, which he found too sweet for his taste. It had been a satisfying meal of lamb and bread at the Taberna of Lunianus.

"So Porcius, what are you doing these days? Are you married?"

His host let out a huge guffaw. "That will never happen. It's too much fun living unattached. If I want Livia, I send for her. If I want Tatiana, I call her. They or other little deliciae come to my house whenever I want and keep me company. They like what they get in return."

I imagine they do, thought Marcus. In appearance Porcius was not at all a desirable man, with his large paunch, his disheveled way of dress, and his intolerable manners. But he had one redeeming feature that many women could not resist. He had money, which he lavished upon anyone pleasing, who would do his bidding.

Money was also something Marcus knew he needed. It was time to get down to business. "How do you maintain such a lavish lifestyle?"

Porcius smiled a sly smile. "I am a publicanus. I collect taxes for the propraetor of Magna Graecia and for our Divine Princeps Nero." He pounded his chest three times with his right fist. "And am I ever good at it. I've got nearly one hundred people working for me. My underlings do all the dirty work. All I need do is please two men—and they are much pleased with me."

Marcus plunged in. "I need a job. If you want to become even better at collecting taxes, then I am your man. I specialize in dirty work."

Abruptly, Porcius countenance changed and he eyed Marcus suspiciously. From previous experience he knew of the younger man's ruthless ambition. *I have a good thing going. If I allow Marcus in on it, he will not hesitate to bury me when the opportunity arises.*

"We are not hiring right now. But there are many jobs to be had here in Syracuse if you're not above brick laying, or serving tables, or working at the docks."

A surge of anger swept through Marcus. "What do you take me for? I am not a man of menial tasks. I am a patrician of noble birth. I could never lower myself to such depths!"

Porcius laughed condescendingly. "When a man is hungry, any job surpasses starving." He rose from the table and summoned the waiter. After handing the waiter a few coins, he turned once more to Marcus.

"I can't help you." With that he toddled out the front door and was gone.

* * * * *

At midday the two families sat down for a meal of chicken, bread, and fruit at the long table in the upstairs common room of the dwelling. Before partaking Antonius beckoned to Paul.

"Would you please honor us by giving thanks for the food that is before us?"

As Paul bowed his head the others followed suit. "Gracious Father from above, Creator of all things. We thank You for Your provision of food, both to enjoy and to strengthen our bodies. Thank You for our wonderful hosts. May we be encouraged, each by the others' faith, in the name of our Savior Jesus Christ. Amen."

As they partook, Paul and his companions listened to learn the names. Antonius' wife Lucia had a bright countenance that matched her name. She was simply fun to be around. Their oldest daughter, sixteen-year old Angelina, exuded a gentle sweetness. Their ten-year-old son Drusus had a seriousness about him that portended accomplishment. Five-year-old Caecitas had a personality that matched her mother's—and then some.

"Caecitas is blind," spoke Lucia. "She has been blind from birth. Hence her name."

Liuni, who headed the other family, was less flamboyant and much more reserved than Antonius. "But he is a master weaver and a great records keeper," spoke Antonius. "We wouldn't have a business without him."

His wife Hilarius was as animated as her husband was quiet." Nine-year-old Aelia, eight-year-old Vitus, five-year old Fausta, and three-year-old Fannia were their children.

"Before it is dark, I would very much like to see the place where you would have us meet people," said Paul.

"Very well," answered Antonius. "We will go there as soon as we are finished with our meal. The shop will be closed for the next three hours anyway. It is some thirty minutes from here on foot."

3

One of those Detestables

Having given his soldiers their instructions, Julius departed the ship and set out to tour the city. It would be for him a solo venture, as it was sacrosanct for an officer to socially fraternize with his subordinates. Paul and his group, whose company he would have preferred, especially because of the girl, were gone to parts unknown.

As he strolled down the main thoroughfare of Via Gelone, he was struck by the emptiness of the people. It was for him a new experience to view people from such a perspective. *Lost, empty people, with no direction or purpose, resigned to their stations in life, dealing with life's many problems, whose only solace is to eat, drink, and be merry—and then to die.*

He pondered his own life. Before his conversion to Christ he had been all soldier, resolute to make his way up the ranks to one day command a legion. But his whole perspective was now changed. He only wanted now to resign from the army as soon as his commitment was finished, to find a worthy trade, to marry and have children, and to serve his Savior.

He thought again of the young maiden he had seen at the dock. He knew nothing about her, other than that she was probably a believer, since she was with a believing family. *But she looks like a believer. Oh Lord, may I have her?*

His practical, logical mind then retreated to more realistic ground. *Those things will have to wait. My immediate job is to convey Paul and his companions safely to Rome.*

As midday approached the heat bore down on him and he became both tired and hungry. Near the edge of Acradina he found a taberna that looked promising. Upon entering, he immediately felt relief from the heat. The eyes of all inside seemed to rise in unison and fall upon him, attired as he was in the uniform of a centurion. But he was used to that. Scanning the taberna for a place to sit, he recognized a familiar face from the ship. What he had not observed before was his impressive head of hair, for the man had always been hooded. Though they had not spoken on the ship, his desolate look prompted Julius to approach him.

"Hello, I am the centurion Julius from the Isis. I saw you on the ship. May I join you?"

The man set down his wine glass without looking up. "Sure. Why not?"

"Have you eaten?"

"Yes," came the short reply.

"What is good here to eat?"

"The lamb with durum wheat bread is good if you can afford it."

A waiter appeared and Julius ordered as recommended. "I am Julius. What is your name?"

"Marcus."

Julius searched his mind. "I believe I know of you from my time on Melitene. I was one of those who was stranded there, courtesy of the great storm."

"I left because of the other great storm."

"What other great storm?"

"The great Christian storm," he replied irritably. "They stormed the island and took over."

Julius knew of his reputation—now again confirmed. "I see. Is that a bad thing?"

Marcus began his reply calmly. But as he spoke, his voice increased in fury. "It is worse than a bad thing. They refuse to pay homage to our Roman gods and our emperor. They spurn pleasure in favor of tedium and knowledge in favor of ignorance. In doing so, they make useless their earthly lives. They foist guilt upon people and think themselves superior to all who aren't them. They fantasize about some afterlife, as if there were one. They lie. They cheat. They steal. They are detestable people. I couldn't wait to get away from them."

A momentary flash of anger welled up in Julius, which he did his best to suppress. *Oh Lord, this is one very lost man. Please give me wisdom in my response.*

"So now that you are free of the Christians, will life be better for you here in Syracuse?"

He smiled a pained smile. "Hopefully."

"What kind of a life are you looking for? I will listen if you care to speak."

Marcus considered the centurion. Julius did not fit his image of a young Roman officer, taking and giving orders dispassionately. He seemed like a real flesh and blood human being.

"I thought I had a good job lined up here. But the man who could offer it to me feared that I would eventually bury him." He snickered. "I would have too."

"So, what are you going to do now?"

"I don't know. I will not wear a loin cloth and load ships."

"Hunger is a powerful persuader." As Julius silently prayed for wisdom, another question entered his mind.

"Was it just the Christians that prompted you to leave Melitene?"

For long moments Marcus hesitated, pondering if he should bare his soul to a stranger. He took in a deep breath and slowly let it out. "I left behind a pregnant girl."

A name popped into Julius' head. "Would her name be Eletia?"

Startled, Marcus looked up. "Do you know her?"

"A little. She is quite a vivacious young lady."

His comment brought him a suspicious look.

"No, she is not my girl, if that is what you are thinking. I have my mind set on someone else. Does your conscience now bother you?"

"It actually does," he sighed. "I wonder how she is going to care for herself and the child. I suppose the Christians will help her. She appears to be one of them. They seem to do that sort of thing."

"So maybe not everything about the Christians is bad?"

"I suppose not," he reluctantly admitted.

"Do you think you'll wonder about the child—your child, as the years go by?"

For the first time a hint of sorrow came to Marcus' countenance. "I will."

"What do you think you should do?"

As quickly as the hint had come, it vanished. His face again hardened. "There were no jobs to be had on Melitene—at least my kind of jobs. The island is too small for me and infested by those detestable Christians. Eletia would constantly nag me to join them. She is better off without me and I without her!"

Calmly Julius nodded. In his spirit he knew that it was now time for him to show his hand. "I with whom you speak am also one of those detestables."

His meal arrived. Before partaking, Julius bowed his head and inaudibly gave thanks. Marcus remained silent until Julius began to eat.

"You think that does any good?"

Julius used the time spent chewing his first bite to ponder his response. "It is a habit I picked up from a man named Paul, while we were on our ship during the giant storm. Do you know of him?"

"Yes, I know of him." He judged it better to leave out his attempt to kill the man.

"We had been battling the elements for nearly two weeks. All of us were miserably cold and seasick. We came to the end of ourselves and were resigned to die until Paul stepped forward. I remember vividly his words."

"Men, you ought to have followed my advice and not to have set sail from Crete, and incurred this damage and loss. And yet now I urge you to keep up your courage, for there shall be no loss of life among you, but only of the ship. For this very night an angel of the God to whom I belong and whom I serve stood before me, saying, 'Do not be afraid, Paul; you must stand before Caesar; and behold, God has granted you all those who are sailing with you.' Therefore, keep up your courage, men, for I believe God, that it will turn out exactly as I have been told. But we must run aground on a certain island." *(*Acts 27:21b-26)

"Early the next morning Paul encouraged us all to eat, for we had eaten nothing for many days, being so seasick. He promised again that we would not perish. With no other place to turn, we chose to believe him. He gave us hope where there was otherwise none. Then before us all he thanked the God he served and ate. So we ate too—and were strengthened.

"Just as day was breaking the next morning, we ran aground on an island, just like he had told us, which turned out to be Melitene. I commanded that those who could swim should jump overboard and make for the land and that those who could not swim should grab on to anything that floated and paddle in. We were 276 aboard that ship. And just as Paul had promised, not a single life was lost. And that is why I thank my God always before eating."

Marcus remained still, visibly moved. "That is the truth of it?"

"That is the truth of it. Paul was a prisoner in my charge—and still is. I had liked him before. I liked him a lot better after we all stood again safely on terra firma. Soon afterwards I embraced his God."

Marcus looked around the taberna. "If Paul is your prisoner, where is he? Why aren't you guarding him?"

"He is somewhere in this city, staying with a couple of Christian families. He will return to the ship before we sail in three days."

"He will just come back on his own when he could be free?"

"He will."

"I wouldn't if I were him. I would be long gone to parts unknown."

"To a follower of Christ, a man's word is his bond."

Marcus nodded. "Tell me, Julius. You are a soldier. You kill people. It appears to me that Christians do not. How do you reconcile your profession with your belief?"

"With difficulty," Julius admitted. "I came to believe in Christ on Melitene while a soldier. I have another five months of obligation to the army and cannot just quit. I do sometimes worry that I will be given an order that I cannot in good conscience carry out."

"What would you do if that happened?"

Julius considered his answer. "So far it hasn't happened. It is a bridge I will cross, if ever I come to it." He took a deep breath. "I formerly had the goal of one day commanding a legion. Now I intend to leave the army at the end of my term. I want to find a wife, maybe the girl I mentioned, and settle down."

Marcus shook his head. "That is one of the things I don't understand about you Christians. You limit yourselves."

"I do not see myself as limited. I see myself as having limitless, God-given potential. I believe that God has much greater things for me than commanding a legion. I don't know just yet what those greater things might be, but the path to discover them excites me. And then there is eternal life, filled with rewards after my earthly life is done."

He pushed his plate back satisfied. As a soldier he was used to eating fast. The chore complete, he fastened his eyes upon Marcus.

"Our ship leaves Syracuse Tuesday morning at the eighth hour. I will be on it, charged as I am with taking Paul and his companions with me to Rome. It seems to me, Marcus, that your life is at a crossroads. You can either remain here and attempt to find what you are looking for, or you can come with us, intent on getting a true idea about what it is to be a follower of Christ. I would be delighted if you would choose the latter, but that is up to you."

He rose from the table and offered his hand to Marcus. After some hesitation Marcus stood in respect and took it.

"Let me pay for your wine."

He paid for his meal and for Marcus' wine. At the door he turned once more to his new friend. "Live, Marcus."

With that he was gone. Marcus remained. There were other matters weighing on him that he had not confided to Julius. Strong drink seemed his only solace.

4

Ille Forum

Before dawn the next morning, the first day of the week, Paul arose and went outside to the veranda that overlooked the street below. The air was warm and all was still, a huge contrast from his tour of the marketplace on Ortygia the afternoon before. He inhaled deeply and raised his arms toward heaven.

"Holy Father, my God and my King. I praise and adore You for Your greatness and Your love. You had mercy on me, the chief of sinners. What would You have me do today?"

For long moments he remained standing, arms upraised, listening for the voice of the Holy Spirit. As he stood and listened, promptings began to enter his mind.

*****

After a delectable breakfast of bread, olives, and spiraea of eggs and cheese, topped by various savory fruits, Paul bid the two families to be seated in the upper common room of the house. "Thank you so much, ladies, for the delightful breakfast. It feels good inside of us."

He looked around the room. All eyes, even of the children, were upon him in anticipation. "You said that you are babes in Christ. There is no shame in being babes as long as you are unwilling to remain such. It is the first day of the week, the traditional time for Christians to gather for worship, for fellowship, and for learning."

He focused his eyes on Antonius. "Do you intend to open your shop today?"

"Should we not?"

"If you keep your shop closed and take Sundays for rest, you will do better on the other six days. It will also serve as a testimony to others. They will ask why you are closed. You can tell them that you honor Christ Jesus the Lord."

"Very well then," spoke Antonius. "We will remain closed today in honor of our Savior."

The children cheered. "Can we go to the beach instead?"

Paul smiled and began his teaching. "Our faith begins with the God who created us. Because He is our Creator, we must naturally assume that He knows more about how we ought to live our lives than ourselves, just as the tentmaker knows more about tentmaking than the tent. The problem is that our natural minds have been skewed because of Adam's sin."

"Who is Adam?" asked Drusus, Antonius' son.

"Adam was the first man God created, after He had created the heavens, the earth, and all other living things. God created Adam first, and then Eve to be his wife. From Adam and Eve, we are all descended. God placed them in a garden called the Garden of Eden and gave them dominion over all the other living things He had created. They were told that they could eat freely from any tree in the garden except from the Tree of the Knowledge of Good and Evil. If they ate from that tree they would die. But the Serpent of Old, Satan, tempted Eve and she ate. She gave some of the fruit to Adam and he ate. Through Adam's sin the entire human race fell into sin and death, which is why we are mortal and which is why we humans are always at odds with one another. It is why the world we live in is such a mess."

For two hours Paul continued to teach the rudiments of the Christian faith until it became obvious that the children could endure no more. Upon completing his teaching, he addressed Antonius and Liuni.

"After the midday meal, would you men please take us back to the Ortygia market place, this time to do more than observe?"

*****

After another savory meal Paul and his companions, along with Antonius and Liuni, set out for the market place. "Our city is set in four sections," explained Antonius. "We live in Acradina. The island of Ortygia is another. A third part is called Tycha. The farthest part to the north is Neapolis, which contains the great amphitheater of which I spoke."

The men crossed the stone bridge over the narrow waterway that linked Ortygia with the rest of the city. To their right loomed Portus Grande. The Isis, still in its berth, stood out as one of the larger ships at the docks. To the left of the bridge was Portus Parvus, a smaller port for smaller ships.

Upon clearing the bridge, they continued straight for five minutes until they came to the Temple of Apollo, the god of youth, archery, music, dance, truth, prophecy, healing, poetry, and the sun. He was revered by both Greeks and Romans as the son of Zeus and Leto and the twin brother of Diana, goddess of the hunt, of the moon, and of chastity. Situated in a garden, the temple measured some 175 feet in width, by 75 feet in depth. Twenty-four large columns surrounded the building, with two rows of smaller interior columns between them. All supported a massive wooden roof. Though the structure was a marvel of human engineering, for Paul it was a revulsion of demonic spirits and false religion.

From the temple the men turned left and went two blocks north to enter the marketplace, a large, wide-open square, flanked on all four sides by olive and sycamore trees. An array of pungent smells greeted them, produced by displays of tomatoes, oranges, lemons, chili peppers, along with various meats and seafoods. Other booths sold idols or practical household items. Hawkers animatedly shouted in differing dialects for people to buy their wares. Some added flair to their pitches. One particular purveyor strummed his sambuca and sang in an attempt to lure clientele to his booth. Customers haggled with vendors in animated tête-à-tête regarding the price.

At the northwest corner of the marketplace stood a raised platform called Ille Forum, where anyone was permitted to speak upon any subject and passersby were just as free to ignore them. Upon the stage stood a wildly gesturing, shouting man, who seemed to think that volume made up for lack of substance. As Paul and his companions made their way toward the stage, they discerned his disjointed rambling to have something to do with Greek freedom from the Romans. None appeared to be listening. The five men politely awaited Paul's turn, hoping for a soon end of the man's incoherent tirade. While waiting Paul silently prayed for wisdom.

Finally, after another fifteen minutes of babble, exhaustion forced the man to yield. Immediately Paul took the stage. He scanned the crowd and prayed one more time before speaking.

"Men of Syracuse, I observe that you are very religious. For only a short distance from here lies the great Temple of Apollo. But magnificent though the temple be, the God whom I worship, the God of all creation, does not dwell in temples made by human hands."

From the crowd a few heads began to turn. On the stage appeared to be a man worth hearing. There was something about the confidence by which he spoke.

"Assembled here this day I observe Greeks, Romans, Jews, Parthians, Medes, Elamites, Egyptians, Cretans, Arabs, and others. Though we are all different, we originate from one blood, created by one God, who created all things, of whom the great philosopher Plato wrote.

'Is the world created or uncreated? That is the first question.
Created, I reply, being visible and tangible and having a body,
And therefore sensible; and if sensible, then created;
and if created, made by a cause, and the cause
is the inexpressible Father of all things…'

"This inexpressible Father of all things I now declare to you. It is He who has made us, and not we ourselves."

To the chagrin of the vendors, a large part of the crowd began to surge toward the stage.

"Yet though He created us to have fellowship with Him, we all like sheep have gone astray. Each of us has turned to his own way, which is why this world is so filled with violence and strife. It is why there is the sting of death for all living things, including ourselves. Yet the God who created us, because of His great love for us, while we were yet sinners, sent His Son Jesus Christ into this lost world to die for us. He was crucified upon a Roman cross and buried. But on the third day, He rose again from the dead, as was prophesied by the great Greek poet Epimenides."

"They fashioned a tomb for You, holy and high One,
But You are not dead: You live and abide forever,
For in You we live and move and have our being."

"Show us a sign, that we may believe in this God," shouted a man from the crowd, who appeared to be a Jew.

Before Paul could respond, another in Greek attire shouted. "Foolishness! Why pay attention to this idle babbler of some strange Deity?"

More shouts arose from the crowd, to the effect that none could be distinguished and none could hear Paul's answers. As chaos descended upon the scene, most of the onlookers turned away, leaving only six who remained.

"I want to hear more about this," spoke one among them, a short, slight, dark complexioned, middle-aged man with matted hair. "My name is Rufus."

"There is a public park just on the other side of the stage overlooking Portus Parvus," spoke Antonius. "There are benches with tables and shade. It is much quieter there."

* * * * *

That night Paul, Luke, Aristarchus and the two Christian families dined together on a meal of fish, bread, fruit, and wine. Among them also was Rufus, whom they had met at the square, he being the only one who appeared serious about knowing Christ.

After dinner Aristarchus got out his lute and taught the assembled group a series of psalms and hymns, which upon learning they sang together, rejoicing in the goodness of their Savior. Especially delightful was Caecitas' singing. It seemed as if she saw God in a way that the other children and even the adults did not.

After the singing, Paul turned to Rufus. "Tell us about yourself, Rufus. How is it that you came to the market place earlier today and heard the message of salvation?"

"It is a long story," answered Rufus. "I will do my best to be brief. I was born in humble circumstances fifty-two years ago in Alexandria, Egypt. My mother was named Drusilla. She lived a pained, difficult life.

Her father was a drunkard, whom she seldom saw. She was only fifteen when her mother died. She found herself alone on the streets and hungry.

"Alexandria is always full of young sailors from all over the world. She met one such man from Ethiopia, who spoke kind words to her and bought her a meal. In return she gave herself to him, which is how I came to be. She never saw him again. I am pretty sure that he never knew of my existence.

"After that no man wanted my mother, seeing that she had a child of mixed race. She was alone for the rest of her life. Her mother was a seamstress. She had taught my mother the trade, which is how she made a living for us.

"She wanted a better life for me. When I was eight years old, she managed to enroll me at the Alexandrian Museum, the best school in the city. It had been founded by Ptolemy I Soter some 200 years before. At first, I was afraid of the large buildings, but over time it became like a home to me. I loved the beautiful gardens and the colonnaded walkways. There I learned to read and to write. I learned mathematics. I did so well in my studies that the school decided to supplement what my mother could pay, enabling me to remain there all through my childhood and youth.

"Upon the completion of my education, they hired me as a professor of philosophy and literature. Over time I helped expand the school's already considerable library. With my earnings I was finally able to provide a better life for my dear mother, but only for a short time. She died when I was twenty-three.

"Like my mother, I never married, but in my case by choice. Marriage wasn't for me. I derived my joy from teaching young students to love learning. I had a comradery with them that made my fellow professors jealous. Though the students loved me, I was never popular with my colleagues.

"A new president priest came to our school from Rome. He decided that my view of a single great Deity, who created all things, was incompatible with the Roman and Greek views of a plethora of gods and goddesses. I was summarily dismissed, which is why I came here to Syracuse, seeking another position. So far, I have come up empty. It seems that my views and my linage are incompatible here too.

"As for how I came to the marketplace, I simply needed to buy some food with what little money I still have. When I heard Paul speaking on the stage, I was immediately drawn. As I listened, I knew that he spoke of the One I have worshipped for years without knowing His name—who somehow rose from the dead to live again, as wrote Epimenides. So here I am, eager to learn all I can about Christ."

All remained silent for a time until Paul spoke. "I find in my journeys that not many mighty or noble respond to the gospel. You Rufus, are a wonderful exception. I hope you will remain among the believers here. They have much to teach you. You have much you can teach them."

He addressed the entire group. "I must depart for Rome the day after tomorrow. It is not much time to teach you, but I want to begin by speaking to you now on what it means to be a Christ follower."

"Let us lay aside every encumbrance, and the sin which so easily entangles us, and let us run with endurance the race that is set before us, fixing our eyes on Jesus, the author and perfecter of faith, who for the joy set before Him endured the cross, despising the shame, and has sat down at the right hand of the throne of God." (Hebrews 12:1b-2)

For a long time, Paul spoke until the hour grew late and the children drifted into slumber.

Angelina, the oldest of the children, arose and carried them to bed one by one as Paul spoke to the adults about the next day.

"Tomorrow is our last full day here. I am by trade a tentmaker. We do not wish to eat anyone's bread without paying for it. In the morning we three would like to help you with your business. I can work with my hands. Aristarchus can fetch and clean. Luke can help with customers."

"I am also good with my hands," spoke Rufus. "My mother taught me the skills of a seamstress. If am allowed to remain among you, I will also earn my keep."

"Have you people been baptized?" spoke Paul.

"What is baptism?" asked Antonius.

"It is an ordinance of the Lord that is to be practiced by all who follow Him. Tomorrow, during the heat of the day, when all the shops are closed, we will head for the beach and take care of that matter."

"Whatever that is, I want to be baptized too," spoke Rufus.

Just as the adults were ready to go to bed themselves, Angelina approached Aristarchus. "I loved the sound of the lute you were playing. Could you teach me the skill?"

Aristarchus considered the young lady's request. "I cannot teach you everything in just one session."

"I do not expect to learn everything in just one session. But I can begin."

"Then ask your parents for permission. If they approve, we will find some time on the veranda tomorrow after the baptisms."

5

Making Blind Eyes See

After breakfast the next morning the entire group went to work, with the children doing chores commiserate with their capabilities. By noontime the front of the shop had a new coat of paint. The interior was clean and organized, with considerably more stock prepared for sale. Sales had been brisk, as the spirit of a people working together in harmony seemed to have had a magnetic effect upon passersby.

After the midday meal, the entire group embarked on the ten-minute walk to Via Elorina, the main thoroughfare along the coast. From Via Elorina they found a narrow dirt foot path that led to the beach, shaded by palm, myrtle, and olive trees. As the beach came into view, the path gave way to sunlight. Lilacs, carnations, wild roses, and snapdragons bloomed on either side in full spring array until they emerged on to the sand just west of the docks. To their right loomed the long flat Portus Grande beach. Innumerable people were already there, spread as far as the eye could see. Many had entered the gently lapping water to cool off.

The believers made their way to the right and found an open spot some ten minutes down the shoreline. There they stopped and settled. With his back to the water Paul delivered a short message to the group on the significance of baptism.

"Christ died for our sins according to the Scriptures…He was buried, and…He was raised on the third day according to the Scriptures." (1 Corinthians 15:3b-4)

"You go under the water, signifying your identification with Christ in His death and the death to your old way of living. You rise from the waters, signifying His resurrection to life and your new way of living as followers of Christ. If you believe that Christ died for your sins and rose again from the dead—if you want henceforth to live only for Christ—then you may be baptized. This is an individual decision. Each of you must decide for yourself if you wish to be baptized. Parents cannot decide for their children. The children must decide for themselves. They must not be coerced."

After considerable conversation Antonius and Lucia came forward with their children, Angelina, Drusus, and Caecitas. "We all want to be baptized," spoke Antonius for his family.

As Paul baptized Antonius' family, starting with the parents, a sizeable crowd began to gather to witness what to them was a strange spectacle. Liuni's entire family came next. Finally came Rufus.

"This is for me an entirely new life. It is what I have sought since my youth."

Upon completion of the baptisms, the children, who could no longer be held back, dashed into the water and began to splash happily. Angelina carefully kept watch, especially for her blind sister Caecitas.

"Angelina appears to be a very responsible young woman," remarked Paul to Lucia.

"She is a great joy to us. She is like a second mother to the younger children. She also seems to have a healing touch that neither I nor Hilarius possess. When any of our children are sick, it is Angelina they want to care for them."

A prompting entered Paul's spirit. "Tell me about Caecitas' blindness."

"She has been blind from birth. I often describe to her how things look. I find it difficult to explain color. She seems happy enough as she is, but she has often told me how wonderful it would be if she could see. Yet I will tell you this. She sees into the spiritual world. She sees things that we who see, do not see."

"Call her," he said.

Upon hearing her mother's call, Caecitas left the water and made for the sound of her voice. "Yes mother?"

"Young child, would you like to see?" asked Paul.

A glowing thrill came to her face. "I would love to see more than anything in the world!"

"Do you believe that Jesus could make you see?"

"I know He could!"

"Then please come to me."

From his sitting position Paul shifted to his knees in order to be at the same level as the child. He placed his left hand behind her head. His right hand covered her face, with his thumb gently over her right eye and his index finger over her left. He began to pray.

"Lord Jesus, You gave sight to the blind. You once restored my sight. I pray now in Your Name, that You will extend that same gift of sight to Caecitas, who loves You and wants to use her eyes to serve You."

For a full minute he held his hands in place before slowly lifting his right hand from her face. As he did so, faint images began to form in the child's eyes. Gradually, the images brightened and sharpened into focus. Caecitas stood still in wonder, allowing the process to continue until she was forced to cover her eyes, as one must do for a time after emerging from a dark cave. Gradually then, she uncovered her eyes until they became fully adjusted to the light. For the first time in her life she looked into the face of her mother.

"Oh Mother! You are so beautiful!" Spontaneously, she threw herself into her mother's arms. After a long hug she pulled away and began to dance rapturously on the sand. "I can see! I can see!"

If the baptisms had attracted curiosity, the healing from blindness did far more. The believers found themselves suddenly inundated with inquisitive people, wanting to know what was going on. What was supposed to have been a two-hour interlude ended up consuming four. By the time the believers began their return trek, the day was well spent. Ten new souls followed them, swelling their party to twenty-five.

On their way back to the shop Aristarchus joined Angelina. "It has been quite a day, hasn't it?"

"That is to say the least."

"Are you still interested in a lesson on the lute?"

"I would love to learn the play the lute."

"Do you have permission from your parents?"

"Yes. I asked them on the way to the beach."

"Then if you are going to get a lesson, it will have to be right after we get back to the shop."

* * * * *

Fifteen minutes later they found themselves on the veranda, with Aristarchus holding the lute in his hands. He was the eldest of the three men bound for Rome. His thinning hair was pure silver, but his mind was sharp and he still possessed the wonder of youth in his spirit.

"It was the Greek mathematician Pythagoras who figured out what is called the octave scale, but only because God invented it first. As God created the heavens and the earth in seven days, so are there seven tones in a major scale. The eighth tone at the top of the scale is a repetition of the bottom tone at the beginning."

He played a simple major scale and then played the bottom and the top tones back and forth. "Do you hear the semblance?"

"Yes."

"That tells me that you have musical aptitude. From the notes of a major scale you can create an endless amount of melodies in what is called a major key."

He played a simple melody.

"But a major scale plays only happy music and the human soul has other dimensions."

He played a minor octave scale.

"From a minor scale you get sadness, using some half tones beneath the notes of a major scale. Not all of life can be happy. Not all of life can be sad. A properly developed human soul knows how to feel either at the appropriate times.

"Just as there were twelve patriarchs of Israel and twelve original apostles of Christ, so are there twelve tones in a chromatic scale."

He played a full chromatic scale.

"From those twelve tones you can reach the entire spectrum of human emotions with music. You can learn to compose your own melodies, based upon your own experiences and moods, that will touch human hearts."

He played a sad melody.

"It makes me want to cry," remarked Angelina.

"Sadness is not a bad thing. From sadness we learn to feel deeply. We learn to empathize with people when they go through sad times in their lives.

"The next thing I must show you is how to create the different tones with your fingers. This particular lute has four strings. Your right fingers pluck the strings. You can vary the volume, loud or soft, by how hard you pluck the strings. Your left fingers press down the strings at differing intervals to change the tones. The further up the neck your fingers go, the lower the tone. The further your fingers go toward the sound box, the higher the tone."

He demonstrated the technique in slow motion before handing her the lute. "Now you try it. Play me a major octave scale."

Clumsily at first, she began to create the differing tones and fought her way up a major scale.

"You learn the fingering positions by playing slowly. Then you gradually pick up speed. Muscle memory begins to take over. Over time, playing the lute will become as natural to you as other things you have already learned, such as walking, in your development from infancy to your present stage. But with a lute you must learn on purpose. You must practice, maybe six days a week, for a couple of hours each day."

"Why not seven days?"

"Because God rested on the seventh day. If God needed rest on the seventh day, then so do we. It is God's way of rejuvenating our bodies and our souls. If we follow God's pattern, we will over the long run produce more in six days than we could have done in seven. We'll be happier, we'll produce more, we'll have better relationships with people, and we'll live longer lives."

"That sounds like it must be true."

For the next forty minutes he coached her as she played both major and minor scales, marveling at how fast she was catching on. "You indeed have a natural aptitude for music that not everyone possesses. That does not make those of us with such an aptitude better than those who do not. God has given us all differing natural abilities. We can't all just make music. Some people have to farm or we would starve. Some are naturally more inclined to build things like this house. Some make and sell tents. The important thing is that we strive to become the best farmers, builders, tentmakers, or lute players that we can be."

*****

A simple evening meal of bread, cheese, and fruit was prepared. After giving thanks the people partook in the upper common room of the crowded house. Upon completing their supper, Aristarchus again got out his lute and repeated the psalms and hymns of the previous night. As the new believers caught on, their collective voices carried to the street outside, where passersby marveled at the joyful sounds. All the while Angelina sang and imagined herself leading such gatherings, bringing joy to human hearts. She resolved to save her earnings until she could purchase her own lute.

"It looks like another series of baptisms are in order," remarked Paul to Antonius after the singing was complete. "That is a wonderful thing. Since you are the leader here and I will be gone, I charge you with performing them."

Paul then addressed the entire group. "Luke, Aristarchus, and I must depart for Rome early tomorrow morning. God has done a great work here today. Caecitas sees. Ten new souls have been added to the kingdom of God."

"Therefore if any man is in Christ, he is a new creature; the old things passed away; behold, new things have come." (2 Corinthians 5:17)

"From henceforth, may you all walk in newness of life."

He changed the subject. "Just as none of us can predict with certainty what will become of us in the future, I do not know what lies ahead for me in Rome, except that my life is in God's hands and that heaven awaits me after I have shed my earthly tent. But I do hope one day to be back among you. In the meantime, Antonius will be in charge of this newly founded church. He is a dear man of God. Listen to him as you have listened to me."

For the next hour Paul spoke of the difference between earthly and heavenly thinking, and of the narrow road that leads to life. When weariness began to overcome attentiveness, he ceased, knowing that the human soul can only take in so much on any given day.

6

The Gift

Before dawn the next morning Antonius and Liuni joined the three Rome bound travelers on the veranda overlooking the street. There they worshipped Christ together before Paul spoke to the two leaders who would remain.

"I am appointing Liuni too, as an elder of the church here. Antonius, you are to be in charge, but I want you the listen to the counsel of Liuni. He is a rock. He will keep you out of trouble. Together you will be strong.

"Do not be deceived. So far you have experienced no persecution. From my experience it usually takes the enemy time to realize what is happening and to organize their counter-attack. But counter-attack they will. Be on guard for your flock. Watch for savage wolves that will come in among you with only destructive intent. Covet no man's silver or gold."

After the time of instruction, the three men laid their hands on Antonius and Liuni, praying love, wisdom, and strength into their lives. Yet Antonius remained anxious. For him, the weight of the world seemed to have been placed upon his shoulders.

* * * * *

Julius paced the deck of the Isis, a jumble of nerves. Again, he anxiously scanned the streets. No sign of Paul and his friends. He knew that they would not purposely betray him.

But what if Paul's preaching has gotten him into trouble? What if he is sitting in a carcer somewhere in the city? My superiors will have no mercy on me.

He also wondered if Marcus would show up. With words barely audible he prayed as he paced. "Lord Jesus, I pray for Marcus. He is such a lost soul. I pray that he finds You, whether he chooses to come with us or not. I pray for Paul and for his friends..."

Just then one of the two sights he wished to see emerged from a cross street on to Via Melitene, the nearest street to the ship. His inner tension immediately dissipated. "Thank you, Jesus."

Among the approaching group his eyes again found the fair young maiden, though he did his best to conceal his delight as he waved to them. Upon seeing him, they returned his greeting. At the foot of the gangway the group stopped. Those who were staying took turns embracing Paul and the others.

Right then, at the last minute, Aristarchus handed Angelina his lute. "I am led by the Holy Spirit of God to give this to you. God has shown me that you will become a great musician. He will use your ability to reach many a human heart."

For a moment Angelina stood speechless as she grasped the instrument in her hands. "I have no words." She began to cry.

"You have a tender human soul, Angelina. You have great compassion for those who suffer. Some day you will make a wonderful wife for a godly man." He gave her a fatherly hug. "I can get another lute for myself in Rome."

With great difficulty Julius remained aboard the ship, allowing the goodbyes to proceed unhindered. Every fiber of his being wanted to approach the girl, but good sense held him back. *I will have time to speak with Paul later. Maybe he can tell me something about her.*

"We depart in five minutes," announced Captain Lucius. "If you are coming with us, come aboard now."

Two hugs later Paul and his traveling companions boarded the ship. There Julius greeted them. "I must confess that I was worried you wouldn't show. I thought that maybe the Jews or someone else had gotten you all thrown into prison for preaching."

Paul laughed. "We arrived too late on the Sabbath. It was too late to get into trouble with the Jews here. But we did have a great time with the Gentile believers."

As Paul waved farewell to the believers standing on the dock, shore workers pulled the gangplank from the ship. They unfastened the ropes from the moorings that bound the Isis and cast them aboard. Long poles backed the ship from its berth. Once away, the wind caught the sails. The Isis wound its bow in the opposite direction and began to move on its own.

All the while Julius fixed his eyes upon the young woman, turning away only when she seemed to return his glances. Through the din of conversation at the dock he had caught some of the words between her and Aristarchus. *If only that husband could be me.*

From the deck Paul continued to wave to the Christians ashore, tears forming in his eyes. "They will suffer greatly for their faith," he remarked to Luke.

7

Ille Perfugium

It had been a perfect day for a wedding, warm but not hot, with a gentle breeze blowing in from the sea. Publius smiled as he watched Theophilus and his bride Flavia board the same carriage he and Amoenitas had used on their wedding day. Nearly the entire church contingent of some five-hundred people, as well as many others, cheered as the carriage departed from the Mathos Amphitheater in route to their home, flanked by an honor guard of six Roman soldiers on horseback.

Inside the carriage Theophilus beamed. The emaciated, bedraggled, nearly terminated Flavia he had carried from her prison cell only five months before was nowhere evident. Her auburn hair, set off by a white orchid, shimmered brilliantly. Around her neck hung the jade amulet her mother had given her. It had been returned anonymously only one week prior by a guilt-ridden Roman official.

He took hold of her left hand. "I am the most blessed of men to have you as my bride."

Flavia cupped his hand between hers with her right. "Gratiana told me that I am a woman of inestimable worth. It is wonderful to have a man who agrees. I must confess that I prefer riding in this carriage with you right now to sitting in the darkness of that cold, desolate cell."

Amoenitas watched the carriage until it was out of sight before turning to Theophilus' three daughters, Benedictus newly nine, Laverna seven, and Accalia four. "Your daddy and your new mommy need some time together. Come on, girls. We're going to our house and we're going to have lots of fun there." She gathered them into another carriage furnished by her husband's father Trebonius.

"I will join you later," spoke Publius before Amoenitas cracked the reins and headed for their home near the Litus Baths.

"You're next," he spoke to Doctor Corbus and Domina Iras Macatus, who stood nearby, arm in arm. "How are things at the hospital?"

"We are doing well," answered the doctor. "Our only problem is a lack of patients, which I guess is a good thing. Since we implemented the sanitation reforms recommended by Doctor Luke, the general populace has become a lot healthier. Clean drinking water and proper sewage disposal have made a tremendous difference."

Together they perused the people who were gathered in groups, showing little sign of wanting to disperse. "It is not just the physical health of the island people that is a blessing. It is the health of our church," remarked Domina Macatus in her high-pitched voice.

Publius nodded. Since Paul's departure the church had increased in both size and power. Those who were serious about following Christ, had grown in depth. The persecution warned about by Paul had so far not materialized as a significant factor. It helped having Publius' father Trebonius as propraetor of the island, to discourage troublemakers.

Yet Publius maintained a healthy concern. For one thing, he was running out of new things to teach the people, limited as was his knowledge of Christ. Both he and Theophilus longed for the promised book from Luke about the life of Christ.

*****

"You have made great progress with your painting skills," spoke Gratiana. "You have a gift from God, which not only consists of an ability to create stunning images, but images that are pregnant with symbolic meaning. You create art that compels people to look and to ask."

"Thank you, avia," answered Eletia. "There is something about painting that brings out my soul and fills it with joy."

"Which is why I have left this one wall here at Ille Perfugium blank. I have taught you all that I can teach you. Soon I must shed my earthly body. It is now time for you to strike out on your own and develop your own painting style. Paint on this wall what comes to you from the Spirit of God, for His glory."

*****

With fresh coats of paint inside and out, breathtaking murals of biblical scenes on all but one of the inner walls of the great room, comfortable furniture, and re-established gardens front and back, the former brothel, newly christened Ille Perfugium, drew some of its former residents like a magnet, this time to more worthy pursuits. After a time of prayer together Gratiana, Amoenitas, and Eletia opened its doors to the seven women who waited outside.

"Welcome," said Gratiana. "We are so glad you have come. We have rooms for you all upstairs. Two to a room for now. One of you will room with Eletia. You may choose your own room assignments and get settled. Please come down to the great room in thirty minutes for our midday meal."

*****

Easy chatter, with Eletia in the lead and Gratiana in support, accompanied the meal of salted bread, eggs, fish, and fresh vegetables and fruit from the outside garden. Amoenitas, strangely troubled in spirit, silently surveyed the women who sat with them on each side of the long rectangular table in the great room. *Hopefully all have come to get their lives back in order.*

Two she had known before when they were children at the gymnasium. Cornelia was bright, but had the same melancholy spirit she had displayed as a child. Amoenitas wondered if she had experienced a dysfunctional home life. Mariana, with her intelligence and beautiful features, had always been a favorite of the teachers. Despite two years of hard living, renting her body to others, she still retained a degree of youthful beauty.

Of those she had not known before, Demetra, aside from being obviously Greek, was an enigma. *I will have to observe more and spend time with her privately.* Fabia, except for her hard-bitten face, was also hard to read. Herminia was subdued, having not said a word so far during the entire meal. Albina was the polar opposite, a worthy match for Eletia when it came to conversation. On the surface Valentina appeared to have her life the most together, but Amoenitas sensed deep scars beneath. *I must pray for wisdom in getting to know these wounded women.*

Gratiana pushed back her chair at the head of the newly refinished wooden table, a long-ago product of her late husband Porcius Caepio. "I hope you have all enjoyed your meal and that you have found your rooms inviting and homey. Again, we are very glad to have each of you."

She smiled. "Now comes the fun part. I must go over the house rules."

A collective groan rose from around the table.

Gratiana waived her right hand in understanding. "I know. But you'll get used to them. These rules are your friends. They will keep you out of trouble. First of all, any men visitors must remain downstairs. The only time men are permitted upstairs is for necessary repairs to any of the rooms. And if that is the case, none of you are to be in a room with them while the repairs are taking place.

"Some of you will think that is no problem. Some of you here might understandably hate men. But not all men are like the ones you have experienced. Hopefully, some or all of you will one day have husbands who will treat you like ladies. In the meantime, no other forms of sexual expression are permitted upstairs either. Do I need to elaborate?" Gratiana's eyes met in turn those of every woman at the table. One by one they nodded.

"We don't charge money for you to live here. Those costs are graciously underwritten by the Mathos church. But that doesn't mean you stay here for free. Your rooms are to be kept clean and orderly at all times. We leave it to those of you who occupy each room to decide who does what. Just keep your rooms in order. An orderly room is conducive to an orderly life.

"Thirdly, meals don't just prepare themselves. We will teach you all how. But within two weeks, on a rotating basis, you will be preparing all of your own meals. Those not assigned to meal preparation will wash dishes, clean the lower part of this house, do laundry, or keep the outside gardens watered and free of weeds. We will change the chore list every second Monday, but everyone will have chores every day. If you fail to do your part, you don't eat. Please don't test us on that.

"After your morning chores are complete, there will be two mandatory class sessions that I, my granddaughter Amoenitas, or other women in the church will teach. The first session each morning will involve the basic skills of reading, writing, and arithmetic. We want all of you to be literate and able to transact business. The second session will involve practical skills, such as sewing, weaving, gardening, nursing, handiwork, or child rearing. There will be no classes on Saturdays or Sundays.

"The things I have outlined are mandatory if you wish to live here. After the noon meal and the after-meal clean-up each day, you will be free until the evening meal preparation to relax here or go about the town. If you can get a job somewhere to earn money doing something worthwhile, so much the better. But by a job, we don't mean doing what you did here before.

"The last two things I have to tell you are voluntary. This is a Christian home. We honor and serve our Savior Jesus Christ here. We do not require that any of you believe as ourselves in order to live here. But every evening in this room we will have a time of singing, prayer, and a look at what few Hebrew Scriptures we have. Your attendance for that is voluntary. If you choose to do something else, we only ask that you not distract those who do attend. Though we encourage it, neither do we require that you attend the Mathos church on Sunday mornings. But if you truly want to become fully free of your old life and to live from henceforth in newness of life, it is Christ who empowers us to do so."

She rose from the table. "We will take care of the clean-up today. The routine begins tomorrow morning. Don't worry, ladies. We will ease you into it. For this afternoon you are free to do as you please."

* * * * *

Alacerius sat beneath the shade of a great oak tree outside his home, high on the sparsely populated eastern side of the island. He had never completely recovered from his bout with island fever. Lingering aches plagued his body and a lack of energy sapped his strength. He looked over at Alexandra, who sat opposite him sipping fruit tea. She wore a fine flowing crimson gown, accented by her signature peacock.

"It is dreadful what the Christians have done to our island these past few months. They must be stopped. They must be destroyed! But how do we accomplish that?"

"We destroy their leaders," answered Alexandra.

"Easier said than done. We have tried. Have you figured out another way?"

Alexandra smiled a sinister smile. "I already have a plan in place. We have a certain young woman planted at Ille Perfugium. But not all of our other pieces are in place just yet. We will make our move when the time is right—when they least expect it."

8

Puteoli

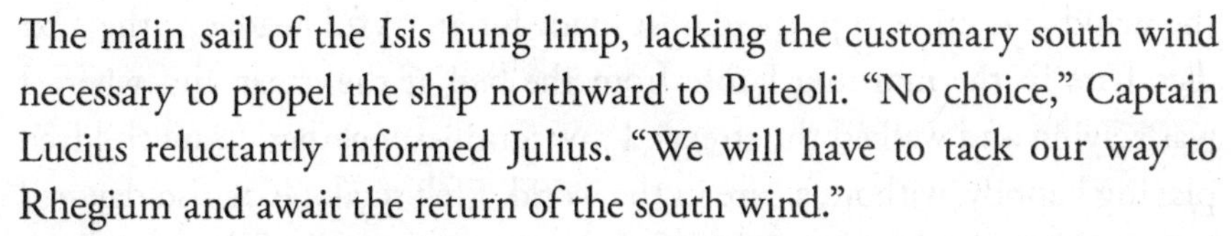

The main sail of the Isis hung limp, lacking the customary south wind necessary to propel the ship northward to Puteoli. "No choice," Captain Lucius reluctantly informed Julius. "We will have to tack our way to Rhegium and await the return of the south wind."

The centurion sighed. He wanted off the choppy waters of the sea and was already five months behind schedule, courtesy of his involuntary stay on Melitene. His superiors in Rome might not be understanding of the reasons for his tardiness. But the circumstances he had faced were beyond his control.

"You are the captain. Do whatever seems best to you."

Immediately after he spoke, someone tapped him on the shoulder from behind. He turned to discover a familiar face looking back at him. "I thought I would take you up on your offer."

"Marcus, I didn't see you come aboard. I figured you had decided to remain in Syracuse."

"I had no reason or place to stay. I came aboard late last night and went directly below. Since my fare is good all the way to Puteoli, here am I."

Inwardly Julius rejoiced. "It looks like we won't make Puteoli by tomorrow, as hoped. No wind. We're putting in at Rhegium, at least for the night." He gestured to his friend. "Come, let's sit down."

The two found an open bench on the starboard side of the ship, where afternoon shade was more readily available. "So, was it just the free bed and food that brought you aboard?"

Marcus chuckled. "Partly that. Maybe something else."

Julius' mind quickened as he peered at his friend. Marcus appeared ready to converse at a deeper level. His eyes communicated a willingness to speak honestly and to listen.

"I can't sleep at night."

"I am sorry to hear that, Marcus. Why is that?"

Knowing Marcus to be a proud man, he waited patiently for a response. Deeper level communication was not easy for him.

"I have hurt people," he finally admitted. "I never used to feel guilty about things like that. Now I am overwhelmed."

"I have hurt people too," replied Julius understandably. "We have that in common. I think I know how you feel."

"Three days ago, after you left the Taberna of Lunianus, I spent the rest of the day sitting at that same table, drinking away the problems of the world and mine in particular. It made for an awful headache the next day. Late in the morning I rose from the bed at the cheap inn where I was staying and walked the streets. I saw families together. I saw children playing happily, without a care in the world. I felt so alone. It also dawned on me that drinking does a lot of things to me and all of them are bad. It numbs my guilt temporarily, but makes me to do more guilty things. I always feel awful the next morning. It costs me money, of which I now have little. And then there's that other thing I have finally come to realize."

"What other thing?"

"It doesn't solve any problems. It only creates them. I need to stop, but I don't know if I can. If I do stop, then I have to face my regrets. So I drink, which only causes more regrets. It is a terrible cycle. Is there a solution to all of this?"

Julius marveled at his openness. He was conversing with a very different person from the arrogant, cock-sure man he had known in passing on Melitene. He looked to his right, toward the stern of the ship. Some fifteen paces away stood Paul, conversing with a group of his friends.

"Shall I ask Paul to join us? He can give you answers better than I."

Marcus shook his head. "He won't want to talk to me. I tried to kill him. I am pretty sure that he knows that."

"You would be surprised. Paul has done worse than you. Innocent people are dead because of him."

"I wouldn't have guessed that," replied Marcus, visibly moved. He took a deep breath. "Innocent people are dead because of me too. You know, I was once intoxicated with joy at the prospect of killing him. Now I have no desire at all to do so."

Julius gave a soft chuckle. "You don't want to kill Paul anymore. That is a good thing. It sounds like God is working on your heart." He patted his friend on the back. "There is a way to be free, Marcus, both of strong drink and of your regrets. There is a way to become the man you would rather be. Christ makes all the difference in a man's life."

Abruptly Marcus stood to his feet. "Thank you for listening to me, Julius. I will go below now."

As Julius watched Marcus disappear down the stairway into the hold of the ship, he silently prayed. *Lord Jesus, work on his tormented heart. Set him free. What can I do to help him get there?*

*****

The stop at Rhegium turned out to be short and uneventful. Rather than pay extra for a room ashore, most of the passengers elected to sleep the night on the ship. When a south wind came up early the next morning, Captain Lucius decided to immediately put off.

But with the wind came inordinately rough seas, which sickened many of the passengers, including Marcus, who found himself embarrassingly among those obligated to lean over the side of the ship. For the next two days they sailed within sight of the rugged coastline of Italy. At least the continuous sight of land was reassuring.

*****

Late in the afternoon on the second day from Rhegium the great concave harbor of Portus Puteoli finally came into view. Before the ship loomed the impressive stone Bridge of Caligula, consisting of six high, wide arches, three on its left side, through which sailed outgoing ships, and three on its right for incoming ships like the Isis. To the left of the bridge was a long stone breakwater that connected it to the land. Upon a causeway on the breakwater stood a large number of people, watching ships enter and leave the harbor.

A large Alexandrian grain ship that had just passed through one of three stone arches on the port side of the Isis temporarily blocked Marcus' view of the smaller harbor of Misenum, home port of the massive Roman fleet of Penteconters, Pemiolias, Liburnas, Triremes, Biremes, and other warships that ruled the great sea. Life for the pirate, he knew, during the Pax Romana was a hazardous profession.

As soon as the Isis passed through the middle arch on the incoming side, the first thing Marcus noticed was a sulfurous stench. *So that's why they call it Puteoli—for its putrid smell. This will take some getting used to.* Compensating somewhat for the smell was the welcome calming of the waters.

As the Isis neared the dock, a group of thirty some people began to enthusiastically cheer for someone on the ship. When the cheers became more distinct, the unmistakable name of Paul told Marcus the reason. *I doubt he's ever met any of those people, yet they greet him like they've been best friends all their lives. Nice touch these Christians have. How did they even know he was coming?*

"Greetings in the name of Jesus Christ," spoke the leader of the group, as Paul and his friends debarked from the ship. "My name is Urbanus. Which of you is Paul?"

"I am," spoke Paul, extending his hand.

"We have lodging for you all," said Urbanus. "How long will you and your companions remain here in Puteoli?"

Paul pointed to Julius, who stood beside him. "This is the centurion Julius, who is charged with seeing me to Rome. He is also one of us, a fellow believer in Christ Jesus. How long will we be here, Julius?"

"Some of my men, which includes me, are pretty sick from the last couple of days. Two of my men have family here that they haven't seen in two years. I think maybe a week is about right."

He placed his right hand on Paul's shoulder. "Enjoy your time with the brethren here. Again, I spare no man to guard you. It will be different once we reach Rome, where I will be obligated to keep up military appearances. Please don't get yourself arrested for preaching or something else. Let us meet here again next Friday morning at the sixth hour. I will have mounts for those of you going with us to Rome. I expect it may take us another six full days to travel the 150 miles from here to there via the Appian Way."

9

Seven Young Women

For Eletia, the practice of rising early each day was a lifelong, if reluctant habit. Life on the Aequitas property had always been hard, especially after her father Andronicus had passed from the world five years before. Milking goats, feeding chickens, collecting eggs, and cleaning the barn were morning chores, which naturally fell to her as the younger of the sisters. Amoenitas had to work the field. Her mother Julia tended to the house in the morning and later helped in the field.

Life for Eletia had taken a dramatic turn the past few months, beginning with her pregnancy. Her mother Julia had passed away during the great storm, compounding her problems and grief. But then came her encounter with Christ. She remembered all too well her close brush with death and the dreadful visions of an afterlife of horror. By the grace of God, she had survived, as had the child within her. Now, as a follower of Christ, rising early was more delight than duty. In the morning all was quiet. In the morning one could hear the voice of God.

It was still dark as she cautiously grasped the railing and felt for the first step down the stairway at Ille Perfugium, where she had lived since its opening. Being now great with child, she knew that she could not afford a fall down the stairway. As she descended, a strange heaviness swept over her soul. *Something isn't right.* She had learned over the past few months not to dismiss such warnings. *But what isn't right*?

Once seated in the great room, she began with simple gratefulness and praise to God, who had saved her, both body and soul. She then began to pray about her premonition.

Oh Lord Jesus, I just have this feeling that something terrible will soon happen. I feel the enemy at work. But I believe in You. You are more powerful than Satan and all his dominion. Whatever it is, I pray You to thwart the wicked schemes of the evil one.

She began to ponder and pray for the seven young women who lived with her in the house. Most, having come from dysfunctional homes, looked to Gratiana as a matriarchal mother figure. Amoenitas, who came later each morning to teach classes on reading, on health, and on nursing, was respected as a model of what a woman could become, if she stayed the course of life at Ille Perfugium and embraced Christ along the way.

But Eletia had a different kind of relationship with the women. For one thing, she actually lived among them, rooming with Cornelia, whom she had vaguely known before. She too had been immoral and suffered grievous consequences. She was someone the other women could touch—whom they knew did not consider herself above them.

Cornelia hardly spoke to anyone except Eletia. *No wonder she is always so morose, with what her father did to her. Lord Jesus, she needs a lot of patience and love. Help me to give that to her.*

Mariana's anger came out at the slightest provocation. She had been a favorite of the customers who visited the former brothel. Now her hatred for men seethed. She had sworn never to marry, never to have children, and never to afford a member of the male gender so much as a kind word. *Oh Lord Jesus, give me wisdom. Help me to know what I can do to reach her. Open her deeply wounded heart.*

Fabia also hated men, which demonstrably showed itself in her appearance. She had gone out of her way to look as unattractive as possible. *Dear Father, I have also hated men. But You have taken away my hatred. I ask You to do the same miracle with Fabia.*

Valentina did her chores faithfully and got along with everyone. She took pride in her appearance and did well in her classes, being the most educated of the women. But there was something. *All I know, Lord Jesus, is to observe her. Please give me wisdom and discernment.*

Demetra was hard to know. She faithfully did her chores and attended the classes. But she only spoke when required and did not appear interested in developing a friendship with anyone, including Eletia. *I don't know what to do with her, Lord Jesus. Help me.*

Herminia was pleasant, but distant. She had the most trouble with the classes, seemingly unable to grasp the simplest concepts. Unlike the others, she had grown up in an outwardly functional, two-parent home. But Eletia surmised that from the perspective of her parents, she had never been able to do anything right. *Lord Jesus, is it just that she is not as intelligent as the others, or is it an acute lack of self-confidence? She needs someone to believe in her, just like You believed in me.*

Albina was outgoing and fun to be around, but had the biggest problem with chores. It wasn't that she defiantly refused to do them. She was the master of incomplete, sloppy work. *Lord, that was me not so long ago. How can we help her learn to take pride in her work?*

She prayed for the child in her womb. *My Savior, help me to be the mother my child needs. I feel so inadequate, especially because I am alone.*

Her prayers turned to a certain man. *Lord Jesus, I don't know where Marcus is, or if I will ever see him again. Part of me despises him. But I wasn't such a paragon of virtue myself. I pray that somehow You will do a miracle in his heart. May he come to know Your love, Your forgiveness, and Your peace, just as I have.*

For a solid hour she continued to pray. During that time the terrible foreboding began to fade, replaced by a sense that though something might soon happen, its effects would be fleeting. She emerged from her contemplations to discover the first light of the new day beginning to fill the house. Quietly, she ascended the stairway.

"It is time to rise, ladies," she called as sweetly as possible through the curtains into each cubiculum. "It is the Lord's day today." Audible groans emanated from the four rooms. Sixth hour wake-up calls had not been a part of their former lives.

*****

"What are you painting, Eletia?" asked Cornelia.

"It is a picture of my life so far. The rock represents the hardships of this world. The earth beneath the rock represents the good soil of Christ. Being rooted in the good soil, God has given the spindly olive tree the ability to split the rock, to leaf, and to bear fruit."

"What do you mean by that?"

"I have faced some hard things in my life, Cornelia, some by circumstances beyond my control and some of my own making. By myself I am too weak and foolish to properly deal with any of it. But if we are willing, God can take any such life and make it strong enough to break a rock and bear fruit."

"Even for me?"

"Even for you, Cornelia. No one's life situation is always ideal. How do we choose to handle what comes our way? Do we live by our wits or by God's wisdom, power, and grace?" Sometimes we bring calamity upon ourselves by our own poor choices. But no matter the reason for the calamity, there is always a path to life, even when it seems that we are hopelessly buried under a rock."

Cornelia looked beneath and to the right of the wall, which was still blank. "What are you going to paint on the rest of the wall?"

"I don't know yet. Those parts of my life have yet to happen. All I know is that if I get right what I am now painting, then God will take care of the rest. All will turn out well in the end."

* * * * *

The morning was cool and still, with a slight overcast. A group of women from Ille Perfugium ambled toward the amphitheater, accompanied by a pattern of continuous gongs from the bell tower, beckoning worshipers to come. At Gratiana's side walked Herminia, who clung to the older woman like a new-born chick. Cornelia walked with Eletia. Behind them trailed the other two women who had consented to attend the Sunday morning worship service, Albina and Valentina.

At the top of the great amphitheater they were greeted by two women of the church. Valentina helped Gratiana descend a few steps until she realized that Gratiana wanted to go no further. The further down they went, the more steps she would have to climb when the service was finished. The women sat together in a group on the far left of the amphitheater, which given its size, seemed sparsely filled. About 300 worshipers were so far present.

"Who were the two women who greeted us when we came in?" Cornelia asked Eletia.

"The older woman is Domina Iras Macatus. She works at the valetudinarium. The younger is Flavia, now newly married to Pastor Theophilus."

"I love the way they greeted me. It was like they actually thought I was worth something. Maybe someday I will have a husband like Pastor Theophilus."

"Flavia had a problem with feeling inferior too. And look how it has turned out for her, albeit through a lot of pain. You too are of great worth to the One who made us. Both of those women had to learn about their worth in the eyes of God—as I am learning."

For another ten minutes they sat, awaiting the beginning of the service. In the meantime, the attendance swelled to nearly 500. Immediately after the tolling of the ninth hour, Publius appeared on the stage.

"Good morning dear brethren in Christ. I have a special treat for you today. Upon hearing about what has taken place on our island, a group of believers from Jerusalem has arrived on a ship from Caesarea. With them they have brought for us complete copies of the ancient Hebrew Scriptures in our language, along with a personal letter from an apostle named Peter, who assures us that they are inspired words from God. In his letter he says that our Savior Jesus Christ often quoted from these same Scriptures. This morning I want to speak to you about two possible ways to live, out of what is called the first Psalm."

"How blessed is the man who does not walk in the counsel of the wicked, nor stand in the path of sinners, nor sit in the seat of scoffers! But his delight is in the law of the Lord, and in His law he meditates day and night. And he will be like a tree firmly planted by streams of water, which yields its fruit in its season, and its leaf does not wither; and in whatever he does, he prospers.

The wicked are not so, but they are like chaff which the wind drives away. Therefore the wicked will not stand in the judgment, nor sinners in the assembly of the righteous. For the Lord knows the way of the righteous, but the way of the wicked will perish." (Psalm 1)

Publius looked up from the scroll and scanned the audience. "It creates quite a visual picture, does it not? I want to be like that tree. Therefore, I have chosen the law of the Lord, as have most of you here. I prefer prospering in all that I do over being chaff which the wind drives away."

As Publius spoke, Eletia drank in the words. *I too prefer God's way, the way of life. It is so much better than the way of death.* She wondered how the women with her were taking in the message of the first Psalm.

10

The Bench by the Road

The sun hung low in the western sky, a welcome relief from the blistering heat of the day. Hungry, thirsty, and sunburned in face, Marcus and his party wearily entered what appeared to be a lively town called the Market of Appius. He was also saddle sore from four days of riding from Puteoli to Sinuessa, from Sinuessa to Minturno, from Minturno to Tarricina, and from Tarricina to the current town. Two more riding days remained to get to Rome. It seemed a daunting task, but for now he could rest.

The Market of Appius was by far the most populated and lively of the stations along the Appian Way he had so far seen. Off-duty soldiers strode the main street in search of a good time. Vendors peddled their wares from makeshift shacks along both sides of the street. Raucous music spilled from a taberna to his right.

Near the far end of the town they came to a large barn, across from which stood an elaborate looking inn called Aurelius Deversorium. It appeared that both the barn and the inn functioned primarily as Roman army facilities. Wearily, Marcus dismounted with the others in his group, nine soldiers and Paul's contingent of three. Walking with his legs still spread wide from being in that position the greater part of the day, he led his equally weary horse to the barn for watering, feeding, and rest.

Just as they emerged from the barn, a group of five men greeted the parched, hungry travelers. "Which of you is Paul?" asked one who appeared to be their leader, a burly, brawny man with a huge expanse of red hair.

"I am," came Paul's answer.

The man greeted him warmly. "My name is Dominic, a home builder by trade. I have been a follower of Christ now for many years. But only recently I read your long letter to our church in Rome. It has revolutionized my life."

"Thank you, Dominic. It revolutionized mine is I wrote it, guided by the Holy Spirit."

"We heard of your coming and have come from Rome to meet you. Perhaps you and I can talk more about your letter along the way, but for now we have made arrangements for you and your entire party to eat and to stay the night at the Aurelius Deversorium. How would you like that?"

A cheer rose from the travelers, soldiers and civilians alike. Readily they followed Dominic and the others into the inn. Once inside they were led to a large private room. Inside were two long tables, already set with dishes and filled cups of water. Eagerly the men found places, seated themselves, and drank. Within minutes a group of gaily attired, smiling women emerged from the kitchen, carrying large platters of savory beef, chicken, and fish, along with bread, vegetables, and fruit. It was all Marcus could do to wait for Paul to finish his prayer of thanksgiving before digging in.

*****

Satisfied, at least in stomach, Marcus decided to take a long walk to help digest his food and to work out the stiffness in his legs before settling into bed. He knew that sleep would allude him if he retired too early anyway. Night had fallen by the time he exited the inn. He turned to his left, anxious to escape the boisterous noise of the Market of Appius night life. As he walked, he reflected upon his changed preference. *I once loved that noise. Why do I want now to avoid it?* He only knew that it went deeper than a lack of money.

The evening cool was a welcome contrast from the heat of the day. Once beyond the confines of the town he also found the going dark, with only a quarter moon reflecting on the cobblestone road to light his way. He figured on walking half a mile in the direction of Rome before turning back.

As he walked and the tumult of the town faded, a great heaviness fell upon his soul, much like the surrounding darkness. To his left lay the

Pontine Marshes, from which frogs croaked and crickets chirped. A voice from within took on greater forcefulness with each step.

You are the vilest of men. Walk out into that marsh, lie down, and sink into the mire. End your miserable life. It is the only way to atone for the many terrible things you have done. No one will ever find you. No one will even care to look.

He stopped and turned in the direction of the marsh. The darkness pressed upon him like an iron vise. Fear gripped his inner being. He began to shake. *But what then will happen to my soul? Do I even have a soul?*

"Do you mind if I join you?" came a startling voice from the direction of the town.

He turned to face the man he had both painstakingly avoided and subtly followed the past two weeks. For reasons he did not understand, he felt relieved to see him. Words formed and somehow escaped his mouth.

"I would be glad for your company."

As the man approached, he marveled at their difference in size. Paul was nearly a foot shorter than himself and slight in build. Yet there was something about his bearing that more than compensated for his perceived physical shortcomings. He reminded Marcus of Solon on the island of Melitene. There was more to both men than met the eye.

"I have been watching you these past two weeks."

"You have?" With great effort he labored to hide his surprise.

"We have met before. Do you remember? I tried to speak with you after Publius worked on your face at the Aequitas property. You were a sorry sight."

"Yes, I suppose I was," he reluctantly agreed.

"I am also aware that you tried to kill me early one morning at the summit of Scopulus Altus. But then you saw something or someone that sent you fleeing for your life."

Marcus kept silent. *How does he know that?*

"I knew that you were with us on the Isis, heading for Syracuse. I knew that you came back aboard for the voyage to Puteoli. I have watched you these past four days on our ride to Rome."

"What have you seen?" he asked somewhat apprehensively.

"A deeply troubled soul."

"Why have you not approached me before?"

"I did not perceive that you were ready to be approached."

They resumed their walk. Marcus remained silent for a time, pondering his response. The dread fear that had pervaded his thoughts seemed to have dissipated in favor of hope. "Do you think I am ready now?"

"The Holy Spirit of God, whom I serve, prompted me to follow you from the town. He told me that it was time to approach you. I am here. Talk to me, Marcus."

Desperately Marcus searched for a response that would deflect the onus of guilt he felt in his soul. "Have you spoken with Julius about me?"

"He spoke to me only briefly that you were among us. He prefers to keep private conversations private."

For the next few minutes, they continued to walk silently side by side, Marcus deep in his thoughts. *Do I dare open my soul to this man?*

"I am troubled by some things I have done," he finally said.

"That is a good sign."

"How is that a good sign? For me it is misery."

"A man must see the wretchedness of his ways and his inability to redeem or reform himself before he can see his need for God."

They came to a bench under a sycamore tree along the side of the road. Feeling that they had walked far enough in one direction, Marcus seated himself.

"Julius told me that you have also done some regretful things. He told me that people are dead because of you."

Paul joined him on the bench. "It is shamefully true. I was called Saul of Tarsus then. I was a Pharisee, a sect of the Jews who are zealous for God, but much misguided. Considering myself too high and mighty to engage in actual stoning, I guarded the cloaks of those who stoned to death a young follower of Christ named Stephen. After that, with authority from the chief priests of Judaism, I rounded up Christians and threw them into prison, to be put on trial for their lives. When their fate came to a vote, I always voted death. Many were put to death. But God had mercy on me. On my way to Damascus to persecute still more followers of Christ, I was felled by a blinding light from heaven."

"Saul, Saul, why are you persecuting Me?" (Acts 9:4b)

"It was Jesus who spoke to me. I was made blind and led by the hand into Damascus, where I spent three days without sight, without food, and without water."

"How did you feel during that time?"

"As badly as a man can feel. I realized all the evil I had done. I prayed much, asking God for the mercy I had never given His people."

"What happened after the three days?"

"A man named Ananias came to me. He laid his hands on me and said, 'Brother Saul, the Lord Jesus, who appeared to you on the road by which you were coming, has sent me so that you may regain your sight, and be filled with the Holy Spirit.' (Acts 9:17b)

"My sight was restored. So grateful was I, that I asked immediately to be baptized as a follower of Christ. I ate and drank. Then some of Jesus' disciples in Damascus looked after me for a few days. I marveled at their forgiveness and love for me."

Marcus nodded thoughtfully. "I have noticed the love you Christians seem to have for one another. The whole dinner thing this evening showed it to me again."

Despite all his efforts to preserve his dignity, tears forced their way into his eyes. "People are dead because of me too. Nothing I can do will ever bring them back. What is there to do about the guilt I feel other than to drink—or to end it all in the marshes?"

"You have asked the right question. The God who created us is holy. Being holy, He cannot tolerate sin or sinners in His presence. 'For the wages of sin is death, but the free gift of God is eternal life in Christ Jesus our Lord'." (Romans 6:23)

"How does that work? How can God give us eternal life in Christ Jesus if we are sinners, deserving of death?"

"God couldn't just wave away our sins like they never happened. His holy nature demands death as the consequence of sin. But He still loves us, Marcus. It is His nature to love."

"I still don't understand. How can God love people and have to destroy them at the same time?"

"You do ask the right questions, my friend. Our sins had to be transferred to someone else who had lived a perfect, sinless life. He who knew no sin was sent by God to die on a Roman cross for our sins. God poured out His wrath upon His Son, as if His Son had committed all of our sins. At the same time, He transferred His Son's sinless life to us to justify us—in effect making us sinless. In one act God both satisfied His wrath against sin and poured out His love for all mankind."

Marcus shook his head. "That all sounds wonderful, but I am still confused. Julius said that Christ lives today. You just said that He died on a Roman cross. How can He be alive if He is dead?"

"Because Christ came back to life. He paid for our sins, satisfying God's wrath. Then having paid for our sins with His death, God raised Him from the dead three days later."

Again, Marcus shook his head. "All of this is mind boggling. I cannot take it in."

"It is an understanding that usually comes to us in increments, Marcus. I am still in the process of trying to fully understand it myself. All I know for sure is that 'If any man is in Christ, he is a new creature; the old things passed away; behold, new things have come'." (2 Corinthians 5:17b)

Despite all resistance the floodgates opened and Marcus surrendered to the tears he had vainly fought. He turned and directly faced Paul through his tears.

"I want this. I want to know this forgiveness for my many sins. I want to be clean. I want to be free of the habits that are destroying me. I want to know this Christ."

*****

That night Marcus lay in his bed, still wide awake, pondering what had just taken place on the Appian Way. For the first time in his life he felt truly loved. He felt the presence of the Lord hovering over him, almost as if he could touch Him. He felt indeed like a new man. *What would you have me do with the rest of my life, Lord?*

His mind went to Eletia. *Lord Jesus, Eletia carries my child. I have hurt her. Oh Lord, I know it. And what I did to her sister Amoenitas! Could either of them ever forgive me? Lord Jesus, my life is now in Your hands. Make me into the man You want me to be.*

For the first time in a long time that Marcus could remember, he drifted into a sound sleep.

11

The Temple Beth Shalom

The first light of the new day greeted his eyes when Marcus opened them the next morning. From beneath his upstairs cubiculum came the muffledsounds of voices and activity. He swung from his bed and stood to his feet. For a moment he stayed in place and considered.

I am the same man I was yesterday at this time—and yet I am not.

He pulled back the curtain covering the open window to the outside to breathe in the fertile spring air. Fragrances of flowers filled his nostrils in a way he had never before noticed. For the first time in many years he actually heard the singing of birds welcoming the new day. Smells of fresh bread from the kitchen wafted upward, tantalizing his senses. Quickly he dressed and made his way downstairs, there to be greeted by several of his party.

"Good morning, Marcus. I hear that you are a new follower of our Savior Jesus Christ," spoke Dominic.

Marcus smiled—another strange new experience for him. "I am indeed."

At his affirmation a spontaneous roar of approval arose from those present. For the next fifteen minutes he found himself bouncing from one man to another, all of whom spoke kindness and encouragement.

"Christ died for you," spoke a man who introduced himself as Tychicus, one of the four others who had come with Dominic from Rome. "If you were to only person on this earth, He would have died just for you."

By the time food came from the kitchen, the entire group of travelers and greeters from Rome had filtered in. Once they were seated at either of the two long tables, Julius rose to speak.

"We have just a short trip of about twelve miles to Three Inns today. Because it is short and we and our horses are much wearied from our travels so far, we will begin our journey one hour later than normal this morning."

He turned to Paul. "Paul, would you please bless the food for us before we partake?"

*****

At the ninth hour the party, now numbering eighteen, resumed their journey to Rome, still two days distant. As they passed it, Marcus eyed the bench under the sycamore tree where he and Paul had sat the night before. It would be a place he would always remember, the place of his new beginning. He gazed at the lush foliage on either side of the road. To his left spread the Pontine Marshes. The mostly low growth enabled him to see all the way to the Great Sea. By contrast to his right was an array of palms, olive trees, cypress, Aleppo pines, and Ravello. Beyond the trees rose the Lepine Mountains, with traces of snow still garlanding its peaks. The entire scene spoke a beauty that heretofore had gone unnoticed for many years. Gone also was his sense of physical weariness. Even the day itself was shaping up to be pleasant, not nearly as hot as the day before.

Twenty minutes later they came to a long stretch of especially dense foliage on both sides of the road, where the light of the sun only sparsely dotted the cobblestones. "This is the most dangerous part of our trip," spoke Dominic in Marcus' hearing. "Highwaymen emerge from any of the innumerable hiding places on either side of the road to pillage travelers. But I don't think we have much to worry about today. It is unlikely they would attack a group our size, especially a group that includes trained soldiers. Even still, we need to stay bunched up."

*****

The remaining two days of travel passed without incident. Late in the afternoon on the second day, the megapolis of Rome finally came into view. From a distance it appeared a jumble of massive buildings, though none were particularly tall. By a shaded area near a stream Julius halted the group to water the horses and to give himself and his soldiers a chance to bath and to shape up their appearance as much as possible.

When it came time to move on, one final distasteful task remained. "I hate to do this, Paul," said Julius. "You pose no flight risk, but you are technically my prisoner and it must appear so when we enter the city or I will no longer be a centurion." With that two of his soldiers shackled him in chains, to which Paul meekly submitted. From that point on he rode between the two soldiers, whose names were Petronius and Decimus.

What appeared captivating at a distance lost much of its sheen as Marcus and the others entered the city. The first thing he noticed was the stench. It wasn't anything in particular. The city just smelled badly in contrast to the fresh air of the countryside. It reminded him of Melitene after Alacerius had taken control of the island.

With Dominic leading the way, the group wound its way through a maze of crowded, dirty, narrow streets until they came to a street called Via Flaminia. On the right they passed a large synagogue.

"That is the Temple Beth Shalom," spoke Dominic to Paul. "The chief rabbi is a man named Isaac Shelemiah. I know him a little bit. He has a good heart."

Just past the synagogue on the left they came to a small, non-descript two story dwelling, connected to a number of other small, non-descript two story dwellings. Julius saluted a detail of twenty-some soldiers who marched by as Dominic unlocked the door and bid Paul and his assigned guard Petronius to enter. There at the door Paul bade farewell to his companions.

"We didn't know about the others with you until we met them at the Market of Appius," explained Dominic. "We have arranged for you and your guard to be quartered here, while arrangements are made with the authorities for you to receive your hearing. I hope you will find this dwelling comfortable and properly furnished. Later today some people will come by to stock your home with food. We will lodge the others with the families of the men who are with me."

"Remove Paul's chains," Julius instructed Petronius. "As long as he is inside and out of sight, no chains are required. But if he goes outside the front of this house for any reason, you must be with him at all times. He must be chained and henceforth connected to an iron ball that will be brought by tomorrow."

He then addressed Paul. "Once I have seen to my men, I will inform the authorities of your presence. It will be up to them to arrange the time and place of your hearing. I pray that you will soon be free. God be with you."

With that the door was shut and Paul found himself alone with his guard Petronius. "Sir, I do not enjoy chaining you any more than you enjoy being chained."

"We will just have to make the best of it," answered Paul. "What do you know about Christ?"

*****

With the others Marcus rode up to the large archway entrance that opened to the great military plaza of Champs-de-Mars. Through the archway Marcus caught glimpses of squads of soldiers marching to the cadence of an assemblage of drummers on a raised stand at the far end of the plaza. Before entering, Julius said his goodbyes to the five men who had come from Rome and to Paul's friends Marcus, Luke, and Aristarchus.

"The soldiers and I must find our lodging on the other side of this archway. You are all dear people. I have much enjoyed our time together. May God keep you in His care until we meet again." The men clasped wrists before Julius and his men rode through the archway into the plaza.

*****

Three days after his arrival, Paul ventured from his dwelling for the first time and made for the Temple Beth Shalom. A low cart on wheels had been thoughtfully furnished by Dominic's people to accommodate the iron ball fastened to a five-foot long chain that was connected on the other end to Paul's right ankle. The temple occupied its own specific, non-symmetrical block, surrounded as it was by curved, narrow streets. The building itself was rectangular in shape and appeared by Paul's reckoning to be pointed toward Jerusalem.

Just outside the entryway to the temple Petronius removed the clasp from around Paul's ankle. The chain around his neck that restricted his arm movements remained in place. Quietly they entered, Paul taking pains to minimize the clanking sound of his chains, which echoed off the walls of the high-ceilinged structure. Before them, at the front was a group of men seated in the first three rows of benches. A rabbi stood before them at a podium, reading a passage in Isaiah from a scroll. To his side was a menorah and a manna jar. As quietly as possible Paul and Petronius came to the fourth row and seated themselves.

The rabbi looked up from his scroll. "Greetings, gentlemen. I am Rabbi Isaac Shelemiah. May I help you?"

Paul stood to his feet. "My name is Paul, formerly Saul of Tarsus, a Jew of the tribe of Benjamin, and an ardent follower of Christ."

The rabbi gazed at him, puzzled. "Go on."

"Brethren, though I had done nothing against our people, or the customs of our fathers, yet I was delivered prisoner from Jerusalem into the hands of the Romans. And when they had examined me, they were willing to release me because there was no ground for putting me to death. But when the Jews objected, I was forced to appeal to Caesar; not that I had any accusation against my nation. For this reason therefore, I requested to see you and to speak with you, for I am wearing this chain for the sake of the hope of Israel." (Acts 28:17b-20)

Rabbi Shelemiah gestured to the men seated before him. "Are any of you here familiar with a Paul or a Saul of Tarsus?" None spoke affirmatively. He again addressed Paul.

"We have neither received letters from Judea concerning you, nor have any of the brethren come here and reported or spoken anything bad about you. But we desire to hear from you what your views are; for concerning this sect, it is known to us that it is spoken against everywhere." (Acts 28:21b-22)

"Very well," answered Paul. "I do not wish to interrupt your study of Isaiah here. Can we set a time for you to come to my dwelling? I am just down this street on the left-hand side of Via Flaminia at number seventeen."

Rabbi Shelemiah addressed his assemblage. "Would three days hence at the eighth hour of the morning be acceptable?"

When the men nodded affirmatively, he asked the same question of Paul, who also nodded agreement. "Until then, I bid you all the peace of God."

With that Petronius rose with him and the two exited the building.

12

The Sign of the Prophet Jonah

Having already been in prayer for over an hour, Paul watched the sun peak above the Theater of Marcellus to the east, bringing with it sunlight and warmth to the upstairs of his rented home. He gazed from the veranda at the columns and arches of the great amphitheater, which he knew to have a capacity for 20,000 spectators. *The Romans certainly know how to build things,* he mused. *But that too must one day crumble.*

A knock came from downstairs, interrupting his contemplations. *Are they here already?* His guard Petronius answered the door. Familiar voices came to his ears as he made his way downstairs.

"Good morning, Paul," spoke Dominic. "We heard that you were going to have guests."

On a table in the middle of the downstairs great room were four leather satchels, each fully laden with provisions, brought by Dominic, Tychicus, Marcus, and a woman he surmised to be Dominic's wife.

"What do we have here?" asked Paul.

"We have brought some things we thought would bring joy to the hearts of your guests," spoke Dominic as he and the others began to unload the contents. Out of the satchels came fresh baked bread, olives, figs, raisons, cheese, fresh caught fish, and bottles of a honeyed wine called mulsum.

Paul beamed. "We were just going to talk. The rest of this never occurred to me."

"Which is why you need a wife," spoke Dominic. "You would be surprised with how food breaks down barriers between people and invites conversation."

He pointed to the woman. "This is Ruth, my Jewish wife, who unlike myself, is wise to the dietary restrictions of her people."

"I am pleased to meet you, Ruth. Your namesake was a great woman of God."

He turned his attention back to Dominic. "I can agree with your point about food. As for a wife, that will never happen to me. Where is Luke?"

"You might not see him for a while," answered Marcus. "He is lost to this world, holed up by himself, involved in some deep writing project. He gave us strict instructions that he is not to be disturbed for at least a month."

"Well then," said Paul. "He must be writing something important. I have some writing I need to do myself."

Ruth handed Marcus a broom. "Dominic and I will prepare the food. Would you please sweep this room? Try not to raise too great a cloud of dust. After that, would you please clean the cultus behind the house? Judging from the condition of this room, I suspect it also needs attention."

Though they were not chores to which Marcus was accustomed, he went immediately to work without a word. Within an hour the house was clean and inviting. The fish was cooked and the entire spread was laid out in an appealing arrangement on the table, which had been moved three feet out from the wall so that partakers could gather food from either side of it. The aromatic aroma of warm mulsum permeated the room, giving it a homey feeling.

No sooner was the project complete when the sound of a large approaching continent preceded a knock on the door. Ruth opened the door to some twenty men, all in traditional Jewish garb, the blue tassels at each corner of their topcoats setting them off.

"Greetings, rabbis," spoke the woman. "Do please enter."

Rabbi Shelemiah laughed as he and the others filed in. "We are not all rabbis here, domina. Most of the men with me are tradesmen of some sort, who have left their shops in the hands of others. We are much curious to hear what Paul has to say."

He spotted the long table, upon which the food was displayed. "What do we have here? You people are very hospitable."

"Rabbi Shelemiah," said Paul. "Since you are the leader of the group, we would be honored if you would ask the blessing before we partake of this wonderful meal."

After breakfast the visiting contingent found spots on the floor, with scarce any space between them. Petronius, having little interest in the subject at hand, retreated upstairs. Ruth found refuge in the culina, where she cleaned up from the morning meal and began preparations for the midday. Dominic, Marcus, and Tychicus seated themselves among the group.

To provide visibility, Paul seated himself on a chair in a corner opposite the table. He gazed upon the assemblage, making eye contact with each, from right to left. Satisfied that he had their undivided attention, he began to speak.

"Brethren, as I stated at the synagogue, having appealed to Caesar, I am here in Rome as a prisoner for the sake of the hope of Israel. I am a Jew, born in Tarsus of Cilicia and educated under Gamaliel. Being zealous for God, I strictly observed His laws, as do all of you here in this room. In my zeal, I thought it service to God to persecute those who followed the way of Christ, binding and casting them into prison. Thus one day, with authority from the Sanhedrin, I was on my way to Damascus, filled with rage and ill intent toward the Christians there."

For the next three hours Paul continued, telling of his encounter with Christ and then speaking from the law and the prophets, demonstrating from the Scriptures that Jesus was the Messiah of Israel. His guests politely listened until the time came for a welcome one-hour break and a simple midday meal of bread, fruit, and cheese.

The afternoon session became less formal, with questions and interchange. "How could this Jesus be our Messiah, if he continually violated the Sabbath?" asked Alexander, who identified himself as a coppersmith.

"As spoke Jesus to the Pharisees in the countryside of Judea, 'The Sabbath was made for man, and not man for the Sabbath'," (Mark 2:27b) answered Paul, who remembered Alexander from Ephesus. "The Scriptures have shut up all men under sin. The Law provides the standard, to which none of us can of ourselves attain. It reveals our sinfulness. The Law serves as our tutor, that leads us to Christ, that we might be justified by faith."

"You argue well from the Scriptures, Paul. But what sign can you show us, proving that this Jesus is our Messiah?" asked Rabbi Shelemiah.

"For just as Jonah was three days and three nights in the belly of the sea monster, so shall the Son of Man be three days and three nights in the heart of the earth,' (Matthew 12:40) having been crucified upon a Roman cross. But just as Jonah was vomited alive upon the shore, so Christ rose from the tomb and became alive again, which authenticated His Messiahship. And as I spoke to you earlier this morning, I myself met Him on the road to Damascus."

As the afternoon interchange wore on, the polite formality of the morning gradually gave way to open dispute and hostility from some of those present. By the late afternoon many appeared ready to leave, but not before Paul spoke to them one final word.

"The Holy Spirit rightly spoke through Isaiah the prophet to your fathers, saying 'Go to this people and say, You will keep on hearing, but will not understand; and you will keep on seeing, but will not perceive; for the heart of this people has become dull, and with their ears they scarcely hear, and they have closed their eyes, lest they should see with their eyes, and hear with their ears, and understand with their heart and return, and I should heal them.' Let it be known to you therefore, that this salvation of God has been sent to the Gentiles; they will also listen." (Acts 28:25b-28)

With that remark the bulk of the men departed, many offended at Paul's reference to the Gentiles. But five remained, having believed in Christ as their Messiah, among whom was a gentile proselyte named Tertius and a young man named Ampliatus. These stayed and partook of the evening meal of poultry, bread, figs, and wine.

13

Chafing at the Bit

Marcus bit off another chunk of chocolate and cherry cerasus as he and Paul sat in shade on the veranda of his rented house. In the stifling heat, the street below was mostly quiet for the afternoon brevis somnus.

"This is really good. Dominic is fortunate to have Ruth as a wife," remarked Marcus.

"He is indeed," answered Paul.

"I have gotten a job now as a carpenter with Dominic."

"Wonderful. Our Savior was also a carpenter. Do you have experience in that trade?"

Marcus shook his head. "No, which is why I am not being paid much initially. But I learn fast." His face became clouded. "I don't know if I can remain much longer in Rome, though."

"Why is that, Marcus?"

He looked down to the floor and slowly brought his eyes back up. "I got a young girl pregnant on Melitene. As near as I can tell, she should be giving birth to my child any time now."

Paul nodded understandably. "Eletia, the sister of Amoenitas, who is now the wife of Publius."

Marcus put down his half-finished dessert and looked directly at Paul. "You knew about this? Why have you not spoken to me about it before?"

"I have known, Marcus. But you have a lot of issues going on right now. Are you thinking that you should go back to Melitene, to try to win her heart and become a husband and a father?"

"Yes. There was a time when I thought it desirous to live free of such encumbrances. But now I am greatly ashamed of my former lifestyle. I shudder at many of the things I have done. I want now only to fulfill my obligations as a man."

Paul took another bite from his cerasus. "That is both good and bad. It is evidence that you have truly been reborn. I also shudder at the things I did in my past life. But I am no longer that man and you are no longer the man who did those past awful deeds."

He put his hand on Marcus' back. "It is important for us to learn to forget those things which are behind and to reach forward to those that are ahead. Our sins are forgiven, having been paid for by Christ on the cross. He rose from the dead to newness of life. We are new men, Marcus, with new natures, living a new life."

Tears began to form in Marcus' eyes. "But Eletia is still pregnant."

"That is true, my son. Sin complicates a man's life. Even after he comes to Christ, he still must often deal with issues from his past life."

"Then what should I do?"

Paul thought for a moment. "I want to encourage you to remain here in Rome, at least for a time. Get grounded in your faith. Learn the carpenter's trade. You need to possess an honest skill. Return to Melitene and to Eletia when you are ready, as a whole and established man, with a trade to offer her as a means to support your family."

"But what if she marries another man in the meantime?"

"That could happen. But even if it does, you will still be ahead. God has a way of working things out far better than we could have imagined, if we choose by faith to live life His way. Right now, it is more important what God is doing in you here, than for you to run off before you are ready, less likely to win Eletia's heart and less able to assume the responsibility of marriage and a family."

Marcus stood to his feet in frustration and raised his voice. "How would you know? You don't have a wife and a child! This is torture to me!"

"You are right, Marcus," Paul answered calmly. "I have neither wife nor child. But please be seated and hear me. I do know something about waiting. When I first came to Christ, I wanted to tell everyone about Him. And I did. But I was like a wild, unbroken stallion. I went after people for Christ the same way I had gone after people against Christ. When people failed to respond the way I thought they should, I shouted at them. I wanted to lock them up in prison for being so stubborn and brainless.

"But then I was led by the Spirit to Arabia for a while, where I learned the humble trade of tentmaker. Every man needs to know a practical trade. For me, tentmaking has come in handy. I have often worked my trade to sustain myself when times were lean. During my time there also, the Lord spoke to me. Over time he tenderized my spirit.

"When I returned to Damascus, I still needed time to learn the importance of working with others. I couldn't be a one man show. I was in Damascus three years before the elders there felt me ready to go up to Jerusalem to meet Peter, who had known Jesus in the flesh while He was on this earth. I stayed with Peter for fifteen days."

"What was he like?"

Paul laughed. "Nothing like the man he told me he used to be, who spoke and acted first, and thought later. We had that trait in common."

"And like me sometimes."

Paul nodded. "Salvation comes to a man at a certain point in time. But like with a newborn child, that is only the starting point. From there it takes time for Christ to truly form in a man. 'But we all, with unveiled face beholding as in a mirror the glory of the Lord, are being transformed into the same image from glory to glory.' (2 Corinthians 3:18a) God is still working on me."

He stood and again placed his hand on Marcus. "You are very different from the man I knew about and observed on Melitene. The man who once thought himself above everyone and who thought only about himself is now greatly humbled. I see in you now a willingness to do the dirty jobs and to treat others with respect. I see you endeavoring to learn an honest trade. Most of all, I see a man hungry for God. Remain with us a while longer. God will make it known when it is time for you to return to Melitene."

"But three years?"

"I do not know the timeframe, Marcus. The only thing I know for sure is that the more you chafe at it, the longer it will take."

"You think I will return to Melitene eventually?"

Paul again patted him on the back. "Yes, my brother. The time will come. Let's pray."

For several minutes the two men prayed together. As they did, a peace settled upon Marcus. He resigned himself to allowing God to work in his life and to become the best carpenter he could be.

A knock came to the front door, interrupting their contemplations. From downstairs Petronius called up to Paul. "Sir, there are two soldiers here who wish to see you. They have a message for you."

"Invite them inside. I will be right down."

As Paul descended the stairs, the face of one of the men, a tall, muscular centurion, went from businesslike to stern. He pointed to Petronius. "Milite! Why is this man not in chains?"

Petronius visibly shuddered before the young officer. Timidly, he replied. "Sir, this man is not a flight risk. I have known him now for several months. Whenever we venture outside this house, I put him in chains, to which he readily submits. But it is not very practical inside the house."

The officer's face softened. "I see your point, milite. Just so you understand that if he ever does make a run for it, you will forfeit your life."

"I am aware of that, sir."

"Very well."

He handed a small scroll to Paul. "In one week, you are directed to appear at the tenth hour at the Mamertine Carcer in the Forum. Should you fail to appear for any reason, you will be hunted and conveyed there by force. The consequences will be severe should you put us to that effort. You will hand this scroll to the duty publicus when you appear."

"If God allows, I will appear," answered Paul.

Visibly irritated by Paul's answer, he turned again to Petronius. "For your sake, he had better appear, and he had better appear in chains if you know what is good for you."

"Yes sir," answered Petronius. He saluted the centurion, who formally reciprocated. The two soldiers turned and left without another word.

14

Damaged Souls

It was all Amoenitas could do to maintain a professional calm as her sister Eletia's screams reached a fever pitch. "It's time to push now, Eletia. You're doing fine. Push! Push!"

The top of a head appeared. "I can see the baby. Push!"

In a woosh the child slid into the world, crying volubly to announce her appearance.

"You have a girl!" exclaimed Amoenitas.

While Amoenitas cut the umbilical cord, Valentina tended to Eletia, who was experiencing mild bleeding. Upon finishing the cord task, Amoenitas began to clean the baby with warm, damp cloths.

"I want to see my baby," clamored her mother.

Amoenitas held the half-cleaned infant up to her sister. "My Julia!" she cried over the screams of her child. *She has Marcus' nose and his lips.*

"I think there is only one way to quiet little Julia down," declared Amoenitas merrily. She positioned the child for nourishment. Julia's Marcus styed lips found their mark and immediately went silent. Neither sister could stifle a laugh as Amoenitas continued cleaning the backside of the baby. "Solving her problems won't always be this easy," she kidded.

Valentina took another warm cloth and wiped the perspiration from Eletia's head. "She is a beautiful child, Eletia. Congratulations."

"You have done an excellent job assisting me, Valentina. You will make a very good mid-wife or curare if either is a direction you want to go."

Valentina smiled. "Thank you, Amoenitas. What a precious baby. Someday, I hope to be a mother too."

"So when are you and Publius going to have a baby?" asked Eletia.

Amoenitas laughed. "I guess I may be next. I am pregnant."

She walked to the entrance of the upstairs bedroom at Ille Perfugium and pulled back the curtain. "It's a girl," she called to the waiting assembly downstairs. "Her name is Julia, after her avia."

A chorus of resounding cheers rose from below.

*****

Affixed at the top of the distaff was a large clump of wool from Publius' sheep herd. Seated on a stool, the young woman secured the long, round wooden pole in her left armpit.

"You're doing fine, Herminia," spoke Gratiana, as she went to work. With her left hand she pulled a small amount of wool down from the clump at the top of the distaff. The tightly wound spindle below her right hand spun rapidly, twisting the strands of wool into fiber. When the spindle played out, she rewound it with newly formed fiber until it was ready to spin again, twisting more strands into fiber from the wool above. As she spun, a huge smile came to her face.

"I can do this!" she cried triumphantly.

"Yes, you can," affirmed Gratiana. She looked at the other six women, who were seated in a semi-circle around Herminia. "Spinning woolen fiber from a distaff and spindle is an important skill for a woman to learn. From the fiber you can make clothing with a loom, a skill I plan to teach you all next week, once you have mastered this first skill. Now, who wants to try this next?"

Timidly, Cornelia raised her hand.

*****

The three women fanned themselves as they sat at one end of the large dining table at Ille Perfugium. With the exception of Cornelia, who was taking a nap upstairs, all the residents of the house were about the town for their afternoon free time. Beside Eletia slept baby Julia in her cunae. The women spoke in low voices, so as not to disturb the child.

"How did your morning class go?" asked Gratiana, looking at Amoenitas.

"I thought pretty well. Valentina both reads and writes very well. It is almost as if her former life never affected her. Demetra, Mariana, and Fabia are catching on. Herminia and Cornelia are both frustrated. So far, they don't get it. Albina isn't interested." She shook her head. "Mariana's caustic remarks toward Herminia and Cornelia do not help."

Gratiana nodded understandably. "Maybe Herminia is slow with reading, but she showed the most skill of all the girls with the distaff. I made sure she knew that when the class was over."

She sighed. "These girls are all damaged—even Valentina. She's just better at hiding it. We've got to love them and be patient. Is there a way to motivate the slower girls—to help them see the value of knowing how to read and write?"

"Maybe I could spend some extra time with the slower girls, away from those who do better," suggested Amoenitas. "At least that would spare them the derision."

*****

Cornelia gazed at Eletia's next offering on the wall, to the right of her first painting of the olive tree splitting the rock, filling the space in the middle of the upper part of the wall. "Is that little Julia?"

"Yes," answered Eletia.

"Do I take it that the woman holding Julia's right hand with her left is you?"

"That is me."

Cornelia eyed the painting with bewilderment. "But she can't walk yet. You have her walking."

"I am envisioning a little into the future. In maybe six months she will be walking."

"Why is Julia's left hand not at her side? Why is it raised partly in the air and to her left?"

Eletia put down her brush and stepped back. "Why so it is." She shook her head. "I don't know. I guess I just subconsciously painted it that way."

Cornelia looked to the right and beneath each painting and noted that those areas were still blank, with ample space for additional offerings. But as Eletia had said, that part of her life was not yet lived.

* * * * *

Amoenitas snuggled close to Publius as they sat together on their special bench, just above the bluff, that marked the spot where Publius had proposed to her. The sun had sunk into the sea. The brightest stars and planets were just beginning to appear in the gathering, cloudless night sky. A cool breeze blew in from the sea, a welcome respite from the heat of the day.

"What will you be speaking about this Sunday to the church?" she asked.

"For this is the will of God, your sanctification; this is that you abstain for sexual immorality…' (1 Thessalonians 4:3) is something Paul told me. When it comes to doing the will of God, there are specific things that are different for each person. But there are general things that are equally applicable to us all. One has to do with sexual purity. Some of our young people are getting a little too flirty with the opposite sex. I worry about some of our married couples too. I see wandering eyes. Maybe something about sexual purity will be in order. It is a positive, empowering thing, but sexual promiscuity destroys individuals and families faster than anything I know, except maybe murder."

Amoenitas rubbed her cheek against Publius' soft beard. "You are the most upright man I have ever known. I am blessed that God gave you to me as a husband."

Publius placed his left arm around her. "I am blessed to have you as my wife." He patted her abdomen with his right hand. "And soon we shall have a child to love."

"What do you think, Publius? Boy or girl?"

"I guess I'd prefer a son, but that is in God's hands."

"I have a feeling that it's a boy. We'll see."

"Yes, we'll see."

Publius took a deep breath and exhaled slowly. "Things are going so well with our church, that I am almost afraid."

"What do you mean?"

"I don't know what I mean. We are still growing in numbers. The people love coming together and serving one another. It's just that Paul warned us of savage wolves and of persecution to come. I don't see any of that on the horizon. It worries me."

Amoenitas pressed her lips close to his. "Let's just enjoy our season of peace while it lasts."

15

The Paradox of Freedom and Bondage

The heat of the day was already telling as Paul, Marcus, Petronius, and the wagon driver made their way through the winding cobblestone streets toward the Forum for Paul's hearing. They had been obliged to secure the services of a wagon at Paul's expense because of the impossibility of Paul making the two-mile journey on foot with a 100-pound iron ball at the end of his chain. The heat expanded his right ankle, causing the clasp around his ankle to bite into his flesh, numbing his right foot. The same was true of his two wrists, clasped with bracelets that connected to his neck chain. Little conversation took place between the men seated in the cargo space of the wagon.

Momentary worry about possible imprisonment and even execution gave way to confidence as Paul prayed. He remembered his time on the ship during the storm when an angel from God had spoken to him. "Do not be afraid, Paul; you must stand before Caesar." (Acts 27:24b) He would stand before Caesar before he could die. How long ago that experience now seemed.

He thought about Petronius and the other soldiers who had guarded him on Petronius' days off. All had heard the gospel. Two had come to faith in Christ. As for Petronius, he had not yet believed, but the two had become fast friends. He constantly prayed for his friend's salvation.

From the Via del Fora Romana the wagon turned right into the massive Forum complex. Immediately to their right was the Temple of Saturn, which also served as the treasury building, where Rome's silver and gold was stored. Six massive pillars adorned the front of the structure, giving it a stately appearance. Between and recessed behind the middle pillars stood a huge wooden door, high enough for a twenty-foot tall person to enter without stooping. *How small those who conceive such buildings want to make the people feel who use them,* thought Paul.

From the temple they continued straight for another 200 yards until they reached the Mamertine Carcer, a less impressive building that served to house criminals on its left side and to hold trials on its right.

Getting out of a wagon fastened to the iron ball was an unwieldy process. Petronius and Marcus lifted the ball from the bed of the wagon and placed it upon a wheeled cart provided by the carcer. For the chain to reach the cart, Paul had to lay on his back and drape his right leg over the side, with his right knee bent at the top. He then had to be awkwardly lifted by the two men and set upon his feet by the cart.

Through the entrance they passed. Once inside they came to the desk of the duty publicus. Without a word Petronius handed the summons scroll to him. The publicus surveyed the contents. Upon finishing, he raised his eyes, handed the scroll back to Petronius, and pointed down the long hallway.

"Second door to your right. Go in and be seated in the back. No talking."

Upon entering the room, a guard escorted them to the seating area. "Release the prisoner from his ankle chain," he intoned evenly. "The neck chain remains in place." He returned to his post by the door.

Petronius inserted his key into a hole by the joint of the ankle bracelet and turned it to the right. Immediately, the bracelet released, much to the relief of Paul. He began to rub the imprinted area and to rotate his numb right foot to return circulation to it.

A hapless looking prisoner in rags stood before the magistratus, who sat high at his judgment seat, a stern look upon his face. He was dressed impressively in a white toga, with a wide purple stripe, signifying his prominence. Five minutes later the prisoner was escorted from the room. From the look on his face, the verdict had not gone well.

"Next case," the magistratus called.

Petronius and Paul rose together and approached the judgment seat.

"The prisoner Paul from Jerusalem," Petronius informed the magistratus. He handed him the scroll.

The judge examined the scroll and gazed down at Paul. "I am aware of your case, which seems to be religious in nature, and therefore out of Roman jurisdiction. But you have appealed to Caesar and so here you stand at your initial hearing. We have sent messengers to Caesarea and to Jerusalem, so far to no avail, calling upon the Jewish religious leaders to send emissaries here to formally charge you. I am sorry to waste your time, but I cannot hear a case against an accused without an accuser. You will return to your quarters, where you are to be held under house arrest until such time as they arrive. You may go."

"Your Excellency? May I make an appeal," asked Petronius humbly.

"Yes, milite?"

"I have been obliged to chain my prisoner for our trip to here from his house. He poses no risk of flight. I have known him now for several months. May we dispense with the chains on our return trip to the house? As you can see from the indent on his ankle, they are most uncomfortable for him."

The judge nodded thoughtfully. "You do realize, milite, that if your prisoner were to escape, your own life would be forfeit?"

"I realize that, Your Excellency."

"Very well then. No chains on his return trip. But take the chains with you."

He scrawled a note with his stylus on a small, thin wooden board, dipped his signet ring into wax, and applied it to the board. "If anyone accosts you about the lack of chains, show them this board. You are dismissed."

Quickly they left the building. Once outside, Petronius removed the neck chain and the bracelets from around his wrists, bringing further relief. Paul flexed his hands to return circulation to them. "Thank you, Petronius, for getting me out of these chains. They are most uncomfortable."

"You are welcome, Paul. I try to look out for my friends."

To get a better look at the entire Forum, Petronius asked the wagon driver to pass through its center down the Via Sacra on their return trip. As they continued down the main street, the tall, round Temple of Vesta, the goddess of home, hearth, and family, stood out on their right. Inside dwelt the six Vestal Virgins, priestesses of the goddess.

"They are selected during childhood," spoke the wagon driver. "The girls have to be deemed pure of physical and character defects. In the temple they serve thirty-year terms, keeping the eternal flame lit in order for Vesta to protect the city and the empire from harm. For the women inside, their status is both an honor and a curse. As long as Rome prospers, they receive honor. Should Rome falter, its bad luck is inevitably attributed to the unfaithfulness of one of the virgins. The College of Pontifices discovers the guilty party through a series of tests. Once the guilty party is ascertained, she is stripped of her vittae and her other badges of office. She is scourged and put in grave clothes. Jeered by the crowd and with all the ceremonies of a funeral, she is carried on a litter through the Forum to the Campus Sceleratus, just inside the city walls, close to the Colline gate. There she is placed in a small underground vault containing a couch, a lamp, a table, and a little food and water. She is then sealed inside forever. No amount of denial or tearful pleading on her part can ever change that. We had such a case just last year."

From the wagon Paul wept as he heard the story. *How cruel are the ways of man*?

Once past the temple they came to an open market area where they stopped to buy provisions for the house. While Paul and Petronius tended to that business, Marcus, who disliked shopping, strolled about the open area. On a bench under a sycamore tree he spotted a young man in rags who looked the picture of despair. A small voice from within told him to approach the man.

"Hello sir," he said pleasantly. "You look like you have been through some hard times."

The young man looked up at him, his face forlorn. "Why should you care?"

Marcus sat down beside him. "Because God cares and you are one of His creations. What is your name?"

"Onesimus. I arrived here from Colossae two weeks ago. It is hard to find a job here in Rome, unless one is willing to return to slavery. And I am too proud to beg."

"Well, I am pleased to meet you, Onesimus. I am Marcus. You were a slave in Colossae?"

"Yes, but never again. No man will ever be master over me again."

"Are you hungry?"

He nodded.

Marcus pointed to the wagon, which Paul and Petronius were loading with provisions. "Let me see if maybe we can spare something for you. Will you come with me?"

Without saying a word Onesimus stood to his feet and followed Marcus to the wagon. "Do we have anything we can spare for a hungry young man?" inquired Marcus.

Paul extended his hand to Onesimus. "My name is Paul. What is yours?"

He took Paul's hand. "Onesimus."

"You look a bit thin and forlorn. Do you have a place to stay tonight?"

Onesimus shook his head.

"Well then, we can either give you a little food here and go our way, or you can come with us. We'll feed you a much better meal at my house and put you up for a night."

The young man eyed Paul suspiciously. "Is this a slave trap?"

Paul laughed. "No. We are more interested in setting people free."

* * * * *

After a much-needed midday meal of chicken, fruit and fresh vegetables, Onesimus followed Paul to the veranda overlooking Via Flaminia. The normally busy thoroughfare was quiet except for the distant barking of dogs.

"That was the best meal I have had in as long as I can remember. Thank you very much, Paul. And thank you for allowing me to spend the night. It will be nice to sleep inside and safe for a change."

Onesimus took a sip of the cool beverage in his cup. "This is really good. What is it?"

"It is called kykeon," answered Paul. "It is a mixture of water, barley, and mint, with a little honey to sweeten the taste. I am getting a little older. I find it helpful in digestion after a meal."

"It tastes like it must be good for you," observed the younger man.

Paul looked directly at Onesimus, his eyes communicating that it was time to get serious. "You told us that you were a slave in Colossae. How did you come into slavery?"

"I was twelve years old. My family fell into hard times. My parents owed a lot of money to a lot of people. We were headed for debtor's prison until a man named Philemon satisfied our debts in exchange for our servitude."

Paul's face perked up. "Philemon?"

"Yes, Philemon. Do you know of him?"

"I know him very well. How is it that you are now free?"

Onesimus gave a haughty chuckle. "I made my freedom. I took a costly necklace that belonged to his wife, sold it in Colossae, and ran for it. Even though I worked hard at being useless to Philemon, I figured it was just payment for the wages he never paid me. I made my way here to Rome. Just two days ago I ran out of money from the necklace. I sure am glad you people came along."

A pained look came to Paul's face. "You had food and a place to stay in Colossae. Do you understand that if you were to be caught, you would be sent back to Philemon and placed at his mercy? He could have your thumbs cut off—or worse."

"I don't intend to be caught."

Paul took another sip of kykeon. "I spent two years in that area, mostly in Ephesus. I know many people there, including Philemon. You could have done a lot worse than him as far as masters go. He saved you and your family from debtor's prison. He is a good man. He would have set you all free upon the satisfaction of your debt."

"I wouldn't know that. He is the only master I have ever had. I didn't like being a slave, having to do what I was told all the time."

"Preferable to debtor's prison?"

Onesimus grudgingly conceded the obvious. "Yes, I suppose so. But freedom here is preferable to slavery."

"If you can find a job. So far that doesn't seem to have worked out for you." For long moments Paul was silent, pondering his next words.

"We are Christians here, Onesimus—followers of Christ Jesus. Marcus, who found you at the market place is a recent believer. Philemon, your former master, is also a Christ follower."

Onesimus suddenly became fearful. "Am I now to be your slave?"

Paul shook his head. "I don't own slaves. Perhaps you do not fully understand my situation here. I am a prisoner of Rome. In the morning you'll be free to go—or free to go now if you prefer. It is I who cannot walk away freely from this house."

"I didn't realize that."

"One of these days I will have a trial. Hopefully afterwards, I will be set free. In the meantime, I only appear free to the casual eye because my guard Petronius allows me as much freedom as he can."

Paul took his final sip of kykeon and set down his cup. "There is another kind slavery and there is another kind of freedom, far exceeding the freedom you suppose yourself to have. In that other sense I am the freest of men, but you are sadly bound. May I speak to you about true freedom?"

A look of puzzlement came across Onesimus' face. "How is it that you, a prisoner, are free, and I, who am free, am yet a prisoner?"

"You are a creation of God, Onesimus. He created you for a purpose beyond anything you can now imagine. A great paradox of life is the natural supposition that freedom from the God who created us equals freedom to do as we please, and that submission to God equals bondage. The opposite is true."

"How could that be?"

"Freedom from God equals bondage to sin in any of its many forms, all of which lead to death. Without God we become slaves to strong drink, or to fornication, or to idolatry, or to hatred, or to something else destructive. We cannot stop doing the thing that is destroying us, but rather need more and more to achieve what still fails to satisfy. Christ sets us free from the addiction and destructiveness of sin to become all that God has made us to be. Life takes on a dynamic of power, of love, and of eternal purpose."

For the next thirty minutes Paul spoke to Onesimus the story of how he had moved from the kingdom of darkness to the kingdom of light. All the while the younger man became increasingly drawn into the story and burdened by his own sense of guilt and shame. In the end, with tears in his eyes, he responded.

"How can I too know this freedom from my wretchedness?"

16

The Twenty-fifth Psalm

The atmosphere buzzed with excitement. From the stage Publius peered out over the throng, which filled the amphitheater nearly to capacity. Many were new people, most of whom he had seen about the island. He was filled with satisfaction. *Our church just keeps growing. Will we soon outgrow the amphitheater?*

At the upper heights of the facility, near the center, he spotted his wife Amoenitas with the Ille Perfugium contingent, which now included Demetra. When their eyes met, she smiled and waved to him. He returned her gesture before raising his right hand, the signal for the service to begin. Immediately, the congregation quieted.

"Good morning, dear people of God. I see that we have a large number of new people in attendance this morning. I hope the regular people here have made you feel welcome. Here we honor and serve our Lord Jesus Christ, who has brought light and hope to our lives. This morning I am led of the Holy Spirit to teach about holiness, an essential ingredient in the Christian life. But before I begin, Linus, who taught me the shepherd's trade, will teach and lead us in a new song he has written, based upon the words of the twenty-third psalm."

Having been introduced, Linus entered the stage from the left wing. He was a tall, impressive looking man, with a well-kept beard. Beside him stood his wife Beatrice, who held a lyre.

"Good morning, dear brothers and sisters in Christ. Since I came to know my Savior, I have also discovered music. Like David of old, I have found that music exalting our Creator, sung at night, has a soothing affect upon my sheep. They relax and huddle together, making it easier for me to protect them from cross foxes and other predators on this island. Since the Lord is our Shepherd and we are His sheep, I thought it might have the same effect upon us. My wife Beatrice and I will sing the twenty-third psalm for you first, and then you can join us the second time."

He took the lyre from his wife's hands and began to strum the strings. After an introduction to the melody they began their duet of praise from the psalm. The catchy tune, overflowing as it was with joyfulness, plus the beckoning of the couple drew the congregation to join in the second time through. A glad chorus filled the air and rose up to heaven. From the left wing of the stage Publius sang, filled with the joy of the Lord.

*****

For ten minutes Publius had been speaking to the hushed congregation. From the stage it appeared that his words were penetrating many a convicted heart. "There is forgiveness for those of you who have fallen," he compassionately proclaimed.

Suddenly, near the center, at the top of the amphitheater, a young woman sprung to her feet. "Liar! Hypocrite!" she screamed. "It is you who have fallen! You raped me! Admit it to everyone here! You raped me!"

Shocked, Amoenitas stood to her feet and turned to the woman who had been seated next to her. "Valentina, what you doing?"

"He cheated on you, Amoenitas!" she shouted to her face. "He forced me. You need to know the truth about your husband!"

Off to the right side of the theater another young woman suddenly stood. "He raped me too! He is a filthy animal! It is time for him to be exposed for what he really is!"

On the opposite side of the theater stood another woman who began to shout the same accusations. The mood of the congregation rapidly turned from contrition, to confusion, to chaos.

A man among a cluster of visitors in the center of the amphitheater stood to his feet and shouted. "If this is Christianity, I want nothing to do with it. Come on people. Away from here!" The large contingent of visitors around him rose collectively, made their way to the center aisle, and climbed the steps to the exit.

Upon their cue, others spaced about the crowd rose up and did likewise, a few of whom had been regular attenders. From the stage Publius looked on in helpless bewilderment. *What is happening here?*

* * * * *

Crestfallen and dispirited, the young pastor and his wife turned their horses from the main road to the lesser trail that led to their home. For a time, they made small talk in a fruitless attempt to ease the trauma of the morning. It was no use. The conversation inevitably made its way back to the ugly subject at hand.

"I have done nothing of what they say, Amoenitas. The charges those women have laid against me are utterly false. I hardly know Valentina. The other two women I don't know at all."

For a while Amoenitas remained silent, attempting to gather her thoughts, her pause raising concern in Publius. *Does she at least in part believe the slanderous accusations?* After what seemed an eternity, her carefully worded response came.

"I know that you have not done any of this, Publius. I will tell you how I know. First of all, I know you. You have proven yourself to me many times. I also wondered why Valentina took her belongings with her to the service. She had moved out of Ille Perfugium. This entire episode was planned.

"I will tell you another reason I know. After the service abruptly ended, she told me to my face that Gratiana, Eletia, and I have been pilfering money from the fund that was set up to run Ille Perfugium. The thing is, she seems to really believe that. It was like it wasn't her speaking, but a foreign spirit inside of her."

Amoenitas shook her head sadly. "She is the brightest of all the women at the refuge. She even helped me deliver Eletia's baby. Yet there was always something about her. I couldn't see it, but I felt it."

Publius sighed. "I am grateful to know that you believe me, Amoenitas, and that you know the charges against me are false. For what it's worth, I know that none of you pilfered from the money box. But look at the damage. A third of the people left in disgust, including a few of the faithful. Those who lingered broke into groups and began arguing with one another. Some shouted ugly words at me. Only a few steadfast souls like Theophilus came to my aid, seeing through the charges for what they were."

"If anyone knows about slander, it is him," answered Amoenitas. "Remember what happened to his wife Flavia? Alacerius is behind this. I have no proof, but I can feel it. Your mother Alexandra too. She is still on this island. I know that in my spirit—and I know how deeply that saddens you."

He shook his head. "My father has promised an investigation. But as an interested party, he cannot preside over the process. He must send for a neutral arbiter from Syracuse. It will likely be two weeks before such an investigation can begin. Meanwhile our church suffers. My reputation is in tatters, as is yours. Will our church ever be the same?"

For the next thirty minutes they rode silently, a great heaviness upon them. When they arrived at their home, they mechanically tended to their horses, Bellator and Castanea, before going inside. Once inside their refuge they spontaneously collapsed to their knees and cried out to God.

"Dear heavenly Father, we are in great distress. In this day of trouble, please conceal us in Your tabernacle. Hide us in the secret place of Your tent. For false witnesses have risen against us, who breathe out violence. Save us! Save our church, Great Shepherd of the sheep!"

As they prayed, gradually their hearts turned from despair to hope.

*****

"We have succeeded beyond our wildest dreams!" chortled Alacerius.

"Praise be to the goddess Juno!" exclaimed Alexandra. She raised her glass. "May my son return to sanity! Death to Amoenitas! Death to the church! May we regain our rightful place as masters of Melitene!"

"When do we get paid?" asked Valentina. The other two accusers, Lucilia and Octavia, chimed their agreement.

Alacerius stared a malevolent look that sent shivers through the women. "You will be paid when your job is complete. We have an investigation to get through. You must convince the arbiter that your charges are credible. Think through your stories. Know when to show anger and when to weep.

Timing is paramount. Once you have succeeded in convincing the arbiter, you will be handsomely rewarded."

He fell into another violent, hacking spell and immediately excused himself. The spells seemed to be increasing of late. But this time was different. This time he coughed up blood.

*****

The young couple rose from the floor and strode hand in hand to the bluff overlooking the Great Sea. Only when they noticed the position of the sun, situated some thirty minutes above the horizon, did they realize how long they had been praying. Neither had they eaten.

At the bluff they closely cuddled on their special bench. The sound of the waves pounding the rocks below soothed their spirits. Silently they sat as the sun gradually made its way into the sea and sank beneath the waters. As stars began to appear, Publius wrapped a blanket around them. Together they sang the twenty-third psalm.

*****

In the gathering twilight a core of people from the church assembled at the home of Theophilus and his wife Flavia. Among them were Gratiana, Demetrius and Phoebe, Doctor Corbus and his new wife Dōmina Macatus, Linus and his wife Beatrice, and Trebonius.

"Thank you all for coming," spoke Theophilus. "What happened this morning at the amphitheater is nothing but a slanderous, satanic attack upon our church. The enemy means to destroy us. Flavia and I are determined not to allow that to happen."

The others responded in agreement.

"Shall we go and comfort them?" asked Linus.

Theophilus shook his head. "They need this night to be alone. We will see them in the morning. This situation won't look as bad to any of us in the morning. But this evening we must pray for our dear pastor and his wife. They are deeply hurting right now. Most painful to them is the knowledge that some of our true church members actually believe the false charges. But the Scriptures say that 'Truthful lips will be established forever, but a lying tongue is only for a moment.' (Proverbs 12:19) Greater is our God than all the powers of hell. As for the accusers, we must covenant together not to express or harbor hatred. We must feel pity for them, for unless they repent, theirs will be a terrible end."

The collective prayers of the faithful ascended heavenward and crossed paths with the peace that descended upon them.

17

The Inquiry

The gathering at the amphitheater after the previous Sunday's debacle was about half the size of the week before. In contrast to the normal sense of excited anticipation, the mood among the attendees was subdued. People conversed with one another in tones barely above a whisper.

With Publius under a cloud, it had been agreed that Theophilus would speak. Publius sat in the audience near the top with his wife, along with Gratiana, Eletia, and several of the Ille Perfugium women. Valentina was conspicuously absent.

"Good morning brethren," began Theophilus. "I am satisfied that the charges leveled against Publius last Sunday are utterly false. The charges against his wife Amoenitas and the ladies who run Ille Perfugium are equally false. Yesterday, I came across a passage from an ancient Hebrew text, written by an ancient Hebrew king. 'Like a sparrow in its flitting, like a swallow in its flying, so a curse without cause does not alight.' (Proverbs 26:2) I am confident that the truth will prevail in these matters and that our church will emerge stronger than ever."

He called for his wife Flavia, who was seated in the first row. As she ascended the steps, Amoenitas noted that she looked lovelier than ever in her blue pastel stola.

"Flavia was also slandered, accused of murder by an evil man. While the great storm raged and the plague was at its peak, she languished in a damp, dark prison cell, awaiting death as her only escape. But God had mercy on her, as He did upon our entire island. And God had mercy on me, bringing into my life one of the two sweetest, kindest human beings who ever lived, the other being my first wife, Livilla. While I have no proof that the slanders against Publius and the women of Ille Perfugium were perpetrated by the same source, I recognize the same spirit of accusation, which comes from the pit of hell."

As Theophilus spoke, a cloud of peace slowly began to descend upon the faithful. All would be well after all.

*****

The two men sipped wine from elegantly crafted goblets in the atrium of the propraetor's villa. "This is the second time I have had to deal with a case involving Christians," spoke Porcius Festus. "I had to deal with a man named Paul in Caesarea, whom the Jews wanted dead. But he appealed to Caesar, and to Caesar I sent him. I don't know what became of him after that."

"Well," answered Trebonius, "I can shed some light on that. His ship was blown off course just a bit during the euraquilo we had last year. It shipwrecked here on Melitene, which proved fortuitous for me."

"How so?"

"I was near death with island fever, but Paul miraculously healed me by the power of his God."

Festus gave him an incredulous look. "You truly were healed?"

"I truly was near death. I truly was healed. I truly have become a follower of Christ."

Festus surveyed the atrium. "I thought something was missing here. I have seen no statues of our Roman gods or goddesses anywhere in or around the villa."

"I had them all removed," declared Trebonius. "After what Christ did for me, how could I not do that? Not only was I healed, but many others on this island were healed of island fever by the same power of Christ. That fact, the fact that Publius is my son, and the fact that all of the accused are Christians is why I had to recuse myself from being a judge regarding the charges against them."

"You do realize, of course, that if Rome were to get wind of your conversion, you would be quickly replaced by another propraetor. Emperor Nero despises Christians." He studied Trebonius' facial response and laughed. "No, Trebonius, the emperor will not find out about your conversion from me. But he will find out. I am sure you are aware that you have plenty of enemies on this island who will see to that. It is only a matter of time."

He stood to his feet. "I will need at least a week to conduct my investigation. Once that is complete, we will have our inquiry."

*****

Together Publius and the stalwarts of the church entered the propraetor's villa through the atrium. The first thing Publius noticed when he strode into the peristylium was that the proconsul's seat had been moved from the middle of the room to its far end in order to accommodate what figured to be a larger than normal crowd. Before the seat was a tall, highly polished oaken table, upon which sat a gavel.

Chairs had been set up on either side before the proconsul's seat with a wide gap in the middle to separate the opposing parties. To the left of the seat as one would face it, sat the accusing women; Valentina, Lucilia, and Octavia in the first row. To their left sat Alacerius with Alexandra. Publius noted that Alacerius looked pale and appeared to have lost weight. A number of others whom Publius recognized sat behind them, including Otho, the soldier who had once posed as a believer in an attempt to assassinate Paul. The tension within the room was palpable.

Despite the atmosphere Publius felt confident and at peace. The prayer time together at the home of Theophilus and Flavia earlier that morning had been encouraging. A sense of the Lord's presence seemed to cloak him and the entire group. He held on to the hand of his wife Amoenitas, who remained close to his side.

"So, you stick by your man," sneered Alacerius from the other side, "even though he has been exposed as a philanderer. But I suppose philanderers and embezzlers do need to stick together." None on the church side chose to respond, but kept their eyes forward.

From the church side of the room a door opened. "All rise," commanded the servientes ad legem, who stood by the side of the door.

In strode Porcius Festus, resplendent in his senatorial tunic, a garland upon his head. *He certainly looks like a magistratus,* noted Publius. He assumed the proconsul's seat and surveyed the room.

"Be seated," he intoned. He pounded his gavel, signifying that the inquiry had begun.

"Good morning to all of you. It has been alleged that the accused, Publius Fabianus, lead pastor of the church in Mathos, sexually forced himself upon each of the three women seated together in the front row to my right. It is further alleged that the three women who run Ille Perfugium, Amoenitas Fabianus, Eletia Aequitas, and Gratiana Caepio have been embezzling the fund that was set up to run their operation. I note that neither Gratiana nor Eletia are present this morning."

Amoenitas stood to her feet and was recognized. "Your Excellency, Gratiana is too old and feeble to withstand the strains of a long court proceeding and Eletia is a young mother, who at present cannot leave her baby. Both have requested that I speak for the three of us."

"Very well," responded Festus. "First, we will deal with the charges against Publius."

* * * * *

"So that's it? We get nothing?" spoke Valentina.

Alacerius glared daggers at the three women. "You couldn't get your stories straight. You contradicted each other. Two of you said one thing at first, and then something else later. Publius was able to prove that he was somewhere else at the time he was supposed to have been with Lucilia. The financial log at Ille Perfugium was checked and found to be in order, with no funds missing. Publius walked away free and Ille Perfugium is still open. Since you failed to produce the desired results, you don't get paid!"

"So what are we supposed to do now?" she asked. "The Christians will have nothing to do with us."

"I know what I would do if I were any of you. I would either jump from Scopulus Altus or flee this island. Because once Felix is gone, if the Christians don't kill you first, you'll all have unfortunate accidents. Now go from me, before the unfortunate happens right now!"

18

The Commission

The day was nearly spent. Upon entering Paul's house, Marcus immediately noticed two large clay jars on the table in the downstairs great room, the same place he had met with the Jewish leaders some five months before. In the middle of the room were four chairs facing each other, three already occupied by Paul, Luke, and Julius. He was greeted by the other three men as he seated himself in the empty chair. For the first time since Marcus had known him, Julius was attired in the clothing of a togatus, a common civilian.

"We ought to begin by asking the favor of our God for the task now before us," began Paul. "Lord Jesus, hear us now and bless our endeavor to take Your word to those who so desperately need to hear it. I pray Your hand of protection upon Julius and Marcus. I ask in Your precious, wonderful name, amen."

Hand of protection upon me and Julius? wondered Marcus. *Something is up.*

Upon completion of his prayer, Paul gestured to Luke, who pointed to the two jars on the table. "Contained in those jars, gentlemen, is what I have been doing these past five months that you have not seen me. Each of those jars contain identical parchment scrolls, one for Publius and the other for Theophilus on Melitene. The scrolls tell the story the Holy Spirit of God directed me to write about the life of Christ upon this earth. Before leaving Melitene, I promised Theophilus that I would send him the story."

He looked directly at Julius and then at Marcus. "It is the two of you whom we wish to task with their safe delivery to Melitene."

A whir of thoughts immediately flashed through Marcus' mind. *Is this the fulfillment of my desire to return to Melitene? What will* come of it? *What if we fail in our mission? Will I be able to see my child? Is Eletia's heart given to another? How will Publius and Amoenitas receive me? Will I be able to get a job? Will I stick with it? Away from Paul, will I be able to stand on my own as a Christ follower?*

"When do we leave?" he managed to ask.

"At first light tomorrow morning," came Luke's response. "Julius is now out of the army, but he still has military connections. He has already secured two sturdy mounts to convey you to Puteoli. You will have money and ample provisions for your journey. You will need to be armed. The trip could be dangerous. Each of you is to carry one of the clay jars in case the other doesn't get through."

* * * * *

The morning sun arced higher in the cloudless sky and beat down mercilessly upon the two men. Marcus removed his outer tunic and stuffed it in the leather bag on the right side of his saddle. He drew a draught of water from his skin. To preserve their horses in the heat, he and Julius rode at an easy pace on the first leg of their journey, from Rome to Three Inns.

"Do you know what really got me on that ship from Syracuse to Puteoli?" asked Marcus.

"No."

"It was two words you spoke to me just before you left the Taberna of Lunianus. You said 'Live, Marcus,'. It dawned on me that the way I was living was not living."

"Well, I am glad that you are living now."

"I am too. I want nothing to do with my old life. So how is life for you, now that you are out of the army?"

"I feel like a free man. I can rise from my bed when I want to. I can go where I want. I can do what I want. No man gives me orders. I don't have to give orders to others and worry if they are the right ones."

"What do you want to do, once our task is complete?"

Julius chuckled. "I want to get married and to settle down."

"Do you have someone in mind to settle down with?"

Julius smiled. "There is a girl whom I saw in Syracuse, on my way to

Rome. We never spoke. I don't even know her name. But I have not been able to get her out of my mind since. Our eyes met and lingered for just a moment. She had the sweetest, kindest face I have ever seen. She's not bad in form and figure either. I assume she must be a believer, since she was with a believing family. I intend to look her up once we get to Syracuse. If I can't find her then, I will return there and look for her later, after we have made our delivery. How about you?"

"Well, I hope your plan works out for you. As for myself, I intend to look up Eletia when we arrive at Melitene. I don't know if she will have me, but I intend to try."

"I think she would do well to have you, Marcus. I would not have said that a few months back."

*****

As Marcus saddled his horse early the next morning, a dread sense of anxiety fell upon him. He remembered Dominic's words of five months before, that the trip from Three Inns to the Market of Appius, which featured dense shrubbery and small rises to hide behind, was the most hazardous part of the journey. Thieves might not attack a party of eighteen, but they were only two.

"We must move fast today despite the heat," spoke Julius, who appeared to have the same apprehension. "No time for easy chatter. The faster we move; the less time thieves will have to attack us."

They set off at a hard pace.

*****

Four men on horseback suddenly appeared out of nowhere, blocking the road a quarter of a mile ahead of them. Julius looked behind to discover six additional horsemen blocking the road an equal distance behind. Their ill intent was obvious. With no place to flee on either side of the road, he drew his sword and spoke decisively.

"Our only chance is to charge straight ahead like wild men, as if we were the aggressors. It will be two against four, rather than two against ten. Yell like we mean to attack, which we do! Cut and slash, but don't stop. We must rip through them and keep riding! If one of us falls, the other must keep going! They will show no mercy."

Unable to think of a better plan, Marcus drew his sword, fear overruled by adrenalin.

"Charge!" Julius cried, as if he were still in the army. In a matter of seconds, they were upon the startled highwaymen. At the last instant Marcus veered to the extreme left of the road so as to allow only one bandit to engage him. He made as if to slash, but instead plunged his sword deep into the torso of his enemy. A piteous cry emanated from the stricken man as Marcus swept by. To his right he saw that Julius had also broken through.

For a time, the highwaymen pursued, but the speed of their two mounts continually widened the gap until they gave up the chase. Taking nothing for granted, he and Julius continued at full gallop the remaining three miles to the Market of Appius.

Upon reaching the near edge of the town, they dismounted at the same stable they had used on their way to Rome, the same place where they had met Dominic and his group.

"Our horses are pretty lathered," spoke Julius to one of the attendees. "Please take good care of them. You will be paid before we leave with them in the morning."

As Marcus trailed behind Julius toward the Aurelius Deversorium, he noticed blood on the ground and his friend's unsteady gait. He overtook Julius for a closer look. A crimson wound stood out prominently through his subucula on the lower right side of his chest.

"Julius, you're wounded."

"One of them got his sword into me," he admitted, trying maintain his composure. "I think it went pretty deep."

*****

A middle-aged woman with a leather carrying case entered their room. "We don't have a fully qualified medicus here in the Market of Appius," she said. "My name is Hortensia. I am a curare. Let me see the wound. Turn on your left side, please."

She took a forfex from her carrying case and gently cut away his subucula. The wound was still fresh. She pointed to Marcus.

"Bring me a clean wash basin filled with warm water and a bottle of wine. Be quick about it." She drew a clean cloth from her case and pressed it to the wound to stop the bleeding.

"What do you think?" asked Julius. "How bad is it?"

"I don't know just yet. It isn't good. How did you get this wound?"

"From a sword fight. We didn't start it."

"Did you get the other man?"

"There were four of them, but yes. I got the man who got me and one other."

She exhaled slowly. "You might have gotten a lot. I will do my best, but you probably need a medicus."

"Will I be able to continue my travel?"

The curare thought for a moment. "Expert care and rest would be best for you, but you'll not find a competent medicus anywhere between here and Rome."

"We are not going to Rome. That's where we came from. And I am not about to turn around and face the highwaymen who did this to me again, especially in my condition. My friend and I are bound for Melitene."

"Melitene? Then if I were you, I would stop at Puteoli. You will find better care there—if you can get there."

Just then Marcus returned with the requested items. Quickly Hortensia took another cloth from her case and immersed it in the warm water. Upon washing the wound, she discovered for the first time the puncture place, about one inch in diameter, just below the ribcage. After cleaning the outside surface, she poured wine on to another cloth and gently swabbed the wound while Julius grimaced. She then took yet another cloth and again applied pressure to stem the bleeding.

"It needs three or four sutures," she explained. "I have cleaned the wound on its surface, but there is likely grime beneath. If I were to close the wound now, it might fester inside and cause greater complications."

"What should we do?" asked Marcus.

"That is a tough call. You need the kind of care I cannot give. If Rome is not an option, then Puteoli is your best bet. But it's a five-day ride from here and I am not sure your friend is up to the task. Watch the wound for redness or swelling or pus. Watch for fever. Cool, damp clothes to his forehead will help lower his fever. Have him drink plenty of water. He has lost a lot of blood. Water will help to replenish it. I will give you ample dressings. Change them at least twice each day and cleanse the area with wine before you apply a new dressing."

"Thank you," said Marcus. He recompensed the woman for her service and then looked anxiously at his friend.

"We are going to Puteoli," declared Julius resolutely. "We have a task to complete."

19

The Vision

Even more than the two-week storm at sea, the five-day ride from the Market of Appius to Puteoli turned out to be the greatest ordeal of Julius' life. The gait of his horse continually aggravated his wound. Every night, staying at the various way stations, his fever would come up. Each night the redness and swelling around his wound became greater than the night before.

But for Marcus the real shock came as they approached Puteoli in the late afternoon of the fifth day. "We will not stop here," announced Julius weakly.

"What?" asked Marcus incredulously. "We have to stop. You need help."

"I had a vision last night. My help will come in Syracuse."

"You were delirious last night. How do you know you had a vision?"

"We must go straight to the docks and find a certain ship. The ship will take us to Syracuse."

"Who is going to help us in Syracuse?"

"An angel of mercy."

As they entered the town, Marcus considered forcing the issue. But Julius had always shown decisiveness and good judgment. Syracuse likely offered better help than Puteoli. It was still on the way to Melitene. *Maybe he did see a vision*. He elected to acquiesce.

* * * * *

Upon leaving the horses at the Puteoli military station, Marcus found a covered cisium for hire, drawn by two horses. "Take us to the ship docks," he told the driver. Gently, he laid Julius in the bed of the wagon. On either side of his friend he laid the two leather bags containing their earthly belongings and the two clay jars.

The trip to the docks took ten jarring minutes over cobblestones. By the time they arrived it was nearly dark. Marcus desperately scanned the dock. Near the end to his right appeared a small ship. As the wagon approached, Marcus perceived that it was about to sail. He bounded from vehicle and ran aboard.

"Who is the captain here?"

"I am," spoke a short, wizened, gray-haired man. "Both captain and the crew. Are you heading for Syracuse?"

Dear God! There must be someone there waiting for us. "That is our destination! I have a friend with me. Are you about to sail?"

"As you see. If you're coming, come aboard now. One denarius apiece."

Quickly, Marcus ran back to the wagon. Three small stones lay in the fare box, designating the price for the ride. "Would you please carry our belongings to the ship while I take care of my friend?" he asked the driver. "Please be careful with the clay jars."

He pulled Julius by his feet from the rear of the wagon, lifted him under his legs and back, and hastily made his way to the ship. Only then did he realize that his solidly built friend was heavier than he looked.

"I need a bunk below for my friend," he told the captain between gasping breaths.

Down the short stairway he carried Julius. The hold was packed nearly to the stairway, but on the starboard side he found an unoccupied bunk and placed Julius upon it. The wagon driver, who had followed them, laid their two leather bags by the bunk. Marcus checked to make sure they still contained the jars.

"Thank you," he said to the driver as he paid him.

*****

It was completely dark by the time the ship passed the Bridge of Caligula and entered the open sea. In the hold Marcus felt Julius' forehead. He was burning hot with fever. He changed the dressing over the wound.

He then dipped a clean cloth in the water barrel and wiped his friend's forehead.

"Oh Lord Jesus," he cried audibly. "Save my friend. Find for us this angel of mercy." Even after praying, doubt permeated his thoughts. *Will Julius even still be alive by the time we get to Syracuse? How am I supposed to find this angel of mercy?* One minor miracle encouraged him. They had found a ship almost immediately.

After tending to him as best he could, Julius fell into a fitful sleep. Knowing he could do no more, Marcus went topside and joined the captain in the pilot house.

"Why are you headed for Syracuse?"

"Welcome to the Tantulus, the captain responded. "I carry a cargo of volcanic sand. They need it in Syracuse to make concrete. There is also another purpose to our voyage."

"When do we expect to arrive there?"

"I have a fast ship. By late afternoon, the day after tomorrow, I hope. Provided the sea remains calm, the winds remain favorable, and Rome does its part."

"How do you navigate at night?"

"We stay close by the shore of Italy. There are certain lights along the shore that I know well. Once we reach the Strait of Messina, we'll guide off the east coast of Magna Graecia until we get to Syracuse. What happened to your friend?"

Marcus closed his eyes. Inwardly, he suddenly realized how traumatized he felt. "We've had a few problems on our trip, which began in Rome and hopefully ends on Melitene. Along the Appian Way we ran into some bandits. We had to fight through them in order to pass. Julius was wounded in the fight."

"Julius?" The captain asked. "I knew a centurion by that name."

"You know my friend?"

"If he is the same Julius. I didn't get a good look at the man you carried below, but a centurion named Julius sailed with me on a much larger Alexandrian grain ship I used to own last winter. We were bound for Italy, but ran into a huge storm and wound up shipwrecked on the island of Melitene. I lost my ship and my cargo, but we all miraculously survived, thanks to a prisoner Julius had with him named Paul. I had no answers to our predicament. We were all resigned to die until Paul basically took over my ship."

"I didn't know those things," said Marcus. "But I do know that it is the same Julius and I also know Paul. What is your name?"

"Marinus. I was aptly named by my parents, for I am of the sea."

"Well Marinus, my friend Julius is in very bad shape. Very honestly, I fear for his life. I wanted to seek help in Puteoli, but he told me he had a vision of someone helping him in Syracuse. What do you think?"

The captain put his right hand to his scruffy chin. "I never used to believe in miracles. But it sure seemed like a miracle that all of us survived that great storm. I saw more miracles once we were ashore on Melitene. Maybe we'll have another miracle for Julius—and for our ship."

Suddenly, Marcus' curiosity was aroused. "What do you mean, about another miracle for our ship? You've hinted at some other purpose for this voyage."

"I would prefer not to go into that right now. The other purpose may not materialize."

"Well, all right then," he answered resignedly. "You saw a miracle with the passengers of your ship and more on Melitene. Are you a believer in Christ?"

Marinus shook his head. "I suppose not. I never attended any of the Christian gatherings while I was stuck on Melitene. Quite honestly, I have never forgiven myself for risking that voyage. Paul had warned us not to go. I put the lives of many people in jeopardy. Then I lost my ship and with it my entire fortune. It has only been these last three months that I have had this ship. It's not much compared to what I had, but it's a start."

Marcus nodded sympathetically. "We have all done stuff we regret. If only you knew my stuff. The thing is, there is forgiveness in Christ. That's all I've got."

Marinus remained silent. When Marcus saw that he wished to converse no further on the subject, he took his leave and went below to check on Julius before getting some much-needed sleep himself. As he descended the stairway, it was evident that Julius was again delirious, as was his nightly pattern.

"Angel of mercy, angel of mercy," he continually repeated.

Marcus poured wine onto a cloth and again massaged the wound on the surface. In the dim light of the hold he could not see the degree of redness around the wound, but noted that it felt more swollen to the touch than ever before. He dampened another cloth from the ship's water barrel and wiped Julius' forehead and face.

Though he still felt unacquainted with prayer, even after his conversion, he knew that Julius would soon die unless they could find his angel of mercy. Unartfully, but sincerely, he spoke to his Savior.

"Lord Jesus, I feel helpless. I cannot fix Julius. I have my doubts we'll find any angel of mercy in Syracuse. But I know that You healed people on Melitene. And I know that You have healed my heart. Please, Lord Jesus. Do a miracle for Julius. He is the best friend I have ever had."

"Live, Julius," he softly uttered before climbing into the other vacant bunk on the port side. Even though he was exhausted from his week of travel, his battle with outlaws, and from constantly tending to Julius, it again occurred to him that Marinus had hinted at another purpose to his voyage. *What is it that I don't know about this ship?* As he lay in his bunk, exhaustion overcame worry and he fell into a deep sleep.

*****

After what seemed mere minutes, Marcus awakened to light filtering down the stairway. The ship rocked easily from side to side. He rose and checked on his friend, who was still sleeping soundly. He felt Julius' forehead. It was considerably cooler than it had been the night before. He ascended the stairway and again joined the captain in the pilot house. To their port side, only a mile distant, appeared the rugged Italian coastline.

"Don't you ever sleep?" he asked.

"Not on this trip." Marinus pointed to a ship before them, some three miles distant. "And now we come to the fun part of our voyage. You ran into bandits on the Appian Way. We have bandits on the sea too. We call them pirates. I just hope my friends show up in time for the party."

Alarms went off inside Marcus. "What are you talking about?"

Marinus scanned his surroundings full circle. No other ships were in sight. "I mentioned another purpose to our voyage. I have to do more than haul volcanic sand if I want to regain my fortune." He pointed again to the ship, which was approaching head-on, closing fast.

"That is the pirate ship that has been troubling commerce in this area.

I am a small ship that appears to be easy prey. The Roman navy has offered me a substantial amount to serve as bait for that ship. Now I just hope that the navy does its part."

"You mean they are about to attack us for our cargo and probably kill us too?"

"If they're successful. Coming about," he warned.

With his steering paddles he turned the Tantulus toward an inlet near the shore. The main sail overhead shifted to the port side of the ship, which then heeled on its side. In his mind Marcus hoped that Julius had not tumbled on to the floor.

"We can't escape from the raider, but we can delay engaging him."

"Why didn't you tell me this when we boarded last night?" Marcus spat out angrily.

"I sort of did. I just didn't tell you everything."

Another ship appeared from a small inlet, just behind the approaching raider. "And there is our help, Marcus. Just the same, you had better retrieve your sword. Things might still get hot."

Hastily Marcus ran into the hold, fuming as he went, to retrieve his and Julius' swords. He hadn't bargained on another fight. To his relief, Julius was still in his bunk. He came again topside and laid Julius' sword on the floor beside the captain.

"Not that you'll be any good with it!" He took another glance at the raider, now only one mile distant. In its fervor to overtake the Tantulus, it appeared that the pirates had not yet spotted the Roman trireme, using both oar and sail power, that was closing fast on its tail.

Marinus breathed a sigh of relief. "They'll not catch us before the trireme catches them. Neither will they escape this time."

He pointed to two additional Roman warships, another trireme and a bireme, emerging from the inlet before them. "They've got the pirates. All we need do now is to keep running until the danger is past."

The pirate ship turned seaward, having finally spotted its peril, but as they did, the trailing, faster trireme matched their move. Coming parallel to the pirate ship, it then began to close on it, forcing it shoreward again, into the jaws of the other two warships. The pirates were trapped and they knew it.

With no place to go, they set a course directly for the bireme, the weakest of the three vessels. It was no use. The trailing trireme closed fast on its port side. When it drew within range, Marcus observed fireballs of burning pitch hurled from the trireme at the pirate ship, which quickly set it afire. Marines aboard the trireme then raked the pirate crew with their crossbows, weakening any resistance they might encounter. After the pitch and crossbow treatment, the warship bore down upon the hapless raider at ramming speed. Resounding cheers erupted from the marines and crew when they rammed the pirate ship below the waterline with their protruding, seven-foot-long bronze ramming spear, nearly breaking the enemy vessel in two.

No boarding was necessary. Two pirate crewmen who tried to board the trireme in surrender were met with a hail of arrows. Both plunged into the sea. The three rows of oarsmen reversed direction, disengaging their ship from the stricken vessel, which quickly sank on its own. Several survivors jumped into the sea and swam for the Roman warship, pleading for the mercy they had never given their victims. None was to be had.

Fifteen minutes later the Tantulus pulled alongside the winning trireme, whose oars had been retracted to allow for docking. Grappling hooks from the larger Roman ship secured them together. When it was safe, Captain Marinus boarded the ship to collect his reward.

"Well done," spoke the trierarchus. "We have been trying to catch these malcontents for a long time. No casualties on our side. No survivors on theirs. No more terrorizing our grain ships. A most satisfying operation."

He handed Marinus two Roman aurei.

*****

Early the next morning the Tantulus entered the narrow Strait of Messina, the most notable landmark on the voyage. To the left of the mile-wide passage was the craggy coastline of Italy. To the right was the relatively flat finger of land that marked the beginning of the great island of Magna Graecia. Once the narrow passageway opened, they would hug the coastline of the island for the rest of the way, rather than that of Italy.

In his right hand Marinus continued to finger the two Roman aurei. He showed one of them to Marcus, which featured the image of Messalina Valeria. "What do you know about Messalina Valeria?" he asked Marcus.

"I have heard of her. That's about it."

"She was the promiscuous third wife of former Emperor Claudius and cousin of Emperor Nero. She was executed some fifteen years ago for allegedly plotting against Claudius."

"It seems like all our emperors and their families do is plot against one another."

Marinus laughed. "That they do, unless they're busy oppressing us. It will take the rest of this day to reach Syracuse. Sorry for the delay. I hope we get there in time for Julius."

Marcus sighed. "I do too."

His friend was in a bad way. If his fever was lessened each morning, his general trend was still downward, with longer deliriums at night and less relief each morning. He would die soon without help.

20

The Angel of Mercy

A strong wind brought the Tantulus into Portus Parvus, the smaller of the two Syracuse harbors, more quickly than expected. With two hours of daylight remaining the ship docked.

Immediately, Marcus swept Julius into his arms, struggled up the stairway, and carried him off the ship to a waiting, two-wheeled cisium. Captain Marinus trailed behind with their belongings and the two precious clay jars. The cisium puller helped Captain Marinus load their belongings aboard his vehicle, while Marcus laid Julius lengthwise on the passenger bench.

Before parting, Captain Marinus returned to Marcus the two silver denarii he had paid for their passage at the beginning of the voyage. "It is the least I can do for you under the circumstances. Good luck to you and to Julius. I hope you find your angel of mercy." The two clasped wrists before Captain Marinus returned to his ship.

"I will walk alongside the cisium," he told the puller. "Please take us to the nearest good medicus."

"I know of no such person," answered the cisiarii. "I know of several corrupt men who call themselves medici. They will take your money, but they aren't good for much else."

A deep sense of helplessness fell upon Marcus. *Dear God, help us! What can I do?*

"Take us to the nearest open marketplace," he told the young man. There had been little food available aboard the Tantulus, as Marinus had not expected passengers. Other than the fact that he was hungry and felt that Julius might also benefit from nourishment, he had no idea why he spoke those words.

"There is a marketplace about fifteen minutes from here," spoke the puller. He glanced at the stricken passenger on the riding bench. "He looks like he really could use a good medicus. Wish I could help you with that." He lifted the two arms of the cart and pulled it forward.

Why she had been sent to the marketplace at this late hour of the day, she did not know. True, they needed fresh fruits and vegetables for their household, but there would be little left and none fresh by the end of the day. Still, she went without protest, needing to get outside anyway.

Upon entering the marketplace, she was surprised to find a single vendor who had just set up his display, while others were packing to go home. "You are just starting?" she asked.

"My wife is ill at home," he explained. "I have been tending to her all day. But she is feeling better now and we still need to sell our produce. So here I am. I figured there might be a few late shoppers like yourself who need a late vendor like myself."

His produce was fresh. As the vendor counted, she began placing oranges, olives, tomatoes, and cucumbers into her leather bag. Upon filling the bag, she did the obligatory haggling before settling on a price. She paid the vendor and made for her home. It would soon be dark and she needed to be indoors before then.

In her way from the square she spotted a cisium, with a beleaguered looking man standing beside it. On the bench of the vehicle lay a man who appeared in need of help. Something inside told her to approach.

"Your friend looks to be in a bad way," she said to the man who stood beside the vehicle.

"You are right about that. I am looking for a good, honest medicus, or maybe an angel of mercy. Do you know of any?"

She took a closer look at the man who lay on the bench and gestured to the cisiarii. "Quickly! Bring him to my house."

*****

The quiet stillness was a welcome relief to Julius in his delirium. A soft female voice, the sensation of warm water on his abdomen, and the smell of vinegar brought a sense of comfort. Tender hands applied a sticky substance to his wound, from which came a soothing awareness of relief. Soft, moist cloths massaged, cooled, and cleansed his body. Two hands then enveloped his right, giving him reassurance. All would be well. He fell asleep peacefully for the first time since his battle with the bandits.

The young woman looked up at Marcus. "The honey will take down the swelling and will help draw out and cleanse his infection. He will sleep now. The constant movement he has experienced the past few days did not allow him to rest the way he needs to rest."

"You have had an effect upon him that neither I, nor a certain curare could accomplish. What is your name?"

"Angelina."

"Angelina?" A look of wonder spread across Marcus' face. "The angel of mercy. My friend saw you in a vision. He has been calling for you since we were in Puteoli."

She marveled at his words. "I have seen him before too. What is his name? What is your name?"

"His name is Julius. I am Marcus."

"Well then, Marcus, I am here. This is my home. Here we fear God and worship our Savior Jesus Christ."

Marcus smiled for the first time since before their encounter with the bandits. "We also are worshipers of Christ." He looked anxiously at her. "Will my friend live?"

She hesitated. "Nothing in this world is certain. But I will do everything in my power to see that he does. The rest is in the hands of God."

"You mentioned your father on the way here, but I have not seen him. Where is he?"

Her countenance fell. "He is in prison."

"Why?"

"By order of a man named Porcius, allegedly for failure to pay his taxes. We have always paid our taxes. The true reason my father is in prison is because Porcius hates our church. Liuni, whose family also lives with us, is trying to hold our church together, but we are floundering in my father's absence. Some of the believers, not wanting to suffer my father's fate, have left our fellowship." Tears formed in her eyes. "They won't let us visit him. I fear for his life."

"You are helping us, Angelina. Perhaps I can help you. I know Porcius. I will try to see him tomorrow. Maybe there is something I can do."

* * * * *

The melodious, haunting, mesmerizing resonance of a plucked instrument penetrated Julius' sub-conscience, projecting wellness into his soul. Gradually, his awareness sharpened until perceived dream became audible reality. He opened his eyes to the early morning light of a new day. By his side stood the young woman of his visions and of his delirium the night before—the same woman he had seen months before by the dock. She smiled and put down her lute, much to his distress.

"Good morning, Julius," she spoke. Even the sound of her voice was heavenly. He stared in awe at her long, shimmery chestnut hair, her gentle features, and the sweetness of her face. Their eyes met. "I need to examine your wound."

She drew back his blanket and gently pulled up his night shirt. "Your wound looks better than it did last night. The swelling is down. The red encircling the wound has receded. I was just going to apply a new topical of honey."

"Honey?"

"Honey cleanses wounds like this. It draws out the poison. It heals the surface skin and the tissues beneath. It soothes pain. It reduces swelling."

She applied vinegar to a cloth and gently massaged the area around the wound before cleansing her hands with additional vinegar. She then poured a liberal amount of honey from a jar, encircling the wound. With her right hand she gently massaged the area around the wound before rubbing honey into the wound itself. Julius grimaced slightly when she touched the punctured surface, but almost immediately afterward felt relief.

"I have seen you before," spoke Julius.

"And I have seen you. My name is Angelina."

"How did I get here?"

She smiled. "Your friend Marcus brought you here. I just happened to meet him at the marketplace last evening. You were too delirious to know anything that was going on."

He glanced around the room. "Where is Marcus?"

"He went off to see a friend."

* * * * *

Upon entering Porcius' home, Marcus was immediately struck by its extravagance. "It is one of the perks of my job," boasted his erstwhile friend. "I have rugs and tapestries from India, linens from Egypt, and furniture from Melitene, made by some master craftsman there."

He gestured to Marcus. "Have a seat." He called toward the kitchen. "Tatiana, bring us some wine."

A moment later an alluring, stunningly picturesque young woman with olive skin and smooth, swarthy hair emerged from the kitchen—genuinely a study in desire. In her two hands she carried two fancy goblets filled with white wine. Flashing a brazen smile at Marcus, she set the two goblets down on the table between the two men.

Each took a sip before Porcius got to the point. "So, you wanted to see me? Here I am. What is your business?"

Taken aback by the abrupt, harsh manner of his address, Marcus searched for the right response. Gone was any sense of their former comradery.

"I am here on behalf of a friend who is in prison, apparently for failure to pay his taxes. I tried to visit him, but was denied. I was hoping you could help him and me."

"And who might this friend be?"

From his tone it did not appear that Porcius would be of any help. Nevertheless, he had to try. "His name is Antonius, a tentmaker. His family lives about a mile from here."

Porcius searched his mind. "Antonius? We have so many men in prison who forgot to pay their taxes. It is hard to distinguish them. You say he is a tentmaker?"

"He is a tentmaker and a believer in Christ."

A hint of recognition came to Porcius' face. "Oh yes, that man. It was more than just taxes in his case. He was making trouble in our city."

"You had him thrown into prison for being a Christian?"

Porcius eyed him suspiciously. "I had him thrown into prison for being a trouble-maker. Don't tell me that you're now one of them."

For a brief moment Marcus considered denial. But he had come too far for that. "I was a very lost soul, Porcius. Christ has brought love and stability to my life."

His former friend let out a derisive laugh. "Have you taken leave of your senses?"

He looked Porcius in the eye. "I don't think so. I have just one question for you on behalf of Antonius and on behalf of all the others you have imprisoned for failure to pay their taxes. How are they to work and to pay their taxes if you keep them locked up?"

For a brief moment Porcius considered Marcus' logic before answering. "You don't understand, Marcus. Holding them in prison is precisely the point. I keep them there until their families can come up with the money to free them. They find ways. Others pay their taxes for fear of suffering the same fate. Rome wins. I win."

"Your victims and their families lose. May I see Antonius?"

"What for?"

Marcus put down his goblet and rose to leave.

"Why be so serious, Marcus? I know just the cure for you. Let's get drunk together. Then I'll fix you up with a girl. Do you want Tatiana? She seems to want you."

"I already have a girl, thank you—at least I hope I do." He looked again around the room. "I can readily see why you place such importance on collecting your tax revenue. I can also see that we are not going to get anywhere. Thank you for the wine." He turned and made for the door.

"Do not make trouble for me, Marcus. You know what I do with trouble-makers." He laughed. "But maybe then you would get your wish. Maybe then you would get to see your friend."

Without another word Marcus closed the front door behind him, glad to be again outside where he could breathe.

*****

At dusk, after the last customer had left, Liuni closed the tentmaker shop and sat down with family and friends that worked at the shop to go over the day. "At least our shop is prospering," he began.

He turned his attention to Rufus. "We miss Antonius, but you are a godsend. We might soon have enough money to satisfy the debt the city officials say we owe to get Antonius out of prison."

"I am glad to be of help," answered Rufus modestly.

"How is Julius doing?" Liuni asked Angelina.

"He is much improved from how I found him last night. I think he will live and will make a full recovery. He just needs continued treatment and rest. Time will take care of the rest."

"Well then, Julius is doing well. Rufus is doing well for us. The shop is doing well. Now if only I could say the same about our church and about Antonius. I feel so inadequate on those accounts."

"I couldn't help regarding Antonius, but perhaps I can help you regarding your church," spoke Marcus. He removed the lid from one of the clay jars that sat beside him. Upon inverting it, out slid a thick, rolled up series of scrolls, held together by two ties of twine. "Julius and I were charged with a mission, which we have yet to fulfill. We are to deliver two identical scrolls to the church on Melitene."

"What is on the scroll?" asked Lucia.

"It is the story of Christ while He was here on this earth, written by a man named Luke. It seems to me that you people need one of the two copies here. The Melitene church will just have to get by with the other."

21

The Way of Grace

Valentina sat hidden in her room at the Remissio Inn, her mind in a quandary. The slander against Publius and against the women who ran Ille Perfugium had failed. Because of its failure, Alacerius had refused to pay her. She now found herself without money or friends, with hideous nightmares haunting her sleep at night.

Who will ever hire me, a prostitute, who falsely accused the best man on this island? I can't go back to Ille Perfugium. They would never have me. I have no money to buy passage away from here to start over somewhere else.

One more dreaded, nightmarish night remained at the inn and then she would be both homeless and destitute. Two dark, inexorable options forced their way to the forefront of her mind. *I must either return to prostitution or take a leap from Scopulus Altus.*

The latter seemed the better choice.

*****

The three men sat together, sipping wine in the atrium of the propraetor's villa. "You have been acquitted of the charges against you, my son. But you are still tainted in the eyes of many."

Publius nodded in unhappy agreement. "Lack of enough evidence to convict. That's all it was. And quite a few members of our church have left to return to their old ways. How are we to recover?"

"I sure wish we had the story about the life of Christ that Luke promised us," spoke Theophilus. "All we have at present is what Paul told us and the ancient Hebrew Scriptures."

"Well, we don't," said Publius. "When they will come, if they come, is anyone's guess. How I will regain my reputation and how Ille Perfugium will regain theirs is also anyone's guess. I suppose time will help, but what we truly need is a miracle. I don't know what else to do right now but pray."

The three men prayed together. As they prayed, along with a sense of peace, ideas began to form in their minds.

*****

After another lurid, nightmarish sleep, Valentina awakened in the early morning darkness to face the dread reality. Within three hours she would have to vacate her room at the Remissio Inn and had no further place to stay. After a meager breakfast her money would be totally gone.

As she rose to dress, a cloud of hopeless despair enveloped her soul. She tried to pray, as Eletia had tried to teach her, but was immediately thwarted by a voice within that screamed condemnation and hideous, vile blasphemies.

She gathered her belongings and made her way downstairs. The morning chill brought a shiver to her body beyond its actual intensity. It was still dark, with just the hint of dawn in the eastern sky. All was silent and dark in the square, save for the shop to her right. She laid her final two bronze assis on the counter of the pistrina.

"One spira please," she told the baker.

Without a word or any eye contact the baker laid a thin dough of flour, eggs, and cheese on a plate. On top of the dough he placed the standard portion of blackberries and set it on the counter. Taking the two coins, he went about his business.

Head down, she sat at the table before the pistrina and began to eat in silence. Her mind was set. There would be no more prostitution. She would eat and then begin her grim journey to Scopulus Altus before anyone else entered the square. She felt like a condemned criminal eating her last meal before facing a brutal execution. A voice inside continually berated her. *You are worthless. You must jump. There is no other way.*

"May I join you?" came a kind, elderly voice.

She knew the voice. She gave no answer and kept her eyes downward. But a glimmer of hope stirred in her soul.

"That spira sure looks good."

A minute later the elderly woman seated herself across from Valentina. After silently giving thanks, she partook. "I love these. A little over a year ago, another young lady introduced me to these at this very same spot."

Her voice was gentle and reassuring. Valentina finally looked up from what was left of her sparse meal. "You are talking to me?"

"I will listen too, if you have anything you want to say."

She began to cry. "I really have made a mess of things."

Gratiana nodded sadly. "Yes, but there is a way back. God forgives. So do God's people."

"I never had a father, or at least one to speak of," she blurted out. "He was a sailor, who was seldom home. It was better that way because whenever he was home, he was never anything but drunk. I was the oldest of the children in my family. When my father was drunk, he beat my mother and us children. Finally, when I was nine years old, he left on another voyage. I've not seen him since. As soon as he left, my mother secretly moved us from Syracuse to Catania on the island of Magna Graecia. Free of my father's abuse, for the next five years I thrived in school. Those were the best years of my life."

She looked at Gratiana. "Do please continue, my dear."

"But one day when I was fourteen, I came home to find a strange, not so savory looking man in our house. He looked me over from head to toe and then circled me. 'This one will do handsomely,' he said to my mother. He handed her a sum of money. My mother would not look at me, but I saw the tears in her eyes.

"The next thing I knew, I was bound and gagged, and placed in a wagon with several other girls similarly confined. One of the other girls was Demetra." Her eyes welled up. "My mother had sold me to be a sex-slave."

"How could any mother do that to her child?" asked Gratiana incredulously.

"We had no father. My family was starving. She had four younger children to feed. We were put on a ship and brought here to Melitene. From the port we were taken in the dead of night to the brothel, where

I lived until recently. I became a favorite of all the richer men, the high government officials, and the military officers on the island."

Oh, you poor girl, cried Gratiana inwardly. "I am so sorry, Valentina. But it can all be redeemed. You are infinitely important to the God who made you. He loves you. He forgives our failings. Through all your sorrows, you can still find His purpose for your life."

Tears she had endeavored to stifle forced their way and began to roll down her cheeks. "It is too late for me. I am about to walk to the cliff behind Scopulus Altus and jump."

"Would you like something more for breakfast?" offered Gratiana. "You look like you could use more."

Without waiting for an answer, Gratiana rose from her chair and returned to the counter. "Vespes, may I please have another spira for my friend?"

She called me friend?

A moment later Gratiana reseated herself and pushed the second plate to Valentina. She ate.

While she ate, the elderly woman spoke. "I have a better idea for you than that other thought you expressed to me. I want you to help us." She handed Valentina a clean cloth from her carrying bag. "Dry your tears now."

The clean cloth felt comforting to her face. She took another bite of the second spira and again looked up. "How could I help you?"

"You can help us by telling the truth, Valentina. Tell us who it was that put you up to this. Our church is hurting. We have lost a lot of people. Publius and his wife are hurting. Ille Perfugium is hurting. This whole island is hurting."

"You ask a hard thing of me."

"Not as hard as the landing you would make upon the rocks below Scopulus Altus." She took Valentina's hand. "Live, Valentina. It is not too late for you. You are a very bright young woman. You are worth the blood of God's Son, the Lord Jesus Christ."

At the mention of the Savior's name Valentina jerked her hand from Gratiana's. Her face suddenly contorted. Vile blasphemies began to pour from her lips.

"She is mine!" came a voice through her mouth. "She will jump! It is her only escape!"

Immediately, Gratiana recognized that an evil spirit was within her. She began to silently, but fervently pray. *Dear God, help me to know what to do!* The answer came instinctively.

"In the name of Jesus Christ, the King of kings and Lord of lords, I command you to be silent and to come out of her!"

At her words Valentina began to convulse violently. She fell from her chair to the cement and began to writhe in agony. Gratiana repeated her command.

"In the name of Jesus Christ, the Son of God and Savior of the world, I again command you to be quiet and to come out of her!"

Abruptly, her body stopped quaking and went limp, as if she were dead. From behind the counter Vespes, who had observed the spectacle, exited the shop and knelt beside her.

"She is still breathing."

She opened her eyes. He helped her to a sitting position. For a few moments she remained in place, dazed. Finally, she nodded to Vespes. He helped her back into her chair. She was sweating profusely. He found a towel from his shop and gave it to her.

"Call out to Jesus," spoke Gratiana gently. She again took Valentina's hand. "Allow His Spirit to enter your body and your soul. Be free to become the woman He created you to be."

Tears again flowed from her eyes. "Would God really forgive even a woman such as myself?"

"He really forgave even me. I too have done much wrong in my life. That is why we need Jesus. He is the way of grace."

The words formed on her lips. "Lord Jesus, I need You. Please enter my life. Please forgive me for my many sins. I need You, I need You, I need You."

Along with the kingdom of heaven, Gratiana rejoiced.

*****

Thirty minutes later, having retrieved her belongings from her rented room and with Gratiana at her side, Valentina, her heart racing, ascended the three steps to the front door of Ille Perfugium. *Gratiana has been gracious and kind to me. But what about the other women here? What will they say to me?*

They entered the house to find the entire company of residents seated around the table in the great room having breakfast, engaged in easy chatter. Upon seeing Valentina, the chatter abruptly stopped.

"Ladies," announced Gratiana. "Valentina has returned to live here among you again."

For what seemed an eternity the women sat in stunned silence. Albina finally took the lead. "What is she doing here? I thought she said that Publius raped her. I thought she said that you and the other leaders here were thieves."

"Why don't you turn right around and leave," added Mariana scornfully. "We don't want you here."

Gratiana's surprisingly strong grip held Valentina in place. "Valentina is sorry for what she has done. She has just become a new creature in Christ. All of us here have also done wrong many times."

She turned her eyes to Valentina. "Speak to the women here. Speak to them what is true."

Trembling, Valentina struggled to compose herself. Tears again streamed down her cheeks. "Publius did not rape me. Neither did he rape his other accusers. Gratiana, Amoenitas, and Eletia did not steal from the Ille Perfugium account. All of what I said were lies. I wanted money, which I never got."

Unable to speak further, she broke down into uncontrollable sobs. Gratiana hugged her.

From the table Eletia arose, approached her distressed friend, and took her by the hand. "You are forgiven, Valentina. I too have done much that needed forgiveness." With her embrace Valentina's trembling subsided. "Welcome back."

Following Eletia's cue, Cornelia and Herminia rose from the table and did likewise. The others remained in place and spoke no further. Together, the three who had risen helped Valentina with her belongings and accompanied her upstairs. Upon entering her old culina, they laid her belongings on her bed.

"It will take some time with the other girls," spoke Eletia compassionately. "Just do your chores quietly and don't say much. Don't answer when unkind words are spoken to you. Don't beg. In time the others will come around. Let them come to you when they are ready."

22

Longings

Angelina helped Julius to a sitting position in his bed and then swung his legs sideways to dangle over the floor. "Good morning, Julius. Drink." She handed him a large cup filled with cool water. "Take it slowly, but take it all. You need plenty of water."

While he drank, she snipped the band around his torso with her forfex and removed the dressing of fig leaves to examine the wound. "The swelling and the redness are almost completely gone."

"I feel a lot better too—like maybe I could get up and walk. I want out of this bed."

Angelina smiled. "That is a good sign."

She rubbed the area around his wound with vinegar before applying another topical of honey. Her fragrance and the feel of her hands upon his body was overwhelming.

"I am grateful for you taking care of me, Angelina. When I am well, I hope you will allow me to repay you."

She applied another dressing of fig leaves in a thin, porous pouch to the wound and wrapped another long cloth bandage around his torso to hold the dressing in place. "The fig leaves also stimulate healing. Tomorrow, if all the redness is gone, I will begin using aloe instead of honey. It is a lot less sticky."

"When can I get out of bed?"

"Maybe tomorrow. We will see how it goes."

She placed a wooden tray on his lap, upon which was a plate of salmon, an orange, and durum wheat bread containing olives, nuts, and raisins. "Eat Julius. Your body needs food to help repair itself."

He prayed silently and partook. While he partook, she sat on a chair opposite him. "The wound will heal on its own, without sutures. It has been too long since you were hurt and the impurities were too deep for me to bind the wound when you got to me. It will close on its own, but it will leave an ugly scar."

Julius began to laugh before abdominal pain stifled him. "I suppose scars for men are different than scars for women. For men, battle scars are a sign of courage. Many of the soldiers I commanded have battle scars. I was in two battles during my time in the army, but never received a sign of courage. Maybe civilian life is more hazardous than I thought. How long will it take before I can do what I have always done?"

"Hopefully, we will be able to take a short walk tomorrow. I think it will be at least a month before you can return to battling highway bandits."

We will take a short walk? Together? He smiled. "If I can help it, I don't intend to battle any more highway bandits, but Marcus and I are supposed to deliver two scrolls to the church on Melitene. They really need them. Winter is approaching. If we don't go soon, ships will stop sailing until next spring."

Though her outward professional countenance remained unchanged, inwardly Angelina winced at his words. *Is that all I am to him—a means to get well and then he leaves? Or is he just being dutiful about a task to accomplish? Am I being selfish, Lord? How do I answer him honestly?*

"You won't be sailing anytime soon, Julius—not if you want to heal properly." She took the tray from his lap. "You eat fast."

"Soldiers are trained to eat fast. It is a difficult habit to break."

When she sat down again on the chair opposite him, he reached out his hand. She took it. "Tell me, Angelina. I saw you at the docks from the ship that took me to Puteoli. Did you see me?"

She blushed. "Yes, I saw you."

"What went through your mind when you saw me?"

Her head dropped, breaking eye contact. *How do I answer that*? She took a deep breath and slowly brought her eyes back up, but not quite to his.

"I saw you interacting with others. I saw how they responded. I thought you looked like a man who knew how to handle people. You conveyed a certain authority that men respected. Did you think anything when you saw me?"

His heart began to race. *What do I say to her?* The words just came.

"I thought you had the kindest, sweetest face I have ever seen. For the past five months I have thought of little else but you. And then I saw you again in a vision after I was wounded."

She stood to her feet, knowing that she had to leave the room before all semblance of professional demeanor was lost. "I must get down to the shop and help with the business. I will check on you again this afternoon."

Rest now, my love, she breathed inaudibly as she exited.

*****

"I got her to smile!" exclaimed Cornelia. "She is so adorable!"

"Let me hold her next," begged Mariana.

Eletia smiled as she watched the women vie to hold her baby Julia. *It makes them want to be mothers themselves. I wish that for them all. Even Fabia is smiling now.*

Out of the corner of her eye she watched Valentina, who sat alone on a couch away from the others. She knew that Valentina wanted to hold her daughter too, but was afraid to ask. *Oh Lord, give the other girls forgiving hearts. It's not like they never did anything wrong.*

As if on cue, upon finishing her turn holding Julia, Herminia stood to her feet and carried the child to Valentina. None of the other women dared comment as Valentina sat enthralled. She ran her right index finger over Julia's cheek and smiled broadly, trying to entice a response.

"Oh!" she cried as Julia obliged.

God bless Herminia. To whom will Valentina hand my child? I doubt any will ask.

Valentina rose and walked tentatively to Mariana, who had been the most scornful of her. She held out the baby. For what seemed an eternity Mariana sat motionless. Finally, she excepted the child.

"Thank you" she simply replied.

At least that's something, thought Eletia. *I am so glad these young women, at least most of them, want to be mothers too. Now if only my little Julia had a father.*

23

A Turn of Events

The next morning Angelina again examined the wound. "It has now been a week since you came. The swelling and the infection are completely gone. Your wound is healing nicely."

She rubbed the first topical of aloe onto the wound. "Do you think you are ready for a short walk?"

Gingerly, Julius rolled to his right, swung his feet to the floor, and sat up. Upon standing, a surge of dizziness immediately forced him down again. "This is going to be harder than I thought."

Angelina handed him a staff. "You will need this for a while."

He stood again to his feet, this time using the staff to stabilize himself. Though his physical wound was healing, his pride was now wounded. He eyed his freshly laundered clothing on a nearby table. Having been embarrassed long enough by her treatments and sponge baths, he spoke decisively. "Let me dress myself and then we can go."

She smiled, brought his clothes to the bed, and left the room.

*****

Upon exiting the shop, Julius found himself wanting to deeply inhale the fresh morning air while his eyes adjusted to the light, but his abdominal pain thwarted him. The warm sun felt good on his skin. He found his legs somewhat clumsy, but the staff reassuring. As he continued to walk, more circulation returned to his legs and he soon found himself moving almost normally.

"How was getting dressed?"

He consciously held back another laugh, knowing the penalty. "It was painful and slow. What normally takes me less than a minute took fifteen. But there was a certain triumphant feeling with accomplishing the task unassisted. Tomorrow I will strive for ten minutes."

"How far do you want to go?"

"I don't know yet. Let's just keep going until I think we need to turn back."

Around them as they walked came the clatter of shops opening for business. The smell of fresh baked bread drifted from a pistrina that had customers lined up at the counter. Children shouted and ran about the street.

But Julius paid little notice to his surroundings, save for the young woman who walked by his side. He had walked with other young women before, but had never experienced the exhilaration that came with her presence.

"How did you get into healing?"

"My avia, my father's mother was a healer. She showed me things. When my brother Drusus got sick, we feared for his life. We treated him together and he got well. My avia told me that I had a healing touch. I learned all that I could from her until she passed away two years ago."

"Where is your father? I have met everyone in your household except for him. Is he still alive?"

"We don't know for sure," answered Angelina sadly. "He has been away from us in prison, without a word now for forty days, allegedly for failure to pay our taxes. I think the real reason is that they don't like our church. They won't let us visit him or allow any correspondence back and forth."

"I'm sorry, Angelina. I wish I could fix that."

"My father ran our shop, though Rufus has filled in nicely. But it has really hurt our church. We don't have a leader now. Liuni tries, but he doesn't have the same gifts as my father."

They came to a park, which featured pleasant trails, grass, benches, trees, and numerous shady arbors. At the entrance of the park was a vendor, selling various treats. One in particular caught Julius' eye. "Would you like a pastiera?

Her face lit up. "They really look good."

He pulled four bronze assis from his pocket and laid them on the vendor's cart. The vendor cut two slices and set them on wooden plates. "Please return the plates when you are finished."

They entered the park and found a shaded bench. Much to Julius' delight, Angelina sat as close to him as propriety allowed. Her gentle fragrance of rose petals soaked in olive oil dizzied him. He took a bite from his tart. "This is as good as it looks," he exclaimed.

Their eyes met and locked. Hers were a deep blue, rare for a Magna Graecia woman. But it was the sparkle in her eyes that enamored him. The sun filtered through her shimmery chestnut hair. He marveled at the shape of her nose and mouth. *If only I could kiss those lips. Are they willing?*

He thought better of trying and retreated to safer ground. "How did you and your family come to believe in Christ?"

"It happened before I was born. My father, who was just my age at the time, was at the market place on the island of Ortygia. A man named Dominic was speaking about Christ on the Ille Forum stage. He said he had just come from Jerusalem, where he had gone for the Jewish Feast of Pentecost. There he heard about Christ from a man named Peter, who said that Christ was nailed to a cross by godless men, but then God raised Him from the dead, putting an end to the agony of death."

"You say Dominic? Did your father tell you what he looked like?"

"He was a young, big, powerful looking man, with a huge head of red hair. He was on his way back to Rome, where he worked as a carpenter."

"Then I have met that same man at a place called the Market of Appius. He is now a prominent leader of the church in Rome."

Angelina smiled. He loved the way she smiled. "I guess it is a small world. Anyway, on that day my father became a follower of Christ. When his marriage to my mother was arranged, he led her to Christ. Liuni came later to my parents' tentmaking shop, looking for a job. My father hired him and then he and his family became followers of Christ too. Such is the world I was born into. I cannot remember a time when I did not believe in Christ."

Julius shuddered. "I can certainly remember my days before Christ.

The things I did. Now I wonder how I could have thought the way I thought."

They finished their pastierae and rose up. Only then did Julius realize his exhaustion. Getting back to the shop would be his second daunting task of the day. They returned their plates to the vendor.

"Those were really good," Angelina told the vendor.

He smiled. "My wife makes them. She makes them and I sell them."

"Well then, tell her that I hope she keeps making them. We'll be back."

We'll be back? Again, her words sent a thrill through Julius' soul. *Is she thinking about the two of us as a couple?*

As they made their way toward the shop, Julius knew that he had indeed overdone his first attempt at walking. But for a man of his mental makeup, if his legs weren't up to the task, determination had to make up the difference.

"So your father is in prison, hopefully still alive, Rufus helps run the shop, and you have no one to lead the church."

"That is where we are. Liuni is humble and good with his hands, but has little ability as a teacher. Rufus is a tremendous teacher, but feels that he is too young in the faith to lead. He does teach the children, including myself, reading and arithmetic. Caecitas especially learns fast. The joy of seeing has not worn off with her. As I said, Rufus is a born teacher, but I perceive that he feels somewhat frustrated teaching children."

"How so?"

"Though he doesn't say it, I can tell that he really would prefer to teach young people my age and older. He has a philosophical bent. You can't get philosophical with children."

Julius shifted his staff to his left hand in preparation for his next move. His right arm needed a rest anyway. For a time, they walked silently side by side while he deliberated. *What if she rejects me?* He had been fearless and decisive in battle. The task literally at hand seemed more daunting.

"But there is something new that is really helping us," spoke Angelina, breaking the silence. "We are now reading our way through the story of Christ's life from the scroll Marcus gave us. I love the story of Christ's birth. I can't wait to hear what comes this evening. You should join us."

"I would love that." He thought again of the Melitene church and how badly they needed the same story. "How are we going to get Luke's story to the church on Melitene if I can't go anywhere? They need it too."

"God will provide a way," she answered simply. He loved her simple, sincere faith.

Finally, he gathered the courage to cross the line from patient to twosome. He grasped her left hand with his right, bracing himself for possible rejection. She gave his hand a slight squeeze, signaling her acceptance. Thrill overcame exhaustion.

As they neared the shop, sounds of laughter and joy came to their ears. Something good was happening. Curiosity quickened their pace. Hands separated. Upon opening the door, they discovered the reason for the laughter standing before them.

"Father!" cried Angelina. She ran into his arms and embraced him, immediately noticing how thin he had become. "What happened? How did you get free?"

"It is a long story," he answered. "Right now, I am hungry. Your mother is fixing me a meal. Can it wait until after I have eaten?"

He recognized the man standing next to his daughter. "I know you. You are the centurion who took Paul with you to Rome."

The two clasped wrists. "That is me, although I am no longer a centurion. I am out of the army."

"He was wounded on his way here from Rome," spoke Angelina. "He and Marcus brought with them a book from Luke about the life of Christ. He was almost dead when he got here. As you can see, he is in much better shape now, as soon you will be."

"I see that there is much I must catch up on. Who is Marcus?"

"I am," said Marcus as he stepped forward. "I am glad to meet you, sir."

Lucia called from upstairs. "Antonius, your food is ready."

"Enough talk for now," said Angelina. "My father needs a meal."

She turned to Julius. "And you need to return to your bed."

Neither party was inclined to dispute.

24

Temptations

The cool overcast of the morning felt like a harbinger of the coming winter as Onesimus hauled his two-wheeled cart from the nearby market place to Paul's house. On it lay provisions for the house, along with paper and ink for Paul's writings. He had been doing much of that lately.

For Onesimus, the past four months had been the best of his life. He had come to know Christ and had found for himself a worthwhile niche in serving Paul that gave him a sense of purpose. Upon reaching the house, he gave the coded knock to the door, three rapid knocks, pause, and then four more rapid knocks. Paul liked sevens. Petronius opened the door.

"Welcome back, Onesimus. Did you get everything?"

"I think so. Writing supplies for Paul. Plenty of fresh fruit, vegetables, and baked breads. Chicken and fish. We ought to cook the fish this morning, while it's still good."

"That sounds like the way to do it."

*****

After a sustaining breakfast of swordfish, olives, cheese, Parthian bread, and cherries, Paul beckoned Onesimus to accompany him upstairs to the veranda overlooking the street. While the young man made his way up the stairway behind Paul, he sensed that something significant was in the offing. Paul never wasted time on trivial conversation. On the veranda

Onesimus noticed a sealed clay jar that looked to have something to do with the coming conversation. The two men seated themselves.

"I am much indebted to you for your service to me these past four months."

From Paul's tone Onesimus surmised that his situation was about to change. An anxious flutter came to his heart. "I would do anything for you, Paul."

"I know you would, which is why I am about to ask of you a very difficult thing."

He swallowed hard. *Maybe I should not have said that.* "What difficult thing?"

"I want you to return to your master Philemon."

I definitely should not have said that. For long moments Onesimus was silent. A sense of dread washed over him. He felt like a man at a tribunal who had just been sentenced to death.

"You ask too much of me, Paul. Philemon is cruel. He will have me maimed for life—or maybe even put to death."

Paul slowly shook his head. "I doubt any of that will be the case. He may have appeared cruel to you because you resisted him. But he worships the same God we worship."

"But it is wrong for one man to own another."

"He spared you and your family from prison. I would worry less about what you think might be wrong for Philemon, and more about what is right for you. You stole a necklace from his wife."

As is wont of youth, Onesimus began to get emotional. "You taught me that Christ calls us to freedom. Why do you now ask me to subject myself again to slavery?"

Paul remained calm. "As I spoke to you the first day you came here. There is a freedom not born of circumstances. I am imprisoned in this house. Yet I am the freest of men."

He opened the jar and pointed inside. "In this jar are two letters. One is written to the church in Colossae. I want you and Tychicus to journey to Colossae together and deliver it. After doing that, I want you to personally deliver the smaller letter to Philemon. It is sealed with wax. I would prefer that you not read it. Just deliver it to him. I want you to apologize to him and to his wife for stealing her necklace. I want you to offer yourself to him to work off your debt. I want you to serve him as you have served me."

Philemon trembled. "You know I cannot do that."

Paul's tone was firm, but fatherly. "I know that you will do it and I know Philemon. He will forgive you and will accept you back into his home, not as a slave, but as a brother in Christ."

Onesimus managed a nervous laugh. "You know, of course, that I could leave here with Tychicus and just disappear somewhere along the way."

The older man nodded thoughtfully. "Yes, you could. I have instructed Tychicus to make no attempt to hold you, should you so choose. If you give in to temptation and choose to run, he will still deliver both letters. But I have every confidence in your obedience. You are a new man in Christ, Onesimus. As a new man, I am confident that you will do the right thing."

The young man took a deep breath. "If I ever see you again, Paul, please remind me never to make you another 'anything promise'."

* * * * *

Content, Antonius pushed back his chair from the supper table in the upstairs great room. "It is so good to eat real food again." He looked around the table at the assemblage of people. "It is even better to be among the people I love." He pointed to Marcus and to Julius. "I am also glad to get to know you two outstanding young men."

"Tell us your story now," spoke Liuni. "How is it that you were set free?"

Antonius put his right hand to his chin in thought. "From what I was told, it seems that Porcius the publicanus may have allotted for himself a hefty portion of the taxes he collected, in addition to his regular pay. When an auditing team from Rome made the discovery, he was immediately dismissed. This morning all of the men, including myself, imprisoned for failure to pay their taxes were released—hence the joyful mood, not only among us, but among many of the people who came into our shop today."

"I cannot recall a better day of sales," spoke Liuni. "What happened to Porcius?"

"I believe he now resides in the same carcer I inhabited. I think he will remain there for a long time, if he manages to escape an even worse fate. Nero does not like being embezzled."

From the clay jar next to him he pulled out the scroll from Luke. "From what you have told me, this is a treasure. I am anxious to read it."

"We have not yet had the time to read through much of it," answered Liuni. "We were hoping you would take up where we left off last night and help us make sense of the next section. It is something about Jesus fasting for forty days."

"Forty days," mused Antonius. "That is how long I was in the prison. Fasting was my involuntarily lot for most of the time. It should be interesting."

*****

After the meal clean-up, the people again assembled at the table in the upstairs great room, as Antonius opened the next scroll from Luke's story. "And Jesus, full of the Holy Spirit, returned from the Jordan and was led about by the Spirit in the wilderness for forty days, being tempted by the devil. And He ate nothing during those days; and when they had ended, He became hungry." (Luke 4:1-2)

He read through the section until he came to the end. "And when the devil had finished every temptation, he departed from Him until an opportune time." (Luke 4:13)

He rolled up the scroll and placed it back in the jar. "This is indeed a treasure. I observe from what I have read this evening that Jesus was weak from the lack of food and that the devil tried to take advantage of the situation to get Him to eat. I think I know how He felt. A man that hungry would do almost anything to eat. Yet Jesus did not. Why wouldn't He turn the stones into bread? Wouldn't He have been justified in doing so?"

He looked around the table. None volunteered to answer. "Angelina, what do you think?"

"Food feeds the body, but the word of God feeds the soul. It is more important to have a fed soul, which is eternal, than a fed body, which is temporal."

Her father nodded approvingly. "That is a good answer. What would be the implication if all of us were actually to live that way? Anyone?"

"I think we would fight less over food," answered Rufus. "I think we would learn to treasure God's ways more than our own understanding of how we should live. We would approach life with the understanding that the One who made us knows more about life than we who are made."

As the evening wore on, the people discussed why it is better to worship God than the devil and why it would be foolish to jump from a height, expecting to be delivered by God. Afterwards, they naturally fell into a time of worship of their Savior.

"Read to us more every night," spoke his son Drusus when they had finished their worship time.

"I will," answered Antonius. "And now it is time for the wives to take the children to bed. I have an important matter I want to discuss with the men here at the table before we do the same."

The mothers rose up and carried their smallest children, who had already fallen asleep, to bed. The older children followed, leaving only the men in the common room, who seated themselves closer to Antonius.

"Would you be willing to run the shop for us tomorrow?" Antonius asked Rufus. "I want to take the time to recover my strength and to read entirely through Luke's story."

"I will do so," he answered.

"Good. I also gather that this scroll was actually not intended for us directly, but for the church on Melitene. Thankfully there is another identical scroll that needs to get to them as soon as possible."

"That is true," affirmed Marcus. "But Julius will be too weak to complete the trip for at least another three weeks."

Julius raised his hand and spoke. "With fall upon us and winter approaching, we are coming to the time when fewer and fewer sea captains will venture upon the Great Sea, risking their lives, their ships, and their cargoes. I know that from personal experience. If we don't go soon, we will be forced to wait until the spring, which I find unacceptable."

Antonius nodded. "I also find that unacceptable. Our fellow believers on Melitene need Luke's story. I have an idea that I believe will satisfy all parties and all concerns." His eyes met everyone in turn. "From what I am told, Rufus filled in well, running our shop during my forced absence. I also understand that he helped our children with their reading and arithmetic."

Liuni nodded. "He did well on both accounts."

"I further understand that he would prefer to teach older students, but that little opportunity to do so is open to him here, at least in part based upon the color of his skin. I wonder if the gymnasium on Melitene might be more accommodating to a man like Rufus."

"I am sure that would be the case," spoke Marcus. "They had an Ethiopian teacher there for many years named Solon, whom I knew personally. I didn't like him at the time, but that was another life. He was the head of the entire school and highly venerated. I think skin color would matter less on Melitene."

Antonius nodded in agreement. "So here is what I propose. "Rufus will accompany Marcus as soon as possible to deliver the scroll to the Melitene church. Julius will remain here to heal."

All nodded their agreement before Rufus spoke. "I will go, but I will miss you all here. This is the first time in my life where I have felt real acceptance—like my ancestry does not matter, but only who and what I am as a man."

"We are Christians here, Rufus," answered Antonius. "We believe that we are all made in the image of God, all fallen, and all redeemed through the sacrifice of Christ on the cross. Christ died for all of us, which means that each of us individually is worth the blood of God's Son. For any of us to despise another man because he is of a different race is in effect to nullify Christ's sacrifice in his heart and to despise the God who made that other man."

"Then it has to work both ways," observed Rufus. "I have known many from my Ethiopian heritage who have despised those with lighter skin, simply for being different. And truly, none of us chose where and how to be born. That was God's choice."

"It was, but we live in a fallen world, Rufus, where humans battle and even kill one another over the most trivial, absurd things. We are God's people. We must show our fellow humans a better way to live. We must even love those who hate us because we are different, whatever that difference might be. It is God's way for us to live."

All present nodded agreement to Antonius' plan. "Then it is settled," spoke Antonius. "Tomorrow I want Marcus to find a ship at the docks bound for Melitene, hopefully on the day after tomorrow, and to book two passages. I want Rufus to run the shop. Lord willing, Marcus and Rufus will depart the next day and I will hopefully be ready by then to re-assume the responsibility of running the shop."

After his words the men prayed together before retiring for the night. As he lay in his bed Rufus felt both excited and saddened. He envisioned himself teaching at the gymnasium on Melitene, guiding young lives in the direction God would have them go. At the same time, he knew he would miss the dear people of the Syracuse church.

25

Polaris

Immediately after breakfast the next morning Marcus set out for the docks on his mission to find a Melitene bound ship. It was work he found more to his liking than being cooped up inside a shop all day. Upon reaching the docks, he first tried the Portus Grande side, figuring that he would more likely find suitable passage there. But the larger ships were going either east or west. None were taking the short jaunt south to Melitene.

After two unproductive hours he turned to the Portus Parvus side. As expected, he found no sea captains willing to venture forth on their smaller ships into the oncoming winter seas. Discouraged, he pondered his options. Returning to the shop fruitlessly was a distasteful prospect. He could perhaps attempt to entice someone to venture upon the seas with a substantial sum of money. *But where am I going to get the money?* He wanted to complete the mission. The prospect of seeing Eletia again also mixed into his thoughts.

Abruptly, it occurred to him that he was on God's mission. He remembered how Paul had prayed before doing anything. He had always considered himself more a man of action than contemplation, but he was changing inside.

He found a bench by the wharf and sat down. There he bowed his head and closed his eyes, as he had often seen Paul do, but which he found awkward and humbling. *What will people think as they pass by?* He forced himself to do it anyway, speaking in a barely audible volume, so as not to attract attention.

"Lord Jesus, the people of Melitene need Luke's story. Please grant me success in finding a ship to take us there. I also want to see..."

"Marcus?"

Embarrassed at being caught praying, he looked up. There before him stood Marinus. A leather bag filled with something was slung over his back. "Well, we meet again," said the sea captain. "What were you doing?"

It seemed no use to lie. "I was praying."

"Really?" Marinus joined him on the bench, setting his bag on the cobblestones in front of him. "What were you praying about?"

"Do you recall that Julius and I were bound for Melitene? We have a story to deliver."

"I do. How is it with Julius?"

"He is much better now. We actually found the angel of mercy he saw in his vision. Julius is healing, but not yet ready to accompany me to Melitene." He took the plunge. "Would the Tantulus by any chance be heading that way?"

Marinus thought for a moment. "It could head that way. From what I understand, they really need commodities there like wheat, barley, rye, olives, figs, oranges, and honey for the coming winter. There are merchants here with a surplus of those items, needing to sell them to a captain willing to risk his ship with the prospect of making a big profit on the other side."

"Would you be game to go?"

Again, he thought. "I need a bigger ship. Bigger ships cost a lot of money. This would help me get a bigger ship."

"Would you have room for two passengers?"

"I could make room. Who is the other passenger if it isn't Julius?"

"His name is Rufus. He is an older man and very scholarly."

Marinus looked around the wharf. "Where is he?"

"He is at a shop about ten minutes from here on foot."

"Then bring him here at daybreak tomorrow. I will have my ship loaded and ready to go."

Marcus searched the wharf with his eyes. "Where is the Tantulus?"

Marinus pointed to his left, further down the wharf. "It is the seventh ship down from here."

"One denarius for each of us?" asked Marcus.

"Deal. I note that you found Julius' angel of mercy. If you were praying for a ship, then I had better comply." The two clasped wrists.

Marcus rose from the bench and began to walk rapidly for the shop. Abruptly, a thought occurred to him. He stopped, turned, and called back. "We aren't going to be bait for another pirate ship this time, are we?"

Marinus laughed. "I could only wish. Not this time—unless one shows up unexpected, in which case we'll just have to outrun it."

*****

The water was surprisingly choppy for so early in the morning once the Tantulus cleared the harbor and reached the open sea. A cold wind blew from west to east, encouraging the two passengers to seek the shelter of the pilot house, which was preferable to the stuffy, cargo-laden hold.

"How do you navigate in the open sea without any landmarks?" asked Rufus. "From what I understand, Melitene is a small island, easy to miss."

"I do have landmarks," answered Marinus. "I try to keep Portus Grande on the starboard stern of my ship. By the time I can no longer see the port distinctly, Melitene should come into view. Once I see Melitene, I will aim a little left of the middle of the island. Then once darkness falls, I can navigate toward Portus Amplus by the signal light from the fortress of Aemilianus, which guards the harbor."

He pointed toward the western horizon. An ominous formation of dark clouds was gathering. "It looks like a storm is coming. Hopefully, we will reach the harbor before the worst of it reaches us."

"Supposing we were out of sight of land altogether?" asked Marcus. "How do you know which direction you are going?"

"By day I can tell at least somewhat by the position of the sun. By night mariners rely upon Polaris, the north star. On a clear night in the open sea I can gauge my direction relative to the position of the star. If I am heading straight for it, I am going north. If I am heading directly away from it, I am going south. If it is to the starboard of my ship, I am going west and if it is to port, I am going east."

"Why the north star? Why not any star?"

"Because just like the sun during the day, all the stars move across the sky from the east to the west during the night. But the north star always remains fixed in the same position."

"How can that be?"

"It just is." Marinus tapped Rufus on the shoulder. "I am told that you are a man of science. Why is the north star uniquely stationary all the time?"

"There are a number of theories," answered Rufus. "None are provable. The theory to which I subscribe is that the earth upon which we dwell is a round ball, spinning about in the heavens. The sun shines upon half of the earth at all times. The sun and the stars do not move around the earth, as appears to be the case, but rather the earth rotates one complete revolution each day, making the other heavenly bodies appear to move. The north star is over the extreme north of our earthly ball, which makes it appear stationary, relative to our position at all times. Therefore, we can rely upon it for navigation, unless it is blocked by clouds."

Marinus chuckled. "That sounds good to me. All I know is that it always stays fixed. It also reminds me of those miserable two weeks at sea when we were caught last year in that euraquilo. No landmarks. No sun or stars for many days. I had no idea where we were—Spain or Egypt, or somewhere in between. Paul said we would run aground on some island. Since I had no answers, I figured we should listen to him. The island turned out to be Melitene."

"Are we in trouble?" asked Marcus. "Will the approaching storm cause us to get lost?"

"Not in terms of navigation, because we will never be out of sight of land either way. But it might get pretty rough on the seas before we reach the harbor, hopefully before midday tomorrow."

"Do you plan to winter there, like you were forced to do last year?"

"Not if I can help it. I hope to sell this cargo, then to take on a full load of wool and get it back to Syracuse before winter. Wool commands the highest price at this time of year."

He yawned deeply. "I will need some sleep if I am going to last the night. How would you like to take over the steering of the ship for two hours, Marcus? I'll refund your denarius."

Momentary fear quickly gave way to challenge. "What do I do?"

"Just keep Portus Grande on the starboard corner of our stern. Once you see Melitene, aim a little to the left of the middle of the island."

"But how do I steer this thing?"

Marinus showed him the two wooden handles on either side of his captain's chair. "These handles go beneath the waterline and extend to the stern of the ship. If you want to go right, or to starboard, you push the right handle away from you and pull the left handle toward yourself."

He demonstrated the maneuver. The ship turned to starboard. "Now you try it. Turn the ship back to port until Portus Grande is on the starboard corner of our stern."

With some apprehension Marcus assumed the captain's seat. He pulled the right handle toward himself and pushed the left handle away, overcorrecting a little. With some adjustment he succeeded in putting the seaport from which they had come on the starboard stern.

"Very good, Marcus. Two hours. You might see Melitene by the time I come back up." He exited the pilot house and disappeared into the hold of the ship.

*****

With the darkness came rain, lightly at first, but soon it morphed into a downpour. Clouds covered the north star, but the light from the fortress of Aemilianus shone brightly in the distance. As the wind and the seas became increasingly violent, Marinus ventured from the pilot house to trim the sail. All the while his two passengers became increasingly queasy.

"We're all right," said Marinus. "I can see the light. But you men ought to go below and try to get some sleep. You won't feel so sick. I am used to this. Just hold on tight along the way and make sure you close the hatch behind you."

Neither man needed prodding. They rose and left the pilot house. Once outside, they grabbed on to anything that would support them, to keep from falling upon the rocking deck, possibly to be washed overboard. Upon reaching the stairway, they clung to the railing and descended the steps into the hold. Once Marcus closed the hatch behind them, they found themselves in murky darkness. They felt their way to their bunks over the swaying floor. Once in their bunks they felt immediate relief. The ship also did not seem to rock quite so much below as it did topside. For a while they talked.

"Something just came to me, Marcus."

"What is that?"

"We need a fixed point like the north star to navigate a ship in the open seas. I wonder if God didn't put Polaris where it is for that very reason? I wonder if it is also a sign?"

"What kind of a sign?"

"Don't we also need a fixed point of reference to navigate our lives?"

"How so?"

"All of my life I have been searching for a fixed point upon which I could judge between truth and error, and between right and wrong."

Marcus chuckled. "You remind me of Solon, the man I used to know on Melitene. He was a lot like you. I despised him at the time."

"I hope you don't despise me now."

"No, Rufus. I do not despise you. I am not the same man I was a year ago. You and I are very different men, but I respect you. I never thought about a fixed point of reference, but I guess you must be right. How can we truly judge right and wrong if it becomes a matter of everyone's personal opinion? You are a thinker, Rufus. In a lot of ways, I wish I could be like you."

"Sometimes I wish I had your vigor and strength."

"Maybe sometimes you can be my wisdom and I can lend you my strength."

Marcus became troubled in spirit. "I look forward to delivering Luke's story to Theophilus, once we have found him. That will be a pleasant task. But then I must seek out a man named Publius and his wife Amoenitas, both of whom I have greatly wronged. I want to make peace with them. I hope they will make peace with me."

"Do they know the Lord?

"Yes. Publius is the leader of the church on Melitene."

"Then I think they will forgive you. When we understand that God has forgiven us for our many sins, it becomes easier for us to forgive others for theirs."

"I think they will forgive me, but there is another matter, which I think may be more difficult."

"What other matter?"

"Amoenitas has a sister named Eletia. She never meant anything to me before, except as an object of my lust. She almost died in a plague we had there, but somehow recovered. Just before I left the island last spring,

I saw her—obviously pregnant. I am pretty sure that I am the one who got her that way. She was among the believers in Christ. Her child, my child, is likely born by now."

"Do you hope to win her heart? Do you hope to become her husband and to be a father to your child?"

"That is what I hope for. What should I do?"

For a moment Rufus was silent, thinking through his answer. "If I were you, I would apologize to her for how I treated her. Then I would give her some money to help support the child without asking for anything in return. I would join the church there and begin to serve. If you were to do those things, then over time you would gain the respect of the people, and of Eletia. You need to prove yourself to be the kind of man a woman would want for a husband."

"That is a tall order, Rufus. I don't know if I can do all that. I can say that I already have some money I have saved that I intend to give to her when I see her."

"That will be a good start. I wonder if I will get a teaching post at the gymnasium. I wonder that if I do get one, if I will be a teacher worthy of my students."

"I think that if we will take on the right challenges, God will grow us into the men we need to be. We ought to pray about these things before we sleep. God knows our worries."

Back and forth the men prayed, each for the other, until they drifted into a peaceful sleep.

26

Seven Denarii

By the time the Tantulus reached port, it was early in the afternoon of the next day. For the two travelers, it was a relief to set foot again upon solid, if not dry ground. Rain was falling heavily, along with a substantial wind. Before leaving the wharf, the men clasped wrists with Marinus.

"I can't say that we enjoyed this voyage," spoke Marcus for the two, "but at least it got us to where we needed to go—and I got some experience in steering a ship."

Marinus smiled. "That you did. It was a pleasure having you men aboard to keep me company." He scanned the darkened sky. "Like it or not, I may have to winter here."

The two men took their leave of Marinus and made their way up the main thoroughfare of the city of Portus Amplus. On the main street they came upon a thermopolium called Festivitas.

"The first thing we need is a good meal and some hot drinks out of the rain," said Marcus. "Then we'll figure out a way to get to Mathos."

Drenched from head to foot, Rufus acquiesced in easy surrender. Upon entering the establishment, they found a table by a front window. When they sat, Marcus immediately put his head down on the table and closed his eyes. Even still, the table seemed to rock and sway, as if they were still on the ship.

Almost immediately his attempted recovery from seasickness was interrupted. "May I take your order please," spoke the famulus.

"Amberjack please," answered Rufus, "along with wheat bread and a glass of mulsum, preferably warm."

"And you, sir?"

"I'll have the same," Marcus answered without raising his head.

"I see that you and the sea don't agree," observed Rufus after the waiter was out of earshot.

Marcus' head remained down. "No, we don't. Not when it's rough like that. For a while, I thought about jumping over the side and just ending it. How about you?"

"I am glad to be on land again, inside and out of the cold. Tonight, I want a hot bath and a warm, clean bed."

For the next fifteen minutes no conversation occurred between them until the waiter returned with their order. When Rufus suggested they thank the Lord for their food before partaking, Marcus head stayed down.

"Lord Jesus," prayed Rufus. "Thank you for this food. Please help us to get back our land legs and to find a way to Mathos. Amen."

They had just begun to partake when a burly, red-haired man approached them. "Did I overhear you men say something about heading for Mathos?"

"We were hoping to get to Mathos before the day is out," answered Marcus. "We need to meet a man there named Theophilus."

"Theophilus? Well then, this is your lucky day. I have a wagon, I am heading to Mathos, and I know just where Theophilus lives. I can take you right to his house."

They gestured for him to seat himself at their table. "I am Marcus and this is my friend Rufus."

"I am Demetrius. I live five miles west of Mathos, near the western end of our island. But I have to pass through Mathos on my way there. Are you men followers of Christ?"

They looked at Demetrius in surprise. "Yes, we are. How did you know?"

"I saw you praying before partaking of your meal. I am also a believer. I am a sutor by trade."

"What are you doing here, so far from your home?"

"The best leather, the best rawhide, and the best cork at the best prices can only be found here in Portus Amplus. I just made my purchases and thought I would get a meal before heading back to my home. I make my shoes at home and sell them, along with my wife Phoebe at the market place in Mathos on Saturdays."

The famulus appeared to take Demetrius' order. "I will have grouper fish covered with garum sauce, along with wheat bread, vegetables, and some non-fermented grape juice."

"Non-fermented, sir?"

"Please. Non-fermented."

"Very well, sir."

"Do you mind if we eat while you are waiting for your meal? We'll wait for you to finish."

"Go ahead. Eat your meals while they are hot."

*****

By the time they exited the thermopolium the rain had stopped, the sun had come out, and the wind had died down. Billowy white clouds floated by in a pristine blue sky that shone vivid in contrast with the buildings and hills below. With room on the buckboard only for one other man, Marcus deferred to Rufus and found himself a cramped spot in the cargo area, which smelled heavily of leather. A hot bath and a clean bed at the end of the day did indeed sound good. Numerous seagulls arced overhead as they made their way west on the cobblestone road toward Mathos.

"I hope I am not being impertinent," spoke Demetrius to Rufus. "But what is your business with Theophilus?"

"We have come from Rome with a story about the life of Christ, written by a man named Luke. From what I understand, Luke promised Theophilus a copy of the story last spring while he was here on Melitene."

Demetrius smiled. "He has often spoken of his need for Luke's story. We have been praying for it to come. He will be delighted to see you. You have come all the way here from Rome?"

"Not I. Marcus is the main courier from Rome. He and a man named Julius were supposed to deliver the story to Theophilus, but Julius was badly wounded in a fight with bandits on the Appian Way. He had to remain in Syracuse to heal. I joined Marcus there to help him complete the trip."

"We know Julius. He is a good man. I hope he fully recovers."

The wagon came to a long upward climb. "This is the hardest part of the trip on my horses. But we'll level off in about five minutes."

While they climbed, he continued his conversation with Rufus. "What about you? Why have you come to Melitene? Marcus could have just finished the trip alone."

"That is true. I hope to become a teacher at the gymnasium in Mathos. No such jobs were available to me in Syracuse. I was informed that they might be amenable to hiring someone like me here."

"They might. You can talk to my wife about that. She works at the gymnasium."

After much inner debate Rufus gathered the nerve to ask the question he had wanted to ask since he heard Demetrius' order at the restaurant. "May I ask you a personal question?"

Demetrius eyed him quizzically. "You may. I may choose not to answer it."

"Why did you specify non-fermented grape juice?"

"Christ saved me from my sins last winter, among which was strong drink, which made me violent. My wife Phoebe knows about that. I don't ever want to be that way again. Therefore, I will not go near strong drink of any kind. I am afraid that one drop would send me back to my old ways."

"Well then, you are better off without it," Rufus agreed.

The wagon reached the top of the hill and leveled off. An hour later they reached Mathos under blue skies. At the end of their ride Demetrius declined any payment.

"You men have brought to us a priceless treasure. I cannot wait to hear from it myself. That is payment enough for me."

*****

Theophilus beamed as he held in his hands the precious scrolls. "I cannot begin to tell you how glad I am to see these. In the next couple of days, I intend to read through them entirely. Then Publius will have a chance to do the same. Thank you, men, for bringing them."

"It wasn't easy," spoke Marcus. "But by the grace of God we got them here."

"I am sure it wasn't easy. Nothing worthwhile is ever easy."

While the men spoke, Flavia entered the great room carrying a tray of savillum. The two visitors stood to their feet as she set the tray on the table before them.

"Thank you, Flavia," said Theophilus. "This is my wife, gentlemen. She is to me another heaven-sent gift from God."

"We are pleased to meet you," said both simultaneously.

She smiled and nodded to the men. Her long, curly auburn hair, fair complexion, blue eyes, and slightly freckled face afforded her a delicate beauty that was not lost on either of the men.

"Before marrying me, she was a baker at the governor's villa. Here you see a sample of what she can do."

He gestured for the men to again be seated and to partake as Flavia retreated back into the culina. Marcus reached for the nearest delectable and took a bite. It tasted as good as it looked. "I can see why she was employed at the villa."

"The day is mostly done," spoke Theophilus. "Where are you men staying tonight?"

"We saw an inn in the square," answered Rufus. "We figured we would stay there."

Theophilus shook his head emphatically. "You don't want to stay at the Remissio. It's a seedy place. Save your money and stay with us. Flavia will feed us a fine dinner. We have a tub. You men can get a bath. We have beds for you. After breakfast tomorrow morning you can go about the rest of your business here on the island."

"You are very kind," spoke Marcus gratefully. "Speaking about the rest of our business, I need to speak with Publius and his wife Amoenitas. Where might I find them?"

"Publius is likely tending sheep on his land four miles west of here. You might still find Amoenitas at Ille Perfugium."

"Ille Perfugium?"

"It's on the main square, not five minutes from here on foot. It used to be a brothel. Now it is a Christian home for some of those same women, helping them to live more worthwhile lives."

Marcus rose to his feet. "Rufus, I need to speak with Amoenitas. You look tired. Why don't you remain here while I attempt to accomplish one more task this day?"

He turned to Theophilus. "I hope you don't mind. There is something I must do. I should be back within an hour."

*****

Standing at the front door of the former brothel, Marcus took a deep breath before knocking. He had visited the place before with less honorable intent. From inside he heard female voices and steps approaching. When the door opened, he froze. There before him stood Eletia. The shock on both faces matched.

"Marcus? What are you doing here?"

He stammered. "I…I came to see Amoenitas."

"Amoenitas is not here. She is gone for the day." He stood before her like a cornered rabbit that knows it is about to become prey for a hungry predator.

"Is there something I can do for you?"

"Do you have a baby?" he blurted out.

"Yes. I have a baby girl." He continued to stand paralyzed. "Are you wondering if the child is yours?"

"Yes."

She eyed him suspiciously. "Do you come in peace?"

"I come in peace."

For a moment she hesitated before opening the door all the way. She gestured for him to enter. As he came inside, he stole furtive glances at her. *She is more beautiful than any woman I have ever seen. Dear God, would it be possible?*

He followed her to a young woman who sat on a couch holding the child. "Herminia, may I please have my baby?"

The exchange was made. Eletia held the sleeping infant before her father. "Her name is Julia, after my mother."

In wonder he gazed at her. *She has my hands. She has my forehead, my nose and my mouth. Oh, I love her already.*

"What is your business, Marcus? Why have you returned to Melitene?"

He looked around the room. Two women were setting the dinner table. Two others could be heard working in the culina. "May we speak privately?"

"We can speak privately here in this room, within sight of the others present."

She motioned for him to take a chair. She seated herself opposite him on a couch. A low table between them served as a barrier.

"What is on your mind, Marcus?"

He drew another deep breath. "I saw you on the dock just before I left Melitene last spring on the same ship that took Paul away. I saw that you were pregnant. I saw that you were among the believers in Christ. I arrived at Portus Amplus early this afternoon, carrying with me the story of Christ's life written by Paul's friend Luke."

Innumerable questions rushed through Eletia's mind. *Oh Lord, he doesn't seem like the Marcus I knew before. Where do I begin?*

"I am aware of the promise of the coming story. Do you still have it with you?"

"No. It is with Theophilus. He was overjoyed to see it. I have just come from his house."

A look of puzzlement came to her face. "Why would you want to bring such a book? Why would anyone trust you with such a book?"

"You ask valid questions, Eletia. I am not the same violent, hard-hearted, bitter man who left here last spring. I had some conversations with Paul and others. I have become a follower of Christ."

For long moments she did not answer. *Is he genuine, or is this all an elaborate charade?* "That's very nice. What do you expect from me, Marcus?"

"I expect nothing from you, Eletia. I have just one more question for you and then I will leave. Where can I find Publius and your sister Amoenitas? I want to make my peace with them."

"They will both be here in the morning by the ninth hour. They will have morning duties until the eleventh hour. You may come here then if you want to speak with them. Do you truly come in peace?"

Marcus rose to his feet. "I truly come in peace, Eletia. I have wronged you. I wronged your sister and I wronged Publius. I hope someday that you all will forgive me."

He opened his leather purse and extracted seven silver denarii. "These I earned in Rome from doing construction work. I have saved them for you. I hope to get a similar job here in Mathos and to be able to help you more."

A hint of tears began to form in her eyes. "Thank you, Marcus. These will help me a lot."

He took one last look at his child and turned to leave. She accompanied him to the door.

"Marcus, I do forgive you, just as God has forgiven me."

*****

After seeing to her needs Eletia put Julia into her cunae for the night. The tiny child was already blissfully asleep, a state Eletia feared would be denied her. She climbed into her bed more from habit than hope, her mind in a quandary.

What do I do, Lord? It is hard for me to believe that Marcus is really different from the man I used to know. He seems different, but is it all an act? He did give me seven denarii.

As she considered her late afternoon meeting with the father of her child, she reflected upon her own conversion. *It took a while for many who knew me to believe that I was genuine too. It took a while for me to believe it myself. Old habits die hard, but a new spirit gradually prevails.*

She envisioned herself married to Marcus, with him being a responsible husband, gentle and kind. Together they would love their daughter. Together they would assemble with their fellow believers at the amphitheater. Together they would cry out to God for wisdom and for strength to live life. Together they would have more children. *Could it be possible, Lord?*

Despite her skepticism about sleeping, all thought faded as weariness overcame doubt.

27

A Fresh Beginning

The welcome summer shade from the now withered passion vines that crisscrossed the lattice of the awning above seemed unnecessary on what was turning out to be a cool, gray, overcast fall day. Gusting winds rustled the trees around Publius, Amoenitas, and Eletia portending another coming storm as they sat at the patio table behind Ille Perfugium.

"When Marcus comes, please send him to us here, Valentina. And please, once he has joined us, we are not to be disturbed."

"It will be as you have asked," she answered, avoiding their eyes. She turned to enter the house.

"Valentina," called Publius. "We forgive you. What was done is done. It is all in the past. We will never speak of it again."

She nodded slightly and disappeared into the house.

"We need to watch out for Valentina," spoke Publius. "I just learned this morning that one of the women who also accused me, Octavia, has been found dead on the rocks below Scopulus Altus. Either she committed suicide, or someone helped her get there."

The two sisters shuddered. "Alacerius," said Eletia. "He did that before with Flavia. We ought to warn her about him, and tell her to never go anywhere out of the sight of people."

"Why can't we have him arrested?" asked Amoenitas.

"It would be hard to pin Octavia's 'accident' on Alacerius, just like we couldn't prove that Alacerius attempted to murder Gratiana. There are no witnesses."

He shifted subjects. "Speaking of Gratiana, where is she? She ought to be with us for a meeting like this."

"I just came from her home," spoke Amoenitas. "She is not feeling well. I need to return to her as soon as we are finished here."

A knock came to the front door that was heard all the way to the back. Publius braced himself. *I wonder how this is going to go—a rematch of our bout last winter or a miracle from God? Lord Jesus, please give us wisdom and discernment.*

They arose. Through the door to the back patio emerged Marcus, followed by Rufus. But it was Rufus who sent a jolt through Amoenitas.

"Solon?"

The older man turned his eyes to her, puzzled. "My name is Rufus, domina. But I have heard of Solon."

Formal greetings were exchanged before the parties sat down around the table. The tension was palpable—like that of a condemned group of five people, one by one awaiting their fate. Publius took the lead in trying to lighten the atmosphere.

"I understand, Marcus, that you came here yesterday and visited with Eletia?"

"I did. Rufus and I arrived from Syracuse yesterday, bearing with us the promised story from Luke to Theophilus about the life of Christ."

"It is here?" Publius looked at Eletia.

"I'm sorry. I forgot to mention that part."

But the revelation had its effect, immediately relieving a considerable part of the tension. "Well," said Publius. "I much look forward to reading it." He turned his attention back to Marcus. "I am informed that you have become a believer in Christ?"

"I have." He looked directly at Amoenitas. "I cruelly struck you last winter when you resisted my advance. Please forgive me. Do you retain any lasting effects from that blow?"

"I felt it for a long time, but it is gone now. Another man struck my mother like that and she never recovered." She nodded to Marcus. "I forgive you."

Marcus returned her nod in grateful acknowledgment. "As you and your husband can readily see from the scar over my left eye, I do bear a lasting mark from that event."

He turned his eyes to Publius. "I deserved what I got, sir. You did well to defend your wife."

Publius gave him a slow understanding acknowledgement. "I forgive you too. I am sorry about the scar. What are your plans, Marcus? Have you come only to deliver Luke's story, or do you plan to remain here?"

"I plan to remain here if I am welcome. I hope to get a job." He stole a quick glance at Eletia. "I plan to see what happens from there."

"You are welcome here on Melitene, Marcus, if you behave yourself. We don't want to see any of what we saw from you here before."

"I hope never again to give you any reason to wish that I were elsewhere."

Publius gestured to Rufus. "What about you, Rufus? What are your plans?"

"I came first to help Marcus get the scrolls delivered. I came also in the hope of getting a teaching position at the gymnasium here. I long to help young minds develop in the right way."

At this point Amoenitas found herself unable to hold back. "You are so much like Solon, who taught at the gymnasium here for many years. Where were you born?"

"In Alexandria, domina."

"Alexandria? That is where Solon lived before he came to Melitene as a young man. How many years have you lived?"

"Fifty-three, domina."

Amoenitas did a mental calculation. "Solon came here from Alexandria at the age of twenty-two. He taught at the gymnasium for nearly fifty years, until last year when he was dismissed. Who is your mother?"

"Her name was Drusilla. She is now gone from this earth." He became misty-eyed. "She lived a hard, joyless life. Her father was a drunkard, whom she hardly knew. Her mother died when she was fifteen years old. She found herself alone on the streets. There she met an Ethiopian sailor. He bought her a meal and gave her some money in return for a certain favor, which is how I came to be. She never saw him again after that one night."

The final hammer dropped. "Solon was an Ethiopian sailor, who lived for a time in Alexandria, about that same time. He told us about his formerly wild days while he lived there. You have the same nose, the same mouth, the same hair, the same mannerisms, the same calling in life, and almost the same voice."

"I knew him too," added Publius. "My wife knew him better. She has to be right about this."

Marcus nodded in agreement. "Do you remember, Rufus, how I told you on the ship that you reminded me of Solon? I suspect we now know the reason."

Rufus shook his head in amazement. "Is he here? Can I meet him?"

"I am sorry," answered Amoenitas. "He was murdered over a year ago. I was with him when he died. You may be the product of a youthful indiscretion, Rufus, but you are the son of a great man."

"Will you men stay for our midday meal here?" asked Publius. "I think we have room."

*****

After a satisfying first meeting and an equally satisfying lunch the two men headed for the gymnasium in search of employment. A slight rain was falling.

"You might as well start looking here too," said Rufus as they entered the grounds. "They might need someone with your skills."

Memories flooded Marcus' mind as he surveyed the grounds while he and Rufus headed for the main officium. From the various buildings came typical classroom chatter. "It doesn't look or sound much different from how I remember it. But it feels totally different," he remarked.

Upon entering the officium, they saw a woman seated behind a desk. Rufus took the lead. "Good afternoon, domina. My name is Rufus and my friend here is Marcus, who used to be a student at this school."

The woman smiled pleasantly. "My name is Phoebe. How may I help you?"

"You wouldn't happen to be the wife of a man named Demetrius, would you?" asked Rufus.

"I am."

He chuckled. "He gave us a ride to here yesterday from Portus Amplus."

"He told me about it. I understand you are looking for a teaching position?"

"That is correct, domina. And my friend Marcus would like to know if there are any construction or maintenance jobs available here."

"Well gentlemen, it seems that your timing is impeccable. We have one opening in each area. You will have to go through an interview with our Concilium, but even there your timing is perfect. They are meeting in one hour to discuss how to fill our openings. Do you men have any local references—people who could vouch for your credentials and your character?"

Marcus shook his head. "I am sure there are a number of people around here who could vouch otherwise for me. But I am a new man, eager for a chance to prove my worthiness."

Rufus pulled two parchment scrolls from his leather bag. "I have here two letters of recommendation, one for each of us, from the pastor of the church at Syracuse. Though I doubt any of you here know the man, maybe the letters will lend some weight to our cause."

"As for Rufus," spoke Marcus, "this is his first time ever on this island. But he is the son of Solon, if that will make any difference."

Phoebe smiled. "It might." She handed each another parchment, along with ink and two styluses. "I need for each of you to write yourselves a resume. Include your name, contact information, experiences, and how you think you could help our school. It's raining outside, but I think there is an empty classroom on the right after you go out the door. Bring your resumes back here, along with your letters of recommendation, in one hour. I will get you into the meeting."

"Thank you," said both simultaneously.

Once out of earshot, Marcus exclaimed his surprise. "I had no idea I had a letter of recommendation from Antonius."

"You earned it," answered Rufus.

* * * * *

"You look funny with that big mark over your eye," remarked the middle of Theophilus' daughters to Marcus. Theophilus and Flavia cringed.

"That's rude," corrected her ten-year old sister. "I'm Benedicta. My rude sister is Laverna." She pointed to her youngest sister. "That's Accalia. She's four and she's very shy."

Marcus smiled as he moved immediately to lighten the atmosphere. "It is an old, ill-earned battle wound. But I have gotten used to it."

"Theophilus, you have yourself quite a wife," remarked Rufus as spooned himself another chunk of timpana.

"The perfect ending for an eventful day." added Marcus. "We have both been hired. We start tomorrow."

"God is good," said Theophilus. "You men have jobs. How did it happen so quickly?"

"They have needs at the school. But even still, our jobs are tentative. They want Rufus to observe a history and a philosophy class with another instructor and then have the instructor observe him before he can be on his own. As for me, I will train under an older man named Phlegon for a month before he retires."

"Well good. That is the best way to ease into a new job. You men need to learn your jobs. They need time to gain confidence in you." Theophilus paused for a moment. "How did it go at Ille Perfugium this afternoon?"

"It has indeed been quite a day," answered Rufus. "I found out that my father was Solon."

Every head around the table came up. "Solon?" asked Flavia. "Your father was Solon?"

"Yes. It is a long story. I never knew my father. They also remarked at the school how much I reminded them of Solon. Apparently, they really respected him. I think that is what got me hired."

He turned his attention back to Theophilus. "Have you had time to read any from Luke's story?"

"Since you men left this morning, that is pretty much all I have been doing. I was just reading a story about a Samaritan man who helped another man, probably a Jew, who had been wounded by thieves when you men came. I cannot begin to describe to you how thrilling it is for me to read these stories about Jesus for the first time. The more I read, the more I love Him. I cannot wait to finish and to give the scrolls to Publius."

He pushed his chair back from the table and smiled at his wife Flavia. "You have done it again, my love. Wish I could keep eating your timpana, but my stomach is full. Do you mind if I take a walk with our guests before we call it a day?"

* * * * *

The air felt heavy, as if another rain might come at any time as the men embarked on a walk around the Mathos square. Few people were out as they passed the bell tower.

"The older I get, the more important I find it for me to get out and walk after a big meal," remarked Theophilus. "Otherwise, I don't sleep well."

"It is the same for me," spoke Rufus.

They passed the lictorum. "I used to work here," said Theophilus. "I was a vigilus before I was a pastor. I find my present job far more satisfying, but my former profession was a good background for it."

It came time to shift gears. He patted Marcus on the back and pointed to Ille Perfugium. "I am aware of your history with Publius, Amoenitas, and Eletia. How did it go with them this afternoon?"

Marcus hesitated, trying to arrange his answer properly. "All the right words were said. I asked them to forgive me. They said they did. But still, I didn't feel a whole lot of warmth."

Theophilus nodded. "That is about how I thought it would go. It will take time, my brother. Forgiveness is given, but trust is earned. It will take time to regain their trust after the experiences they have had with you. Show up on time for work every morning. Humbly learn your job. Give Eletia some of your earnings and ask her for nothing in return. Come to the church faithfully and serve. If you do those things, then over time those relationships will change for the better."

28

The Sweet and the Bitter

In the wan evening sun of the late fall, Julius breathed in the invigorating salty sea air as he walked alongside Angelina on the Portus Grande beach. It felt good to breathe deeply without pain again. A gentle breeze blew in from the sea. Small waves lapped the shore, whispering calm to his anxious spirit. The sand under his bare feet afforded him a sense of well-being. They passed a fisherman standing calf deep in the water. Few others were present.

He felt as if he drew strength from the hand he held, as if life were flowing into him from the woman he loved. He wondered if she felt the same flowing into her. All the while he trembled inwardly. *What if she rejects me? How will I walk her back to the shop if she rejects me? How will I live, if not with her?* He recalled his discussion the night before with her father Antonius.

*****

"I like you, Julius. You are a good worker. But I sense that shop work like ours will not be your life's work. What will you do? How will you support my daughter?"

"You are right about shop work, sir. It cannot be my life's work, though I will do it for a time until I find my way. It won't be the army either. I want to be with Angelina—not off in some distant land fighting barbarians. I want something stationary, challenging, and rewarding."

"What about your father? Have you been in contact with him about this? What does he say?"

Julius shook his head sadly. "I have no father or mother, sir. Both died in a plague when I was ten years old."

Antonius was visibly moved. "I see. Then their approval is not a factor. I would be proud to have you as a gener. You have my blessing to ask my daughter. I think she likes you, but she must make up her own mind."

* * * * *

He peered into the distance and selected the fateful spot, a lonely stretch of beach that included a bench. A myrtle tree leaned over the bench from behind that afforded shade for a part of the day, though none was necessary in the gathering dusk. He wondered if Angelina could hear his heart pounding in his chest. The distance continued to close. *What do I say to her?* He had rehearsed his words innumerable times. Nothing seemed to come out right. He had never been a man of words.

They arrived at the fateful place. "Let's sit for a time."

Is this the time? she wondered. *Is he about to ask me what I hope more than all the world he is about to ask me? Dear God, I have wanted Julius since the day I first saw him at the docks, not knowing if I would ever see him again. What if he doesn't ask me? Is he too afraid to ask? How can I allay his fear without being too obvious?*

She sat closer to him than ever before. Together they gazed outward to the sea. A solitary two-sailed Roman bireme was making its way into the harbor. The sun was still shining half-way up its main sail. No ships were departing. No stars or planets were yet visible in the approaching night sky.

He opened a little distance between them and turned to her. He cupped her left hand between both of his. He looked into her eyes, searching for a positive signal, but saw only mystery.

"Angelina, I cannot tell you how much it meant to me when you saw my suffering. Your first touch brought hope to me—that I would live after all. Your music from the lute fed my soul. I could give back to you nothing at the time. But now I want to spend the rest of my life giving back to you."

She began to pant audibly, unable to hold back. "Julius, are you asking me what I hope you are asking me?"

If he needed a signal, he had it. "Angelina, will you be my wife? Will you join your life to mine and journey with me—together for the rest of our lives?"

"I will, Julius! I will!"

No more words. They stood and faced each other. Simultaneously, they embraced, hearts pounding together. Slowly their faces moved until their lips found each other and joined.

*****

Tears welled in her eyes as Amoenitas struggled for control. Before her sat a packed to capacity crowd in the amphitheater, their somber mood matching the gray, overcast sky. A light mist fell from the heavens.

"She was my avia—one of the greatest human beings I have ever known. She was the wife of Porcius Caepio, whose furniture still adorns the homes of many of us. She was an artist; whose paintings demand more than a cursory look. She was the friend of many, always encouraging, always helping to draw out potential, including my own. And now she is with our Savior, whom she loved with every bone of her being."

Not since the memorial of Solon had there been such a gathering on Melitene. One by one, people like Flavia, Valentina, and Doctor Corbus spoke of the mark Gratiana Caepio had made upon their lives.

At the conclusion of the service the bell tower rang a slow, continuous gong as her body was conveyed by wagon to its final resting place in a rock-hewn tomb next to her husband's, near the summit of Scopulus Altus.

*****

The balmy winter sun shone through an assortment of barren deciduous trees, interspersed by tall Italian cypresses pointing majestically to the sky. On a grass clearing, dulled slightly in color by the winter, an assemblage of fifty-some family and church members were gathered. It was the same park Julius Galerius Hirpinius and Angelina had visited some months before on his first outside foray while healing from his battle wound. Now it was the sight of their wedding. Twin Italian cypresses book-ended the setting for the ceremony. Behind the chairs stood a bright red, ten by ten-foot tent that had been set up to accommodate the bride and her attendants.

On the left side of the book-ends as one faced the front, Liuni lit a torch, not in honor of Ceres, but of Christ to begin the ceremony. At the center stood Julius, with Antonius to his left.

"This is the proudest moment of my life," whispered Antonius to Julius.

"This is the happiest moment of mine," came the reply.

The pleasing timbre of a lute brought Caecitas from the tent. She was wearing a pink tunica, with a white garland in her hair. Down the center aisle she traipsed, tossing flower pedals to the spectators on both sides. The look on her face clearly communicated that she still marveled in her relatively new ability to see.

As soon as she sat down on an empty chair in the front row, a fanfare from three hired trumpets and a drummer sounded. From the tent Angelina emerged, wearing a grand white tunica. Her hair was shaped high in a tutulus, with a garland of marjoram, lavender, sage, and white lilies fastened at the top. Around her waist was tied the traditional gold cord, bound by a Knot of Hercules, a symbol of her virginity. The audience stood to their feet. She strode down the center aisle, regal in her steps and demeanor.

There is no beauty I can conceive of greater than the beauty of Angelina, thought Julius as she made her way to the front. *Dear God, I do not deserve her, but I will take her just the same. Oh, that I might be worthy of her.*

*****

After a sumptuous feast in the upper great room of the shop, Julius and Angelina made their way, hand in hand, to the nearby hired house where they would live for at least the first three months of their marriage. It was all the dowry Antonius and Lucia could afford, gained during their attempt to ransom Antonius from prison.

As they walked toward the house, two overwhelming thoughts dominated Julius' mind. *I was a single man, only responsible for myself until this day. Life for me now will never be the same. I am responsible for another human being. Dear God, help me to be the man I need to be.*

The other was anticipation of what was coming after they entered the house.

29

Lost and Found

Long before it was light in the morning, by the light of a single candle, Amoenitas dipped her stylus into the inkwell to continue with her writing project.

"And a woman who had a hemorrhage for twelve years, and could not be healed by anyone, came up behind Him, and touched the fringe of His cloak; and immediately her hemorrhage stopped." (Luke 8:43-44)

She shifted uncomfortably in her chair. The new baby, coming sometime within the next two months, made finding a comfortable sitting position difficult. She continued.

"And Jesus said, 'Who is the one who touched Me?' And while they were all denying it, Peter said, 'Master, the multitudes are crowding and pressing upon You.'

"But Jesus said 'Someone did touch Me, for I was aware that power had gone out of Me.'

"And when the woman saw that she had not escaped notice, she came trembling and fell down before Him, and declared in the presence of all the people the reason why she had touched Him, and how she had been immediately healed.

"And He said to her, 'Daughter, your faith has made you well; go in peace'." Luke 8:45-48)

Upon finishing the small section of her copying project, she put down her stylus and wept. For Amoenitas, the tedium of producing a personal copy of Luke's story for her husband was more than compensated by the stories about Christ she was reading for the first time.

That poor woman. She suffered non-stop bleeding for twelve years. She was probably destitute from paying many physicians who could not help her. Anemic and socially outcast. Constantly soiling her clothing. Embarrassing situations. What man would have wanted her?

A further troubling thought invaded her soul. *What if such a woman were to come to me? I wouldn't know how to help her either. I wouldn't take her money, but aside from that, how would I be any different from all those other physicians she probably saw?*

But she came to Jesus. She just touched His cloak and was made well. Jesus felt power going out of Him. How does that work? Could I ever gain such a power? Paul had it. I do not. At least I do not at this time. How does one get it?

She continued with the story of Jairus' twelve-year-old daughter, who had died. Again, she wept. *Oh Lord Jesus, there is no shortage of suffering and heartache in this world. But Jesus brought her back to life. She was lost and then was found. Oh Jesus, You have the power over death. Could you use me also to do miracles—to relieve at least a small amount of the suffering I see all around me?*

* * * * *

Cornelia examined the next addition to Eletia's mural, on the far right of the top row on the wall. This time she had painted a narrow, tall jar with rolled parchments protruding from its top. On the floor just to its right was what looked to be the cap, the object of Eletia's concentration at the moment.

"I see that you are painting again, Eletia. What does the jar mean?"

"It is not so much the jar, but the parchments that peek from the top of the jar."

"What are the parchments?"

"The word of God. They are the Scriptures brought to us from Judea and of Luke's story about the life of Christ. What few Scriptures I am able to get my hands on thrill me. They tell of the God who created us, revealing to us what He is like. They tell us the path we should travel in our lives."

* * * * *

From the arched entrance of the school the older man stood and surveyed the large square courtyard inside. The trees were neatly trimmed. The grounds were raked and the walkways swept. The stone tables were clear of debris and bird droppings. He patted Marcus on the back.

"I must admit, your reputation made me skeptical about you at first, Marcus. But now I can retire in peace, knowing that I have left the gymnasium in good hands. Your apprenticeship is over. You are both a fast learner and a good worker. The job is now yours."

"Thank you, Dominus Phlegon."

"I will inform Phoebe that as of tomorrow, you will be fully in charge. I expect that with your promotion will also come a substantial raise in your pay."

Marcus smiled. "Now I can give more to help Eletia and my child."

Phlegon nodded approvingly. "How is it going with Eletia?"

"I think she is less afraid of me than at first. She let me hold little Julia for the first time yesterday."

He patted Marcus on the back. "That is a good sign. Keep up the good work. You have convinced me. In time you will convince her."

* * * * *

The beckoning gongs had stopped. The Sunday morning overcast was lifting and the sun just beginning to peek through as Marcus scanned the audience from the center of the amphitheater. His mind was filled with joy. It had taken three months since he had landed on the island. Now, for the first time, he found himself seated next to Eletia, having been invited to do so the evening before. On Eletia's other side sat her sister Amoenitas. He wanted to move closer and to put his arm around her, but good sense held him back.

The audience hushed as Publius took the stage. "Good morning, dear brethren in Christ. Before saying anything else, I want to acknowledge my wife Amoenitas, who just finished making my copy of Luke's story about Christ last night. I now have a copy for myself. It was for her a long, tedious process, mitigated by her learning much more about Christ than she knew before. I am the most blessed of men to have her as my wife. Well done, Amoenitas. Please stand and be recognized."

Feeling somewhat embarrassed, she stood. Resounding applause erupted from the audience, with many shouting words of praise and appreciation her way. She remained standing for what she felt was the minimal time required and sat down again. Publius waited for the applause to die down before beginning his message.

"This morning I wish to begin our time together with a simple question. When do we most treasure a possession?"

He gestured to the audience, inviting answers. A young man near the front to Publius' left timidly raised his hand and was recognized.

"When it is new."

Publius nodded thoughtfully. "Yes, we all love new things, new clothing, a new wagon, a new home. But what is the problem with newness alone?" He recognized another hand, this time from a middle-aged woman.

"Newness wears off. What is new eventually becomes old."

"That is true. Newness is fleeting. Any other ideas? When do we most treasure a possession?"

"When it is obtained by great effort," spoke an older man from the audience.

Publius made like he was going to clap his hands together, but stopped just short. "That is a good answer, Phlegon. We are getting closer. What is gained by great effort, is commonly treasured more than what took little effort. That truth is at the root of what I am looking for. But I want something more."

He moved his right hand back and forth across the assembly, seeking another volunteer. No further hands were raised. From the stage Publius observed the people looking at one another in bewilderment. After a time, they turned their eyes back to him as if to say *"give us the answer."*

"Well then, I am glad you asked. The answer comes from a story in Luke's book about the life of Christ. It is a story that I have been pondering all week. It is a story that leaves me in tears every time I read through it. It is a story that speaks to our human experience. Everyone here who has lived any length of days knows its truth. What I am going to read to you this morning and then speak about is actually a collection of three stories, all with the same point, but with an added truth in the final story. It is the story of a lost sheep, a lost coin, and a lost son. It begins with our Savior sharing a meal with people whose lives were not so virtuous, and being criticized by the religious leaders of Judea for doing so." His eyes lowered to the scroll upon the lectern before him, lovingly copied in his wife's picturesque handwriting.

"Now all the tax-gatherers and the sinners were coming near Him to listen to Him. And both the Pharisees and the scribes began to grumble, saying 'This man receives sinners and eats with them.' And He told them this parable, saying, 'What man among you, if he has a hundred sheep and has lost one of them, does not leave the ninety-nine in the open pasture, and go after the one which is lost, until he finds it?" (Luke 15:1-4)

As he continued through the three stories, his eyes began to well up, clouding his vision. Overcome by emotion, he found it difficult to maintain his composure. From the audience the same feeling began to overcome the people, most of whom could identify with the experience of loss—a lost pet, a lost coin, a lost marriage, a lost loved one.

When he came to the story of the lost son, he broke down and had to ask Theophilus to finish reading through the story. With some difficulty his friend managed to accomplish the task before allowing Publius to continue his message.

"I am sorry, dear people. As a shepherd, I know first-hand what it is to lose a sheep. I know all of my sheep by name. I also once lost Amoenitas, I feared forever, until I found her in a prison cell, unjustly placed therein by a cruel man. But she was set free. I know the joy of getting back what once was lost.

"Some of you parents here can identify with the story of the lost son. The thing to understand is that the father in the story would never have known the joy of getting back his son, had he not first known the sorrow of losing him.

"So it is with our heavenly Father. With Adam's fall He lost us all. With Christ's sacrifice He lost His Son. But through the losing of His Son He regained Adam's helpless race, which includes you and me. And then He regained His Son.

"From the standpoint of the son in the story, he was restored to full sonship, though he knew that he did not deserve it. Such is the heart of our God. This is why we love Him—because he loved us first, and forgave us for our many sins. He restored us to full sonship.

"There is a final point to the last story. The son had an older brother who was angry. He fancied himself as better than his younger brother because he had never gone off to squander his estate with loose living. To whom was Jesus referring?"

From the center of the amphitheater came an upraised hand. "The Pharisees and scribes at the beginning of the story?"

"Yes, Marcus. Those men and all who consider themselves morally superior to the rest of us—who see no need of forgiveness. How their attitude breaks the heart of God! But how heaven rejoices when one sinner repents and turns to Christ! What was lost has been found! Such is the heart of God, reflected in our hearts. To know full joy, one must first know great sorrow."

From his place in the amphitheater Marcus tearfully bowed his head. *Dear God, I was that lost son. How I wasted my life! But You have restored me, though I don't deserve it. I once had Eletia. She who was so easily gained was just as easily cast aside. But now I want her more than anything in the world. Please, dear Father, let me also know the joy of receiving back what was lost.*

30

Ponderings and Stirrings

Amoenitas gazed at her sleeping niece Julia, securely nestled in her sister's arms. *Soon I will be a mother too. Oh, how blessed am I. I love my child already.*

"We are alone here this afternoon at Ille Perfugium, Eletia. How I miss these times with our avia. She had a wisdom born of experience that neither of us possess. I soon will have a child to care for. Who will take charge of this house?"

"I can think of only one person. Valentina."

Amoenitas tentatively nodded. "She is truly repentant over what she did. She is like that woman we have read about in Luke's story, the one who wet Jesus' feet with her tears. She loves like few people I have ever known. I think it is because the one who is forgiven much, the same loves much. The women here have accepted her again. She is also a born leader. But has there been enough time? Shepherding these girls and maintaining this place is a huge responsibility."

"It is not like she'll be alone. We will still be around at least some to help her."

"But our hearts will be first for our children."

"As they should be. Do you know what I miss, Amoenitas? I have been thinking about our home where we grew up."

Amoenitas chuckled. "I well remember how you used to hate the place. You couldn't wait to obtain the age to leave."

"That was then. This is now. I miss our parents. I miss the rooms.

I even miss the chickens and the coup. I miss our ox Origan. I miss the goats. Now all we have are the memories."

"We have changed much, Eletia. I miss our old house too. Publius and I stopped by there two days ago. Except for our vegetable and herb garden, the outside land is cared for. Marceles has seen to that. But our house is in ill repair. The roof leaks. It is moldy, dusty, and cobwebbed inside."

She went to another subject that she knew was prominent in her sister's heart. "How did it go with Marcus seated next to you at the amphitheater this morning?"

"He was in tears at the end of the meeting. I think he identified with the lost son. He is so changed from the man I knew before. He was selfish. Now he keeps just enough of what he earns at the school to live on, and gives the rest to me. He was arrogant. Now he is humble."

Amoenitas laughed. "You are changed. He is changed. I am changed. Life has a way of humbling us, helping us to see our need for Jesus."

Eletia fixed her eyes upon her sister. "What do you think, Amoenitas? Should I give my heart to him?"

For a moment Amoenitas did not speak. "Love is dangerous," she finally replied. "When we love, we become vulnerable to being hurt. But we cannot live without love. I think the answer regarding Marcus is the same as with Valentina. Has there been enough time for us to place our full confidence in them?"

The two sat silently—deliberating—fearing a wrong decision. At length, an answer came to Amoenitas "These decisions are too big for us alone. I will speak later with my husband about them. Right now, we will speak with our God."

Together they cried out to God for wisdom.

*****

Having left her child in the care of Herminia, Eletia went out the front door of Ille Perfugium and joined Marcus, who was waiting for her. In the evening cool, the two began a stroll side by side around the Mathos square. The torches had just been lit. Teems of couples and families were also out for a stroll along the cobblestone walkway, talking, or going in and out of the shops.

"Marcus?" asked Eletia. "How was Publius' message for you this morning?"

"More than I am able to express to you, Eletia. I was that younger son, though I never had a father like that father. But I did squander all I had with loose living. I don't deserve it, but God has welcomed me back, as have His people."

"You have shown me a lot, Marcus. You are a very different man from the man I knew a year ago. I think I am also a different woman."

They came to Vespes' pistrina. The offerings on display appeared too tempting to pass up. "We have both had a good dinner," spoke Marcus. "How about some dessert?"

"Can you afford it?"

"Yes, I can afford it." He turned to Vespes. "Sir, what do you have special for this evening?"

Vespes smiled. "I have libum." He placed a plate with a round pastry on the counter before their eyes. "It is a cheesecake made of flour, cheese, eggs, bay leaves, and honey. It is very popular. I will give you two for only three assis."

Marcus pulled three small bronze coins from his leather bag and laid them on the counter. A second pastry was added to the plate. The two sat down at a table in front of the pistrina that had just been vacated.

"I could eat ten of these," remarked Marcus after taking his first bite.

Eletia licked her lips. "Vespes has been in business for a long time. It is simply because he is honest and because he bakes good things to eat."

Is it time, Lord, to speak my heart to Eletia? Here? Now? What do I say to her?

He finished his pastry. "I said I could eat ten of these. I could too, but I cannot afford ten. I look forward to a time when money isn't so tight."

He looked into the eyes of Eletia. The girl he had known the year before was now a woman—and more beautiful than ever. *What are her eyes saying?*

He took the plunge. "Is there a future for us, Eletia? Is there any possibility for us?"

Eletia returned his gaze, doing her best to betray no emotion—giving him the respect that his question deserved, but holding back on the answer he so wanted to hear. Yet inwardly her heart was pounding. "Would you like there to be?"

"I would like that more than anything."

"Let's walk some more." They rose from the table to continue their stroll around the square. *Lord, how do I answer him?*

"It is possible," she finally spoke as they passed the amphitheater. "Do you understand that this is a lifelong commitment? No more adventures with other women—a stable job—a father little Julia can respect."

"The life I lived before has become abhorrent to me. I remember it only with great shame. I want to be a man worthy of your respect."

They walked silently past the school. *They trust him at the school*, she thought. "Marcus, I am not saying no, but I am not yet ready to say yes. Can you give me a little more time?"

Every sinew of his soul and body wanted to wrap her in his arms and make her his, but he held back. She had given him hope. Hope would have to be sufficient for the time being. She was too great a prize to lose through impatience. He would wait and continue to become more the man he knew God wanted him to be.

31

The Ultimate Question

Even at his age Rufus felt a sense of excitement tinged with apprehension as he walked into his early morning philosophy classroom, his first solo teaching experience on his first solo day. He had taught on his own in Alexandria before. It also helped that he knew most of the students by name already from other classroom situations. Still, this was a new situation. His faith in Christ had also dramatically altered and sharpened his philosophy.

He greeted each student as they filed in until all fourteen stools were filled with twelve boys and two girls, all between the ages of fifteen and eighteen. He waited for the bell tower to completely gong in the eighth hour before beginning.

"Good morning, young people. Welcome to our philosophy class. For those of you who do not know me, I am Rufus Hamadi, originally from Alexandria, Egypt."

He looked out at his students, making eye contact with them all, one by one. Some, he perceived, were more afraid than he was. Silently, he prayed for a way to ease the apprehension.

"I want to begin with the most basic of all questions. Why do we exist? Why are we here in this world?"

Immediately, he saw a sense of perplexity. Possibly none of the students had ever before considered the question. Neither were any yet brave enough to hazard a guess that might make them look foolish before the others.

"Let me help you a little bit with the question. Why do you exist? Are you simply an accident that just happened in a purposeless universe, or is there intelligence behind your creation? And if there is intelligence, is there then a reason for your existence?"

A timorous hand came up. "Yes Nicabar. Why are you here?"

"I am here because my parents made me come."

Instantly the entire class erupted in laughter. Rufus smiled broadly. "That is actually a very good first answer, Nicabar. It is honest. You are here because your parents made you come."

He held up his right hand. "The first thing we need in this classroom is for all of us to relax. I want our classroom times to have an atmosphere of mutual respect, with everyone present feeling free to express his or her opinion. No unkind taunts. You're all young, trying to figure out life and that's okay. I have asked a hard question that maybe few of you have ever considered."

He again scanned the classroom. "Someone else. Why are we here? We do we exist? Why does the sun travel across the sky each day? Why do we have seasons? Why did everything come into existence? Or is there no rhyme or reason to anything?"

Another hand came up. "I vote for your final question. There is no why. Everything is just here, including us."

Rufus gave an acknowledging nod. "That certainly is one answer to the question, Caius. Quite a few philosophers would agree with you. But if that answer is the correct answer, what does that do to our value as human beings? What is the point of living if there is no point?"

"You just eat, drink, and be merry—and then you die," he answered.

"I suppose that would be the conclusion of many who believe as you have stated. What are some other thoughts, people? Come on, don't be shy."

One of the two girls raised her hand. "Since we could not make ourselves, we had to have been made by an intelligence greater than ourselves. The stool upon which I am sitting was intelligently fashioned of wood from a tree by someone for the purpose of providing me with a place to sit. It did not fashion itself. Since I am much more complicated than my stool, someone had to fashion me."

Rufus nodded. "Thank you, Marilla. The Greek philosopher Aristotle would agree with you. Everything must have a cause, culminating in an ultimate uncaused cause. If Aristotle was right, who or what might this uncaused cause be? Anyone?"

"The uncaused cause could not be a what," answered the other girl, who was seated at the back of the classroom. "Only a who can have intelligence. I am Aeliana. I can say 'I am Aeliana' only because an 'I am' created me."

The entire classroom turned their heads back toward her in awe, perhaps mixed with some jealousy among the boys, not used to being outthought by a girl.

"But who or what made this ultimate being?" asked Nicabar.

"If Aristotle is right, this ultimate being is the uncaused cause of all things," answered Rufus. "Think about this. How could anything that potentially exists come into actual existence, unless someone who already existed could bring it into existence? If there is anything that actually exists, then there logically must be at least one entity that could not, not exist. It must have always existed. This what is called Aristotle's unmoved mover or uncaused cause."

"What about the Greek and Roman gods and goddesses?" asked a student whom Rufus did not know. "What do we do about Zeus or Jupiter? What about Neptune, the god of the sea? What about Minerva, the goddess of wisdom?"

"What is your name, young man?"

"I am Tarquin, recently come from Rome with my family, now wondering who Tarquin is."

"What about the Greek and Roman gods and goddesses?" repeated Rufus to the class. "Did they as a committee create us, or did we create them?"

Aeliana again raised her hand and was recognized. "I must say that we created them, for they are simply more powerful versions of ourselves, filled with the same foibles that plague us. Our true Creator has to be like us in terms of being able to say 'I am.' But He would have to be above us in His nature. He would have to be all-powerful, yet pure in mind, for only the most powerful and purest of mind could conceive of and create so complex and beautiful a world, that yet fits together so perfectly."

"If Aristotle were here, I think he would clap his hands at what you say, Aeliana," spoke Rufus.

He again scanned the class. "The answer each of you comes up with regarding the why of your existence will profoundly affect your philosophy and how you choose to live your life. If we are biological accidents in a universe that somehow sprang into existence out of nothing for no reason, then I suppose one philosophy is as good as another. But if there is a Creator behind all that is, then we are beholden to Him—or Her. We will speak more on this subject tomorrow."

* * * * *

"How did your first day of solo teaching go?" asked Marcus as Rufus entered their rented house on Via Domicilium.

Rufus fell into the couch in the great room. "I thought pretty well. I have two interesting philosophy classes, two history classes, and a class in rhetoric. I think I was able to establish a good learning atmosphere in each. The students need to know that they are important to me and that they should treat one another with respect. I have always thought that was the best atmosphere for learning."

"Did you speak to them about Christ?"

Rufus laughed softly. "It was hard for me to hold back. But the kids must learn to think for themselves. It is not my job to do their thinking for them. I try to treat them the way God would have me treat them. Without actually saying it, that by itself conveys to them my belief that they are more than mere accidents."

Marcus pointed to the kitchen. "There is some leftover dinner for you on the stove—some bread and soup. I hope that it will at least keep you alive. I am not exactly the world's greatest cook."

"Thank you, Marcus. I know you would prefer to eat something from Eletia's hand. It will happen, my friend. Just be patient."

He rose to retrieve his dinner.

"So when are you going to get married, Rufus?"

He placed his dinner on the dining room table. "Probably never. What woman would want an old philosophy professor anyway?"

* * * * *

Together in the great room at Ille Perfugium, the two women watched little Julia struggle to her feet, using the low wooden table to support herself. "She is almost walking now," beamed Eletia.

"I have a question," spoke Cornelia. She led Eletia to her mural painting on the wall. "I see that just this morning you have sketched in the faint image of a man holding little Julia's left hand with his right. Is that why some months back you painted Julia's hand upraised to the left?"

"I guess so. I wasn't really thinking anything at the time. It just happened that way."

"I know something else that is about to happen, just as you showed in your painting. Little Julia is about to walk."

32

Devious Plans

"You're doing fine, Amoenitas. Just a couple more contractions and we'll have the baby. What do you want, a boy or a girl?"

"Whatever God gives us," she sputtered through gritted teeth.

Eletia wiped her sister's forehead with another dry cloth and massaged the outer part of the birth canal with warm olive oil.

"I've done enough of these myself," gasped Amoenitas. "Now I know how it feels to be on the other side." She clutched the two pegs on either side of the birth chair as another contraction set in.

"Go ahead and scream, sister. I know how bad it hurts."

Amoenitas obliged.

Outside the cubiculum Publius paced back and forth, unnerved by the screams—on the verge of panic. "Dear God! Is this bad? Spare my wife! Spare my child!"

For two seemingly unending minutes the unsettling screams continued until they abruptly stopped, replaced by the lusty wails of a newborn child. He tried to no avail to discern the gender from the sound of the cries.

"You have a boy, Publius!" Eletia called through the curtain. "He is beautiful! Everything is all right."

Eletia cut the umbilical cord and went to work cleaning the baby with warm moist clothes, while Valentina tended to Amoenitas. Upon completing her task, Eletia held the child before her mother, cementing an instant bond. "We need to quiet this little guy down."

She placed the child just where Amoenitas had placed Julia some months before, with the same result. All was suddenly quiet.

"What is his name?

"Trebonius. His name is Trebonius, in honor of his avus."

Outside the bedroom Publius found a chair and sat before he knew he would faint. For several minutes he held his head down with his eyes closed, knowing that both he and his wife needed some time. As soon as he felt he was ready, he spoke.

"Are you ready, Amoenitas? May I enter now and see my son?"

*****

Publius looked up from his desk in the small room that had been allotted to him at the gymnasium for his office. Upon seeing his visitor, he stood to his feet.

"I am glad to see you, Marcus. The people at the school here speak highly of you. I myself have noticed the orderliness of the grounds. I also see that you have begun construction of a new stone classroom." The two sat down, the desk between them.

"We have had a recent influx of new students, hence the need for an extra classroom. I hope to have it ready for occupancy within two weeks."

"Well done, Marcus." He tilted his chair back to help relax his visitor, who appeared somewhat nervous. "Now, what is on your mind?"

"I want to marry Eletia, your wife's sister. I asked Amoenitas about it, and she told me to ask you."

Publius nodded thoughtfully. "Well, I think she would do well to have you, but I don't decide for Eletia. Are you asking me what I would suggest you do to win her heart?"

Marcus nodded. "That is exactly what I am looking for."

He tapped his right finger on his desk. "Do you know the Aequitas property, the place where my wife and her sister used to live?"

"Oh yes," he chuckled. "You and I had an unpleasant encounter there. How could I forget?"

Publius laughed. "Well, that is in the past. The point is, no one lives there now, though the property still belongs to my wife and to her sister. Do you know what completely won the heart of their mother Julia to their father Andronicus? He built that home. It is the only home Amoenitas and Eletia knew during their growing up years. Both of their parents are now gone from this world, but their childhood memories linger. Their parents were there. That home and the surrounding property has a deep connection to them."

"What do you suggest?"

"The home has now been unoccupied for nearly a year and has fallen into disrepair. The roof leaks. There is water on the floor and mildew inside. If you were to go down there on your days off without telling Eletia, and to put that home back into first class shape, how do you think she would respond?"

Marcus joined his hands behind his head in thought. "I think she would respond positively. That is a terrific idea. There is just one problem."

"What is that?"

"I am sure the school here would allow me to borrow the tools I need to do the job, but I have no money to purchase any needed materials. I already give most of my income to Eletia."

"As well you should." Publius contemplated for a moment. "I have quite a few materials left over from building projects I have done on my property. You may sort through them and take what you need free of charge. Look over the house first to ascertain what you need. Then come get at least some of the materials from me. I even have a horse and a wagon you can use to transport them. Then you just go to work."

Another idea sprang into Publius' head. "Their matertera Arianna and her husband Marceles live just up the hill from that house. He is also an expert builder. He might have some materials I lack." He considered further for a moment. "If you're real nice to him, he might even help you with the labor."

Marcus' mind began to race. "That sounds like the plan. I will begin this Saturday. Thank you for your wisdom and for your generosity."

* * * * *

Alacerius coughed violently and cursed. "It never seems to go away!" He surveyed the gathering around the table in his home. Present was Alexandra, the soldier Otho, another soldier he had recruited named Sergius, and Livius, a Roman official new to the island.

"It appears that despite our efforts at destroying Publius and the church, they have come back stronger than ever because of that traitor Valentina. Maybe she needs to have an accident, like Octavia's unfortunate fall. But regarding the Christians in general, we must try something else. What? Anybody?"

"What if somehow Ille Perfugium were to burn down in the middle of the night?" suggested Otho. "Valentina might unfortunately burn to death. Some of the others there might sadly suffer the same fate too."

Alacerius considered the idea thoughtfully before shaking his head. "We'll find another way to deal with Valentina. As for Ille Perfugium, I have always treasured the idea of returning the brothel to its former glory, albeit with a classier facade. That wouldn't work well if the place were ashes. Come on people, think."

"Our emperor Nero hates Christians," remarked Alexandra. "If he truly knew what was going on here, I think he would take immediate remedial action."

Alacerius' face suddenly lit up. "Now we are getting somewhere. Do you happen to know Nero personally?"

"I met him a couple of times early in his reign. We even had ourselves a brief dalliance. He is quite the lover."

"Are you on good terms with him?"

"Umm, pretty good. I try never to get personal about those sorts of things. We just had a good time and that was it."

Alacerius' mind began to whir. "What if you were to write a letter to him about the terrible state of affairs on our island. Would he listen to you?"

"I am sure he would. As I said, he hates Christians."

"Then write the letter."

Alexandra smiled. "I will. I will tell him about my traitorous former husband, who has removed all the statues of our gods and goddesses from the propraetor's villa. I will tell him how the temple grounds of the goddess Juno have been desecrated. It is now being used as a picnic area for the church. Her statue is also gone, with a cross replacing it on the same platform. I will tell him that the church is using the amphitheater for their anti-Roman meetings. I will tell him that the church has taken over the school, which is right beside the amphitheater."

"My son Tarquin attends that school," interjected Livius. "He told me that his philosophy teacher, a man named Rufus, rejects our Roman gods in favor of the Christian God."

"Rufus? Who is he?"

"Tarquin tells me that he hears other teachers there comparing Rufus to another teacher they had a while back named Solon."

Alacerius scowled. "That's all we need at the school—another Solon." He turned to Alexandra. "Put something about Rufus in your letter too. He needs to be dead."

"I can deliver the letter," spoke Otho. "I have been ordered back to Rome anyway, to be assigned to a new cohort. I leave in three days."

"Very well. Alexandra, can you have the letter written within three days?"

She laughed her cackling laugh. "I can. It will be delicious."

33

The Letter

Thick slices of fresh crusted bread were already on the table. Angelina ladled a hefty portion of mutton stew into her husband's bowl and a lesser portion for herself. The two sat down before Julius prayed a blessing over their meal. Upon finishing the blessing, he spooned the first bite into his mouth.

"Oh Angelina, this is heavenly after a hard day of work. Thank you."

She smiled. "How was your day today?"

"It was busy. Many customers. I am much happier working than I was languishing in that bed. How was your day?"

"I delivered a baby for a woman named Tanaquil. It went fine for both. Another woman named Decima will have her child in a week or so."

While Julius ate, Angelina sensed an agitation in her husband's spirit, as if he were holding back on saying something he wanted to say, fearing her response. For several minutes they ate in silence before she could bear the tension no longer.

"Is something on your mind, Julius? Please say it."

He swallowed the last of the stew and sat back in his chair. "You can always tell when I need to say something." He gathered his thoughts. "How would you feel about us moving to Melitene?"

Even though she knew there was something big on his mind, the question still jolted her. *How do I respond?* "Why Melitene?"

"I spoke with your father before we were married. He knows that I can never be happy working in a tent shop all my life."

"What would you like to do, Julius?"

"I don't want to denigrate tentmaking. It is an honest, useful profession. But I want something more for my life. I want something challenging and rewarding. I also dislike big cities. The more I know Christ, the less I like Rome and Roman rule. There is more freedom on Melitene. I also have a lot of friends there."

"What kind of challenging, rewarding thing would you want to do on Melitene?"

"I would like to become a vigilus, with the goal of eventually becoming a praefectus. From my experience in the army, I think I know how to handle men. I would love the challenge of keeping law and order, and peace in a community."

A sudden spirit of apprehension descended upon her. She had never before ventured off the island of Magna Graecia. "I would miss my family."

"I would miss your family too—and all the other friends we have made here. They are all dear people. But we could still visit. The voyage between here and Melitene usually takes only one full day and night."

Angelina was quiet for a moment, searching for the right response. "Well Julius, if you feel led of God to move to Melitene, then I will go with you. I am sure they need midwives and healers there too."

"You would love Amoenitas. She does those things."

"Who is Amoenitas?"

"A fellow believer in Christ. A healer and a midwife. The wife of my good friend Publius, who leads the church there. She is a dear woman."

"When would we go?"

"Not right away. Right now, your father still needs me. The rent for our home is paid for a time. We will know when the time is right."

As she thought on the subject, her initial fear began to give way to a sense of anticipation. As long as she had known Julius, he had always shown good judgment. *Maybe we need something like this to take our lives to a higher level.*

*****

Sextus Afranius Burrus, former commander of the praetorians, surveyed the conference room in Domus Transitoria, Emperor Nero's underground palace on Palatine Hill in Rome. The walls and ceiling were trimmed at the edges with gold and precious stones. Inside the trim were frescos of Roman gods and goddesses in various levels of undress. He tapped the marble table with one of its golden candlestands. Even the echo bounding off the marble walls sounded lavish.

He wondered why he had been summoned to the palace so abruptly from his necessary afternoon nap. He wanted to sit and rest his old, weary body, but dared not be found sitting when Nero entered. He placed his hands on the table, using his arms to help support him in a standing position.

The sound of rapid footsteps, resonating off the marble floor, told him that an angry Nero was approaching. He removed his hands from the table and stood upright as the emperor stormed into the conference room. Immediately he handed a parchment scroll to Burrus.

"Burrus, you are my most trusted advisor. Read this letter. Tell me that my eyes have lied to me!"

He calmly took the scroll from his emperor's hand. Twenty-five-year old Nero Claudius Caesar Augustus Germanicus was of average height, with wavy reddish blond hair, blue eyes, and a short neck. *He might be handsome if he weren't so angry all the time*, thought the older man. He laid the scroll on a table and weighted each corner with candlestands.

"Of course, Your Divinity. May I please sit while I read?"

Nero gestured for Burrus to seat himself. He carefully lowered himself into a chair by the table and began to read aloud the letter.

> *Greetings most Divine Emperor Nero,*
>
> *I am sure you remember me as both wife of Trebonius and as your loyal friend. I remain on the island of Melitene, to which we were sent to govern two years ago. I am now alone, having been abandoned by my treacherous former husband. He has embraced the way of the Christians and removed all the statues of our revered gods and goddesses from the propraetor's villa. In truth, no such statues can now be found anywhere on the island, including the temple grounds of our beloved goddess Juno, which has been desecrated by the Christians. Her statue has been replaced by their despised*

cross. They have taken over the Mathos Amphitheater, formerly a public gathering place, for their sinister meetings. They control the local gymnasium, which now disparages Roman laws and customs. Most egregious of all, they malign your most excellent name. A philosophy professor there named Rufus is the worst offender.

With a few brave, like-minded souls, I have done my best to thwart their sedition. They are led by my equally traitorous former son, a charismatic and authoritarian despot named Publius, who wants to turn Melitene into an autonomous island, free from the empire of Rome.

Please, Your Excellency, help us. Help us before it is too late.

I am as always, your loyal servant, Alexandra.

Burrus looked up from the scroll and braced himself for the inevitable tirade.

"And now my ears have confirmed what my eyes have seen. This is treason, Burrus! I will at once send an entire legion to Melitene and crush this rebellion! Those who have fomented this treason must die. It is only a question of the slowest, most humiliating, painful way for them to die."

Burrus remained calm. He had learned that calmness was the best way to help his young emperor see reason, to stay on his good side, and to remain alive. He knew that Nero's mother Agrippina, his step brother Britannicus, and his wife Octavia had failed to follow that policy and had forfeited their lives. He replied in even, measured tones.

"If you value my opinion, most Divine Majesty, I must point out that with all the trouble we at present are having in Judea, in Parthia, and in Britain, we can ill afford to dispatch an entire legion to Melitene. I must also point out that we are getting only one side of what appears to be a great controversy on that island. First of all, I know Trebonius. He is a loyal Roman, if somewhat lacking in leadership skills. I also know Christians here in Rome. For the most part they behave well and are honest in their business dealings. None that I know of speak and act as Alexandra has characterized them."

Nero's initial rage began to dissipate. "What so you suggest I do instead?"

"It might be prudent to send a more forceful propraetor to Melitene, along with a new cohort to replace the present garrison there. Recall Trebonius to Rome, where he can speak to you for himself. It is, after all, the Roman way for an accused to have a chance to answer his accuser before we come to a conclusion."

Nero seated himself opposite Burrus and nodded. "Your counsel is good, Burrus. Perhaps I have spoken too hastily."

*****

The winter chill caused Paul to bundle up with an extra blanket as he sat on the veranda overlooking Via Flaminia. The street and the rooftops before him were coated in newly fallen snow. It was quiet outside, with barely a soul on the streets. Flakes of snow continued to drift silently down from the heavens above. He knew that the snow would likely be gone by the tenth hour the next morning, but for now its pristine purity was something to be enjoyed. He took another sip of his warm kykeon.

A solitary, cloaked figure approached from the south, walking rapidly. From the gait it appeared to be the walk of a man. The closer he came, the more Paul perceived that he was coming to his house, number seventeen. A knock on his door confirmed his observation.

"Who comes?" called Paul from above.

The figure below backed away from the door and answered just loud enough for Paul to hear. "It is Rabbi Isaac Shelemiah. I would like to speak with you."

From the top of the stairway Paul called downstairs. "Petronius. Would you please open the door and allow Rabbi Shelemiah to enter?"

The two met at the top of the stairway and clasped hands. "I am glad to see you, Rabbi Shelemiah. What can I do for you?" He gestured to the veranda, but the rabbi stayed in place.

"Perhaps we could speak alone and indoors?"

"Of course. It is cold outside. Would you like a cup of kykeon?"

"Please."

He removed his outer cloak while Paul poured him a cup from the pitcher over his candle warmer. The two were seated. "Now again, what can I do for you?"

The rabbi took a sip of the drink. "This is very good."

"I have had the involuntary chance this past year and a half to perfect the temperature and the mixture. I find that it does wonders for my digestion. How has it been at the synagogue since last we met?"

Rabbi Shelemiah chuckled. "As you can imagine, our meeting here at your house caused quite a stir. A couple of our people embraced your Christian faith, much to the chagrin of others in our fellowship. Some expressed vehement opposition after we left, Alexander the coppersmith especially."

"He was pretty vociferous when you were all here. I have dealt with him before in Ephesus."

"He was new to us here, a gentile proselyte. But then I discovered after our meeting that he was also an idol maker."

"The Christian faith is also bad for the idol business," added Paul.

"I would think that to be true. When I pointed out to him the incompatibility of God's law with idol making, he left our synagogue."

"What fellowship has God with idols?" answered Paul. He fixed his eyes on the rabbi. "What specifically brings you to me this evening, my friend?"

The rabbi took a deep breath. "I just finished reading your letter to the church in Rome. Dominic gave me a copy of it."

"I see. How did you find it?"

"I found it inspiring, refreshing, joyful, triumphant, confusing, and in many places incomprehensible."

Paul nodded. "I wrote it under the inspiration of the Holy Spirit of God. His ways and thoughts are higher than ours. One must be born again to even begin to understand His mind."

A look of puzzlement came to the rabbi's face. "Born again? What is that? We can only be born once."

"That is true in the physical realm, but I speak of a rebirth in the spirit."

"How can that be?"

Silently, Paul prayed for wisdom before answering. "I have an old friend who lives in Jerusalem named John. I often saw him when I went there. He is one of Jesus' original followers. We still keep in touch by letter. He once told me the story of a rabbi very much like you named Nicodemus. Nicodemus also visited Jesus alone and by night, just as you have done. Jesus spoke to him about his need to be born again."

"I still do not understand," spoke the rabbi. "What is this born again?"

"Nicodemus did not understand either. To be born again is not something that comes through scholarly pursuit. It spawns from a deep consciousness of personal sin and a deep sense of need for God."

"I pursue God every day. I keep His commandments."

"And yet you have come to me because in your heart, you know that something is missing."

Rabbi Shelemiah's face fell. "Yes, something is missing. I pursue God, but I do not find Him."

At that moment a great spirit of compassion for the rabbi fell upon Paul. "Now we are getting somewhere, Isaac. Isaiah the prophet spoke of our human predicament—the why of why we cannot find Him."

"Behold, the Lord's hand is not so short that it cannot save; neither is His ear so dull that it cannot hear. But your iniquities have made a separation between you and your God, and your sins have hidden His face from you, so that He does not hear." (Isaiah 59:1-2)

"What can I do about that?" asked the rabbi pleadingly.

"We cannot find Him on our own, but He has made a way to find us. Listen again to the prophet Isaiah, for he prophesied of the Messiah who was to come, who was to be crucified upon a Roman cross. 'But He was pierced through for our transgressions, He was crushed for our iniquities; the chastening for our well-being fell upon Him, and by His scourging we are healed. All of us like sheep have gone astray, each of us has turned to his own way; but the Lord has caused the iniquity of us all to fall on Him'." (Isaiah 53:5-6)

"He spoke of Jesus," observed the rabbi. "I know the passage of which you speak, but I never saw that before."

"You have now correctly ascertained. The iniquities of us all fell upon our Messiah. Jesus is the Lamb of God, who takes away the sin of the world, including my sins and yours. It is He who has opened the way to God for us and given us life."

Tears came to the rabbi's eyes. "But He died. How can life come from death?"

"Because Christ rose again from the dead on the third day, as was prophesied by King David. 'Therefore my heart is glad, and my glory rejoices; my flesh also will dwell securely. For Thou wilt not abandon my soul to Sheol; neither wilt Thou allow Thy Holy One to undergo decay.' (Psalm 16:9-10)

"Our earthly bodies will one day perish, but He will not abandon us to the grave, just as He did not allow His Holy One to undergo decay."

"I want God!" cried the rabbi. "I want to know this Jesus who died for me and rose again from the dead!"

The two men prayed together. As they prayed, another soul saw the kingdom of God.

34

The Greatest of all Prizes

After a Sunday afternoon meal of chicken, with bread and fruit, Publius saddled up the Fabianus horses, Bellator and Castanea, for Marcus and Eletia. With baby Julia left in the care of Amoenitas, the two rode down to the beach by the Litus Baths. Along the eastern prong of the V-shaped bay area they went at an easy lope in deference to Eletia's limited riding ability.

Once at the beach, the first thing Eletia noticed was the contrast between the summer heat at the home of her sister and the milder temperature near the water. A cool breeze blew in, bringing with it the refreshing smell of the salty sea air. The two rode silently, side by side, though the thoughts of both were a hum of activity.

For Eletia, her resistance to Marcus' overtures was rapidly crumbling. It wasn't based only upon her opinion. Others were now encouraging her to give her heart to a man who was rising in stature before their eyes. He did steady, excellent work at the school. He gave most of his pay to Eletia. He was kind and considerate of others, a huge departure from what those same others had known before. Still, in her heart she needed something more to become fully convinced. For Marcus it was different.

"This is fun, Marcus. I have walked this beach a number of times, but I have never ridden a horse along it."

Half a mile down the beach they came to a mound that served as a natural back rest for those who wanted to sit facing the water. They stopped, still on their horses, as she pointed to the backrest. "The spring before last, I had a long conversation there with my sister Amoenitas. We tossed rocks into the water as we talked. We had become almost enemies, but we made up with each other and became sisters again that very day. That is also where I told my sister that I was pregnant with your child."

At her words a sense of satisfaction flowed into Marcus. It was the first time Eletia had referred to Julia as his child. "I suppose you both talked about me too?"

"We talked about my sister maybe marrying Publius. He proposed to her that very night and she accepted. We talked about my desire to become an artist. I did some of the art work you have seen on the walls at Ille Perfugium. And yes Marcus, we talked about you. I was afraid of you then. I was afraid you might want to kill our child. I couldn't imagine then that I would ever be with you again, talking in this same place. Quite honestly, at the time I hoped to never see you again."

"Did you think of me often after that?"

"I did, Marcus. Over time I began to pray for you. As I prayed for you, my heart changed. I didn't know what might happen later between us, but the Lord impressed upon me the need to keep my heart open to the possibility, just in case. I also wondered how I would be able to raise little Julia on my own."

It is time, thought Marcus. He turned Bellator back to the way they had come. "Ride with me this way, Eletia. I have something I want to show you."

Eletia followed, wondering about the sudden change of direction, but more wondering what he wanted to show her. From the beach they rode back into the summer heat. *This had better be good*, she thought. He spoke not another word, heightening her curiosity. Fifteen minutes later they rode by the house of her sister and Publius.

"We are not stopping here?"

"No," was Marcus' single word response.

Ten minutes later they rode into the clearing between the house and the barn of her old home, the home that her father Andronicus had built for her mother Julia. A flood of memories swept into Eletia. She felt as if she could sense the presence of both her parents on the property. Marcus dismounted at the very place he had experienced his unpleasant confrontation with Publius. He then helped Eletia from her horse.

Only then did she begin to notice significant differences to the property. A new gabled roof lay above her former home, this time with timbers spanning the roof. Clay had been inserted in the gaps to help seal out rain. A thick coat of red tinged varnish gave further protection from leaks and waterproofed the wood.

The garden off to the side, where they had grown food and medicinal herbs was cleared of weeds and newly planted. Rotting timbers on the barn had been replaced. The entire structure sported a new coat of barn red paint.

Marcus opened the door to the house. "Enter," he simply said.

Once inside her heart began to race. The home was swept and put in order. The bathtub had been refinished. The stove was clean. The pantry off to the side was filled with necessary pots, pans, and dishes. She looked at Marcus in wonder.

"How did this happen?"

He smiled. "I did much of it. But I got a lot of help also from Marceles and their son Trophimus. Marceles and Publius gave me the needed materials. Arianna supplied the kitchen necessities."

She inspected the brand-new bed, big enough for two, which was covered with a brand-new muslin blanket. "The work of the ladies at Ille Perfugium," he declared.

At that very moment all reserve vanished. She flung her arms around Marcus and planted a passionate kiss upon his lips.

"Oh, Marcus! Yes! Yes! I want more than all the world for you to be my husband and the father of our child!"

As he held Eletia in his arms, Marcus remembered the words Publius had spoken about prized possessions. *We prize what is new, but newness quickly wears off. We prize more what is obtained by great effort. We prize most what was lost and then is found.*

*****

Except for Cornelia, Ille Perfugium was deserted during the afternoon lull. She preferred the solitary joy of working the loom, making clothing for herself and others, to the innocuous chit-chat of the other women who lived at the home, as they went in and out of shops around the Mathos square. At present she was working on a small outdoor garment for little Julia, who was now walking very well.

After a long period of sitting she got up to walk herself, to work out the kinks in her back. She found herself again gravitating to Eletia's mural painting, which always fascinated her. Immediately, she noticed another change.

Walking opposite of Eletia, with little Julia between them, the faint image of a man holding little Julia's left hand was his right had been painted in.

*****

Because of the circumstances regarding their past and the fact that they already had a child, neither Eletia nor Marcus desired a large-scale wedding. Instead they opted for a simple ceremony in the home of Publius and Amoenitas, with only family, Marceles and Arianna, and their close friends Rufus, Linus and Beatrice, Doctor Corbus and Domina Macatus, Demetrius and Phoebe, and Theophilus and Flavia present.

Upon completion of the ceremony, they sat down to a meal of rabbit stew and biscuits prepared by Amoenitas, with a domed sponge cake called prinjolata for dessert. Afterwards, the twin toddlers Paul and Luke, along with Laelia, and the babies Julia and Trebonius all went down for naps. Only seven-year-old Trophimus among the children remained awake. But Arianna thoughtfully provided a book of simple words and pictures to entertain him while the adults spoke.

If the ceremony and dinner had been low-key, the aftermath more than made up for it. It was time for the bestowment of wedding gifts. From Doctor Corbus and Domina Macatus, newly married themselves, had come the new bed, large enough for two people.

"It is already in your new home," spoke Doctor Corbus.

From Rufus came a wooden placard to put over the doorpost of their home that he had carved and stained himself: "As for me and my house, we will serve the Lord." (Joshua 24:15b)

From Theophilus and Flavia came three goats, a buck and two does. "The buck will see to it that you get more goats from there," noted Theophilus.

From Demetrius and Phoebe came new pairs of leather shoes for each of them, both for more formal occasions. From Linus and Beatrice came matching tunics to keep them warm upon the onset of colder weather.

After the bestowment of those gifts, Amoenitas reached into her purse and pulled out a short scroll, held in its rolled position by two ties of twine. She handed it to Eletia.

"What is this?" her sister asked.

"It is our wedding gift to you and to Marcus. It is a deed transferring the full ownership of our childhood home to the two of you. I already have another home. Now you and Marcus fully own yours."

Eletia handed the deed to her newly minted husband and rose up to hug her sister. "Oh, thank you, Amoenitas. I love the place. All of my memories are there. It will remain in our family for many generations."

Finally came Marceles' turn. He stood to his feet and beckoned for Marcus to follow him out the back door. The early fall day was mostly spent, but still warm as the two men made their way along a newly laid stone pathway to the barn. Once inside the barn, Marceles led Marcus to a magnificent, ink-black stallion not quite full grown.

"That is quite a horse," remarked Marcus.

Marceles pointed, first to Marcus and then to the horse. "This is your wedding gift from Arianna and me."

Marcus gasped. "This horse? For me?"

"You'll have to give him a name."

In awe Marcus placed his right hand on the mane and felt his way across the back of the young stallion. "He is strong and probably very spirited. It will take some time to break him. Thank you, Marceles. I do not know what to say except that I do not deserve such a gift."

"But you need such a gift. We figured that you would need transportation from your new home to the school and back every day."

He then pointed to a finely polished leather saddle, draped over a stall fence, along with reins and a bit. "You'll need something to help you ride your new horse," he declared.

Marcus ran his hand over the saddle, which had two large horns in the front and two smaller horns in back to help hold him in position while on the horse. Beneath the fine leather was a frame of wood to help the saddle hold its shape.

"Then Fulgur will be his name," declared Marcus. "For he looks to be as fast as lightning." He grabbed a handful of oats from the nearby barrel and flattened his hand to feed Fulgur in a beginning attempt to befriend the stallion.

"You will indeed need to break him. He is young and very spirited as you say. But you have a week off from your job at the school, both to know Eletia better and to train your horse."

Marcus clasped hands with Marceles. "You probably saved my life, not that I deserved it, on that day when Publius pounded on me. You helped me with materials and labor on the Aequitas house. Now you give me this horse. How can I ever repay you?"

Marceles answered short and to the point. "Be to Eletia a husband worthy of her. That will be payment enough."

35

Gaius Ovidius Bellirus

With neither forewarning nor fanfare a huge quinquiremus emerged through the thick early morning fog, sailing past the fortress of Aemilianus and into the harbor of Portus Amplus. As it neared the docks, another identical ship materialized from the fog, followed by another, and then another, and then another. Upon docking, soldiers poured from each ship to form ranks from shouted commands. With duteous efficiency five centuries organized, a total contingent of over four-hundred men. To the throbbing cadence of drums, they began to march with military precision up the cobblestone street into the center of the town. All traffic on the street scrambled to clear a path. From the sides, townsfolk watched in awe mixed with fear. It appeared that these soldiers meant business. No interaction between them and the islanders was forthcoming—at least for the time.

At the Roman barracks at the edge of Portus Amplus, the rear century halted and disappeared into the grounds. Just beyond, at a fork in the road, the first three centuries marched west. The last continued uphill and south, in the direction of the propraetor's villa.

Hearing the familiar cadence from a distance, Trebonius peered from the window of the upstairs cubiculum that had once been his son's. He swallowed hard and hastily donned his best tunic. That something big was up, there could be no doubt. In his heart he knew that his days as governor of Melitene were finished. He wondered if more than that would be finished.

* * * * *

From the nearby barracks emerged a tall, authoritatively attired man. He approached the villa, accompanied by another who appeared to be the Pilus Prior, the overall commander of the cohort, along with several other soldiers. From the dress of the tall man Trebonius knew that what he had feared was realized. He again swallowed hard. *I have been replaced. I will have to appear before Nero. He will not be pleased with me.*

He descended the stairs and entered the peristylium. Upon the proconsul's seat he stationed himself, knowing that it would be his last time. He did his best to summon a professional demeanor. Any hint of fear would not become him.

Without awaiting an invitation, the contingent entered the villa through the atrium and proceeded straight for the peristylium. Their marched cadence echoed off the walls. Upon entering, the tall man stood before Trebonius, gave a cursory bow, and stood rigidly erect. He appeared to be in his middle thirties. Clean shaven, with immaculately groomed tawny hair, he appeared every inch the ideal propraetor. His eyes quickly scanned the room before he handed a scroll to Trebonius.

"Greetings, Trebonius Minicius Fabianus. I am Gaius Ovidius Bellirus. Effective tomorrow, at first light, I will be the new propraetor of Melitene. You have until that time to vacate the villa. You are directed by our Most Divine Emperor Nero Claudius Caesar Augustus Germanicus to depart this-island with your entire garrison within three days. You and your entire contingent are to sail directly to Puteoli via the five quinquiremae at the port, and then to march to Rome, where your soldiers will await further assignment. You are to personally appear before his Divine Excellency at the earliest possible date. It is all written on the scroll and sealed by the emperor's signet ring."

The new propraetor again surveyed the peristylium. "I cannot help but notice the absence of any statues of our revered Roman gods and goddesses. I hope for your sake that they are not destroyed."

Trebonius trembled inwardly. "They are not destroyed, Your Excellency. They are stored in a room at the barracks from which you just came."

"That is good." Gaius gave Trebonius another perfunctory bow, turned, and exited the villa.

*****

By the end of the day, with the help of his soldiers, Trebonius had moved all but the essentials of his personal belongings to the guest house for important dignitaries by the soldier's barracks. The move had been performed purely to keep up appearances. With one final night allowed in the villa, he determined to remain while he pondered his options.

To obey the order and to face Nero meant almost certain death. He knew from the tone of the new propraetor that Gaius' report of him and on the state of the island would be far from favorable. He also would not be able to deny that he now belonged to Christ, an admission that he knew would enrage the emperor. He had greatly feared death when it appeared inevitable during his illness of more than two years before. The healing power of Christ had greatly diminished in him that fear.

But there were other considerations. He had a son and daughter-in-law whom he loved dearly. He had a grandson who had been named for him. His son still looked to him for a wisdom that can only be obtained through the experience of years. *Lord what shall I do?*

As he pondered the subject, a plan began to form in his mind, based in part upon his recollection of Solon's escape from his home some two years before. He would not return to Rome. That would only mean death. He would escape the villa, remain on the island, at least for the time being, and hide somewhere. But where? Publius would know. If he didn't, then Amoenitas or others would know.

It came to him that his best chance lay in escaping the villa before Gaius had time to assert his control over the island—and the Christians. It would have to be under the cover of darkness, best around midnight, when eyes watching him would be wearier and minimal. He dared not attempt to retrieve his horse. The barn would be guarded. Even if he were to somehow pull that off, the sound of galloping hooves would give him away. He would have to escape by stealth on foot, yet he would need as much distance as possible between himself and the villa before his absence was discovered. He reckoned that the ten-mile journey to Publius' house would take three to four hours, time enough to arrive before dawn, before anyone realized that he was gone. Gaius would not know of Publius or the location of his house for at least a day.

But now, with a rough plan in place, came the torturous hours of waiting. Outwardly calm, he went about his regular duties at the villa, interacting with his house staff, issuing orders to Titinius, his hastatus posterior, penning mundane briefs to town officials, and sending them off by couriers.

In the afternoon he took his customary nap in his downstairs bedroom. Before lying down, he opened his outside window, figuring that it would attract less attention if he opened it during the daytime rather than at night. At dinnertime he consumed a little more than usual for extra energy.

After dinner he called together his house staff. "I have been replaced and recalled to Rome. In three days, I must sail. You have all been loyal, conscientious workers. Serve the new propraetor as you have served me and I am sure that all will be well for you."

He gave each an affectionate hug and dismissed them. He hated lying to them about his intention, but none of his house staff could know his plan. They would need genuine deniability.

He retired in a vain attempt at sleep, knowing that his gathering adrenalin would likely forbid the luxury. He listened for the sentries, ostensively posted to guard him from intruders. There were three pairs. One of the four sides of the villa would always be unmonitored for a brief time. He timed the duration between their passing's of his outside window. There would be scant room to disappear unseen.

36

The Flight

The bell tower from the distance tolled the ninth hour of the evening. Trebonius briefly considered going right away, but stifled the notion. *The guard will be more alert and will probably move faster earlier than they will later. Newly arrived soldiers will be out on the town after having been cooped up on their ships. They will be traveling back on the road, albeit mostly drunk.*

He dosed in snatches until finally the bell tolled the midnight hour. Silently, he rose from his bed and carried his few essential possessions in a bag to the base of the inside window. Poised at the window behind the curtain, he waited for the next steps to pass and to fade around the corner. He opened the curtain and peered out. No one was visible. A gentle mist descended from the cloud covered sky, fortuitously blocking the moonlight. As inaudibly as possible, he set his bag outside. He then climbed out the window himself and planted his feet on the ground. He steadied the curtain with his right hand, picked up his bag, and immediately made for a bush about ten feet from the villa. Behind the bush he crouched just as the next pair of sentries appeared from around the corner. Once they were past, he opened the distance between himself and the villa, hiding behind another bush before the next pair appeared. He repeated the pattern until he came to a narrow path through the sage that he knew led to the main road, about a quarter of a mile west of the villa. Crouching low, he made his way along the path until he came to the road.

Before entering the road, he glanced in both directions. Finding it clear, he made for Mathos at a rapid walk, a pace he knew he could sustain, at least for a time. He trained his ears for sound. His eyes strained forward, searching for movement in the darkness. Continually he swiveled to see if anyone might be following.

Voices and singing came from ahead. Immediately, he scrambled behind a sage on the right. From the sound he surmised four or five soldiers bawdily returning to the villa barracks. He waited for them to pass before resuming his flight.

Two hours of rapid walking brought him to the valetudinarium, where his friends Doctor Corbus and Domina Macatus worked. From the hospital until he passed Mathos, the road would be more illuminated, increasing his chances of detection. He knew that there was a watchman at the top of the bell tower, the same man who gonged in each hour of the night. Upon reaching the edge of the city, he kept to the shadows behind the back wall of the town square.

Once he cleared Mathos, breathing hard, with both sweat and mist mixed upon his forehead, he slowed his pace. The road from Mathos to Publius' house would be less traveled. Behind him the bell tower tolled the third hour of the morning. He had made good time. It also told him that his absence had not yet been discovered. He continued his journey.

Just as the clock tolled the fourth hour, he came to the dirt path off the main road that led to Publius' house and to the Litus Baths beyond. He had planned to cobblestone the path within the next year, to make it easier to move troops to and from the baths in the event of rain. But that obviously was no longer his concern. He relaxed somewhat. The dirt path was even less likely to wield travelers in the wee hours of the morning. The mist abated. A half-moon emerged, now low in the western sky.

Finally, he reached Publius' house, which prompted an inner debate. It was not yet the fifth hour of the morning. *Should I awaken them and seek shelter inside? What will they think if someone knocks on their door at this time in the morning?* He elected to remain on the porch, at least for a time. He collapsed onto the front porch bench, breathing hard, exhausted from his ten-mile journey.

"Who is there?" came a quiet, but challenging voice.

"It is your father," came the whispered reply.

The door opened. "Enter quickly."

Once inside the two embraced. "Your outer tunic is soaked," remarked Publius. "You need a whole change of clothes."

Amoenitas emerged sleepily from their bedroom. "I will fix you something hot to drink."

"We need to fix him a breakfast right now," spoke Publius urgently.

He addressed his father. "We know what is going on. I am glad to see you, but you know that you cannot remain here. We are the first place they will look."

Trebonius sadly acknowledged his son. "I feel bad about putting you and Amoenitas in danger."

"We knew we were in danger yesterday when we watched two new centuries march past our home toward the barracks by the Litus Baths. We are all in danger. But we also belong to Christ. Nothing can happen to us unless God allows. And even if we die, we go to be with Him in heaven forever."

"So where do you propose I go before heaven?"

"Get some food in you. Then we must go to the home of Demetrius and Phoebe before the Litus Bath soldiers become aware of your escape. A messenger could pass by our house and inform them at any time. Demetrius and Phoebe are less conspicuous than us. But their home cannot be your permanent hiding place either. Eventually, they will get around to searching every house."

He examined his father's clothing. "Come to our bedroom. You need to get out of that clothing and into something more common, like what I wear when I tend my sheep. What you have on now must be burned immediately."

In the bedroom he handed his father a common shepherd's robe with a rope to tie around his waist, and a head covering. "Put these on. You don't need to look like a propraetor. It might be helpful also to refrain from shaving for a time."

A minute later Trebonius sat down to a hastily prepared breakfast of eggs, bread, and fruit, along with a warm cup of non-fermented mulsum. He ate quickly. Publius grabbed his cloak and gestured his father out the back door. "I know a little used trail that will take us to Demetrius' house."

Before departing he addressed his wife. "Please burn his clothing in the fireplace right away."

As they emerged from the back door, the first hint of dawn was showing in the eastern sky.

37

The Fugitive

"I know the perfect place to hide you, sir," spoke Demetrius. He gave his wife Phoebe a sheepish grin. "There is a small cave about a mile from here that used to be my drinking place. I hung out there with Hermes and some of my other drinking buddies. There is a large shrub planted above the mouth of the cave that covers the entrance. I only discovered it by accident. They'll be unlikely to find you there, at least for a time."

Trebonius sighed. "It is not exactly what I am used to, but I guess beggars can't be choosy."

Publius patted his father on the back. "Someone will look in on you every night and keep you supplied. We'll bring you some creature comforts. It won't be forever, father. Better days will come."

*****

"The sole reason I am only busting you all down to tiro is because there is no lower rank!" thundered Gaius to the six soldiers who trembled before him. "I ought to have you crucified! From henceforth, as long as you are under my command, you are barracks and latrine cleaners. Should you fail in the slightest in those duties, you may consider yourselves dead. Now get out of my sight while you still can!"

The soldiers saluted and beat a hasty retreat from the peristylium. They had failed to prevent Trebonius' escape. Their careers as soldiers would forever be tainted. They would find employment difficult, even in civilian life. But at least they were alive—for the time being.

*****

Gaius looked down from his proconsul's seat at whom he figured to be his two main allies on the island. "I am glad to make your acquaintances. At present you know Melitene much better than I. How have you faired these past couple of years?"

"Not well, but tolerably," answered Alacerius. "The Christians have not gone after us like we intend to go after them."

Gaius nodded approvingly. "I understand, Alacerius, that you were once the praecipuus of the Mathos gymnasium?"

"That is true, Your Excellency."

"Well then. As soon as you can get to the gymnasium, you are again, if you wish to be."

Alacerius smiled. "I would wish to be."

"Then I will send some soldiers with you to help gently persuade the current praecipuus to step aside. I want the professor Rufus immediately dismissed from his position. I further understand that the Melitene church has been meeting at the amphitheater on Sundays?"

"That is again true, Your Excellency."

"That will cease at once. We will post a guard there tomorrow morning. No one may enter the amphitheater. Those who protest will be arrested on the spot. As of now, there is no such thing as a Melitene church."

"That is excellent, Your Excellency."

The new propraetor turned his attention to Alexandra. "Now, how do we find that traitorous former husband of yours?"

"I suggest you straightaway send a messenger to the centuries at the Litus Baths. They should immediately visit the nearby home of my equally traitorous former son Publius. Trebonius almost certainly went there."

"It will be done." Gaius gave her what appeared to be a somewhat leering smile. "I understand that your talents are many and considerable. What is to be your function in mending the affairs of this most unhappy island?"

She responded with her slow, cackling laugh. "Put me in charge of restoring the temple grounds of our beloved goddess Juno. Put me in charge of the carcer, which will soon be empty of those the Christians call criminals, and filled with the true criminals—they themselves. I have some reforms in mind that will surely persuade many of them to renounce their Christ. And let me deal with that place the Christians call Ille Perfugium. I will turn it into a refuge of another sort."

"That is much you wish to take on," observed Gaius.

"She can handle it," spoke Alacerius. "She has plenty of drive and has had plenty of rest."

A stirring came from the atrium. A moment later four soldiers appeared in the peristylium, carefully wheeling in a statue of Jupiter on a cart. Upon seeing that a meeting was taking place, the lead soldier immediately apologized.

"I am sorry, Your Excellency. We will return later."

Gaius gestured for them to enter. "We had just finished anyway. Proceed with your work. You do well. I want every statue restored to its proper place before this day is out."

* * * * *

"Where is he?"

"Where is who, Primi Ordine?"

The centurion glared at the pastor. "You know who I am talking about. Your father, the former propraetor of Melitene. Where is he?"

"He isn't at the villa?"

"We will have to search your house."

Publius gave the soldier a stern look. "It has been government policy here up to now, that soldiers do not search civilian homes without a written, court-ordered warrant."

"As of today, that is no longer the policy."

The centurion turned to the squad of ten men who stood behind him, pointed, and issued directions. "You two search the barn. You two watch the back door. The rest of you search the house."

Six men barged through the front door, followed by the centurion. Publius, knowing that resistance would have dire consequences, had no choice but the yield. "My father is not here. You will not find him. Please go easy on our home."

The centurion nodded and signaled to his men to go easy on the home. "Unless we find his father."

38

Two Kinds of Freedom

Paul breathed in the cool, crisp early spring air. It felt good to be out in the sun again, even as a prisoner. He wondered if this latest hearing at the Forum would have the same inconclusive result as had the previous three. The two years of house arrest had been wearing on him. Yes, many had come to him seeking counsel for their lives, including even Rabbi Shelemiah. He had written four important letters that he thought would stand the test of time, one each to the churches of Colossae, Ephesus, and Philippi, and one to his old friend Philemon.

But just as any man, he yearned to be free to come and go as he wished. He longed to be free of the chain around his neck and the ball and chain fastened to his right ankle, albeit placed reluctantly by his friend Petronius. He longed to visit the churches of Asia Minor and Greece to see how they were really doing. Letters could never tell the whole story. He knew in his heart that he would never be able to return to Jerusalem. Still, it felt good to be outside, even in the not so fresh air of Rome, to which he had become accustomed.

Lord Jesus, could I be free at last? Could I travel again? I feel like my work here on earth is not yet finished—that there is more of the good fight to fight. But as You please, Lord. I am Your servant.

The wagon upon which he rode turned right from Via del Fora Romana on to Via Sacra and passed the Colline gate. Ahead loomed the marketplace, the largest in the city, already in full swing, with hundreds of people milling about buying and selling their wares. Smells of food, spices, and incense alternately tantalized and offended his nostrils. They passed the Temple of Vesta and finally came to the Mamertine Carcer.

Petronius and the wagon driver went through the same ponderous process of extricating Paul from the wagon. Upon entering the building, Petronius handed the latest summons to the duty publicus, who pointed down the hallway. They entered the courtroom and were again directed to the seating area to await the call from the magistratus. While they waited, as inconspicuously as possible, Petronius unfastened the clasp around Paul's right ankle. The apostle again rubbed his ankle at the indentation and rotated his foot a few times in an attempt to restore circulation. For long minutes they sat silently.

"Next case," the magistratus finally called.

Summons in hand, Petronius stood to his feet and approached the judge with Paul at his right side. The silver haired magistratus was not someone they had seen before, though he certainly looked the part. He scanned the summons and compared it to another document on his rostrum that only he could see. Upon looking up he spoke.

"Good morning, vir honesti." The respectful, almost friendly greeting took both men by surprise. "I am Judge Amadeus Galbus Egnatius. I see that your prisoner Paul has been under house arrest here in Rome for the past two years."

"That is correct, sir," answered Petronius.

The judge shook his head. "Paul's accusers have had two full years to journey from Judea to Rome to formally charge him. It appears that they have either forgotten him, or don't consider him worth the bother. Without accusers there can be no case."

He pounded his gavel and fastened his eyes upon the prisoner. "You are a free man, Paul. No more chains. No more house arrest. You may come and go as you please, just as any other Roman citizen."

"Thank you, sir," answered Paul. "I am grateful for your decision."

The face of the judge grew serious. "So I have decreed. But I know of you, Paul. For your own sake, I strongly recommend that you leave Rome as soon as possible. The atmosphere in this city is growing increasingly hostile to people such as yourself. Leave before you are again arrested and face a fate worse than you have known so far."

"Thank you for your counsel, sir. I am indeed anxious to leave this city."

The two men bowed respectfully and departed the courtroom.

*****

Luke gave his longtime friend a congratulatory hug. "God's timing is perfect, my brother. I have recently finished writing the history of our church up to this time. Each of these three clay jars contain a copy of the story. One I promised to Theophilus. Another I would like you to give to Publius. I thought you might want to give the third copy to the church of your choice on your journey, maybe to the Syracuse people. The fourth I wish to keep with myself here in Rome."

Paul finished stuffing his few belongings into his tattered leather sack. "You will not go with me this time, brother Luke?"

Luke shook his head. "I am led by the Holy Spirit to remain here in Rome. It will be all right for me, my brother. I don't attract as much attention as you." The two again hugged.

In the lower great room Paul hugged his guard. "You have been a dear friend to me, Petronius. Keep following our Savior."

"I have concluded that there is for me no other life," answered Petronius. "As soon as I can leave the army, I want to join you on your journeys."

"If I am still on this earth at that time, I would love to have you."

In turn Paul hugged his friends Tertius, Linus, and Dominic's wife Ruth. "Perhaps I will see you all again."

Dominic, who was among them, pointed outside. "We have a sturdy mount for you, Paul. My friends are already mounted. We will escort you all the way to Puteoli, in order to protect you from highway bandits."

He bade his final farewells and went outside. Into a large leather saddle bag on the left side of the horse, he stuffed his personal bag and one clay jar. Into the right saddle bag, he placed the other two clay jars, with padding between them to keep the jars from breaking. Upon mounting his horse, his escort of ten riders, all heavily armed, began to move. As they passed the synagogue, Rabbi Shelemiah came out the front door and waved to Paul.

"I see that you are at last a free man, Paul. I will miss our times together, but I am glad for you. Shalom to you and long life."

"Shalom and long life to you, Rabbi Shelemiah," returned Paul as he rode by. In his heart he prayed once more that the gentle, learned rabbi would profess his Messiah in the synagogue, despite the personal and professional consequences. So far, he had not done so.

*****

The ride from Rome to Puteoli consumed an uneventful week. In the late afternoon on the seventh day they arrived at the wharf of the coast city. Once there Paul emptied the saddle bags on his horse. He transferred the jars containing the scrolls, along with the padding of his personal belongings, into a new large leather bag given him by Dominic.

"You are all dear men," he told his escorts. "Thank you for looking out for me these past two years. Perhaps we will meet again on this earth. If not, I will see you all in heaven."

Dominic dismounted his horse and pulled a long staff from a leather sheaf, which he held out to Paul. "You are not the youngest of men anymore, my brother. I thought you might need this to give you some stability."

Paul ran his right hand down the finely crafted staff. The entire outer surface had been smoothed and lacquered to prevent splinters. "Thank you, Dominic. Now I feel like Moses. I would open up the Great Sea and walk all the way to Syracuse, except that I think my legs aren't up to the task. Using a staff will be a first for me, but you are right. It is time."

The two hugged for the last time before Dominic remounted his horse. After final waves the horsemen turned to begin their homeward journey, leaving Paul alone and on foot.

He surveyed the wharf and prayed. ***Lord Jesus, You know the ship I should pick. I only want to make Your name known as I journey to Syracuse.***

He strode down the wharf, making inquiry as he went among the dozen or so ships that appeared available. None of the first ten ships were heading to his destination, but on the eleventh ship he spotted a familiar face.

"Captain Marinus?"

The grizzled old captain looked up from his ship and instantly recognized the caller. "Paul!" The two walked toward one another and hugged. "It has been a long time," remarked Marinus.

"Yes indeed. We had quite an adventure together."

Paul examined his ship. It looks like a fine ship. It is yours?"

"Just recently. I had a much smaller ship for a long time."

Seeing the large bag, he surmised that Paul needed a ship to take him somewhere. "Where are you heading?"

"To Syracuse and then to Melitene. From there to Asia and to Greece."

"Well then, I can get you to Syracuse. I am heavily laden with a cargo of volcanic sand, of which the merchants in Syracuse cannot get enough. How about I take you there for free? I would like to make up for our last voyage together."

Paul breathed a prayer of thanksgiving to God, before giving Captain Marinus a wary look. "You are not going to put me through another experience like last time, are you?"

Captain Marinus laughed. "Let's hope not. I lost my ship at Melitene, though thankfully no lives. It has taken me more than two years to obtain this ship, which I have no intention of losing. I have a crew of four, all veteran seamen. You will be my only passenger."

He called to one of his crewmen. "Kosmos, would you please find my friend Paul a place to bunk and to store his belongings?"

"I will sir," Kosmos replied. He gestured for Paul to follow him.

As Paul trailed behind the short, bronze skinned sailor down the stairway into the hold of the ship, the distinct odor of a man not used to bathing or social occasions unsettled his nostrils. Only twelve feet of open space remained in the hull as living space for the crew. The rest was filled to the stern with bags of volcanic sand. Kosmos pointed to the last bunk on the starboard side.

"You can sleep there." He pointed to the open space under the bunk. "You can store your things there. No one will bother them."

* * * * *

Night had fallen by the time the ship cleared the harbor and entered the open sea. Paul sat on the port side of the deck, preferring the fresh night air, the stars above, and the coastline of Italy to the stuffiness of the hold. He had been far too long inside. The waters were surprisingly and pleasantly calm. It felt good to be off the horse and off his feet, watching the flickering lights along the coast go by. Yet his mind remained a storm of activity.

Lord Jesus, I pray right now for the soul of Captain Marinus. I believe You have brought us together again for a purpose. May salvation come to him before this voyage is complete.

After a time, he felt led of the Spirit to make his way to the pilot house where Captain Marinus was finally alone. Once inside the cabin he seated himself on a bench behind the captain.

"So, is life better for you now, Marinus, since the last time we were together?"

"It is. This is Tantulus II. Until recently I had Tantulus I, a much smaller ship. With this ship I can now take much longer trips on the Great Sea."

"I am glad for you."

Marinus nodded. "It might interest you to know that about a year ago I transported your friends Marcus and Julius from Puteoli to Syracuse."

Paul's ears perked up. "Really?"

"Really. Your friend Julius was in very bad shape. He was wounded in a fight on the Appian Way and close to death by the time we got to Syracuse. I helped them get to a cisium."

"I got a letter from a man named Antonius, who is the leader of the Syracuse church. He told me that his daughter Angelina had nursed him back to health. And then they were married."

"Yes, I knew about that. Marcus told me that Julius had a vision about being helped by an angel of mercy. Her name turned out to be Angelina. I later ferried Marcus and a man named Rufus to Melitene, while Julius stayed behind to heal. It seems like everything about you Christians eventually works out."

"God causes all things to work together for good to those who love God.' (Romans 8:28b) That is true even in death. For in death we only leave this earth to be with Christ."

For a time, there was silence. Paul felt tempted to break the silence with more conversation, but adhered to a check in his spirit. It seemed better to wait and to pray.

After what seemed an eternity, Marinus finally broke the silence. "So, it's kind of like you Christians win either way. God either does miracles for you on earth, or He takes you to His heaven."

Inwardly, Paul rejoiced. Here was his opening. "That is how it works,

Marinus. Eventually, we must all leave this earth, believers and non-believers alike. And then we either go to be with Christ forever if we have believed in Him, or we go to the place of everlasting torment if we have not believed, away from the presence of the Lord forever."

Marinus shook his head. "That sounds severe, Paul. Can't we just go into the earth and cease to exist, except as compost?"

"That is what many believe, but it is not so. The prophet Daniel spoke about that issue. 'And there will be a time of distress such as never occurred since there was a nation until that time; and at the time our people, everyone who is found written in the book, will be rescued. And many of those who sleep in the dust of the ground will awake, these to everlasting life, but the others to disgrace and everlasting contempt'." (Daniel 12:1b-2)

"I have recently thought much about these things, Paul. Being no longer a young man, I am increasingly aware of my mortality. I have also done much wrong in my life and fear that I may be bound for that place of everlasting contempt. How do I change that? How do I get my name written in the book?"

In his spirit Paul again rejoiced. "You repent of the life you have been living. You turn from it and believe in the Lord Jesus Christ. He sets you free to become the man you wish you could be."

"What does it mean to believe?"

"Christ was crucified on a Roman cross some thirty years ago. But on that cross, He took upon Himself the sins of the entire world, including yours and mine. On the third day He rose again from the dead. You believe that those events truly happened. You believe that Christ died to take away your sins in order to make you right before a just God. You believe that He rose again from the dead to eternal life. In believing you surrender every aspect of your life to Him. If Christ rose again from the dead to eternal life, then we too who believe in Him will one day rise again from the dead to eternal life."

"I want to believe those things, Paul."

"Then let us together call upon the name of the Lord."

Right there in the pilot house, while Marinus continued to steer the ship, the two men prayed together and all heaven rejoiced.

39

The Upper Room

The early dawn of the second day was the ideal time for Tantulus II to reach Portus Grande at Syracuse. The shoremen who loaded and unloaded ships preferred to work from first light until midday, after which the heat became unbearable. Little activity would again occur until the late afternoon and end only with darkness. Almost as soon as Tantulus II docked, workmen in loincloths clambered aboard to unload Marinus' cargo of volcanic sand.

Having gathered his things, Paul, leaning upon his staff, watched from the dock as the workers went down the stairway into the hold and began to bring up the bags of sand one by one. Another worker opened the rear cargo hatch. He momentarily disappeared into the hold and then began lifting bags from there. He and a partner on the deck built up a pile of four bags, before others began to carry the top bag to the dock to lay in wheeled carts. As they continued, the two workers who remained on the ship maintained the pile at four bags, in what appeared to be a back-saving technique. Each cart was filled with twelve bags before being wheeled to the wharf to be set by previously filled carts.

Behind the carts on the wharf Paul observed four men in knee length linen tunics of various colors and designs. Each wore a wide-brimmed hat to protect his head from the withering sun and leather sandals on his feet.

After a short conference with his crewmen, who remained aboard the ship, Captain Marinus approached Paul. "Those men you see counting the bags are my potential buyers. Each represents a different business that needs volcanic sand. Each wants to get the lowest possible price. Of course, I want the highest. I will sell my cargo to the highest bidder among them."

"What are your plans here?" asked Paul.

"I intend to remain for three days. My crewmen will want some shore time after I pay them. As for myself, if you are willing to wait until after I have negotiated a price for my cargo and then paid my crew, I would love to accompany you to meet your friends here. It shouldn't be long."

"Then I will wait for you. I would love to have you meet the people here."

Once the unloading was complete, Paul watched from a distance as Captain Marinus negotiated with the buyers, who were arranged in a semi-circle around him, each in animated gesture. Marinus remained calm. *He seems to know how to conduct business.* He glanced back at the ship and noticed how far it had risen in the water.

After a few minutes the captain clasped wrists with a merchant who wore a violet tunic with gold embossed patterns. While the other three men parted to examine other cargoes, the winning bidder handed Captain Marinus a number of coins to complete the transaction. When Marinus turned, the smile on his face told Paul that his friend had gotten a good price.

"It must be God's blessing on my life," he said upon returning Paul. "I got the best price I have ever gotten. Just one more matter of business remains."

He re-boarded the ship and handed several coins to each of his crewmen. After securing the ship, he fetched a few personal belongings and rejoined Paul at the dock. "How far are we from Antonius' house? Do we hire a cisium or do we walk?"

"I would prefer to walk," answered Paul, slinging the bag Dominic had given him over his shoulder. "I haven't been able to do much walking for two years."

*****

"Do you have any tents for sale?" asked Paul casually as he entered the shop with Marinus.

It took a moment for Antonius to shift from storekeeper to friend once recognition kicked in. "Paul!" he exclaimed. "Welcome, my dear brother!"

Immediately, the other workers in the shop mobbed Paul, hugging and kissing him on his cheeks. Captain Marinus stood off to the side, marveling at the greeting his friend was receiving."

"Hi Paul!" gleamed Caecitas, as she skittered down the stairway. "I can still see!" She threw her arms around him.

"And I am glad, sweet Caecitas. My, how you have grown. Have you been telling everyone what Jesus did for you?"

"The whole city knows about her," answered Antonius. "It has been both a blessing and a curse. Others have come to us seeking similar miracles, but other than what Angelina can do, we don't know how to help them."

"Julius," said Paul. "I heard that you were hurt. I am glad to see you now so well."

"I am well, Paul, and also married to the angel Angelina. She is not here right now. She is a midwife and healer, out and about her business."

After the initial tide of greetings had receded, Paul introduced his friend. "This is Captain Marinus, whose ship brought me here from Puteoli. He is now one of us, a fellow believer in Christ Jesus."

At Paul's words Captain Marinus began to get the same treatment, which he found overwhelming.

"Let me take you men upstairs and find you a place to sleep," spoke Liuni. "You probably need some rest and we must tend to our business today. But this evening we will have a grand meal together and then some fellowship time."

* * * * *

After a welcome meal of lentil soup with fresh bread the two families, along with Paul, Marinus, and a few other church members packed the upper room for an evening of rejoicing. It began with psalms and hymns the people had learned over the past couple of years, worshipping together as Angelina led them on her lute. It was obvious to Paul that she had become an accomplished musician since last he saw her.

After the period of singing, several testified of blessings Jesus had brought to their lives; a restored marriage, a new baby, a better job, and friends coming to faith in Christ. All the while Marinus, feeling intimidated as a newcomer, kept silent, fearing that the others would want to hear his story. When a lull came, his fear was realized as Antonius prodded him.

"You probably feel shy, Marinus. But you are among friends. We would love to hear your story."

With much trepidation, Marinus inhaled deeply and let the air out slowly before he began to speak. "I have lived now for fifty-three years. Of most of my life I am not proud. I once had a wife and five children. We lived right here in Syracuse. I have no idea now where they are or what any of them are doing.

"During my married years I did what sailors do from port to port. When I came home, which wasn't often, I drank, I abused my wife and I beat my children. Then after one voyage I returned home to find my house occupied by another family. They told me that my wife and children had left while I was gone and that they had no idea where they went. I made no attempt to locate them. It seemed at the time that I had been set free to carouse all the more."

Tears began to form in his eyes. "In recent years I have moderated somewhat on the drinking and carousing, yielding to the vicissitudes of age. But it was only two nights ago that I gave my heart to Christ. Now suddenly I find myself greatly ashamed of my former life. I only wish there were some way I could find my wife and my children, and make it up to them. All of my children have to be grown by now—if even they are still alive."

"We have all done things of which we are now ashamed," spoke Antonius. "I shudder at my former life. But in Christ we are new creations. I am no longer the man I was. You are no longer the man you were. We will pray for you regarding the finding of your family."

He turned to Paul. "Do you have a word for us? Do you have something to encourage us in our faith?"

Paul removed the top from one of the clay jars that sat beside him on the floor. From the jar he removed a large, bound roll of parchment scrolls.

"My friend Luke has penned a history of the church which, lacking proper light and always being on the move, I have been unable yet to read myself. It is quite a long story. I thought I would simply read to you this evening the beginning of the story of the first Christians." With his words the room grew quiet in anticipation.

"The first account I composed, Theophilus, about all that Jesus began to do and teach, until the day when He was taken up, after He had by the Holy Spirit given orders to the apostles whom He had chosen. To these He also presented Himself alive, after His suffering, by many convincing proofs, appearing to them over a period of forty days, and speaking of the things concerning the kingdom of God." (Acts 1:1-3)

He continued to read until the point where Matthias was numbered with the eleven apostles.

"Why aren't you in the story?"

Paul smiled. "I suspect that I will appear later, Caecitas. At the time I did not know Christ. In fact, I was a great enemy of Christ and His people."

"When is Jesus going to come back?" she asked.

"We don't know. But it is always good to be ready for His return."

"Could you read to us some of the story every night until it is done?"

Paul again smiled. "I wish I could, Caecitas. But as I said, it is a big long story and I must leave in three days. But maybe your father can take up reading it after I am gone."

"Do you mean that we may keep the scrolls?" asked Antonius.

"Yes, the scrolls in this jar are for you."

"Who is Theophilus?" asked Drusus.

"He is an elder for the church on Melitene. Luke addressed the story to him, but it is for all of us. I look forward to seeing Theophilus in a few days. He will also get a copy of this story."

"The first Christians continually devoted themselves to prayer in an upper room," Antonius noted. "I note that we too are in an upper room. Why don't we now do as they did?"

For the next forty-five minutes the gathering lifted their voices in praise and worship of their Savior, their spirits being drawn together as they prayed. One by one during that time the children fell asleep.

That night Marinus lay on his bed, his mind racing, both in regret and in anticipation. *How I have wasted these first fifty-three years of my life. But all I want now is to follow Christ. I want to make whatever time is left for me on this earth to count for Him.*

His mind turned to his family. *Is there any way, Lord, that I can again see my family? Is there any way I can make things right with my wife and my children?*

An assurance came to him that it would one day be so. But for now, it was time to sleep.

40

Impartations

Long before first light the next morning Paul arose and went out to the veranda overlooking the street. There he lit a single candle on the outside table and began to read the scrolls of Luke's history of the church from where he had left off the previous evening.

Two hours later he stood to his feet, having finished the entire story. He did a few stretching exercises before lifting his arms to heaven.

"O Lord Jesus, what a story is this! How in the world did You have grace on me? May this story become an inspiration to your saints, not only in this present time, but for the entire age of Your church before You return to this earth. May many throughout all generations take up the challenge to be Your 'witnesses both in Jerusalem, and in all Judea and Samaria, and even to the remotest part of the earth.' (Acts 1:8b)

"It was such a special time with Your people last night. Your saints are indeed the majestic ones upon this earth. Thank You again for showing mercy to me, allowing me to become one of Your people. I pray for Your church here in Syracuse. May the people grow together and become strong in the faith. May new people be constantly added to their number. Protect them, I pray, from those who hate Your gospel. May the book from Luke thrill their hearts as it has mine.

"Father, I am torn between so many desires. I do not know how much longer I shall be a free man or how long I shall remain upon this earth. So many places to go. I want to see the brethren on Melitene, in Asia, and in

Greece. I want to go to Spain, for the Iberians have yet to hear the gospel. As you guided me into Macedonia, so guide me now.

"I pray for Antonius. Yesterday I heard that the church is accomplishing great things, but that it lacks miracles of healing. How am I help them with such miracles? How can I help Antonius become fully the shepherd he both wants and needs to be?

"I pray for Liuni. Lord, I confess that right now I do not have a strong reading on him. I know that he knows and loves You, but what is to be his place in the church here?

"I pray for Julius. He looks so happy to be married to Angelina. But I see that Julius needs greater worlds to conquer. I pray for Angelina too. She is such a choice young woman. May she be to Julius the helper suitable for him. May she also develop fully into the woman You have created her to be."

For nearly an hour Paul continued to worship his Savior and to pray for the Syracuse church. Near the end of the hour, in increments, God spoke to him.

At the sixth hour, one by one, the leading men of the church, Antonius, Liuni, and Julius joined him on the veranda. "Good morning," Paul greeted each man as they came. "I have read through the entirety of Luke's story. It is a precious gift to the people of God."

He fixed his eyes on Antonius. "Read it to your people, Antonius. Read a portion every evening until you are finished. Your people will come alive, as will you."

He turned to Julius. "Would you please ask your wife to join us? What I have to say concerns her too."

After Angelina had joined them, Paul opened their time together in prayer before addressing the leaders of the church. "The older I get, the more aware I am of my mortality. It is written, 'As for the days of our life, they contain seventy years, or if due to strength, eighty years, yet their pride is but labor and sorrow; for soon it is gone and we fly away.' (Psalm 90:10)

"I believe that I have maybe three or four more years remaining upon this earth, which I intend to spend as profitably as possible for the cause of Christ. The only question is how may I best redeem the time still allotted to me? As much as possible, I want to pour my life into younger men and women, such as yourselves, who will likely remain long after I am gone."

He addressed Antonius. "You mentioned yesterday that people have come to your church for healing from blindness and other maladies, but that other than what Angelina can do, you cannot help them. Last night people testified of healed marriages, better jobs, new births, and people coming to Christ. Those are all wonderful things, but you don't have to disappoint those who come to you for physical healing, if they have the faith to be healed."

"What do we do?" asked Antonius. "It is not in me to heal people. Maybe my daughter."

"The Holy Spirit has shown me that it is in both of you the perform acts of healing through the power of Jesus Christ."

He turned to Liuni. "As I prayed for you this morning, it came to me that you have the gift of administrations. I note that you are a keen businessman and that you keep the shop below well organized. While Antonius feeds and shepherds the flock, it is you who are gifted to organize and to run its various ministries, such as helping the poor, evangelizing the community, following up on new believers, and seeing to the temporal interests of the church, such as its finances."

He then turned his attention to Julius and to Angelina. "I am led of the Holy Spirit to journey to Asia by ship within two days. There are a number of churches there that require my urgent attention. After that, I am bound for Greece. At the same time, I am charged with delivering Luke's story to the believers on Melitene. You know those people, Julius. I believe they are as dear to you as they are to me. Would you and Angelina be willing to take Luke's story to the Melitene believers in my stead? One copy is for Theophilus and the other for Publius. Perhaps you and Angelina might even desire to settle there."

A sense of thrill and amazement filled Julius' soul. "That is the very thing Angelina and I have been praying about for several months. It has been our heart's desire to settle on Melitene."

"He has spoken to me about returning Melitene several times," vouched Antonius. "I have known for a long time that he cannot spend his life in a tentmaking shop."

"I will speak with Captain Marinus later this morning about him possibly taking a cargo to Melitene, with you and Angelina along as passengers."

He stood to his feet. "And now it is time for me to impart some spiritual gifts to each of you."

He laid his hands on Antonius. "Father in heaven above, Your servant Antonius is Your called to lead the church here in Syracuse. I thank You for his shepherd's heart. I ask You now to impart to him the gift of miracles and healings, that many who are sick may be made well, both within the church and without. May those miracles attest to Your power. May many believe, not only because they hear Your word, but because they see Your power."

He laid his hands on Liuni. "Lord Jesus, churches always need men like Liuni to manage their ministries and their finances. I pray Your heart and Your wisdom into him. Like glue that is only noticed when it fails to do its job, the gift of administrations is an often overlooked, but imperative gift. I also impart to him the gift of the distinguishing of spirits regarding those who ask to serve, or whom he asks to serve in different ministries."

He laid one hand upon Julius and the other upon his wife. "Lord Jesus, I pray that You will give good success to Julius and Angelina in delivering Luke's story to the church on Melitene. I impart to Julius the gifts of wisdom and knowledge. May he become an oak of righteousness. I impart to Angelina the gift of miracles and healings. May she be used of You to restore many to health, that Your name may be glorified. Help Julius and Angelina to bond ever closer as a couple. Do in their lives far beyond all they could ask or think on that island and beyond.

"Impart to all of these dear leaders a hunger and a thirst for You and for Your word. Place in them a love for people and a hatred of sin. Make each of these into all You have made them to be."

When he had finished his commissioning of the four, they continued to pray together until the noise of children and the smell of fresh baked bread drew them to breakfast and to the duties of the day.

41

Into the Cauldron

As planned, Paul departed for Asia two days later after tearful goodbyes from the church. Captain Marinus agreed to take Julius and Angelina to Melitene with the precious scrolls as soon as he was able to find cargo needed on Melitene.

It took nearly a week to fill his ship with bags of Timilia, Maiorca, and Russello wheats left over from the previous fall's harvest. At the dock on the appointed day, shortly after first light, the two families, along with other church members experienced another round of tearful goodbyes, especially for Angelina, who had never before ventured from the island of Magna Graecia.

"Take care of my daughter," Antonius admonished Julius.

"I will, sir."

"Write to us," Lucia charged her daughter.

"I will, mother."

After more kisses and hugs they boarded the ship. The lines were cast from the moorings to the ship. Long poles backed Tantulus II from its berth. Once it was well clear of the berth, Captain Marinus wound the ship through a series of steering oar maneuvers. When his ship finally faced the direction it needed to go, crewmen hoisted the sails. Once the wind caught the sails, Tantulus II began to move. The entire church remained at the dock waving until the ship disappeared from sight behind the island of Ortygia.

Once out to sea, Julius placed his right arm around his wife Angelina.

In response she put her left arm around Julius and cuddled close to him. He felt her fear and the need to reassure her. "For the first time I feel like we are truly on our own. Do not worry, Angelina. Just as you took care of me, I will take care of you."

*****

Though the voyage from Syracuse to Melitene was uneventful, the arrival early the next day portended trouble despite the calm waters. The atmosphere on the island felt different from the moment Tantulus II docked. Dock workers moored the ship. Others unloaded the cargo. Merchants counted the bags.

But no was smiling. The workers labored ponderously, with no spring in their steps. The wharf appeared dirtier than the last time Julius and Marinus had been there. Neither was Marinus able to gain as high a price for the grain as he had hoped, for money seemed in short supply. The profit margin would be slim—barely acceptable. The captain had no choice but to accept.

After tending to his business, Marinus joined Julius and Angelina. The first priority was to get a good meal while they sized up the situation. Soldiers in precise columns marched about the city, more than either Marinus or Julius had seen before. Few children were on the streets. The city was strangely quiet. A pervading atmosphere of fear seemed to hold the populace in its grip.

They found a thermopolium called Festivitas. "It looks anything but festive right now," remarked Julius. Nevertheless, they went inside to get a needed meal.

*****

To travel the five miles from Portus Amplus to Mathos on foot while carrying all their worldly possessions, some of which were still on the ship, was impractical. After inquiring into the best way, Julius hired a wagon drawn by two horses, with just enough room to carry Angelina, their belongings, and Marinus, who had decided to remain a few days before returning to Syracuse. Julius himself would walk alongside. The high cost of the wagon was offset somewhat by Marinus' offer to pay a portion for their transportation.

It was well into the afternoon before they finally reached Theophilus' house. A voice called through the door after they knocked. "Who is there?"

"It is Julius, my brother, along with my wife Angelina, and a friend named Marinus."

The door opened quickly. "Please come in." Upon their entry Theophilus embraced Julius. "I am so glad to see you again."

"And I you," answered Julius. "As you can see, I am now married to the joy of my life."

"She is beautiful," my brother. "Welcome, Angelina."

"Thank you," she answered warmly.

Theophilus gave Marinus a long gaze. "And you are Marinus? I have seen you before."

"I am, and yes, you have seen me before. I was marooned on this island because of the great storm a couple of years back. I was the captain of the ship that ran aground here with Paul."

"When was the last time you people ate?" asked Flavia, who had just entered the great room.

"Not since this morning," spoke Julius.

"Well then, I will fix you all a meal." She gestured to Angelina. "Do you want to join me in the culina while the men unload the wagon?" Angelina nodded and the two women disappeared into the kitchen.

After unloading the wagon, bringing the goods into the house and paying the driver, the men gathered again in the great room. Flavia brought in a tray of four cups and a large beaker of water, flavored with lemon, while Angelina brought a round of fresh garlic bread and a bowl filled with olive oil for dipping. She set the tray on a low table between their two couches.

"Thank you, ladies," the men said, nearly in unison.

After taking a drink, Julius emptied one of the clay jars that had been brought inside and presented to Theophilus a bundle of scrolls bound with twine. "This is the promised early history of the church, straight from the hand of Luke."

Theophilus' face lit up. "Wonderful! I can hardly wait to read these."

"The other jar we have with us is for Publius when we see him."

"He will be glad too."

Julius sat back on the couch. "So, what is going on here? The whole atmosphere of this island is different from when I left. The people seem tense."

"They are tense," answered Theophilus. "Trebonius has been replaced and is in hiding. We have a new propraetor here named Gaius. Fedorata Civitas has been abolished and crippling taxes have been levied upon us. Our church has been forced to vacate the amphitheater and declared not to exist. We aren't legally allowed to meet in groups greater than five. Alacerius has again taken over the gymnasium, where attendance by all children up to age eighteen is now compulsory and our Christian faith is declared seditious. Both Marcus and Rufus have been fired from employment there. Ille Refugium has been shut down in favor of a new 'House of Entertainment,' which is just a fancier version of what it was before. Doctor Corbus and Domina Macatus have been fired from the hospital, which has again become a place of death for the elderly, for newborns, and for 'undesirables' like us if we unfortunately become sick or injured. Swords and spears have been confiscated from the entire citizenry. We are all commanded now to worship the emperor Nero, along with the Roman gods. Other than that, everything is normal."

Julius shook his head sadly. "No wonder everyone is so fearful. What is the church here doing about all this?"

"We still meet in homes and usually in groups greater than five, but we don't talk about it. We still have most of our weapons, but we don't talk about them. We refuse to worship Nero and the gods, but we don't outwardly talk about that either. A large black market has sprung up in an attempt to avoid taxes."

"How are you all bearing up under this pressure? Is the church still strong?"

"We are actually stronger than ever, though fewer in number. Those who weren't fully committed have fallen away. For those of us who have remained steadfast, our faith has become more precious, now that it costs us to believe. The Scriptures from Luke on the life of Christ have been a great encouragement to us.

"If anyone wishes to come after Me, let him deny himself, and take up his cross daily, and follow Me. For whoever wishes to save his life shall lose it, but whoever loses his life for My sake, he is the one who will save it." (Luke 9:23b)

"It comes down to the question of whether or not we truly believe."

"The meal is ready," called Flavia from the kitchen.

"Enough of the burdensome stuff for now," spoke Theophilus. "Let us enjoy a meal together as we celebrate your coming."

* * * * *

Julius pushed back his plate and rubbed his stomach. "Thank you, Flavia. We didn't get much at the thermopolium at Portus Amplus this morning. We were starved."

"Angelina helped me," she modestly replied.

Julius grasped the hand of his wife. "What do you think, deliciae? Have we come to the right place?"

"I believe God has called us here," she answered resolutely. "Being within God's calling is always the right place to be."

"What about you, Marinus?" asked Julius.

"Count me in. I figure I have pretty much wasted my life until now. I might as well make something out of the rest of it. Tomorrow, I am going to move my ship to one of the long-term, winter moorings. They cost a lot less this time of year and my crewmen can always catch on with another ship."

Julius turned his attention back to Theophilus. "We are at your service, my brother, however we can fit in. We are here to stay. I will need to find a job. We will need to find a house."

"What would you like to do for a job?" asked Theophilus.

"I would like to be a vigilus."

Theophilus gave an approving nod. "That would be a good job for you. As you know, I was a vigilus before I was a pastor. Unfortunately, that would not be a good job for you at the present time. Your number one priority would be to discover illegal Christian gatherings and to arrest the participants on the spot. Those who are caught go to the carcer, where Publius' mother Alexandra has devised a number of sadistic tortures in an attempt to force our people to renounce Christ. Quite a few of our people are there right now."

Julius shook his head sadly. "Then what is available to me that won't get God's people in trouble?"

"Your friend Marcus has found jobs repairing people's homes. He says that he has more work than he can do. Do you know the carpenter's trade?"

"Not well, but I am a fast learner."

"Well, the two of you can discuss that possibility when you see him, maybe this evening."

"What is this evening?"

Theophilus took a deep breath. "This is going to be awkward, but this question must be asked. Is Marinus here trustworthy?"

"I have known Marinus for a long time," spoke Julius. "And now he is one of us. We can trust him."

"Very well. The key leaders of the church will be meeting tonight in a cave about an hour's walk from here. If the three of us men come, we will be twelve in all, just like the apostles, but hopefully without a Judas. You can deliver Luke's story to Publius at that time and speak with Marcus about a job."

"What will we do in the cave?"

"We will read God's word. Maybe we will read the first part of what you have just brought us. We will pray together. We will seek the leading of the Holy Spirit for how we should deal with our current situation."

Just then the three children of Theophilus and Flavia; Benedicta, Laverna, and Accalia came through the front door from the gymnasium. Immediately their presence lightened the somber mood that had prevailed in the house.

"I'm Benedicta," proclaimed the oldest of the three to the three guests. "I just turned eleven. I keep my younger sisters out of trouble." She pointed to her next younger sister. "This is Laverna. She's eight and she's rude sometimes."

"I am not," protested Laverna.

"And this is Accalia. She's five."

Accalia smiled and waved to the guests. "Hi."

*****

After feeding the children, Theophilus read to them about Zacchaeus from Luke's story about the life of Christ.

"And He entered and was passing through Jericho. And behold, there was a man called by the name of Zacchaeus; and he was a chief tax-gatherer, and he was rich. And he was trying to see who Jesus was, and he was unable because of the crowd, for he was small in stature…" (Luke 19:1-3)

"What do you think, girls?" he asked upon completing the story.

"Zacchaeus was mean. But Jesus made him be nice," proclaimed Laverna.

"I don't think Jesus made him be nice," corrected Benedicta. "I think Jesus was nice to him first, which made him want to be nice."

"What do you think?" spoke Theophilus to his youngest daughter.

"Zacchaeus was little, like me."

He nodded approvingly to his three daughters. "You have all understood a part of the story. Zacchaeus was a sinner, just like all of us. But Jesus loved him anyway, just like He loves us anyway. The story ends with 'For the Son of Man has come to seek and to save that which was lost'." (Luke 19:10)

"What about the mean tax-collectors here who take all our money?" asked Laverna.

"We must not hate them," answered their father. "They are lost people who need Jesus. We must look for opportunities to do good to them."

42

The Cave

Darkness had descended upon the island. As was his habit before they went to bed, Theophilus read another passage from Luke's story to his daughters, this time about the ten leprous men.

"Ten were healed of their leprosy," spoke Theophilus. "But only one expressed his thankfulness to God. And then Jesus said to him 'Rise, and go your way; your faith has made you well.' (Luke 17:19b) How was his healing different from the other nine?"

"Maybe because his heart was healed too?"

"Very good, Benedicta. I think you are right. A grateful heart makes for a healthy heart. We must always live our lives in gratefulness to God, even when bad things happen to us. Otherwise we become increasingly bitter as we journey through the stages of life. Bitterness is a canker to the soul."

* * * * *

Once the three girls were off to bed, it was decided that Angelina would remain at the house in order to get to know Flavia better. Already, the two women felt like they had become fast friends. The husbands kissed their respective wives and, along with Marinus, silently set out into the darkness from the back door of the house.

For the first ten minutes they followed a dimly moonlit trail until they came to another lesser used trail that led to the cave. None spoke for a time, knowing how easily sound travels at night. Only when they were safety out of earshot from Mathos did they engage in whispered, minimal communications with one another.

*****

From inside the cave Trebonius heard three taps from sticks beaten together. "He is risen," he called through the brush in a voice barely above a whisper."

"He is risen indeed," came the response.

He held his cloak in front of the single candle that burned inside the cave. "Enter," he called.

The brush pealed back to one side, revealing the three men from Theophilus' house, the first to arrive. "Welcome to my humble home," spoke Trebonius.

Julius could barely stifle a laugh. It was indeed a humble home and Spartan in its furnishings compared to the villa. In length, his "home" stretched some fifteen feet to the end, with about ten feet of width at its widest point. Inside was a mat, two blankets, a chair, several candles, a flint, a few foodstuffs, and portions of Luke's account on the life of Christ.

Within the next few minutes, the others arrived in small groups until twelve were present: Publius, Theophilus, Julius, Marinus, Trebonius, Doctor Corbus and Domina Macatus, Demetrius and Phoebe, Rufus, Marcus, and Valentina. Absent among the leaders were the women Amoenitas, Eletia, Beatrice, and Flavia, all of whom had children to watch. Linus was imprisoned for creating a public disturbance by playing his lyre at night for his sheep.

It was agreed that for the session Marcus would remain outside the cave and sound the alarm if danger approached. The malevolent, ever probing eyes of the Roman garrison on the island was relentlessly searching for Trebonius. All present in the cave kept their voices low, barely audible enough to hear one another. After warm but subdued greetings Publius opened their time with prayer.

"Lord Jesus Christ, we the leaders of Your church here on Melitene are gathered to seek Your face about our present state of affairs. Fill us, we pray, with Your love, Your wisdom, Your courage, and Your leading on what we should do. We know that ultimately Yours is the victory. We pray for Linus and for our other brothers and sisters in the carcer. Give them courage to remain steadfast in the face of torture. May they soon be free. We pray for our enemies, who are more victims of Satan's deceptions than enemies. May they too find Your salvation. We remember that we too were once Your enemies. We worship You alone as our Lord and Savior. We pray all of these things in Your precious name, amen."

When he had finished the opening prayer, Publius looked upon the gathering, circled around the single candle that burned in their midst. "Welcome Julius. I see that you have brought a visitor, though I think I have seen him before."

"This is Marinus," answered Julius. "He captained the ship that brought Paul and me originally to Melitene in the great storm. He brought us here from Syracuse this morning. Just a few days ago he embraced our Savior."

"Then welcome, Captain Marinus. We are glad to have you among us."

"I am glad to be here," Marinus answered sincerely. From where he sat, he became aware that the eyes of one of the women present, were staring at him.

Julius handed the clay jar he had brought with him to Publius. "Inside is Luke's story of the early church. Theophilus also has one. This is your personal copy from Luke's hand."

Publius smiled broadly. "Thank you, Julius. I look forward to reading it as soon as I can."

He turned his attention to the subject at hand. "We are twelve here in number, including Marcus outside. I recall that there were twelve gathered in the upper room for Christ's last meal with His disciples before He went to the cross. But among them was a traitor. I pray that it is not so this evening. I recall that Jesus spoke to them regarding a dispute among them about which of them was the greatest. What was Jesus' answer? Anyone?"

"But let him who is the greatest among you become as the youngest, and the leader as the servant," (Luke 22:26b) spoke Demetrius.

"Just so," answered Publius. "He who created all things, including the human race, who has every right to rule us with a rod of iron, has chosen instead to be our servant. The way up is down. To become great in God's economy, one must go low and serve others. Such must be our attitude toward one another and toward all people."

As Publius continued to speak, Marinus finally returned the glances of the woman, likely the youngest of the three present. Her face was enigmatic. He did not know her name, for she had not yet spoken or been addressed. *Why does she keep staring at me?* he wondered.

After the discussion on servanthood, the strategy session began. "Although we have weapons, albeit now illegally, just as the disciples had two swords, the use of weapons against the Roman garrison must be an absolute last resort. We don't want to kill Roman soldiers and send them to hell. We prefer to win them to Christ and send them to heaven. When he was here with us, Paul taught me that 'though we walk in the flesh, we do not war according to the flesh, for the weapons of our warfare are not of the flesh, but divinely powerful for the destruction of fortresses.' (2 Corinthians 10:3b-4) God's weapons are divinely powerful for the destruction of Roman garrisons. We plot our strategy by His wisdom. We fight our fight by His power. Our God is greater than Satan. God wins. Satan loses. We win. Rome loses. Such is the inevitable outcome if we fight God's way."

"How do we fight God's way?"

"Your question takes us to the crux of our strategy, Valentina."

Valentina? Marinus took another hard look at the young woman while Publius continued to speak.

"We fight by praying for our enemies. We pray for the salvation of their souls. When we pray that way, God warms our hearts toward them. He fills us with wisdom on how to treat them. When we get the chance, we do good to our enemies. If they are hungry, we feed them. If they are thirsty, we give them a drink. If they are wounded, we bind their wounds. If we do those things, they may not respond positively at the time, but we open the door for them to come to us later, perhaps privately, when they come again into distress. That must be our heart attitude at all times. When we are cursed, we bless. 'By forbearance a ruler may be persuaded, and a soft tongue breaks the bone.' (Proverbs 25:15)

"At the same time, we must also be wise. It is one thing to love people. It is another to trust them. We must be careful about what we say among the general, unbelieving populace of our island. If any of us are questioned by interrogators from the Roman garrison, they will tell us that as Christians we must always tell them the truth—not that any of them live by such a standard. They will want the names of the people and the places of the dwellings where we assemble together. They will assure you that they mean no harm to the rest of us. They just need the information. They will offer you favors if you give them the information they seek. Do not trust them. How you refrain from giving out information about the rest of us, the Holy Spirit will teach you at the time. But set it in your hearts now that you will not be Judas's. I was questioned at my home about my father's whereabouts a few days ago. I said I didn't know where he was."

"But isn't lying wrong?"

"Lying is wrong, Phoebe, when we do it to cover our sins, to slander others, or to gain unfair advantage over people. We must never lie to one another. But I have been much studying the Hebrew Scriptures since they were brought here from Jerusalem. I note that the Hebrew midwives lied to protect newly born Hebrew boys from being murdered because they feared God. And God blessed the midwives for doing so.

"I note that later Rahab the harlot of Jericho lied to protect two Hebrew spies from capture and certain death. God blessed her and saved her family from destruction for doing so. Rahab then became a member of the Hebrew nation and a part of the royal line that led from Adam to Christ. Therefore, I lied to protect my father from evil men, who only meant him harm."

For the next thirty minutes the believers discussed other homes to meet in, how large the groups should be, people to avoid, what was to be done about the murder of innocent babies and the aged at the valetudinarium, and covering the trails that led to the cave. After the strategy session ended came a time of prayer that reached an intensity few had ever experienced.

When the time ended, the people began to leave in small groups. Julius went outside to speak with Marcus. Within the cave remained only Trebonius, the other two from Theophilus' house, and Valentina.

At that time Valentina approached Marinus and uttered two simple words. "Hello father."

43

Until Better Times

While his wife Poppaea bathed in her marble tub, Nero continued to serenade her with his lyre. "Why do you bathe every day in milk?" he asked as he strummed the strings.

She smiled her alluring smile and answered with her equally alluring voice. "Because milk has a magic that dispels all diseases and blights to my beauty."

Though dubious of her claim, Nero could not dispute her appearance. She was indeed an object of admiration. "When are you going to bear me another child?"

"That is another reason for my milk baths. We lost our little Claudia Augusta last year because I stopped doing them."

"I want a son this time," he declared in his juvenile manner. "Bear me a son."

She laughed. "I will try. May our beloved goddess Juno favor me."

He laid aside his lyre. "I don't like Domus Transitoria anymore. The acoustics are not right for my immeasurable musical talent."

"You are divinity, my husband. Build your Domus Aurea, your golden house."

"How do I justify to the people so expensive a project, when they think we live too lavishly already?"

"You answer to the gods, Nero Claudius Caesar Augustus Germanicus. You do not answer to the common people."

Nero began to pace the floor back and forth. "Where are Seneca and Burrus when I need them?"

Poppaea rose from the tub and positioned herself on the orange marble spot on the floor that marked the shower. She pulled a cord from the ceiling that brought upon her an immediate cascade of warm water to wash away the milk. After a thorough rinse she released the cord and began to dry herself.

A servant entered the chamber. Seeing Poppaea, he immediately placed himself between emperor and wife, his back turned discretely to the wife. He bowed deeply.

"Your divinity, Prefect Faenius Rufus has come to see you."

"Tell him I will meet him in the grotto. Bring to us each a goblet of wine." The servant bowed and exited.

He sighed. "Duty calls, Poppaea." He turned full circle in the chamber. "Maybe I could justify building my new house if Domus Transitoria no longer existed. After all, an emperor has to live somewhere. Maybe Domus Transitoria will have a fire. Wouldn't that be tragic?"

He made his way down a long portico until he emerged into the grotto, his favorite spot in his not so favorite, mostly underground home. Light shone through the clear glass ceiling above. He breathed in the fragrant air from tropical hibiscus, amaryllis, lilies, bromeliads, begonias, and purple orchids. At the far end of the grotto he observed Faenius admiring the plants.

"Why have you found it necessary to disturb me, Faenius?"

"Forgive me, your divinity. I have received a letter from Gaius Ovidius Bellirus, propraetor for the island of Melitene. In it he says that Trebonius has refused your summons to Rome and is currently in hiding somewhere on the island. He desires your instructions as to what he should do once Trebonius is apprehended."

The servant entered with the two goblets of wine. The first he gave to Nero and the second to Faenius. Nero took a sip of wine from his goblet and set it down before going into his tirade.

"This is treason, Faenius! No one disobeys a summons from my hand! Tell Gaius that I want the head of Trebonius brought to me on a platter!"

"It will be done, divinity."

"It is those Christians!" he fumed. "Has Gaius put them in their place?"

"He says he has closed the amphitheater to them. He has forbidden them to meet in groups greater than five."

"Why are any permitted to meet at all? Why aren't their leaders being arrested?"

"To arrest their leaders, your divinity, Gaius requires a legal excuse. So far, they haven't given him that excuse. It is the same here in Rome."

Nero drank down the entire contents of his goblet and flung it into the far wall. "Oh, where is Seneca or Burrus for a time like this? They always gave me good counsel."

"Unfortunately, princeps, Seneca you had executed. Burrus is gone from this earth from natural causes."

He pounded his right fist into the cup of his left hand three times. "Tell Gaius to find an excuse to arrest the Christian leaders. Any excuse! That is what I intend to do here. I'll have them tied to stakes above the ground. Then I will have boiling pitch, wax, and tallow, poured on them. And then I will personally set them afire to light my gardens at night! I can hear their screams even now! It will be glorious! You are dismissed."

*****

In the dead of night two cloaked figures approached and lightly knocked on the front door.

"Give thanks to the Lord, for He is good," (Psalm 136:1a) called Publius from inside his home.

"For His lovingkindness is everlasting," (Psalm 136:1b) came the answer.

He opened the door to his father Trebonius and to Marcus, who quickly entered.

"Welcome. Come and be seated."

They prayed together.

"Is everything in order?" asked Publius after they had finished praying. "Is the boat in place?"

"It is in place—hidden under brush at the very eastern tip of the bay where Paul landed."

"Then let's go."

The three men silently slipped from the house to begin their two-mile journey. Once outside, none dared speak for fear of discovery. Walking rapidly, they reached their destination in twenty minutes.

Publius removed his cloak and used it to cover a lantern, which he then lit with his flint. The flame flickered up. He lifted the seaward side of his cloak three times in rapid succession. A similar light answered three times from the inky blackness of the sea. Upon the response he quickly doused his lantern. The three men pulled the boat from under the brush and slid it down the short slope into the water. With Trebonius seated at the bow, Publius and Marcus each took an oar and rowed swiftly toward the faint image of the waiting ship. In five minutes, they reached Tantulus II.

Publius helped his father board the ship and then handed to him his sparse belongings. "Good bye, father," he whispered. "Until better times."

"Farewell, my son," he whispered in return. "Until better times. God be with you."

"We must get going," spoke Marinus in low tones. "The sooner we put distance between ourselves and this island, the better."

They parted. Tantulus II turned for Syracuse while the two rowers returned to the shore. Once ashore, Marcus drilled two holes in the bottom of the boat with his hand drill. The two men gave the boat a hard shove back into the sea, where it slowly sank beneath the waters.

* * * * *

For a brief time Trebonius sat in the pilot house with Marinus and his daughter. "Thank you for taking me off the island. I am grateful."

"You are welcome, sir. I know a place in Syracuse where you can stay and assume a new identity. Have you ever done any tentmaking?"

Trebonius laughed. "No."

"Well, they'll find something for you to do. Have you ever been crew for a sailing ship?"

Again, Trebonius laughed. "No."

"We'll, we're all right for this evening, but I may need your help tomorrow morning. It's a big ship and I don't have any crew. The less people who know about your escape, the better."

"I'll do my best. The job of propraetor doesn't usually include tentmaking or sailoring."

Knowing of the situation between father and daughter, he excused himself and went below, leaving them to talk alone. He needed the sleep anyway.

After he was gone Valentina studied the face of her father while he piloted Tantulus II toward Syracuse. He seemed so different from the man she had only known in debauched snatches during her growing up years. She wondered where to begin.

"Father?" It felt good to Valentina to use that word. Even though she had been a grown woman for some time, having a real father still filled a void in her life. "May I call you father?"

"Of course, you may, Valentina. May I call you daughter?"

"Please do. I have a question, father. How do you know where we are going in this darkness?"

"I have the light from Portus Amplus on my stern and the north star ahead of me, daughter. I am sorry we haven't had much chance to talk since you announced yourself to me in the cave."

"Well, father, now we can do some catching up. It certainly helps to know that we are now both followers of Christ."

"Yes, it does." He turned to face her. "I have been maybe the worst father who ever lived. Will you forgive me, Valentina?"

"I forgive you, father. I too have done much that needs forgiveness. I find it hard to forgive myself."

He nodded. "I know what you mean by that. Why are you leaving Melitene?"

She hadn't thought through the reasons, but had only known that it had to be. Now, as she answered, her own jumbled thoughts began to sort themselves out.

"Because I had less reasons to stay and greater reasons to go. To begin with, I was overseeing the women at Ille Perfugium until the new propraetor closed us down in favor of his new entertainment house. An old woman named Gratiana was a dear friend to me, but she is now gone from this world. There are people on Melitene who have been looking for a way to kill me after I exposed them. I also wanted to get away from my old life. Everywhere I went on Melitene, I saw men who reminded me of my past. I don't want to remember that past.

"What I want is to find my family again, starting with renewing my relationship with you. I have prayed much for my mother. I know in my heart that she is overcome with remorse about selling me, even though she felt at the time that it was the only way to feed my younger brothers and sisters. I want her to know Christ's forgiveness, just as we have come to know it. I want my brothers and sisters to know about Him too."

"What do you know about the rest of our family?"

"I have not heard from my mother or any of my siblings since she sold me into sex slavery some ten years ago. We were living in Catania. I can find our house—or what might now be our former house there. That is the place to start."

He eyed her anxiously. "Could we look together? If we can find them, and if I can win again your mother's heart, then I intend to become for the first time a real husband. I will sell my ship. I will find a land job and be the man God created me to be." He shook his head sadly. "I guess all of my children are grown now, with lives of their own—if even they still live."

"The youngest, Mercurius, would be eighteen years old now."

"We will search for them, Valentina. But first things first. Once we get to Syracuse, I have a man to deliver to the church house there. I imagine Trebonius will want to grow a full beard and to assume a new name."

He shook his head sadly. "It would be nice if we humans weren't so greedy, so devious, and so selfish. We sure know how to make a mess of our lives—and of the world we live in."

"That we do," she agreed. "But Christ has a way of fixing all that, if only we will give our hearts to Him."

She clung hard to her father as he piloted the ship northward. Both wept.

44

An Issue of Blood

Faenius Rufus shook his head sadly as he and Nero surveyed the smoldering ruins of Rome from Palatine Hill. "Why did you sing 'The Sack of Ilium' in stage costume before the citizenry while Rome burned?" he asked the emperor.

"I wanted to inspire the firefighters to greater efforts and to comfort the citizenry at the same time," answered Nero childishly. "There is always a method to what others equate to my madness."

"Some of the people think that you set this fire deliberately to find an excuse to build your Domus Aurea."

"Is that what some think? What do you think Faenius?"

Faenius trembled inwardly, knowing that a wrong answer might cost him his life. "It is not for me to say, divinity. All I know is that the fire began at the southeastern end of the Circus Maximus. I did not see who might have set it. I do not possess an all-seeing eye."

"But I do possess such an eye," proclaimed Nero. "And I will tell you now who did this treachery. It was the Christians! And now we have our excuse to obliterate them. I understand that Paul has returned to Rome?"

"He has from what I understand, but finding him may be difficult."

"Why was he released in the first place?"

"He was released by order of Magistratus Amadeus Galbus Egnatius for lack of charges. Since no one appeared to charge him in the two years he was imprisoned here, there could be no crime."

"Well, there are at least two crimes now. The first is treason! He forbids his followers to worship me. The second is arson. He either set the fire himself or instigated others to do it. Either way he is guilty. I want him found and arrested, Faenius. Immediately! And this time no house arrest. I want him confined at the Mamertine Carcer until I decide his fate. I want the other Christians rounded up. I want them either thrown to the lions at the Circus Maximus, crucified, or made into torches to light our streets at night! They are a scourge to our society!"

"It will be as you say, divinity."

* * * * *

Amoenitas, Flavia, and Angelina sat across from each other in Amoenitas' home making new winter tunics for their husbands from a pattern Flavia had designed. From Publius' sheep Amoenitas, Cornelia, and Herminia had spun woolen fiber from their distaffs. Flavia had taken the fiber and created material for garments on her loom, from which she had cut her pattern. Together Amoenitas and Flavia were teaching the art of garment making to Angelina.

The three women had become fast friends. It would have been four, but Eletia was tasked with taking care of little Julia, feeding the chickens and the goats, and preparing meals for the men who were harvesting their fall crops of wheat and rye, which included all of their husbands.

While the women worked, they spoke of stories from Luke's gospel. "Why didn't the priest and the Levite help the man who had been beaten by thieves?" asked Amoenitas. "He was probably a fellow Jew."

"I guess maybe they were busy with their lives and didn't want to be bothered with a disruption," answered Flavia.

"But then a Samaritan stopped and helped him," spoke Amoenitas. "He probably saved the man's life. But from what I understand, Jews and Samaritans hated each other. Why would a Samaritan save the life of a man who was his enemy?"

"Maybe the Samaritan was God-fearing," said Angelina. "Maybe he realized that they were fellow human beings, created by the same God above. It is the Christian way to love what some might consider unlovely."

A knock came to the door. Amoenitas rose to answer. Before opening, she called through the door. "Who is there?"

"It is Lucilia," domina.

"Lucilia? Why have you come?"

"Please, Amoenitas. Help me!"

The sound of a body collapsing on the porch hastened Amoenitas to open the door. There before her lay the last of Publius' accusers. Her eyes were glassy. The front part of her garment was soiled from bleeding.

"Ladies, come and help me," called Amoenitas. Immediately, the other two women came to the front door. Both gasped at what they saw. "We'll carry her inside and lay her on the bed in our extra bedroom."

The task of carrying the young woman proved easier than expected, for Lucilia was emaciated, either from lack of food and water, or from whatever infirmity plagued her—or possibly from all three. Once she was upon the bed, Amoenitas filled a pitcher of water from the pump in the kitchen. She filled a cup and brought both into the bedroom. The other two women propped Lucilia to a sitting position while Amoenitas held the cup to her mouth.

"Drink, Lucilia. Your body needs water, but drink slowly."

She filled the cup again after it was downed. Lucilia emptied the second cup. Her spirit partially revived, she spoke. "Thank you. I knew you would help me."

"You have given us a chance to be good Samaritans," answered Amoenitas. "I will get you some food."

Five minutes later she returned to the bedroom with bread, already cooked chicken, and an orange. "Eat slowly, Lucilia. Eat slowly, or your body will reject the food."

As she ate Amoenitas questioned her. "We haven't seen you since that day in the peristylium at the villa. Where have you been?"

"Out of sight as much as possible," she answered. "Octavia fell from the top of Scopulus Altus—probably helped. I knew that I would be next if Alacerius could find me. I didn't think the Christians wanted me. I just stayed out of sight."

"How have you lived these past few months?"

"As you see. I have slept in bushes. I have lived on trash others have thrown away. And then I started bleeding."

When she had finished eating Amoenitas had her lie down again. With a scissors she cut away Lucilia's entire outer garment, which was hopelessly soiled and threadbare anyway. From where the blood had come out, it was obvious that she had an internal issue. Amoenitas' mind flashed to the woman who had been hemorrhaging in Luke's story.

Dear God, I thought at the time that I had nothing to help such a woman. And now You bring one to me?

"Flavia? Would you please get some water boiling in the kitchen? We need to clean Lucilia up. She rose to retrieve some clean clothes from her bedroom. But beyond food and water, cleaning her up on the outside, and putting her in clean clothes, she had no idea how to help the poor distressed woman with her bleeding problem. *If only Gratiana were here.* Silently, she prayed.

When she returned to the guest bedroom, she found Angelina kneeling by the side of the bed, her right hand upon Lucilia's abdomen and her left upon her forehead. "Lord Jesus," she spoke. "You healed people when You were here on this earth. I saw You use Paul to give sight to my blind sister Caecitas. Through Your power Paul bestowed upon me the gift of healing, which I now attempt to use for the first time. I proclaim healing for this poor woman, just like You healed the bleeding woman in Luke's story. Please do it again for this woman, Lord Jesus. I ask in Your wonderful, powerful name. Amen."

From her inner being Angelina felt power flowing from her into Lucilia. Before her eyes the color of Lucilia's skin began to turn from a chalky gray to a healthy glow. Her eyes brightened.

"What is happening?" she asked wondrously. "I feel better!" She lay still, allowing the process to play out to its fullest.

All the while Amoenitas looked on amazed. "Praise the Lord!" was all she knew to say.

A few minutes later Flavia announced that the water was hot. Amoenitas took clean cloths and soaked them in the water. She wrung them out partially, nearly scalding her hands in the process. Upon bringing them into the bedroom, the three women went to work on cleaning up Lucilia. After finishing the job, they allowed her to sleep.

Two hours later Lucilia sat at the table in the kitchen, partaking of the noonday meal with the three other women. She had on a much newer garment that Amoenitas had given her.

"I am amazed that you all have been so kind to me, despite what I said about Publius and the church."

"We are kind to you because God has been kind to us," answered Flavia. "It is the way of our faith."

"And now we must figure out how to keep you hidden, but provided for," spoke Amoenitas. "Alacerius is still out there, wanting his revenge."

*****

Alexandra looked down with disdain at the stricken man writhing in agony upon his bed. Gaunt and with the pallor of death upon his face, Alacerius was a pitiful contrast to his once handsome, powerful, dynamic personage.

"Water! Give me some water," he piteously moaned.

Alexandra remained in place; her expression unmoved. "You are going to die anyway. What good will water do you?"

He glowered at her in helpless hatred. Terrifying voices from malevolent spirits taunted him. Dread fear of the darkness of death and of torment beyond permeated his thoughts.

He gasped for breath. "I don't want to die!" he shrieked. "I don't want to die!"

Darkness closed in upon him. His voice faded. The sensation of his inner systems shutting down enveloped him. He gasped for breath until the ability failed. He felt himself hurtling through darkness—terrified of his fate.

"At last he is gone," spoke Alexandra with great relief.

"And now you can return to your former home, this time to be with a real man."

Arm in arm, Gaius and Alexandra boarded the carriage that would take them from the hospital to the villa.

45

Acting Elder

At the end of the day, a beet red Marcus collapsed into his favorite chair, which immediately brought searing pain to his back. Eletia fetched him a cup of water from the kitchen pump and went out to the garden for some aloe.

During the fall harvest all hands, including his and Julius', were needed to bring in the crops of wheat and rye. He much preferred work at the school, where there was abundant shade during the hottest parts of the year, but like Rufus, he had lost his job under the new island regime. Other repair and construction jobs had to be postponed while the harvest was brought in.

Within two minutes Eletia returned with several large snips from the aloe plants in her garden. With a rolling pin upon her cutting board she squeezed paste from the stems, which she then applied to his back. Immediately, the paste brought soothing relief.

Too bad about my proposal, he thought, as Eletia administered more aloe paste to his neck and face. He had envisioned himself approaching the school administration with a new class concept, that of teaching some of the students the practical skills of construction work. Philosophy and rhetoric were fine, but they didn't create buildings, build ox carts, or produce food. He had a practical mind. *Maybe someday I'll be able to put my idea to work.*

"If you are going to work the field tomorrow, you must keep your shirt on," she admonished him.

"It's too hot for a shirt," he protested.

"Wear it anyway," she ordered. "I can't afford to care for a stubborn, skin blistered husband and a constantly demanding daughter, while being sick myself most of the time, particularly in the morning."

Marcus' ears perked up. "Sick most of the time, particularly in the morning?"

Eletia smiled. "Yes, Marcus. I am pregnant."

*****

"What are the charges, Primi Ordine?" protested Publius.

"Treason against Rome and harboring a fugitive," answered the centurion. "Do you come with us peaceably, or must we do this the hard way?"

"I go peaceably, but may I have ten minutes to pack some things to take with me and to say goodbye to my family?"

The centurion gestured to his soldiers. "Surround the house." He addressed Publius. "You have ten minutes. Do not try to escape. Do not try any treachery."

"No escape, no treachery. It will be as you say." He knew that at the present time, neither attempted escape nor resistance would yield a good result. He retreated back into his house, his mind in a quandary. *What do I take? Amoenitas will know better than I.*

While baby Trebonius wailed for his needs, oblivious of the trauma taking place around him, Amoenitas retrieved a large leather sack. At the bottom she placed a change of clothes and the cloak she had made for him. She gathered some foodstuffs and soap from the pantry. Publius selected several scrolls from Luke's histories of Christ and the early church. He fetched a stylus, ink, and a large roll of unused parchment. He gathered several candles and a flint. Amoenitas filled three large containers with water.

When all had been placed into the bag, he retrieved his wailing son from his cunae. Immediately his crying stopped. He placed Trebonius into his wife's arms before surrounding both with a hug.

"I knew this day would come, Amoenitas. All will be well. Our God is in control."

They prayed a tearful prayer. Publius kissed his wife. Slinging the bag over his back, he walked out the front door in submission to his fate.

Standing in the doorway of their house, Amoenitas watched and wept as they took her husband away.

* * * * *

The cave where Trebonius had been hidden had never been discovered by the island regime. Hence it could still function as a meeting place for the dwindling number of faithful leaders of the church not yet imprisoned. Late that night an assemblage of twenty gathered. Missing among the leaders was only Phoebe, who had been given the task of caring for the babies of the young mothers.

"Publius, Theophilus, and Rufus are now in prison," spoke Marcus. "I was able to visit them all earlier today. Publius is doing as well as can be expected under the circumstances. They keep him isolated from the others. He has asked me to take over the leadership of the church while the other leaders are absent. I feel totally inadequate for this task, but I will not shrink from it. Our God will always make up the difference."

He rolled out a scroll, placed it on a blanket covering the dirt floor of the cave, and weighted each corner. "I found a passage in Luke's account of the history of our church that I think is appropriate for the situation we find ourselves in at this time."

"So Peter was kept in prison, but prayer for him was being made fervently by the church to God…." (Acts 12:5) He continued reading to the end of the story. "But motioning to them with his hand to be silent, he described to them how the Lord had led him out of the prison." (Acts 12:17a)

"So Peter was imprisoned, the church prayed for him, and an angel got him out of the prison. He went to the mother of John's house where they were praying for his release, but then they didn't believe that God had really answered their prayer?" asked Marceles.

"That's what it looks like to me—not until they actually saw him," answered Marcus.

"Isn't that kind of like us?" spoke Doctor Corbus.

Marcus nodded. "It is like us. What do you all think we should do about these imprisonments? I think it would be difficult for us to successfully storm the place."

"We ought to do what they did in Jerusalem," answered Amoenitas. "We must pray for their release, even if we have doubts that God will actually do it."

"Then let's do just that," spoke Marcus.

For over an hour the saints of God prayed fervently for the release of all those imprisoned for their faith. Increasingly, the prayers gained in intensity until at last they stopped, somehow with the assurance that God would do as they had asked. It was only a question of how and when?

*****

Finally, the much-needed horses arrived on two Roman quinquiremae. For Gaius it meant two things. Now a number of his soldiers could rapidly move from one end of the island to the other, making it easier to surprise and to stamp out wayward Christian activity.

The other was that he was at last reunited with his great stallion Validus. More than once he had been told how majestic he looked upon the back of his horse. Giddy with excitement, he mounted Validus for the first time in nearly six months.

46

Two Prisoners, One God

The warm fall morning was calm and pleasant, in marked contrast to what Amoenitas knew she was about to experience. After tying Castanea to a post in front of the prison, she entered the building. The irony of the situation was not lost upon her. *Publius twice visited me in this prison more than three years ago. Now I visit him.*

Upon entering with her bag of supplies, she found an overweight duty publicus asleep behind his table. "Sir," she called. He did not stir. She repeated her address more loudly. Still he did not stir. She placed her left hand upon his right shoulder and jostled him. Finally, he awakened, only to erupt in anger.

"How dare you place your hand upon me!"

"I am sorry, sir. There seemed no other way to awaken you."

"What do you want?"

"It took months of petitioning, but I have finally been granted permission to visit my husband, the prisoner Publius Fabianus."

"What makes you think he wants to see you?"

Ignoring the caustic remark, she handed him the document, signed and sealed by the propraetor.

"I will have to examine the contents of your bag."

As he went through the contents, he helped himself to some bread and cheese before calling to a guard down the hallway. "Artemus, escort this woman to the cell of Publius Fabianus."

The guard came to the front of the hallway and gestured to Amoenitas. "Follow me, please."

The same unpleasantly familiar smells of mildew, vomit, urine, and excrement affronted her as she made her way down the hallway. The temperature noticeably dropped. She donned her cloak. When they came to his cell, the guard opened the door to loudly protesting hinges. "You have one hour," he spoke before closing the door behind her. A single candle illuminated the cell. She embraced her husband.

"Oh Amoenitas!" Publius wept. Her pleasant scent overwhelmed him. "I am so glad to hold you in my arms."

"And I you," she returned. She refrained from making mention of his now not so broad shoulders. "I brought you some food and water, some more candles, and some different Scriptures to read. I am sorry about the meager food. The duty publicus took some of it."

"I am glad for anything," he answered gratefully.

The two sat on the thin mat that served as Publius' bed. He resumed speaking to her in a low whisper. "We must keep our voices down. The sound travels up to the window. They are probably listening to us outside, trying to get information on where to find those of us who continue to meet secretly. That is likely the only reason Gaius granted your request to visit me."

"Our second child is born," she whispered back. "We have a little girl. I named her Mariana, after the mother of Jesus, not after the girl we had at Ille Perfugium. She has your fingers and toes. And her smile! I love her!"

"I can't wait to see her. Who is watching her and little Trebonius right now?"

"Eletia, at her house."

She looked hard into the dimly lit, gaunt face of her husband. "We are fewer, but more fervent. We have prayed. God is about to do something. We all know it."

"I also have that assurance in me. I don't know what or when, but He will act."

The two prayed together for what seemed mere minutes before the guard returned to announce that their visit was over. No second visit had been authorized.

*****

"I have to examine the contents before I can allow you to give this bag to the prisoner," intoned the duty publicus at the Mamertine Carcer. "Sometimes visitors try to smuggle in weapons." He rifled through the contents, which consisted of oranges, olives, fresh baked bread, dried mutton and chicken, a blanket, and a letter. He appropriated one of the oranges before handing the bag back to the visitor. "Follow me."

He led the visitor down the long corridor. Behind one of the cell doors the visitor could hear a man wailing piteously. "Let me out! I have done no wrong. Let me out!" The guard continued walking, impervious to his cries. At the end of the corridor he turned to his left. At the third cell on the right he inserted his key into the lock. The door swung open.

"You have one hour," he informed the visitor.

"Thank you."

The door closed behind him as he entered the cell. It was about eight by eight feet in area, with a tall ceiling. High above him on the opposite side was a single, uncovered window to the outside that allowed in fresh air and a measure of light, but also an abundance of late fall cold. On the right side was a dilapidated desk, upon which was flattened parchment scroll with writing on it, a burning candle, a stylus, and an inkwell. A thin mat lay by the left wall.

But it was the occupant who shocked the visitor. He was stooped, haggard, and much thinned from lack of adequate food. He was chained by the right ankle to a heavy iron ball and appeared to be shivering. *Why the ball and chain?* he thought. *He can't go anywhere.*

The two embraced. "Doctor Luke, my old, faithful friend. I am so glad to see you."

"And I am glad to see you, Paul. How are you feeling?"

"I suppose about as bad as I must look. In my old age and in this cold, I can feel all of the beatings I have received over the years. My body indeed groans, eagerly awaiting its adoption as a son."

"Maybe not like yours, but my body groans too, my brother. Oh, to be young again in the new bodies that await us."

He opened the bag he had brought with him. From the bottom he pulled the blanket and wrapped it around Paul. "I just heard that you had been imprisoned, right after I returned from Neapolis. The church there needed Scriptures and encouragement. How did they get you this time?"

Paul shook his head sadly. "Someone, I suspect Demas, betrayed me, probably for a substantial sum of money. He is gone now to Thessalonica, having loved this present world." He began to weep. "I invested so much of my life into him."

Luke glanced at the desk. "What are you writing now? And why are your letters so big?"

Paul shrugged. "My hand shakes too much to write small. Also, my eyes are failing and I have to write big so I can see what I have written or I'll lose my place. The letter is to my dear friend Timothy in Ephesus. Remember him? I pray that my words will encourage him to fulfill his calling."

He again wept. "I think this letter will be the last thing I ever write. It is almost finished. Will you return tomorrow and take it with you, to send through the postal system? I have no one left to personally take it to him. I pray that he will get it."

"I will. How did your court hearing go?"

"Not well. No one came to speak on my behalf. Most of the stalwarts such as Crescens and Titus are off ministering in other places. Many of those who remain in Rome, such as Dominic and Aristarchus are in prison themselves, probably in this carcer. The guards won't tell me anything. Those still free, I suppose, are too afraid to support me, for fear of losing their freedom. But I proclaimed loudly the gospel of God. I know that some heard.

"Alexander the coppersmith, do you remember him? He did me much harm. He made up slanderous stories about sexual escapades and drunken parties I supposedly arranged during the time I was under house arrest near the Temple Beth Shalom. The iudices believed him—or more likely they were too afraid not to believe him. I was found guilty."

"Have you been sentenced?"

"Not yet. But Nero won't hesitate to give me a thumbs down when I appear before him. No matter. I will again boldly proclaim the truth of salvation only through Christ Jesus. Then I will either die by his hand or God will take me first. Either way, I will soon be with Christ, which is very much better."

Luke pulled the letter from his bag. "I have a letter here from Marcus on the island of Melitene. He sent it to me because he had no idea where you might be. Since your eyes are failing, shall I read it to you?"

"Please."

Marcus the unworthy to Paul, my esteemed father in the faith, greetings.

You will be happy to know that I was able to deliver Luke's story of the church to Theophilus and to Publius here on Melitene, as directed. I gave the other copy to the church in Syracuse. I am now married to Eletia. We have a daughter named Julia and another child on the way. Eletia is very much the joy of my life. She shines with the love of Jesus.

We are having a hard time here. The new propraetor Gaius is determined to destroy all traces of Christian faith on our island. Publius, Theophilus, and Rufus are all in prison. If you can imagine it, I am now the shepherd of what is left of our church that remains free. We meet secretly in different places to pray and to read the Scriptures. We have come to a place where we believe that God is about to do a great thing on our island. What that great thing will be, we have no idea.

We pray that you are well. We understand that the situation for Christians is as hard or harder for those of you in Rome, as it is here. Perhaps we will never again meet upon this earth. If not, then we here on Melitene will see you in heaven. Farewell.

"We must pray for them, Luke. We must pray for them and for Timothy. We must pray for the church in Syracuse. Will you join me?"

For the remaining time the men prayed, until the prison door opened and the guard instructed Luke to leave. Nevertheless, both parted encouraged, each by the other's faith.

47

Mystery Patient

Myriad question marks filled Doctor Corbus' mind as he proceeded to the valetudinarium shortly after his midday meal. *Why do they so urgently need me now?* He had been dismissed from the hospital nearly a year before. Though the reason had never been given, he knew that his Christian faith had factored heavily in the decision.

He passed the bare-chested statue of Asclepius as he neared the entrance. It had been removed during the time Paul was on the island and restored under Gaius. He hated the statue, but now was not the time to deal with it.

At the entrance he came upon an anxious looking centurion, who greeted him tersely. "Follow me." He followed the centurion, uncomfortably upping his pace to keep up. They turned left at the reception desk and entered the long hallway. At the end of the hallway to the right they came to the solitudo, the quarantine room, where few ventured. The suspense of who might be on the other side of the door reached its pinnacle.

Upon entering, he encountered a man lying flat on his back on a high bed, motionless. "Sir, Doctor Corbus has come," the centurion informed the patient.

The patient remained motionless, but spoke. "Doctor Corbus, I am so glad to see you."

"Propraetor Gaius? Doctor Corbus moved to the far side of the bed and leaned over the stricken man in order to make eye contact. Immediately, his mind went to one thing. A few simple questions would confirm his suspicion.

"Can you move your feet?"

"No," came the reply.

"Can you move your hands?"

"Yes, but with great difficulty. I can turn my head, but only with excruciating pain."

"How are you breathing?"

"With great difficulty."

He took a small hammer from the medical tray and administered three light taps to each shin. "Can you feel any of this?

"No."

"Are you able to control your bowl and bladder?"

"No."

"How did this happen?"

"I fell from my horse this morning. I was riding through the brush at nearly full speed. Neither I nor my horse saw the ditch behind a large bush. I was thrown forward and landed on my head. The next thing I remember is waking up in here."

Doctor Corbus' face was grim. "You either have a fracture in the lower part of your neck, or a bad bruise. Allow me to feel the back part of your neck."

Gently, he felt along the vertebrae of his neck with his right hand. While he did so, Gaius winced in sharp pain. He finished his probing and gave the propraetor the grim news.

"I can feel the separations in the lower part of your neck. You have at least two fractures. Your condition is permanent. There are no known medical cures. You may get some use of your hands and arms with time, but you will not get your legs back."

Gaius took the news stoically—at least outwardly. "I was afraid you might say something like that. What do you recommend for me?"

"There isn't much anyone can do right now. We can arrange for someone to feed you, to give you drink, and to keep you clean. We can wait to see how much your upper body condition improves. I can promise you nothing."

Doctor Corbus removed the sheet covering Gaius and searched for other wounds. He found several cuts and abrasions. He felt up the legs and then the arms for other breakages and found none. "It doesn't appear that you have any other major injuries. I can treat the cuts and abrasions. They will heal."

"Fine. Everything will heal except that I will be paralyzed from the waist down for the rest of my life, which may not be much longer. I would rather die than live paralyzed."

"There are ways to adjust," answered Doctor Corbus. While he went to work on cleaning the cuts and abrasions, another possibility quietly entered his mind. "There is another option."

Gaius' eyes brightened. "What other option?"

"I know a couple of healing women on this island, but they are Christians, as am I."

"What can they do that you cannot?"

"Gaius? May I call you Gaius?"

"Sure."

"I was summarily dismissed from this hospital shortly after you arrived, I suspect because of my Christian faith. Was that the reason?"

"Yes. I am charged by the emperor himself to obliterate all traces of Christianity from this island."

"Thank you for your honesty. I am sure you are aware that you can dismiss people from positions. You can forbid people from assembling. You can close an amphitheater. You can imprison or even kill Christians for their faith. But you cannot eradicate the Christian faith. I belong to Christ. He has transformed my life. I have a step-daughter named Laelia, who was near death from island fever. She was healed in the name of Christ. Many others on this island were also healed of island fever. The two women I speak of possess the power to heal, but only in the name of Christ. Do you wish to see them?"

For long moments Gaius lay deep in thought. "Have them come," he finally responded, "but don't tell them why. Have them come at night—secretly. If they can truly heal me, then they will be greatly rewarded. If they cannot…"

"Sir. If you say what I think you are about to say, then I will not ask the women to come. You must give me your word that they come in safety and may leave in safety, no matter the result. I cannot give you any guarantee of healing and they must not be punished if healing fails to occur. You'll be no worse off than you are now. I will try to bring them at night, but they have the right to know beforehand the reason for my bringing them. There are a couple of things you must understand. The power does not come from the women. It goes through them, but the power comes from Christ, who is the King of kings and the Lord of lords. Secondly, there has to be an element of faith on your part. You must believe that you can be healed through the power of Christ."

"Bring them," he said decisively. "I give you my word. No harm will befall them if I am not healed."

Doctor Corbus nodded. "I do not know their plans. If it is possible, I will try to bring them tonight."

*****

Toward the hospital the three road, Doctor Corbus on Bellator, Amoenitas on Castanea, and Angelina on a borrowed horse from Marcellus named Ovid. For Amoenitas, her mind was in turmoil. She and Angelina were being asked to heal the man who had put her husband into prison, among many other things he had done in his attempt to eradicate the church. Yet she knew her oath, to do her best to heal anyone who needed help. She also knew her Christian faith.

But she wondered what she personally could do. She had her bag of medical tools and supplies with her, but wondered what good any of that would do, given Doctor Corbus' grim diagnosis of Gaius' problem. Angelina had less knowledge of herbal remedies and less experience with situations like broken bones, but she had demonstrated a definite spiritual gift of healing, of which Amoenitas knew little. Perhaps their combined efforts, along with Doctor Corbus' knowledge and expertise would be enough. Silently she prayed.

They came to the wooden railing in front of the hospital and secured their horses. A different centurion was waiting for them out front. He briskly led them to the solitudo. For the time being, the less people who knew about Gaius' condition, the better.

"Gaius," spoke Doctor Corbus as they entered the room. "The two healing women are here." He pointed to Amoenitas. "This is Amoenitas, who has worked with me before. I have great respect for her abilities." He pointed to Angelina. "This is Angelina, whom I do not know as well. But Amoenitas tells me that she has a great gift of healing."

Unable to nod without great pain, he welcomed them only with words. "I am glad you have come. Can you help me?"

"We come in the name of Jesus Christ, our Lord and Savior," spoke Amoenitas. "If you wish to be healed, it is to His Name that you must look. We are only humble instruments in His hands."

Gaius' tone was humble. "I must confess to a degree of skepticism, ladies, but also to a great desire to be healed. Would you be willing to ask Him to help me with my unbelief?"

"We would," answered Amoenitas. She gestured to Angelina. "Would you pray for this man?"

"Gladly." With her left hand she felt the vertebrae behind his neck. Her touch brought reassurance to Gaius, as opposed to the pain of Doctor Corbus' examination. "There is definitely at least one fracture," she announced.

She gently rubbed anointing oil on his forehead and then clasped his right hand between both of hers. Immediately, all the tension within Gaius dissolved, replaced by a sense of comfort. Anticipation flowed into his being. She reached her left hand under his neck, while her right hand continued to clasp his right.

"Lord Jesus," she prayed. "I claim Your healing for this man Gaius. May Your Spirit of healing flow into his body. Heal the broken vertebrae in his neck and realign them back into their proper positions. May he be returned again to perfect health through the power of Your name, the name that is above all names, Jesus Christ, the King of kings and Lord of lords. Amen."

She continued to hold her hands in their positions. Surging from both he felt a strong pulse of wellness and healing, flowing throughout his entire body. He moved his feet. In his mind he knew that he was healed.

"In the name of Jesus Christ of Nazareth, rise up Gaius," she proclaimed.

From his bed he propped himself up by his forearms. He placed his hands upon the bed and sat to a full upright position. He moved his legs to the right side of the bed. Dangling over the floor, he gently swung them back and forth.

"They move!" he proclaimed joyfully. He turned his head in both directions. No pain and complete freedom of movement. He gingerly placed his feet upon the floor. The centurion sprang to his side, just in case. His hands left the bed. Tentatively he placed the entire weight of his body on his feet. He took one step and then another.

"I can walk!" Involuntary tears of delight poured from him. He walked full circle around his bed. "I can walk! I have my life back!"

He turned to the women. "Thank you! Thank you! How can I repay you?"

The answer from Amoenitas was quick in coming. "You can release my husband Publius from prison. You can release Theophilus too—and all the others you have imprisoned for the 'crime' of being Christians. You can restore Rufus and Marcus to their jobs at the school. You can restore Ille Perfugium to its intended purpose of helping women trapped in sexual slavery to reclaim their lives, just as yours has been reclaimed. You can allow God's people to assemble openly, without interference."

Gaius turned to the centurion. "Adolphus, I want you to ride to the carcer and inform the chief jailer that all men and women imprisoned for the 'crime' of being Christians are to be released immediately. Tell him that he is so ordered by Propraetor Gaius Ovidius Bellirus. I will furnish the written order to him within an hour. But tell him that if he values his position, he will not wait for the written order to carry out my instruction."

The centurion gave him an upraised salute. "I am much glad that you are healed, sir. It will be as you have ordered." He disappeared behind the door.

In the privacy of the solitudo Gaius turned again to the three physicians. "I would know more about this Christ whom you serve, who makes people well."

48

The Uncertain Future

The sound of a rooster, a sound he had not heard in nearly a year, awakened Publius while it was still dark the next morning. He felt to his side for Amoenitas, hoping to snuggle closely with her. She was already up and about her day, most likely preparing a meal for him. He rose from his bed and made his way out to find her. His walk was unsteady. It would take time the recover his weight and his strength, but at least he was clean, a luxury that had not been afforded him all the time he was in the carcer.

Neither child had yet stirred. Upon seeing her husband in the kitchen, Amoenitas immediately dropped her meal preparation in favor of a long squeeze. For Publius her smell was dizzying and her embrace comforting. Suddenly lightheaded, he found a chair, put his head down, and closed his eyes.

"This morning I thought we would start with food for you first, just this once," she declared. He easily acquiesced.

"I feel like I have risen from the dead," he proclaimed while they ate together in the quiet darkness. He marveled at how quickly she had gotten back her shape after the birth of their second child.

After the meal he felt better. For Scripture reading he chose Luke's account of Jesus' resurrection to read to Amoenitas. "I knew there would come a time for my freedom and that of our fellow worshippers of Christ. Yet when it happened, I was like those women in the story. I could hardly believe the good news."

"I feel just the same way," she answered. "I only wonder now if Gaius will fulfill the rest of his promise."

"We will see. Just like myself, the other people who were imprisoned will need some time to recover. But as soon as possible, I would like to call a meeting here in our home with all the leaders. Perhaps by then we will know where we stand with Gaius Ovidius Bellirus. I intend to ask for a personal audience with him in the next day or two."

The two prayed together with a calm assurance. If God could do what He had already done, then surely, He could do the rest.

*****

"You did what?" scowled Alexandra.

"I released all the Christians from the prison."

"Why? We had almost gotten our island back to normal. I was hoping you would put them all to death."

Gaius sighed. "You're talking about your son. And I was hoping you would demonstrate a little gladness that I was back on my feet. Does that not count for something?"

"Not at the price you paid for it! And I have no son!"

At that moment Gaius knew that his relationship with Alexandra was over. Inwardly, he rejoiced. *How could I ever have wanted this awful woman?*

"I will pack my things and be gone on the first ship to Puteoli—and then on to Rome. Nero will hear of your treachery!"

She stormed from his sight. His joy at her departure was suddenly tempered by the realization that his career in government would soon be forfeit, if not his life.

*****

The distant bell was tolling the tenth hour as Gaius' carriage pulled up before Publius' house. Publius and Amoenitas immediately went out their front door to greet the propraetor.

"Welcome to our home! It was so considerate of you to come to us, rather than making me go to you."

"You were greatly wronged, Publius—and are much weakened from your imprisonment. I felt that this was the least I could do to repay you and your wonderful wife Amoenitas."

He turned to the carriage driver and his escorts. "I won't be more than fifteen minutes. Please wait where you are."

They entered the house. In the great room the two men sat while Amoenitas scurried into the kitchen. A moment later she emerged with spira treats for the two men and for the five who waited outside.

"Thank you," spoke Gaius. "You are very considerate, Amoenitas."

He turned to the matter at hand. "I walk a fine line, Publius. Nominally, I am still at war with Christ and the church here. Such is my assignment from Nero. But I am whole again, thanks to the power of Christ and the love of His people."

"So which side do you choose, sir?"

Gaius shook his head sadly. "It is complicated. For now, I must at least appear to choose Nero. On the one hand, I will pay lip service to the emperor. My stance will appear as before. On the other hand, I have released the prisoners. I have seen to it that Rufus and Marcus have been restored to their positions. As you know, Alacerius is no longer a factor on this island. I have instructed those who now run and those who live at what you called Ille Perfugium to leave by tomorrow. Your people may again do with it as they wish. Neither will I interfere with your gatherings, as long as they aren't too obvious. By obvious, I mean that I cannot allow you to gather again at the amphitheater."

"I understand your reasons," replied Publius. "I am beginning to think that it wasn't such a good idea for us to meet there anyway."

"Your mother Alexandra has departed for Rome. It will take some time for her to get there and to complain about me before Nero. It will take more time for Nero to bring his response here to Melitene. But it will come. If I were to openly go to your side, I would not only be a dead man, but I would be replaced by someone who will again make life miserable for you and the church. It may be that Nero will allow me to remain in place if I keep up appearances."

Silently, Publius prayed for wisdom in his response. "Very well, Gaius. I hear what you are saying. Yet God has done a great miracle in your life. If He could heal you of an injury that would have left you paralyzed for the rest of your life, do you not think He could preserve you, no matter what others might do?"

"You mean like with your father Trebonius?"

"Well, yes."

"I won't be looking too hard for him either."

Publius laughed. "I can tell you this much. You will not find him here on Melitene."

He changed the subject. "God has done a miracle for you. Amoenitas told me that you wanted to know more about Christ. I would be happy to meet privately with you once a week to help you get to know Him."

"How can I know someone I cannot see?"

"It is the mystery of faith. Those who truly seek God will find Him."

He nodded in partial understanding. "Then please. Let us meet."

*****

The two sat together for the midday meal at one of the stone tables under the shade of a large sycamore tree. "How does it feel to be back teaching at the school?" asked Marcus.

"Most of the students were glad to see me," answered Rufus. "I was glad to see them. It feels good to teach again. How long this will last, I don't know. How was it for you this morning?"

Marcus could barely contain himself. "Do you remember my proposal to teach a class on building?"

"Yes."

He pointed to the northwest corner of the school property that backed up to the amphitheater on the other side of the high wall. "It is approved. Tomorrow I will receive a group of students who are less inclined to academic rigors and more inclined to work with their hands. Together we will commence the construction of the Caepio Building in that corner. When it is finished, it will become a classroom for practical skills like construction, furniture making, and handcrafts like basket weaving or clothes making. I will bring in some women like Herminia from Ille Perfugium to teach clothes making. But first things first. This afternoon I will start to move tools and materials there. It has been my dream ever since I began working here."

Rufus nodded, but was skeptical. "How are you going to build such a building with a bunch of beginners?"

"I will teach them. It will go slow, but there is no rush. Some of the kids may already have some experience from projects at their homes. I intend to do as little of the actual construction work as possible and only coach the kids on how to do it. It will be for them a matter of pride. It's a great deal for the school too. They will get paid tuition for the kids to build them a building."

"What about you? Does this also mean a raise in your pay?"

Marcus laughed. "Probably. Eletia won't mind. We are about to have child number two."

"I only hope," spoke Rufus seriously, "that this will last. I am out of prison. We have our jobs back. You have your dream job. Life is easier for now on our church. But how long will this last? Nero still doesn't like us."

* * * * *

As Eletia stood back from her just completed work, Cornelia gazed in wonder at the left side of the bottom part of her mural collage. Before her was an elegantly attired young woman descending upon a pathway of stone steps, her hair blowing in the wind. In her hands she held a lamp that illumined the path before her. Her sash held two long cylindrical leather pouches that appeared to contain scrolls. The tempestuous sea, upon which was a ship, stirred behind her as a new day dawned from over the hills to shine upon a city. Before her and to her right was a gnarled, yet stately old olive tree. Behind her another spindly olive tree was just beginning its new life. At her feet on either side of the narrow pathway were aloe plants that appeared to be thriving.

"Is that you in the painting?" she asked.

"Yes."

"I have never seen you so royally dressed. What does it mean?"

Eletia smiled a broad smile. "I am a child of the King of kings, in whose eyes I appear as royalty. Recently, Publius spoke about a passage from Psalm 119, 'Thy word is a lamp to my feet, and a light to my path.' (Psalm 119:105) The lamp I am holding represents the word of God that lights my path ahead. The steps behind me represent life that has already been lived, in my case, both before I knew Christ and up to the present time. Those steps, many of which deviated from God's path, are in the past. I can do nothing to change them, but I can use even my bad experiences to enrich my future. The steps ahead represent my life that will be."

"Why only three steps? The area beyond them is still dark."

"God's word guides us forward one step at a time. Only when we obediently take the steps He has shown us, are new steps then illuminated. We do not know what our earthly future will bring, but we know the One in whose hands we are held."

"Why is the sea behind you so agitated? Why does your hair blow in the wind?"

"Because life can be tempestuous and unpredictable. Only the steps upon which God's word guides us remain solid and stable in the midst of turmoil."

"What about the ship?"

"It too has endured turbulent seas, but is coming into port. In my case it has brought to me a man who has known his own unsavory past, but who now also walks God's path. The aloe plants on either side of my path represent healing. As aloe helps heal wounded bodies, so Christ heals broken lives. The sun coming up from behind the hills represents a new day. A new day has dawned upon both of our lives. The city upon which the sun has begun to shine represents the church, of which we are a part.

"The baby olive tree behind me represents fragile new life, yet with limitless potential. So can it be for every sincere follower of Christ. We can become like the gnarled old olive tree before me that has weathered many a storm, yet still bears fruit."

"What are the two pouches held by your sash?"

"They represent the two stories written by Luke, first the story of Christ upon this earth and then the story of His early church. As I hear them spoken and read them for myself, they add fuel to the lamp. The sash that holds them represents truth."

49

The Life of Faith

At the ninth hour, three days later, the leaders of the Melitene church, Theophilus, Marcus, Rufus, Julius and Angelina, Demetrius and Phoebe, Linus and Beatrice, and Doctor Corbus with his wife Domina Macatus, began to assemble at Publius' home. After a time of social interaction Publius commenced the meeting.

"It is so good for us all to be together again. It is so good to be free. We ought to begin our time together with some singing. It has been so long since we have been able to sing." He pointed to the young woman who held the lute. "Angelina, would you please lead us?"

One by one, she taught them the songs she had either learned from Aristarchus or composed herself. As the people caught on, they began to sing with conviction. There was something about the experience of singing together, so long denied by the need to meet in stealth, that brought great joy to the people. After the time of singing Publius was able to put his finger on the difference when he spoke to the group.

"Worship of our Savior is made all the sweeter when it has cost us something to do so, just like it cost Him to save us."

Publius then called Marcus and Theophilus to the front of the room from where he sat. "This man Marcus was once an enemy of the gospel, but so too were we all. God has transformed him into a mighty warrior for his kingdom."

He patted Marcus on the back. "Well done, good and faithful warrior, in leading our flock during my involuntary absence. For nearly a year you held our church together. After speaking and praying together, Theophilus and I have felt led to anoint you as an elder of our church here on Melitene. Will you accept the commission?"

For long moments Marcus stood silent. "I feel unworthy of such a commission," he finally answered.

"We are all unworthy," spoke Publius. "But by the grace of God, we are what we are. You have proven yourself a fearless, decisive, and compassionate leader. You have already been doing the job of an elder. We only affirm what you have in fact become."

Marcus took a deep breath. "Then I humbly accept the commission."

He went to his knees while the two elders laid their hands upon his head and shoulders. "Gracious heavenly Father," Theophilus began. "In response to the leading of Your Holy Spirit, we commission your servant Marcus as an elder of our church here on Melitene. May he love You with all his heart and hate sin. May You expand his ministry and use him to reach many who are lost and win them for Your kingdom, setting them free from the shackles of sin and death, to become all that You have made them to be. We pray that You will bless and expand his ministry in our church, at the school, upon our island, and throughout the entire world. Keep his marriage to Eletia strong. Help him to be the father You would have him be. We humbly ask these things in the name of Your Son, our Lord and Savior Jesus Christ. Amen."

When he rose up, both Publius and Theophilus hugged him. "Welcome, Marcus, as a fellow elder," spoke Publius.

He then addressed the entire group. "Through a miracle from God we now have a respite from the persecution that was upon us. We now have a sympathetic propraetor living at the villa. How long our situation will last, only God knows. Even as we speak, my mother Alexandra is heading for Rome, where she will undoubtedly inform Emperor Nero of what in her mind is a travesty. If Nero responds as he has before, we may find ourselves right back where we were—or worse. But our God can do miracles. He is greater than all the forces arrayed against us. He did a miracle to bring us this period of freedom, at least for a time. He can do it again. Meanwhile, I am heartbroken regarding my mother.

"We are in a war, dear people. There is God and there is Satan. There is right and there is wrong. There is truth and there is error. There is light and there is darkness. There is love and there is hate. There is a heaven and there is a hell. God sent His only Son into this world to save us from our sins. Christ taught us how to live and then how to die. He was buried and He rose again from the dead on the third day, having triumphed over sin and death. He is the only means God has provided by which the sin of Adam, which brought sin and death into this world can be rectified. It is a message that Satan hates. He will do everything he can to block the message of salvation because he lives only to hate and to destroy. We must never be 'ashamed of the gospel, for it is the power of God for salvation to everyone who believes.' (Romans 1:16b) We must never be ashamed of the truth, of righteousness, of love, of joy, of kindness, or of eternal life. In the end our God wins and we win with Him. Satan loses. Our job in the meantime is to rescue as many as possible from the kingdom of darkness into God's kingdom of light. What else is there to live for?

"We have been informed that we still cannot use the amphitheater. I have come to the conclusion that that is actually a good thing. When Gaius closed the amphitheater to us, our body scattered. We lost a lot of people. We are going to continue doing what the closing of the amphitheater forced upon us. We are going to maintain and form numerous other small house churches. If you do not already have one going, I want each couple here, or single leader to form a small house church. You gather the believers in your area where you live, to come to your homes on Sunday mornings. You lead your churches, but keep changing the locations where you meet for security reasons. Meet at least once between Sundays to keep the fires burning. Develop leaders within your groups to form still more house churches. We in this room and other leaders we develop will still meet once a week to report on the progress of our smaller churches.

"Once we have formed our churches, we won't be so easy to find and be shut down, as we were last time. Our church will grow deeper rather than wider for a time. But once we are established in this new model, we will grow both wider and deeper at the same time."

He again scanned the assembled group. "Shall we do as I have suggested?"

"Yes!" came the resounding reply.

"Do we really believe that Christ died for us, was buried, and rose again on the third day? Do we really believe that He alone has the words of eternal life?"

"Yes!" came the resounding reply.

"Then let us live every day for the glory of God, and not just to please ourselves. And let us now pray together and worship our Savior."

For the next hour the people prayed. They prayed for the reestablishment of Ille Perfugium and for more damaged women to avail themselves to healing. They prayed for the newly forming house churches, for the salvation of Gaius and for all of the lost on Melitene. They prayed for Trebonius and for the church at Syracuse, to whom they owed much. They prayed for Paul, for Luke, and for the church in Rome. They prayed for one another, that they would be good parents, raising their children in the fear of the Lord. They prayed for health. They prayed for courage in the face of a relentless enemy. And while they prayed together, the home of Publius Fabianus shook with a holy fire.

At the conclusion of the prayer time the people sat for a midday meal of rabbit stew, bread, fruit, and a dessert called konnalli, made more sumptuous by the spirit of the people. What might lay ahead, they did not know. But they knew who would be with them.

50

A Time of Decision

As Publius sat with Gaius in the atrium of the propraetor's villa, everything appeared as it had since Gaius Ovidius Bellirus had taken over the governorship of Melitene. "We have been meeting now for six months, Gaius. I have spoken to you everything I know about Christ and the Christian life. Have you come to a decision as to which way you want to go? Jesus said 'He who is not with me is against Me; and he who does not gather with Me, scatters'." (Luke 11:23)

"Yes, I have come to a decision, Publius, helped by a letter I just received from Nero. I have two pieces of news that I want to give you before I tell you my decision. I am afraid that the news for you may be a double-edge sword."

"Please, let's hear it."

"Your mentor Paul has been beheaded at the behest of Nero. He wanted a much more gruesome, slower death, but Paul's Roman citizenship and his standing with many in Rome forbade it. Nevertheless, Nero boasts in his letter about Paul's death. He thinks it has been his greatest achievement as emperor."

A deep feeling of numbness and sorrow fell upon Publius. Paul had been a great man. He knew of no more sincere servant of God. But he also knew Paul's heart, that for him to live was Christ and to die was gain.

"What is the other news?"

"Apparently, your mother never reached Rome. I don't know why.

But Nero asked how she was doing here. He would not have asked had he seen her."

Further sorrow fell upon Publius. If she had never reached Rome, the most likely explanation was that she had died somewhere along the way. There were any number of ways it could have happened—and also the possibility that she could still be alive. They had had no relationship for years, but she was still his mother. There had been good times together during his early childhood. Yet the news also meant that she had not been able to disparage Gaius.

"He also wants to know why he hasn't yet received your father's head on a platter."

"How are you going to answer Nero's letter?"

The propraetor gave him a wry smile. "I believe that my best answer is no answer. I do not intend to write back. I believe that Nero's days as emperor of Rome are numbered. No man can be so cruel and vain as he has been and not experience a great downfall. I get news from couriers from Rome. The Roman people have reached the point where they are determined to be rid of him. Soon and inevitably, he will be overthrown. I am just going to wait him out."

"So where does this news place you with Christ?"

"I am for Him, not against Him. Just before you came this morning, I gave the order to take down all the statues of the Roman gods and goddesses throughout our island. The work commences tomorrow. I want to be a part of one of your house churches. You can even have the amphitheater back if you want it."

"We will be glad to put you in one of our house churches and I thank you for the offer of the amphitheater, but we will not make it our regular Sunday morning meeting place. We might use it for weddings and funerals, or other big events when such occasions occur."

"I think you are wise, Publius. That will make it much more difficult for a future propraetor to shut you down."

"My thoughts exactly. And what about you, Gaius? What will you do if and when you are replaced and ordered to appear before a new emperor?"

"Most likely, I will do what your father did."

*****

It appeared that Eletia's mural painting was finished, or was it? On the far bottom right of the painting were the images of three crosses at the top of a high hill. At the bottom was an open, rock hewn tomb, with a large round rock rolled to one side.

"What is this, Eletia?" asked Cornelia.

"The middle cross is where our Savior Jesus Christ died for our sins. The tomb below is where He was buried. But on the third day the stone was rolled away and Christ rose again from the dead, 'the first fruits of those who are asleep.' (1 Corinthians 15:20b)

"What does that mean?"

"You will notice the large gap between myself on the illumined steps and my final offering on the far right. The gap represents the remainder of my earthly life, which is still a mystery. We do not know what will take place in our earthly futures. That is true for myself and for Marcus, for Publius and for Amoenitas, for Theophilus and for Flavia, for Julius and for Angelina, for Marinus and for Valentina, for Doctor Corbus and for Domina Macatus, and for Gaius. It is true for all of us who follow Christ. It is true for you. But we do know our final outcome.

"One day we must all shed our earthly tents and be buried in the ground, just as Christ Jesus was buried in the ground. But just as He rose from the dead, to be with His Father forever, so too will all who have followed Christ one day be raised from the dead to be with our Father in heaven forever. We do not know for certain our earthly future, but we know our eternal destiny. For now, we take the steps that He by His word has illumined before us on this earth. It is the life of faith. For me, there is no other way to live."

Epilogue

Nero was as cruel and brutal a dictator as ever lived. During his reign as emperor from A.D. 54 to 68 he had his mother Agrippina put to death, along with his first wife Octavia, his step-brother Britannicus, his advisor Seneca, and countless other high officials he suspected of disloyalty. He is further suspected of having kicked his second wife Poppaea to death. In A.D. 65, after Poppaea's death, he had a freeman named Pythagoras castrated—and then married him.

Nero began work on his Domus Aurea shortly after the great fire of Rome in A.D. 64., supervising every detail of the project. It was an enormously grand, expensive undertaking. To this day no one knows for sure how much area his palace and grounds actually covered, because not all has been excavated. Estimates range from a little under one hundred acres to over three hundred. The entire complex covered parts of the slopes of the Palatine, Oppian, and Caelian Hills. Between them was a man-made lake. There were tree groves, pastures for flocks, and vineyards to give the grounds the feel of country life within the great city.

In the atrium before the palace entrance, Nero had a 100-foot-high bronze statue made of himself. Inside the palace were some 300 rooms, trimmed in gold leaf, with highly polished white marble flooring and frescoes on the walls. Some had pools built into the floor. The ceilings contained semi-precious stones with ivory veneers. Numerous fountains adorned the corridors. Two enormous dining rooms had mosaics in their vaulted ceilings. When it was nearly finished, he occupied it.

"At last I have begun to live like a human being," he is reported to have said.

Nero's extravagance and brutality finally caught up with him. He was overthrown by Governor Servius Sulpicius Galba, who then reigned in his place. He was condemned to death by the Roman Senate. Rather than allow himself to be beaten to death on their terms, he committed suicide with the help of his secretary Epaphroditus.

"What an artist dies in me!" he exclaimed as he died. Few in Rome mourned his passing.

Tradition has it that Paul was beheaded in Rome in A.D. 66 at the behest of Nero, shortly after he had completed Second Timothy, his final book.

Galba relaxed restrictions on the Christian faith all through the empire, but persecution returned after his reign, which lasted less than a year. Rome continued to exert increasing pressure on the people of Melitene to abandon Christianity, in favor of emperor worship.

Finally, about 125 A.D. Emperor Hadrian sent two cohorts of soldiers to round up and kill the Christian leaders and to completely subdue the island. Publius was martyred at the age of eighty-five. Over the centuries the name Melitene evolved into Malta, as it is now known. The Maltese continue to honor Publius as their first Christian pastor.

About the Author

Robert Alan Ward served in the United States Air Force from 1969-1972 before earning a B.S. in Christian Education from San Diego Christian College. A twenty-seven-year career with the United Parcel Service followed.

Now retired, he and his wife Gisela live in the White Mountains of Arizona, where he serves in his church as a home group leader and in the youth department. He and Gisela love to hike the many forested trails of the area. Together they have five children, fourteen grandchildren, and three great-grandchildren.

Robert writes from a decidedly biblical Christian worldview. His consuming passion is to communicate biblical truth in a spirit of love to a confused, frightened, angry world through compelling stories. His other published books include "The Lifestyle Shoppe," "Forged from the Wilderness," "Between Two Seas," "Delivered" and "A Cry for Freedom" (assisting F.L.M. Khokhar), and "Through Fear and Trembling" (co-authored with David Ross). He has also thirteen published drama titles to his credit that are performed all over the English-speaking world.

Website address: www.absorbingtales4u.com